Elric:
The Sailor on the Seas of Fate

The Michael Moorcock Collection

The Michael Moorcock Collection is the definitive library of acclaimed author Michael Moorcock's SF & fantasy, including the entirety of his Eternal Champion work. It is prepared and edited by John Davey, the author's long-time bibliographer and editor, and will be published, over the course of two years, in the following print omnibus editions by Gollancz, and as individual eBooks by the SF Gateway (see http://www.sfgateway.com/authors/m/moorcock-michael/ for a complete list of available eBooks).

ELRIC

Elric of Melniboné and Other Stories

Elric: The Fortress of the Pearl

Elric: The Sailor on the Seas of Fate

Elric: The Sleeping Sorceress

Elric: The Revenge of the Rose

Elric: Stormbringer!

Elric: The Moonbeam Roads
comprising –
Daughter of Dreams
Destiny's Brother
Son of the Wolf

CORUM

Corum: The Prince in the Scarlet Robe
comprising –
The Knight of the Swords
The Queen of the Swords
The King of the Swords

Corum: The Prince with the Silver Hand
comprising –
The Bull and the Spear
The Oak and the Ram
The Sword and the Stallion

HAWKMOON

Hawkmoon: The History of the Runestaff
comprising –
The Jewel in the Skull
The Mad God's Amulet
The Sword of the Dawn
The Runestaff

Hawkmoon: Count Brass
comprising –
Count Brass
The Champion of Garathorm
The Quest for Tanelorn

JERRY CORNELIUS

The Cornelius Quartet
comprising –
The Final Programme
A Cure for Cancer
The English Assassin
The Condition of Muzak

Jerry Cornelius: His Lives and His Times (short-fiction collection)

A Cornelius Calendar
comprising –
The Adventures of Una Persson and Catherine Cornelius in the Twentieth Century
The Entropy Tango
The Great Rock 'n' Roll Swindle
The Alchemist's Question
Firing the Cathedral/Modem Times 2.0

Von Bek
comprising –
The War Hound and the World's Pain
The City in the Autumn Stars

The Eternal Champion
comprising –
The Eternal Champion
Phoenix in Obsidian
The Dragon in the Sword

The Dancers at the End of Time
comprising –
An Alien Heat
The Hollow Lands
The End of all Songs

Kane of Old Mars
comprising –
Warriors of Mars
Blades of Mars
Barbarians of Mars

Moorcock's Multiverse
comprising –
The Sundered Worlds
The Winds of Limbo
The Shores of Death

The Nomad of Time
comprising –
The Warlord of the Air
The Land Leviathan
The Steel Tsar

Travelling to Utopia
comprising –
The Wrecks of Time
The Ice Schooner
The Black Corridor

The War Amongst the Angels
comprising –
Blood: A Southern Fantasy
Fabulous Harbours
The War Amongst the Angels

Tales From the End of Time
comprising –
Legends from the End of Time
Constant Fire
Elric at the End of Time

Behold the Man

Gloriana; or, The Unfulfill'd Queen

SHORT FICTION

My Experiences in the Third World War and Other Stories: The Best Short Fiction of Michael Moorcock Volume 1

The Brothel in Rosenstrasse and Other Stories: The Best Short Fiction of Michael Moorcock Volume 2

Breakfast in the Ruins and Other Stories: The Best Short Fiction of Michael Moorcock Volume 3

Elric: The Sailor on the Seas of Fate

MICHAEL MOORCOCK

Edited by John Davey

This edition published in Great Britain in 2013 by
Gollancz
An imprint of the Orion Publishing Group
Orion House, 5 Upper St Martin's Lane,
London WC2H 9EA
An Hachette UK Company

3 5 7 9 10 8 6 4 2

A CIP catalogue record for this book is
available from the British Library

ISBN 978 0 575 11360 2

Typeset by Jouve (UK), Milton Keynes

Printed and bound by Clays Ltd, Elcograf S.p.A.

The Orion Publishing Group's policy is to use papers that are natural, renewable and recyclable products and made from wood grown in sustainable forests. The logging and manufacturing processes are expected to conform to the environmental regulations of the country of origin.

www.multiverse.org
www.sfgateway.com
www.gollancz.co.uk
www.orionbooks.co.uk

Introduction to *The Michael Moorcock Collection*

John Clute

He is now over 70, enough time for most careers to start and end in, enough time to fit in an occasional half-decade or so of silence to mark off the big years. Silence happens. I don't think I know an author who doesn't fear silence like the plague; most of us, if we live long enough, can remember a bad blank year or so, or more. Not Michael Moorcock. Except for some worrying surgery on his toes in recent years, he seems not to have taken time off to breathe the air of peace and panic. There has been no time to spare. The nearly 60 years of his active career seems to have been too short to fit everything in: the teenage comics; the editing jobs; the pulp fiction; the reinvented heroic fantasies; the Eternal Champion; the deep Jerry Cornelius riffs; New Worlds; the 1970s/1980s flow of stories and novels, dozens upon dozens of them in every category of modern fantastika; the tales of the dying Earth and the possessing of Jesus; the exercises in postmodernism that turned the world inside out before most of us had begun to guess we were living on the wrong side of things; the invention (more or less) of steampunk; the alternate histories; the *Mitteleuropean* tales of sexual terror; the deep-city London riffs: the turns and changes and returns and reconfigurations to which he has subjected his oeuvre over the years (he expects this new Collected Edition will fix these transformations in place for good); the late tales where he has been remodelling the intersecting worlds he created in the 1960s in terms of twenty-first-century physics: for starters. If you can't take the heat, I guess, stay out of the multiverse.

His life has been full and complicated, a life he has exposed and hidden (like many other prolific authors) throughout his work. In *Mother London* (1988), though, a nonfantastic novel published at what is now something like the midpoint of his career, it may be possible to find the key to all the other selves who made the 100 books. There are three protagonists in the tale, which is set from about 1940 to about 1988 in the suburbs and inner runnels of the vast metropolis of Charles Dickens and Robert Louis Stevenson. The oldest of these protagonists is Joseph Kiss, a flamboyant self-advertising fin-de-siècle figure of substantial girth and a fantasticating relationship to the world: he is Michael Moorcock, seen with genial bite as a kind of G.K. Chesterton without the wearying punch-line paradoxes. The youngest of the three is David Mummery, a haunted introspective half-insane denizen of a secret London of trials and runes and codes and magic: he too is Michael Moorcock, seen through a glass, darkly. And there is Mary Gasalee, a kind of holy-innocent and survivor, blessed with a luminous clarity of insight, so that in all her apparent ignorance of the onrushing secular world she is more deeply wise than other folk: she is also Michael Moorcock, Moorcock when young as viewed from the wry middle years of 1988. When we read the book, we are reading a book of instructions for the assembly of a London writer. The Moorcock we put together from this choice of portraits is amused and bemused at the vision of himself; he is a phenomenon of flamboyance and introspection, a poseur and a solitary, a dreamer and a doer, a multitude and a singleton. But only the three Moorcocks in this book, working together, could have written all the other books.

It all began – as it does for David Mummery in *Mother London* – in South London, in a subtopian stretch of villas called Mitcham, in 1939. In early childhood, he experienced the Blitz, and never forgot the extraordinariness of being a participant – however minute – in the great drama; all around him, as though the world were being dismantled nightly, darkness and blackout would descend, bombs fall, buildings and streets disappear; and in the morning, as though a new universe had taken over from the old one and the world had become portals, the sun would rise on glinting rubble, abandoned tricycles, men and women going about their daily tasks as though nothing had happened, strange shards of ruin poking into altered air. From a very early age, Michael Moorcock's security reposed in a sense that everything might change, in the blinking of an eye, and be *rejourneyed* the next day (or the next book). Though as a writer he has certainly elucidated the fears and alarums of life in Aftermath Britain, it does seem that his very early years were marked by the epiphanies of war, rather than the inflictions of despair and beclouding amnesia most adults necessarily experienced. After the war ended, his parents separated, and the young Moorcock began to attend a pretty wide variety of schools, several of which he seems to have been expelled from, and as soon as he could legally do so he began to work full time, up north in London's heart, which he only left when he moved to Texas (with intervals in Paris) in the early 1990s, from where (to jump briefly up the decades) he continues to cast a Martian eye: as with most exiles, Moorcock's intensest anatomies of his homeland date from after his cunning departure.

But back again to the beginning (just as though we were rimming a multiverse). Starting in the 1950s there was the comics and pulp work for Fleetway Publications; there was the first book (*Caribbean Crisis*, 1962) as by Desmond Reid, co-written with his early friend the artist James Cawthorn (1929–2008); there was marriage, with the writer Hilary Bailey (they divorced in 1978), three children, a heated existence in the Ladbroke Grove/Notting Hill Gate region of London he was later to populate with Jerry Cornelius and his vast family; there was the editing of NEW WORLDS, which began in 1964 and became the heartbeat of the British New Wave two years later as writers like Brian W. Aldiss and J.G. Ballard, reaching their early prime, made it into a tympanum, as young American writers like Thomas M. Disch, John T. Sladek, Norman Spinrad and Pamela Zoline found a home in London for material they could not publish in America, and new British writers like M. John Harrison and Charles Platt began their careers in its pages; but before that there was Elric. With *The Stealer of Souls* (1963) and

Stormbringer (1965), the multiverse began to flicker into view, and the Eternal Champion (whom Elric parodied and embodied) began properly to ransack the worlds in his fight against a greater Chaos than the great dance could sustain. There was also the first SF novel, *The Sundered Worlds* (1965), but in the 1960s SF was a difficult nut to demolish for Moorcock: he would bide his time.

We come to the heart of the matter. Jerry Cornelius, who first appears in *The Final Programme* (1968) – which assembles and co-ordinates material first published a few years earlier in NEW WORLDS – is a deliberate solarisation of the albino Elric, who was himself a mocking solarisation of Robert E. Howard's Conan, or rather of the mighty-thew-headed Conan created for profit by Howard epigones: Moorcock rarely mocks the true quill. Cornelius, who reaches his first and most telling apotheosis in the four novels comprising *The Cornelius Quartet*, remains his most distinctive and perhaps most original single creation: a wide boy, an agent, a *flaneur*, a bad musician, a shopper, a shapechanger, a trans, a spy in the house of London: a toxic palimpsest on whom and through whom the *zeitgeist* inscribes surreal conjugations of 'message'. Jerry Cornelius gives head to Elric.

The life continued apace. By 1970, with NEW WORLDS on its last legs, multiverse fantasies and experimental novels poured forth; Moorcock and Hilary Bailey began to live separately, though he moved, in fact, only around the corner, where he set up house with Jill Riches, who would become his second wife; there was a second home in Yorkshire, but London remained his central base. *The Condition of Muzak* (1977), which is the fourth Cornelius novel, and *Gloriana; or, The Unfulfill'd Queen* (1978), which transfigures the first Elizabeth into a kinked Astraea, marked perhaps the high point of his career as a writer of fiction whose font lay in genre or its mutations – marked perhaps the furthest bournes he could transgress while remaining within the perimeters of fantasy (though *within* those bournes vast stretches of territory remained and would, continually, be explored). During these years he sometimes wore a leather jacket constructed out of numerous patches of varicoloured material, and it sometimes seemed perfectly fitting that he bore the semblance, as his jacket flickered and fuzzed from across a room or road, of an illustrated man, a map, a thing of shreds and patches, a student fleshed from dreams. Like the stories he told, he seemed to be more than one thing. To use a term frequently applied (by me at least) to twenty-first-century fiction, he seemed equipoisal: which is to say that, through all his genre-hopping and genre-mixing and genre-transcending and genre-loyal returnings to old pitches, *he was never still*, because 'equipoise' is all about *making stories move*. As with his stories, he cannot be pinned down, because he is not in one place. In person and in his work, it has always been sink or swim: like a shark, or a dancer, or an equilibrist...

The marriage with Jill Riches came to an end. He married Linda Steele in 1983; they remain married. The Colonel Pyat books, *Byzantium Endures* (1981), *The Laughter of Carthage* (1984), *Jerusalem Commands* (1992) and *The Vengeance of Rome* (2006), dominated these years, along with *Mother London*. As these books, which are non-fantastic, are not included in the current *Michael Moorcock Collection*, it might be worth noting here that, in their insistence on the irreducible difficulty of gaining anything like true sight, they represent Moorcock's mature modernist take on what one might call the rag-and-bone shop of the world itself; and that the huge ornate postmodern edifice of his multiverse *loosens* us from that world, gives us room to breathe, to juggle our strategies for living – allows us ultimately to escape from prison (to use a phrase from a writer he does not respect, J.R.R. Tolkien, for whom the twentieth century was a prison train bound for hell). What Moorcock may best be remembered for in the end is the (perhaps unique) interplay between modernism and postmodernism in his work. (But a plethora of discordant understandings makes these terms hard to use; so enough of them.) In the end, one might just say that Moorcock's work as a whole represents an extraordinarily multifarious execution of the fantasist's main task: which is to *get us out of here*.

Recent decades saw a continuation of the multifarious, but with a more intensely applied methodology. The late volumes of the long Elric saga, and the Second Ether sequence of meta-fantasies – *Blood: A Southern Fantasy* (1995), *Fabulous Harbours* (1995) and *The War Amongst the Angels: An Autobiographical Story* (1996) – brood on the real world and the multiverse through the lens of Chaos Theory: the closer you get to the world, the less you describe it. *The Metatemporal Detective* (2007) – a narrative in the Steampunk mode Moorcock had previewed as long ago as *The Warlord of the Air* (1971) and *The Land Leviathan* (1974) – continues the process, sometimes dizzyingly: as though the reader inhabited the eye of a camera increasing its focus on a closely observed reality while its bogey simultaneously wheels it backwards from the desired rapport: an old Kurasawa trick here amplified into a tool of conspectus, fantasy eyed and (once again) rejourneyed, this time through the lens of SF.

We reach the second decade of the twenty-first century, time still to make things new, but also time to sort. There are dozens of titles in *The Michael Moorcock Collection* that have not been listed in this short space, much less trawled for tidbits. The various avatars of the Eternal Champion – Elric, Kane of Old Mars, Hawkmoon, Count Brass, Corum, Von Bek – differ vastly from one another. Hawkmoon is a bit of a berk; Corum is a steely solitary at the End of Time: the joys and doleurs of the interplays amongst them can only be experienced through immersion. And the Dancers at the End of Time books, and the Nomad of the Time Stream books, and the Karl Glogauer books, and all the others. They are here now, a 100 books that make up one book. They have been fixed for reading. It is time to enter the multiverse and see the world.

September 2012

Introduction to *The Michael Moorcock Collection*

Michael Moorcock

By 1964, AFTER I had been editing NEW WORLDS for some months and had published several science fiction and fantasy novels, including *Stormbringer*, I realised that my run as a writer was over. About the only new ideas I'd come up with were miniature computers, the multiverse and black holes, all very crudely realised, in *The Sundered Worlds*. No doubt I would have to return to journalism, writing features and editing. 'My career,' I told my friend J.G. Ballard, 'is finished.' He sympathised and told me he only had a few SF stories left in him, then he, too, wasn't sure what he'd do.

In January 1965, living in Colville Terrace, Notting Hill, then an infamous slum, best known for its race riots, I sat down at the typewriter in our kitchen-cum-bathroom and began a locally based book, designed to be accompanied by music and graphics. *The Final Programme* featured a character based on a young man I'd seen around the area and whom I named after a local greengrocer, Jerry Cornelius, 'Messiah to the Age of Science'. Jerry was as much a technique as a character. Not the 'spy' some critics described him as but an urban adventurer as interested in his psychic environment as the contemporary physical world. My influences were English and French absurdists, American noir novels. My inspiration was William Burroughs with whom I'd recently begun a correspondence. I also borrowed a few SF ideas, though I was adamant that I was not writing in any established genre. I felt I had at last found my own authentic voice.

I had already written a short novel, *The Golden Barge*, set in a nowhere, no-time world very much influenced by Peake and the surrealists, which I had not attempted to publish. An earlier autobiographical novel, *The Hungry Dreamers*, set in Soho, was eaten by rats in a Ladbroke Grove basement. I remained unsatisfied with my style and my technique. *The Final Programme* took nine days to complete (by 20 January, 1965) with my baby daughters sometimes cradled with their bottles while I typed on. This, I should say, is my memory of events; my then wife scoffed at this story when I recounted it. Whatever the truth, the fact is I only believed I might be a serious writer after I had finished that novel, with all its flaws. But Jerry Cornelius, probably my most successful sustained attempt at unconventional fiction, was born then and ever since has remained a useful means of telling complex stories. Associated with the 60s and 70s, he has been equally at home in all the following decades. Through novels and novellas I developed a means of carrying several narratives and viewpoints on what appeared to be a very light (but tight) structure which dispensed with some of the earlier methods of fiction. In the sense that it took for granted the understanding that the novel is among other things an internal dialogue and I did not feel the need to repeat by now commonly understood modernist conventions, this fiction was post-modern.

Not all my fiction looked for new forms for the new century. Like many 'revolutionaries' I looked back as well as forward. As George Meredith looked to the eighteenth century for inspiration for his experiments with narrative, I looked to Meredith, popular Edwardian realists like Pett Ridge and Zangwill and the writers of the *fin de siècle* for methods and inspiration. An almost obsessive interest in the Fabians, several of whom believed in the possibility of benign imperialism, ultimately led to my Bastable books which examined our enduring British notion that an empire could be essentially a force for good. The first was *The Warlord of the Air*.

I also wrote my *Dancers at the End of Time* stories and novels under the influence of Edwardian humourists and absurdists like Jerome or Firbank. Together with more conventional generic books like *The Ice Schooner* or *The Black Corridor*, most of that work was done in the 1960s and 70s when I wrote the Eternal Champion supernatural adventure novels which helped support my own and others' experiments via NEW WORLDS, allowing me also to keep a family while writing books in which action and fantastic invention were paramount. Though I did them quickly, I didn't write them cynically. I have always believed, somewhat puritanically, in giving the audience good value for money. I enjoyed writing them, tried to avoid repetition, and through each new one was able to develop a few more ideas. They also continued to teach me how to express myself through image and metaphor. My Everyman became the Eternal Champion, his dreams and ambitions represented by the multiverse. He could be an ordinary person struggling with familiar problems in a contemporary setting or he could be a swordsman fighting monsters on a far-away world.

Long before I wrote *Gloriana* (in four parts reflecting the seasons) I had learned to think in images and symbols through reading John Bunyan's *Pilgrim's Progress*, Milton and others, understanding early on that the visual could be the most important part of a book and was often in itself a story as, for instance, a famous personality could also, through everything associated with their name, function as narrative. I wanted to find ways of carrying as many stories as possible in one. From the cinema I also learned how to use images as connecting themes. Images, colours, music, and even popular magazine headlines can all add coherence to an apparently random story, underpinning it and giving the reader a sense of internal logic and a satisfactory resolution, dispensing with certain familiar literary conventions.

When the story required it, I also began writing neo-realist fiction exploring the interface of character and environment, especially the city, especially London. In some books I condensed, manipulated and randomised time to achieve what I wanted, but in others the sense of 'real time' as we all generally perceive it was more suitable and could best be achieved by traditional nineteenth-century means. For the Pyat books I first looked back to the great German classic, Grimmelshausen's *Simplicissimus* and other early picaresques. I then examined the roots of a certain kind of moral fiction from Defoe through Thackeray and Meredith then to modern times where the picaresque (or rogue tale) can take the form of a road movie, for instance. While it's probably fair to say that Pyat and *Byzantium Endures* precipitated the end of my second marriage (echoed to a degree in *The Brothel in Rosenstrasse*), the late 70s and the 80s were exhilarating times for me, with *Mother London* being perhaps my own favourite novel of that period. I wanted to write something celebratory.

By the 90s I was again attempting to unite several kinds of fiction in one novel with my Second Ether trilogy. With Mandelbrot, Chaos Theory and String Theory I felt, as I said at the time, as if I were being offered a chart of my own brain. That chart made it easier for me to develop the notion of the multiverse as representing both the internal and the external, as a metaphor and as a means of structuring and rationalising an outrageously inventive and quasi-realistic narrative. The worlds of the multiverse move up and down scales or 'planes' explained in terms of mass, allowing entire universes to exist in the 'same' space. The result of developing this idea was the *War Amongst the Angels* sequence which added absurdist elements also functioning as a kind of mythology and folklore for a world beginning to understand itself in terms of new metaphysics and theoretical physics. As the cosmos becomes denser and almost infinite before our eyes, with black holes and dark matter affecting our own reality, we can explore them and observe them as our ancestors explored our planet and observed the heavens.

At the end of the 90s I'd returned to realism, sometimes with a dash of fantasy, with *King of the City* and the stories collected in *London Bone*. I also wrote a new Elric/Eternal Champion sequence, beginning with *Daughter of Dreams*, which brought the fantasy worlds of Hawkmoon, Bastable and Co. in line with my realistic and autobiographical stories, another attempt to unify all my fiction, and also offer a way in which disparate genres could be reunited, through notions developed from the multiverse and the Eternal Champion, as one giant novel. At the time I was finishing the Pyat sequence which attempted to look at the roots of the Nazi Holocaust in our European, Middle Eastern and American cultures and to ground my strange survival guilt while at the same time examining my own cultural roots in the light of an enduring anti-Semitism.

By the 2000s I was exploring various conventional ways of story-telling in the last parts of *The Metatemporal Detective* and through other homages, comics, parodies and games. I also looked back at my earliest influences. I had reached retirement age and felt like a rest. I wrote a 'prequel' to the Elric series as a graphic novel with Walter Simonson, *The Making of a Sorcerer*, and did a little online editing with FANTASTIC METROPOLIS.

By 2010 I had written a novel featuring Doctor Who, *The Coming of the Terraphiles*, with a nod to P.G. Wodehouse (a boyhood favourite), continued to write short stories and novellas and to work on the beginning of a new sequence combining pure fantasy and straight autobiography called *The Whispering Swarm* while still writing more Cornelius stories trying to unite all the various genres and sub-genres into which contemporary fiction has fallen.

Throughout my career critics have announced that I'm 'abandoning' fantasy and concentrating on literary fiction. The truth is, however, that all my life, since I became a professional writer and editor at the age of 16, I've written in whatever mode suits a story best and where necessary created a new form if an old one didn't work for me. Certain ideas are best carried on a Jerry Cornelius story, others work better as realism and others as fantasy or science fiction. Some work best as a combination. I'm sure I'll write whatever I like and will continue to experiment with all the ways there are of telling stories and carrying as many themes as possible. Whether I write about a widow coping with loneliness in her cottage or a massive, universe-size sentient spaceship searching for her children, I'll no doubt die trying to tell them all. I hope you'll find at least some of them to your taste.

One thing a reader can be sure of about these new editions is that they would not have been possible without the tremendous and indispensable help of my old friend and bibliographer John Davey. John has ensured that these Gollancz editions are definitive. I am indebted to John for many things, including his work at

Moorcock's Miscellany, my website, but his work on this edition has been outstanding. As well as being an accomplished novelist in his own right John is an astonishingly good editor who has worked with Gollancz and myself to point out every error and flaw in all previous editions, some of them not corrected since their first publication, and has enabled me to correct or revise them. I couldn't have completed this project without him. Together, I think, Gollancz, John Davey and myself have produced what will be the best editions possible and I am very grateful to him, to Malcolm Edwards, Darren Nash and Marcus Gipps for all the considerable hard work they have done to make this edition what it is.

Michael Moorcock

Contents

ELRIC IN

MYYRRHN
THE VALE OF XANYAW
THE HEWN CITY OF NIHRAIN
SEQUALORIS
NARGESSER
JHARKOR
THOKORA
DHAKOS
TARKESH
NIO
BANARVA
DHARIJOR
GROMOORVA
STRAITS of CHAOS
PAN TANG
HWAMGAARL
SHAZAAR
MARSHES OF THE MIST
AFLITAIN
THE SERPENT'S TEETH
THE SILENT LAND
THE DRAGON SEA
MELNIBONE
SORCERER'S ISLE
R'LIN K'REN A'A
THE BOILING SEA
ASHANELOON
DHOZ-KAM
OIN
RIVER AR
YU
TO KANELOON AND WORLD'S EDGE

E YOUNG
NGDOMS
THE SIGHING DESERT
THE RAGGED PILLARS
TO PHVM AND YESHDOTOOM KAHLAI
ELWHER
ESHMIR
TANELORN
QVARZHASAAT
THE WEEPING WASTE
ILMAR
KARLAAK
ILMIORA
GORJHAN
KSHAAN
ORG
FOREST OF TROOS
NADSOKOR
RIGNARIOM
JADMAR
OLD HROLMAR
VILMIR
TO OKARA CHANG SHAI
STRAITS of VILMIR
THE FORTRESS of EVENING
MENII
THE ISLE of THE PVRPLE TOWNS
TREPESAZ
CHALAL
RASCHIL
STAGASAZ
ARGIMILIAR
FILKHAR
RIVER CHA
RIVER ZAPHRA-TREPEK
R SCHLAN
IOSAZ
PIKARAYD
ALORASAZ
J. CAWTHORN · 92
ADAPTED FROM THE MAP BY
JOHN COLLIER & WALTER ROMANSKI

To the memory of Ted Carnell,
who supplied the medium

Foreword
by Michael Chabon

THE MINOR MASTERPIECE at the heart of this volume, *The Sailor on the Seas of Fate*, like almost all of Michael Moorcock's efforts in the subgenre of heroic fantasy, is a complicated work, in the original sense of the term: that is, it *folds together*, with an insight both sophisticated and intuitive, 1) an apparently simple adventure story told in three episodes that are themselves interleaved in puzzling ways; 2) a sharp critique, of adventure stories generally (with their traditional freight of cruelty, wish-fulfillment, sexism and violence), and of the heroic fantasy mode in particular; and 3) a remarkable working out (independently one feels of the work of Joseph Campbell) of the Transcendentalist premise that, as Emerson wrote, 'one person wrote all the books.' Moorcock took this literary universalism, with its implied corollary that one person *reads* all the books, and in *Sailor* began his career-long demonstration of the logical conclusion that all the books are one book, and all the heroes one hero (or antihero). From here it is only a short step, which the reader of heroic fantasy is eager to make, to the proposition that all readers and all writers are Odysseus, or Kull, or Elric of Melniboné, sharing through the acts of reading and writing a single essential, eternal heroic nature. This nature links us – all we heroes and Moorcocks – across all eras and lands. One might even attempt to chart these interconnections of story, hero, reader and writer on a single map: Moorcock is such a cartographer. He called his map of our story-shaped world 'the Multiverse.'

It was Moorcock's insight, and it has been his remarkable artistic accomplishment, not just to complicate all this apparatus and insight and storytelling prowess, packing into one short novel such diverting fare as speculation on ontology and determinism, gory subterranean duels with giant killer baboons, literary criticism (the murmuring soul-vampiric sword Stormbringer offers what is essentially a running commentary on the equivocal nature of heroic swordsmen in fiction), buildings that are really alien beings, and ruminations on the self-similar or endlessly reflective interrelationship of hero, writer, and reader; but to do so with an almost offhanded ease, with a strong, plain and unaffected English prose style that was nearing its peak in the mid-seventies.

That's part of what I would have liked to tell to Michael Moorcock, when I recently had the good fortune to attend the Nebula Awards ceremony, in Austin, Texas, and watch him receive a Grandmaster Award. I would have liked to tell him that when I was fourteen years old I found profound comfort in feeling that I shared in the nature of lost and wandering Elric, isolated but hungering for connection, heroically curious, apparently weak but capable of surprising power, unready and unwilling to sit on the moldering throne of his fathers but having nothing certain to offer in its stead. I would have liked to tell him that his work as a critic, as an editor and as a writer has made it easier for me and a whole generation of us to roam the 'moonbeam roads' of the literary multiverse. But as Mike rose to accept his award all I could do was sit there, next to him – marveling down to the deepest most twisted strands of my literary DNA – and applaud.

Michael Chabon
May 2008

Introduction

to the AudioRealms version of The Sailor on the Seas of Fate

There is a subject discussed frequently by Melniboné's philosophers concerning the number of worlds in the universe and how many universes make up the multiverse. ('Planes' is a more common word they employ, since they do not have the notion of worlds as globes.)

Some believe these can be visited in dreams and reached by the moonbeam roads which run between the worlds. Thus they have developed their sophisticated method of the dream couches, where certain privileged aristocrats lie to dream the dreams of years, centuries, even millennia, in a few hours.

Elric, who had in his youth learned his sorcerous skills on the dream couches of Imrryr, no longer remembered his experience of the moonbeam roads, so the nature of the universe was again a mystery to him, though sometimes a memory would return as a nightmare which would bring him screaming back to wakefulness.

After the events already recorded, Elric determined to explore the lands which surrounded his own, deeming it a matter of common sense to understand the nature of those who, realistically, were planning the destruction of his world and his family with it.

In fact, it is likely the young albino was moved as much by curiosity as moral purpose. Yet who of us at his age is entirely sure of the reason for their actions? Let us accept the reasons he gave and concern ourselves instead with other matters.

Elric had one recurring dream which disturbed his nights. He dreamed he returned to a Melniboné made even stranger and more bizarre under his cousin Yyrkoon's rule. Almost nothing was entirely familiar to him. The great towers of Imrryr were warped and twisted into a troubling architecture which seemed to reflect the mental states of those gone entirely mad. Unnatural beasts prowled the serpentine streets and gigantic, demonic creatures lolled in the city squares. The palaces had grown huge, to accommodate those newcomers, and Melnibonéans were dwarfed to the size of ants in comparison.

Where Elric's kinfolk had once lived now dwelled creatures of cryptic biology, with carapaces encrusted in carbuncular jewels and organs which throbbed upon the surface of their bodies, with vast, multifaceted eyes which seemed blind and yet looked into worlds no other could see, with a multitude of arms and legs and other limbs whose function was impossible to guess. Bizarre creatures of Chaos ran through corridors which had become labyrinths, and in the re-wrought chambers of the towers Melnibonéans driven mad by their exposure to these new demons feasted on unnatural food and pleasured themselves in even stranger ways. Cries of horror and pain were the perpetual music filling this Melniboné.

In this dream, Elric made his way to the great throne chamber where Yyrkoon, gaunt and crazed, enjoyed intercourse with his demonic allies and lived in a state of perpetual celebration. Clearly he took no delight in Elric's arrival.

'Where is your sister?' demanded the albino. 'Where is my betrothed?'

And Yyrkoon at last, reluctantly, sent for her. The woman who came to the throne chamber was only barely recognisable to Elric. She was dressed in heavy clothing encrusted with gold, silver and platinum. She could barely move, and her eyes were drugged. Little, dwarfish creatures carried her train and crept in and out of her clothing, adjusting this, altering that. When she saw Elric she smiled, and it was a hideous travesty, clear to Elric that she was under an enchantment.

In the dream, Elric led his beloved away from the throne chamber, past ornamental pools where his dragon brothers, the Phoorn, seemed imprisoned. Once, Flamefang, his closest dragon kin, rose from the coruscating liquid and addressed him.

'We are all slaves of Chaos now, dear lord. All slaves of this nightmare.' But he promised that when Elric and Cymoril wished to leave he would try to carry them on his back to safety. *'Though this stuff which is not water, it corrodes us in such strange ways.'*

Then Elric found himself in a great chamber filled by an enormous bed carved with obscene figures. Cymoril spoke to him in an unfamiliar language. Her love-making was that of a stranger. When he did understand her words, he scarcely understood their meaning. Her tongue was thick, as if she had forgotten the High Speech of Melniboné.

'He told me that Arioch had killed you, and eaten your sword.'

And when Elric looked up through the canopy of that strange bed, he saw eyes he recognised. They were the mocking, triumphant, sardonic eyes of Arioch himself.

They lay together in that bridal chamber. Some might have considered it ostentatious. Some might have found it terrifying. Elric hardly saw the carvings and the decorations for he was filled with complex premonitions.

'We shall be married, now you are returned to Melniboné,' said Cymoril.

And on those words, always, Elric would awake, wondering in panic if he should not return at once to Melniboné, break his word and reclaim his throne. He feared that his actions had already produced cosmic reverberations of unprecedented significance. But circumstances led him in other directions. Try as he might, he could not find the way home. And eventually he reconciled himself to the fact that his destiny lay elsewhere, that there were things he must do, things he must learn, before he could ever return.

In his wakeful moments, when his sense of reality was restored, he told himself that only by mingling with the people of the Young Kingdoms would he learn what he needed. But as is often the case when the powerful design to learn the secrets of the powerless, his condescension was resented, his company rejected. Like so many before and after him, he discovered what a distance his power put between himself and those he envied.

Envy comprised much of what he felt for people he regarded as less complicated souls, leading simpler lives than his own, and carrying less complex burdens. Elric was too young, too self-involved, to realise that only to him were those problems less complex, and that those he envied actually envied him his power which, from their particular perspective, would if possessed by them entirely simplify and improve their lives.

Beyond the walls of Elric's particular plane, the Lords of the Higher Worlds continued to plot and plan not only Elric's fate, but that of his people, their friends and enemies. The machinations of those called 'gods' would lead Elric to explore some of the other worlds of the multiverse, falling into the power of legendary Agak and Gagak, encountering the dead Melnibonéan earl, Saxif D'Aan, and learning still more of his people's past. Of the mysterious blind captain who steered the ship of fate. And, most importantly, of the Eternal Champion, of whom he was an avatar.

Other avatars he would meet were called Corum, Erekosë, Hawkmoon, champions whom some knew as the Three Who Are One, before his joining them. Whereupon, naturally enough, they became the Four Who Are One. All these men were bound upon quests of their own. All sought fabled Tanelorn, where it is said the Champion Eternal shall find eternal peace.

They dreamed of Tanelorn. They desired Tanelorn as some men desired women, and others desired wealth. They longed for Tanelorn as a place they had lost, perhaps before they were born. As a place which, like Paradise, might not by definition exist at all.

Tanelorn. Some called it the City of Eternal Rest, beloved of those who welcome death. Some, of a simpler and perhaps more cynical disposition, say it is indeed no more than another name for the grave.

But I can tell you that Tanelorn is a powerful dream. It is what causes great heroes and heroines to perform great deeds. It is what raises us above the Lords of the Higher Worlds and makes us, poor mortals that we are, something nobler and more powerful than any who seek to control our destinies.

Dream Tanelorn might be to some of us, but to others it is

a reality, a reality we have moulded from the stuff of imagination and which stands for all our idealism, all our fine ambitions, all our yearnings and all our nobler selves. Though we spend many lifetimes seeking Tanelorn, find her at last we shall. And there, as we are promised, we shall know not only peace, but wisdom and security.

But the building of that city shall take many great dreams, and much courage, and you can be sure that not a single drop of savagely spilled blood will taint a single brick or stone of her.

So now begins another tale of the albino.

Forgetting as best he could his cousin Yyrkoon sitting as regent upon the Ruby Throne of Melniboné, suppressing all thoughts of his beautiful cousin Cymoril weeping for him and despairing of his ever returning, Elric went to seek an unknown goal in the worlds of the Young Kingdoms where Melnibonéans were, at best, disliked.

And it would not be long before he found himself sailing upon the mysterious seas of fate. What he found upon those seas is the substance of this story.

The Sailor on the Seas of Fate

For Bill Butler, Mike and Tony,
and all at Unicorn Books, Wales.

Book One

Sailing to the Future

Chapter One

It was as if the man stood in a vast cavern whose walls and roof were composed of gloomy, unstable colours which would occasionally break and admit rays of light from the moon. That these walls were mere clouds massed above mountains and ocean was hard to believe, for all that the moonlight pierced them, stained them and revealed the black and turbulent sea washing the shore on which the man now stood.

Distant thunder rolled; distant lightning flickered. A thin rain fell. And the clouds were never still. From dusky jet to deadly white they swirled slowly, like the cloaks of men and women engaged in a trancelike and formalistic minuet; the man standing on the shingle of the grim beach was reminded of giants dancing to the music of the faraway storm and felt as one must feel who walks unwittingly into a hall where the gods are at play. He turned his gaze from the clouds to the ocean.

The sea seemed weary. Great waves heaved themselves together with difficulty and collapsed as if in relief, gasping as they struck sharp rocks.

The man pulled his hood closer about his face and he looked over his leathern shoulder more than once as he trudged closer to the sea and let the surf spill upon the toes of his knee-length black boots. He tried to peer into the cavern formed by the clouds but could see only a short distance. There was no way of telling what lay on the other side of the ocean or, indeed, how far the water extended. He put his head on one side, listening carefully, but could hear nothing but the sounds of the sky and the sea. He sighed. For a moment a moonbeam touched him and from the white flesh of his face there glowed two crimson, tormented eyes; then darkness came back. Again the man turned, plainly fearing that the light had revealed him to some enemy. Making as little sound as possible, he headed towards the shelter of the rocks on his left.

Elric was tired. In the city of Ryfel in the land of Pikarayd he had naïvely sought acceptance by offering his services as a mercenary in the army of the governor of that place. For his foolishness he had been imprisoned as a Melnibonéan spy (it was obvious to the governor that Elric could be nothing else) and had but recently escaped with the aid of bribes and some minor sorcery.

The pursuit, however, had been almost immediate. Dogs of great cunning had been employed and the governor himself had led the hunt beyond the borders of Pikarayd and into the lonely, uninhabited shale valleys of a world locally called the Dead Hills, in which little grew or tried to live.

Up the steep sides of small mountains, whose slopes consisted of grey, crumbling slate, which made a clatter to be heard a mile or more away, the white-faced one had ridden. Along dales all but grassless and whose river-bottoms had seen no water for scores of years, through cave-tunnels bare of even a stalactite, over plateaux from which rose cairns of stones erected by a forgotten folk, he had sought to escape his pursuers, and soon it seemed to him that he had left the world he knew for ever, that he had crossed a supernatural frontier and had arrived in one of those bleak places of which he had read in the legends of his people, where once Law and Chaos had fought each other to a stalemate, leaving their battleground empty of life and the possibility of life.

And at last he had ridden his horse so hard that its heart had burst and he had abandoned its corpse and continued on foot, panting, to the sea, to this narrow beach, unable to go farther forward and fearing to return lest his enemies should be lying in wait for him.

He would give much for a boat now. It would not be long before the dogs discovered his scent and led their masters to the beach. He shrugged. Best to die here alone, perhaps, slaughtered by those who did not even know his name. His only regret would be that Cymoril would wonder why he had not returned at the end of the year.

He had no food and few of the drugs which had of late sustained his energy. Without renewed energy he could not contemplate working a sorcery which might conjure for him some means of crossing the sea and making, perhaps, for the Isle of the Purple Towns where the people were least unfriendly to Melnibonéans.

It had been months since he had left behind his Court and his queen-to-be, letting Yyrkoon sit on the throne of Melniboné until his return. He had thought he might learn more of the human folk of the Young Kingdoms by mixing with them, but they had rejected him either with outright hatred or wary and insincere humility. Nowhere had he found one willing to believe that a Melnibonéan (and they did not know he was the emperor) would willingly throw in his lot with the human beings who had once been in thrall to that cruel and ancient race. And now, as he stood beside a bleak sea feeling trapped and already defeated, he knew himself to be alone in a malevolent universe, bereft of friends and purpose, a useless, sickly anachronism, a fool brought low by his own insufficiencies of character, by his profound inability to believe wholly in the rightness or the wrongness of anything at all. He lacked faith in his race, in his birthright, in gods or men, and above all he lacked faith in himself.

His pace slackened; his hand fell upon the pommel of his black runesword. Stormbringer, seemingly half-sentient, was now his only companion, his only confidant, and it had become his neurotic habit to talk to the sword as another might talk to his horse or as a prisoner might share his thoughts with a cockroach in his cell.

'Well, Stormbringer, shall we walk into the sea and end it now?' His voice was dead, barely a whisper. 'At least we shall have the pleasure of thwarting those who follow us.'

He made a half-hearted movement toward the sea, but to his fatigued brain it seemed that the sword murmured, stirred against his hip, pulled back. The albino chuckled. 'You exist to live and to take lives. Do I exist, then, to die and bring both those I love and hate the mercy of death? Sometimes I think so. A sad pattern, if that should be the pattern. Yet there must be more to all this...'

He turned his back upon the sea, peering upward at the monstrous clouds forming and re-forming above his head, letting the light rain fall upon his face, listening to the complex, melancholy music which the sea made as it washed over rocks and shingle and was carried this way and that by conflicting currents. The rain did little to refresh him. He had not slept at all for two nights and had slept hardly at all for several more. He must have ridden for almost a week before his horse collapsed.

At the base of a damp granite crag which rose nearly thirty feet above his head, he found a depression in the ground in which he could squat and be protected from the worst of the wind and the rain. Wrapping his heavy leather cloak tightly about him, he eased himself into the hole and was immediately asleep. Let them find him while he slept. He wanted no warning of his death.

Harsh, grey light struck his eyes as he stirred. He raised his neck, holding back a groan at the stiffness of his muscles, and he opened his eyes. He blinked. It was morning – perhaps even later, for the sun was invisible – and a cold mist covered the beach. Through the mist the darker clouds could still be seen above, increasing the effect of his being inside a huge cavern. Muffled a little, the sea continued to splash and hiss, though it seemed calmer than it had on the previous night, and there were now no sounds of a storm. The air was very cold.

Elric began to stand up, leaning on his sword for support, listening carefully, but there was no sign that his enemies were close by. Doubtless they had given up the chase, perhaps after finding his dead horse.

He reached into his belt pouch and took from it a sliver of smoked bacon and a vial of yellowish liquid. He sipped from the vial, replaced the stopper and returned the vial to his pouch as he chewed on the meat. He was thirsty. He trudged further up the beach and found a pool of rainwater not too tainted with salt. He drank his fill, staring around him. The mist was fairly thick and if he moved too far from the beach he knew he would become immediately lost. Yet did that matter? He had nowhere to go. Those who had pursued him must have realised that. Without a horse he could not cross back to Pikarayd, the most easterly of the Young Kingdoms. Without a boat he could not venture onto that sea and try to steer a course back to the Isle of the Purple Towns. He recalled no map which showed an eastern sea and he had little idea of how far he had travelled from Pikarayd. He decided that his only hope of surviving was to go north, following the coast in the trust that sooner or later he would come upon a port or a fishing village where he might trade his few remaining belongings for a passage on a boat. Yet that hope was a small one, for his food and his drugs could hardly last more than a day or so.

He took a deep breath to steel himself for the march and then regretted it; the mist cut at his throat and his lungs like a thousand tiny knives. He coughed. He spat upon the shingle.

And he heard something: something other than the moody whisperings of the sea; a regular creaking sound, as of a man walking in stiff leather. His right hand went to his left hip and the sword which rested there. He turned about, peering in every direction for the source of the noise, but the mist distorted it. It could have come from anywhere.

Elric crept back to the rock where he had sheltered. He leaned against it so that no swordsman could take him unawares from behind. He waited.

The creaking came again, but other sounds were added. He heard a clanking; a splash; perhaps a voice, perhaps a footfall on timber; and he guessed that either he was experiencing a hallucination as a side effect of the drug he had just swallowed or he had heard a ship coming towards the beach and dropping its anchor.

He felt relieved and he was tempted to laugh at himself for assuming so readily that this coast must be uninhabited. He had thought that the bleak cliffs stretched for miles – perhaps hundreds of miles – in all directions. The assumption could easily have been the subjective result of his depression, his weariness. It occurred to him that he might as easily have discovered a land not shown on maps, yet with a sophisticated culture of its own: with sailing ships, for instance, and harbours for them. Yet still he did not reveal himself.

Instead he withdrew behind the rock, peering into the mist towards the sea. And at last he discerned a shadow which had not been there the previous night. A black, angular shadow which could only be a ship. He made out the suggestion of ropes, he heard men grunting, he heard the creak and the rasp of a yard as it travelled up a mast. The sail was being furled.

Elric waited at least an hour, expecting the crew of the ship to disembark. They could have no other reason for entering this treacherous bay. But a silence had descended, as if the whole ship slept.

Cautiously Elric emerged from behind the rock and walked down to the edge of the sea. Now he could see the ship a little more clearly. Red sunlight was behind it, thin and watery, diffused by the mist. It was a good-sized ship and fashioned throughout of the same dark wood. Its design was baroque and unfamiliar, with high decks fore and aft and no evidence of rowing ports. This was unusual in a ship either of Melnibonéan or Young Kingdoms design and it tended to prove his theory that he had stumbled upon a civilisation for some reason cut off from the rest of the world, just as Elwher and the Unmapped East were cut off by the vast stretches of the Sighing Desert and the Weeping Waste. He saw no movement aboard, heard none of the sounds one might usually expect to hear on a seagoing ship, even if the larger part of the crew was resting. The mist eddied and more of the red light poured through to illuminate the vessel, revealing the large wheels on both the foredeck and the reardeck, the slender mast with its furled sail, the complicated geometrical carvings of its rails and its figurehead, the great, curving prow which gave the ship its main impression of power and strength and made Elric think it must be a warship rather than a trading vessel. But who was there to fight in such waters as these?

He cast aside his wariness and cupped his hands about his mouth, calling out:

'Hail, the ship!'

The answering silence seemed to him to take on a peculiar hesitancy as if those on board heard him and wondered if they should answer.

'Hail, the ship!'

Then a figure appeared on the port rail and, leaning over, looked casually towards him. The figure had on armour as dark and as strange as the design of his ship; he had a helmet obscuring most of his face and the main feature that Elric could distinguish was a thick, golden beard and sharp blue eyes.

'Hail, the shore,' said the armoured man. His accent was unknown to Elric, his tone was as casual as his manner. Elric thought he smiled. 'What do you seek with us?'

'Aid,' said Elric. 'I am stranded here. My horse is dead. I am lost.'

'Lost? Aha!' The man's voice echoed in the mist. 'Lost. And you wish to come aboard?'

'I can pay a little. I can give my services in return for a passage, either to your next port of call or to some land close to the Young Kingdoms where maps are available so that I could make my own way thereafter...'

'Well,' said the other slowly, 'there's work for a swordsman.'

'I have a sword,' said Elric.

'I see it. A good, big battle-blade.'

'Then I can come aboard?'

'We must confer first. If you would be good enough to wait a while...'

'Of course,' said Elric. He was nonplussed by the man's manner, but the prospect of warmth and food on board the ship was cheering. He waited patiently until the blond-bearded warrior came back to the rail.

'Your name, sir?' said the warrior.

'I am Elric of Melniboné.'

The warrior seemed to be consulting a parchment, running his finger down a list until he nodded, satisfied, and put the list into his large-buckled belt.

'Well,' he said, 'there was some point in waiting here, after all. I found it difficult to believe.'

'What was the dispute and why did you wait?'

'For you,' said the warrior, heaving a rope ladder over the side so that its end fell into the sea. 'Will you board now, Elric of Melniboné?'

Chapter Two

Elric was surprised by how shallow the water was and he wondered by what means such a large vessel could come so close to the shore. Shoulder-deep in the sea he reached up to grasp the ebony rungs of the ladder. He had great difficulty heaving himself from the water and was further hampered by the swaying of the ship and the weight of his runesword, but eventually he had clambered awkwardly over the side and stood on the deck with the water running from his clothes to the timbers and his body shivering with cold. He looked about him. Shining, red-tinted mist clung about the ship's dark yards and rigging, white mist spread itself over the roofs and sides of the two large cabins set fore and aft of the mast, and this mist was not of the same character as the mist beyond the ship. Elric, for a moment, had the fanciful notion that the mist travelled permanently wherever the ship travelled. He smiled to himself, putting the dreamlike quality of his experience down to lack of food and sleep. When the ship sailed into sunnier waters he would see it for the relatively ordinary vessel it was.

The blond warrior took Elric's arm. The man was as tall as Elric and massively built. Within his helm he smiled, saying:

'Let us go below.'

They went to the cabin forward of the mast and the warrior drew back a sliding door, standing aside to let Elric enter first. Elric ducked his head and went into the warmth of the cabin. A lamp of red-grey glass gleamed, hanging from four silver chains attached to the roof, revealing several more bulky figures, fully dressed in a variety of armours, seated about a square and sturdy sea-table. All faces turned to regard Elric as he came in, followed by the blond warrior who said:

'This is he.'

J. CAWTHORN 79

One of the occupants of the cabin, who sat in the farthest corner and whose features were completely hidden by the shadow, nodded. 'Aye,' he said. 'That is he.'

'You know me, sir?' said Elric, seating himself at the end of the bench and removing his sodden leather cloak. The warrior nearest him passed him a metal cup of hot wine and Elric accepted it gratefully, sipping at the spiced liquid and marvelling at how quickly it dispersed the chill within him.

'In a sense,' said the man in the shadows. His voice was sardonic and at the same time had a melancholy ring, and Elric was not offended, for the bitterness in the voice seemed directed more at the owner than at any he addressed.

The blond warrior seated himself opposite Elric. 'I am Brut,' he said, 'once of Lashmar, where my family still holds land, but it is many a year since I have been there.'

'From the Young Kingdoms, then?' said Elric.

'Aye. Once.'

'This ship journeys nowhere near those nations?' Elric asked.

'I believe it does not,' said Brut. 'It is not so long, I think, since I myself came aboard. I was seeking Tanelorn, but found this craft, instead.'

'Tanelorn?' Elric smiled. 'How many must seek that mythical place? Do you know of one called Rackhir, once a Warrior Priest of Phum? We adventured together once. He left to look for Tanelorn.'

'I do not know him,' said Brut of Lashmar.

'And these waters,' said Elric, 'do they lie far from the Young Kingdoms?'

'Very far,' said the man in the shadows.

'Are you from Elwher, perhaps?' asked Elric. 'Or from any other of what we in the West call the Unmapped East?'

'Most of our lands are not on your maps,' said the man in the shadows. And he laughed. Again Elric found that he was not offended. And he was not particularly troubled by the mysteries hinted at by the man in the shadows. Soldiers of fortune, as he deemed these men to be, were fond of their private jokes and references; it was usually all that united them save a common willingness to hire their swords to whomever could pay.

Outside the anchor was rattling and the ship rolled. Elric heard the yard being lowered and he heard the smack of the sail as it was unfurled. He wondered how they hoped to leave the bay with so little wind available. He noticed that the faces of the other warriors, where their faces were visible, had taken on a rather set look as the ship began to move. He looked from one grim, haunted face to another and he wondered if his own features bore the same cast.

'For where do we sail?' he asked.

Brut shrugged. 'I know only that we had to stop to wait for you, Elric of Melniboné.'

'You knew I would be there?'

The man in the shadows stirred and helped himself to more hot wine from the jug set into a hole in the centre of the table. 'You are the last one we need,' he said. 'I was the first taken aboard. So far I have not regretted my decision to make the voyage.'

'Your name, sir?' Elric decided he would no longer be at that particular disadvantage.

'Oh, names? Names? I have so many. The one I favour is Erekosë. But I have been called Urlik Skarsol and John Daker and Ilian of Garathorm to my certain knowledge. Some would have me believe that I have been Elric Womanslayer...'

'Womanslayer? An unpleasant nickname. Who is this other Elric?'

'That I cannot completely answer,' said Erekosë. 'But I share a name, it seems, with more than one aboard this ship. I, like Brut, sought Tanelorn and found myself here instead.'

'We have that in common,' said another. He was a black-skinned warrior, the tallest of the company, his features oddly enhanced by a scar running like an inverted 'V' from his forehead and over both eyes, down his cheeks to his jawbones. 'I was in a land called Ghaja-Ki, a most unpleasant, swampy place, filled with perverse and diseased life. I had heard of a city said to exist there and I thought it might be Tanelorn. It was not. And it was inhabited by a blue-skinned, hermaphroditic race who determined to cure me of what they considered my malformations of hue and sexuality. This scar you see was their work. The pain of their operation gave me strength to escape them and I ran naked into the swamps, floundering for many a mile until the swamp became a lake feeding a broad river over which hung black clouds of insects which set upon me hungrily. This ship appeared and I was more than glad to seek its sanctuary. I am Otto Blendker, once a scholar of Brunse, now a hireling sword for my sins.'

'This Brunse? Does it lie near Elwher?' said Elric. He had never heard of such a place, nor such an outlandish name, in the Young Kingdoms.

The black man shook his head. 'I know nought of Elwher.'

'Then the world is a considerably larger place than I imagined,' said Elric.

'Indeed it is,' said Erekosë. 'What would you say if I offered you the theory that the sea on which we sail spans more than one world?'

'I would be inclined to believe you.' Elric smiled. 'I have studied such theories. More, I have experienced adventures in worlds other than my own.'

'It is a relief to hear it,' said Erekosë. 'Not all on board this ship are willing to accept my theory.'

'I come closer to accepting it,' said Otto Blendker, 'though I find it terrifying.'

'It is that,' agreed Erekosë. 'More terrifying than you can imagine, friend Otto.'

Elric leaned across the table and helped himself to a further mug of wine. His clothes were already drying and physically he had a sense of well-being. 'I'll be glad to leave this misty shore behind.'

'The shore has been left already,' said Brut, 'But as for the mist, it is ever with us. Mist appears to follow the ship – or else the ship creates the mist wherever it travels. It is rare that we see land at all and when we do see it, as we saw it today, it is usually obscured, like a reflection in a dull and buckled shield.'

'We sail on a supernatural sea,' said another, holding out a gloved hand for the jug. Elric passed it to him. 'In Hasghan, where I come from, we have a legend of a Bewitched Sea. If a mariner finds himself sailing in those waters he may never return and will be lost for eternity.'

'Your legend contains at least some truth, I fear, Terndrik of Hasghan,' Brut said.

'How many warriors are on board?' Elric asked.

'Sixteen other than the Four,' said Erekosë. 'Twenty in all. The crew numbers about ten and then there is the Captain. You will see him soon, doubtless.'

'The Four? Who are they?'

Erekosë laughed. 'You and I are two of them. The other two occupy the aft cabin. And if you wish to know *why* we are called the Four, you must ask the Captain, though I warn you his answers are rarely satisfying.'

Elric realised that he was being pressed slightly to one side. 'The ship makes good speed,' he said laconically, 'considering how poor the wind was.'

'Excellent speed,' agreed Erekosë. He rose from his corner, a broad-shouldered man with an ageless face bearing the evidence of considerable experience. He was handsome and he had plainly seen much conflict, for both his hands and his face were heavily scarred, though not disfigured. His eyes, though deep-set and dark, seemed of no particular colour and yet were familiar to Elric. He felt that he might have seen those eyes in a dream once.

'Have we met before?' Elric asked him.

'Oh, possibly – or shall meet. What does it matter? Our fates are the same. We share an identical doom. And possibly we share more than that.'

'More? I hardly comprehend the first part of your statement.'

'Then it is for the best,' said Erekosë, inching past his comrades and emerging on the other side of the table. He laid a surprisingly gentle hand on Elric's shoulder. 'Come, we must seek audience with the Captain. He expressed a wish to see you shortly after you came aboard.'

Elric nodded and rose. 'This captain – what is his name?'

'He has none he will reveal to us,' said Erekosë. Together they emerged onto the deck. The mist was if anything thicker and of the same deathly whiteness, no longer tinted by the sun's rays. It was hard to see to the far ends of the ship and for all that they were evidently moving rapidly, there was no hint of a wind. Yet it was warmer than Elric might have expected. He followed Erekosë forward to the cabin set under the deck on which one of the ship's twin wheels stood, tended by a tall man in sea-coat and leggings of quilted deerskin who was so still as to resemble a statue. The red-haired steersman did not look around or down as they advanced towards the cabin, but Elric caught a glimpse of his face.

The door seemed built of some kind of smooth metal possessing a sheen almost like the healthy coat of an animal. It was reddish-brown and the most colourful thing Elric had so far seen on the ship. Erekosë knocked softly upon the door. 'Captain,' he said. 'Elric is here.'

'Enter,' said a voice at once melodious and distant.

The door opened. Rosy light flooded out, half-blinding Elric as he walked in. As his eyes adapted, he could see a very tall, pale-clad man standing upon a richly hued carpet in the middle of the cabin. Elric heard the door close and realised that Erekosë had not accompanied him inside.

'Are you refreshed, Elric?' said the Captain.

'I am, sir, thanks to your wine.'

The Captain's features were no more human than were Elric's. They were at once finer and more powerful than those of the Melnibonéan, yet bore a slight resemblance in that the eyes were inclined to taper, as did the face, toward the chin. The Captain's long hair fell to his shoulders in red-gold waves and was kept back from his brow by a circlet of blue jade. His body was clad in buff-coloured tunic and hose and there were sandals of silver and silver-thread laced to his calves. Apart from his clothing, he was twin to the steersman Elric had recently seen.

'Will you have more wine?'

The Captain moved towards a chest on the far side of the cabin, near the porthole, which was closed.

'Thank you,' said Elric. And now he realised why the eyes had not focused on him. The Captain was blind. For all that his movements were deft and assured, it was obvious that he could not see at all. He poured the wine from a silver jug into a silver cup and began to cross towards Elric, holding the cup out before him. Elric stepped forward and accepted it.

'I am grateful for your decision to join us,' said the Captain. 'I am much relieved, sir.'

'You are courteous,' said Elric, 'though I must add that my decision was not difficult to make. I had nowhere else to go.'

'I understand that. It is why we put into shore when and where we did. You will find that all your companions were in a similar position before they, too, came aboard.'

'You appear to have considerable knowledge of the movements of many men,' said Elric. He held the wine untasted in his left hand.

'Many,' agreed the Captain, 'on many worlds. I understand that you are a person of culture, sir, so you will be aware of something of the nature of the sea upon which my ship sails.'

'I think so.'

'She sails between the worlds, for the most part – between the planes of a variety of aspects of the same world, to be a little more exact.' The Captain hesitated, turning his blind face away from Elric. 'Please know that I do not deliberately mystify you. There are some things I do not understand and other things which I may not completely reveal. It is a trust I have and I hope you feel you can respect it.'

'I have no reason as yet to do otherwise,' replied the albino. And he took a sip of the wine.

'I find myself with a fine company,' said the Captain. 'I hope that you continue to think it worthwhile honouring my trust when we reach our destination.'

'And what is that, Captain?'

'An island indigenous to these waters.'

'That must be a rarity.'

'Indeed, it is, and once undiscovered, uninhabited by those we must count our enemies. Now that they have found it and realise its power, we are in great danger.'

'We? You mean your race or those aboard your ship?'

The Captain smiled. 'I have no race, save myself. I speak, I suppose, of all humanity.'

'These enemies are not human, then?'

'No. They are inextricably involved in human affairs, but this fact has not instilled in them any loyalty to us. I use "humanity", of course, in its broader sense, to include yourself and myself.'

'I understood,' said Elric. 'What is this folk called?'

'Many things,' said the Captain. 'Forgive me, but I cannot continue longer now. If you will ready yourself for battle I assure you that I will reveal more to you as soon as the time is right.'

Only when Elric stood again outside the reddish-brown door, watching Erekosë advancing up the deck through the mist, did the albino wonder if the Captain had charmed him to the point where he had forgotten all common sense. Yet the blind man had impressed him and he had, after all, nothing better to do than to sail on to the island. He shrugged. He could always alter his decision if he discovered that those upon the island were not, in his opinion, enemies.

'Are you more mystified or less, Elric?' said Erekosë, smiling.

'More mystified in some ways, less in others,' Elric told him. 'And, for some reason, I do not care.'

'Then you share the feeling of the whole company,' Erekosë told him.

It was only when Erekosë led him to the cabin aft of the mast that Elric realised he had not asked the Captain what the significance of the Four might be.

Chapter Three

Save that it faced in the opposite direction, the other cabin resembled the first in almost every detail. Here, too, were seated some dozen men, all experienced soldiers of fortune by their features and their clothing. Two sat together at the centre of the table's starboard side. One was bareheaded, fair and careworn, the other had features resembling Elric's own and he seemed to be wearing a silver gauntlet on his left hand while the right hand was naked; his armour was delicate and outlandish. He looked up as Elric entered and there was recognition in his single eye (the other was covered by a brocade-work patch).

'Elric of Melniboné!' he exclaimed. 'My theories become more meaningful!' He turned to his companion. 'See, Hawkmoon, this is the one of whom I spoke.'

'You know me, sir?' Elric was nonplussed.

'You recognise me, Elric. You must! At the Tower of Voilodion Ghagnasdiak? With Erekosë – though a different Erekosë. I am Corum.'

'I know of no such tower, no name which resembles that, and this is the first I have seen of Erekosë. You know me and you know my name, but I do not know you. I find this disconcerting, sir.'

'I, too, had never met Prince Corum before he came aboard,' said Erekosë, 'yet he insists we fought together once. I am inclined to believe him. Time on the different planes does not always run concurrently. Prince Corum might well exist in what we would term the future.'

'I had thought to find some relief from such paradoxes here,' said Hawkmoon, passing his hand over his face. He smiled bleakly. 'But it seems there is none at this present moment in the history of the planes. Everything is in flux and even our identities, it seems, are prone to alter at any moment.'

'We were Three,' said Corum. 'Do you not recall it, Elric? The Three Who Are One?'

Elric shook his head.

Corum shrugged, saying softly to himself, 'Well, now we are Four. Did the Captain say anything of an island we are supposed to invade?'

'He did,' said Elric. 'Do you know who these enemies might be?'

'We know no more or less than do you, Elric,' said Hawkmoon. 'I seek a place called Tanelorn and two children. Perhaps I seek the Runestaff, too. Of that I am not entirely sure.'

'We found it once,' said Corum. 'We three. In the Tower of Voilodion Ghagnasdiak. It was of considerable help to us.'

'As it might be to me,' Hawkmoon told him. 'I served it once. I gave it a great deal.'

'We have much in common,' Erekosë put in, 'as I told you, Elric. Perhaps we share masters in common, too?'

Elric shrugged. 'I serve no master but myself.'

And he wondered why they all smiled in the same strange way.

Erekosë said quietly, 'On such ventures as these one is inclined to forget much, as one forgets a dream.'

'This *is* a dream,' said Hawkmoon. 'Of late I've dreamed many such.'

'It is all dreaming, if you like,' said Corum. 'All existence.'

Elric was not interested in such philosophising. 'Dream or reality, the experience amounts to the same, does it not?'

'Quite right,' said Erekosë with a wan smile.

They talked on for another hour or two until Corum stretched and yawned and commented that he was feeling sleepy. The others agreed that they were all tired and so they left the cabin and went forward and below where there were bunks for all the warriors. As he stretched himself out in one of the bunks, Elric said to Brut of Lashmar, who had climbed into the bunk above:

'It would help to know when this fight begins.'

Brut looked over the edge, down at the prone albino. 'I think it will be soon,' he said.

*

Elric stood alone upon the deck, leaning upon the rail and trying to make out the sea, but the sea, like the rest of the world, was hidden by white curling mist. Elric wondered if there were waters flowing under the ship's keel at all. He looked up to where the sail was tight and swollen at the mast, filled with a warm and powerful wind. It was light, but again it was not possible to tell the hour of the day. Puzzled by Corum's comments concerning an earlier meeting, Elric wondered if there had been other dreams in his life such as this might be – dreams he had forgotten completely upon awakening. But the uselessness of such speculation became quickly evident and he turned his attention to more immediate matters, wondering at the origin of the Captain and his strange ship sailing on a stranger ocean.

'The Captain,' said Hawkmoon's voice, and Elric turned to bid good morning to the tall, fair-haired man who bore a strange, regular scar in the centre of his forehead, 'has requested that we four visit him in his cabin.'

The other two emerged from the mist and together they made their way to the prow, knocking on the reddish-brown door and being at once admitted into the presence of the blind captain, who had four silver wine-cups already poured for them. He gestured them towards the great chest on which the wine stood. 'Please help yourselves, my friends.'

They did so, standing there with the cups in their hands, four tall, doom-haunted swordsmen, each of a strikingly different cast of features, yet each bearing a certain stamp which marked them as being of a like kind. Elric noticed it, for all that he was one of them, and he tried to recall the details of what Corum had told him on the previous evening.

'We are nearing our destination,' said the Captain. 'It will not be long before we disembark. I do not believe our enemies expect us, yet it will be a hard fight against those two.'

'Two?' said Hawkmoon. 'Only two?'

'Only two.' The Captain smiled. 'A brother and a sister. Sorcerers from quite another universe than ours. Due to recent disruptions in the fabric of our worlds – of which you know something,

Hawkmoon, and you, too, Corum – certain beings have been released who would not otherwise have the power they now possess. And possessing great power, they crave for more – for all the power that there is in our universe. These beings are amoral in a way in which the Lords of Law or Chaos are not. They do not fight for influence upon the Earth, as those gods do; their only wish is to convert the essential energy of our universe to their own uses. I believe they foster some ambition in their particular universe which would be furthered if they could achieve their wish. At present, in spite of conditions highly favourable to them, they have not attained their full strength, but the time is not far off before they do attain it. Agak and Gagak is how they are called in human tongue and they are outside the power of any of our gods, so a more powerful group has been summoned – yourselves. The Champion Eternal in four of his incarnations (and four is the maximum number we can risk without precipitating further unwelcome disruptions among the planes of Earth) – Erekosë, Elric, Corum and Hawkmoon. Each of you will command four others, whose fates are linked with your own and who are great fighters in their own right, though they do not share your destinies in every sense. You may each pick the four with whom you wish to fight. I think you will find it easy enough to decide. We make landfall quite shortly now.'

'You will lead us?' Hawkmoon said.

'I cannot. I can only take you to the island and wait for those who survive – if any survive.'

Elric frowned. 'This fight is not mine, I think.'

'It is yours,' said the Captain soberly. 'And it is mine. I would land with you if that were permitted me, but it is not.'

'Why so?' asked Corum.

'You will learn that one day. I have not the courage to tell you. I bear you nothing but good will, however. Be assured of that.'

Erekosë rubbed his jaw. 'Well, since it is my destiny to fight, and since I, like Hawkmoon, continue to seek Tanelorn, and since I gather there is some chance of my fulfilling my ambition if

I am successful, I for one agree to go against these two, Agak and Gagak.'

Hawkmoon nodded. 'I go with Erekosë, for similar reasons.'

'And I,' said Corum.

'Not long since,' said Elric, 'I counted myself without comrades. Now I have many. For that reason alone I will fight with them.'

'It is perhaps the best of reasons,' said Erekosë approvingly.

'There is no reward for this work, save my assurance that your success will save the world much misery,' said the Captain. 'And for you, Elric, there is less reward than the rest may hope for.'

'Perhaps not,' said Elric.

'As you say.' The Captain gestured towards the jug of wine. 'More wine, my friends?'

They each accepted, while the Captain continued, his blind face staring upward at the roof of the cabin.

'Upon this island is a ruin – perhaps it was once a city called Tanelorn – and at the centre of the ruin stands one whole building. It is this building which Agak and his sister use. It is that which you must attack. You will recognise it, I hope, at once.'

'And we must slay this pair?' said Erekosë.

'If you can. They have servants who help them. These must be slain, also. Then the building must be fired. This is important.' The Captain paused. 'Fired. It must be destroyed in no other way.'

Elric smiled a dry smile. 'There are few other ways of destroying buildings, Sir Captain.'

The Captain returned his smile and made a slight bow of acknowledgement. 'Aye, it's so. Nonetheless, it is worth remembering what I have said.'

'Do you know what these two look like, these Agak and Gagak?' Corum asked.

'No. It is possible that they resemble creatures of our own worlds; it is possible that they do not. Few have seen them. It is only recently that they have been able to materialise at all.'

'And how may they best be overwhelmed?' asked Hawkmoon.

'By courage and ingenuity,' said the Captain.

'You are not very explicit, sir,' said Elric.

'I am as explicit as I can be. Now, my friends, I suggest you rest and prepare your arms.'

As they returned to their cabins, Erekosë sighed.

'We are fated,' he said. 'We have little free will, for all we deceive ourselves otherwise. If we perish or live through this venture, it will not count for much in the overall scheme of things.'

'I think you are of a gloomy turn of mind, friend,' said Hawkmoon.

The mist snaked through the branches of the mast, writhing in the rigging, flooding the deck. It swirled across the faces of the other three men as Elric looked at them.

'A realistic turn of mind,' said Corum.

The mist massed more thickly upon the deck, mantling each man like a shroud. The timbers of the ship creaked and to Elric's ears took on the sound of a raven's croak. It was colder now. In silence they went to their cabins to test the hooks and buckles of their armour, to polish and to sharpen their weapons and to pretend to sleep.

'Oh, I've no liking for sorcery,' said Brut of Lashmar, tugging at his golden beard, 'for sorcery it was resulted in my shame.' Elric had told him all that the Captain had said and had asked Brut to be one of the four who fought with him when they landed.

'It is all sorcery here,' Otto Blendker said. And he smiled wanly as he gave Elric his hand. 'I'll fight beside you, Elric.'

His sea-green armour shimmering faintly in the lantern light, another rose, his casque pushed back from his face. It was a face almost as white as Elric's, though the eyes were deep and near-black. 'And I,' said Hown Serpent-tamer, 'though I fear I'm little use on still land.'

The last to rise, at Elric's glance, was a warrior who had said little during their earlier conversations. His voice was deep and hesitant. He wore a plain iron battle-cap and the red hair beneath it was braided. At the end of each braid was a small finger-bone which rattled on the shoulders of his byrnie as he moved. This was Ashnar the Lynx, whose eyes were rarely less than fierce. 'I lack the eloquence or the breeding of you other gentlemen,' said Ashnar. 'And I've no familiarity with sorcery or those other things of which you speak, but I'm a good soldier and my joy is in fighting. I'll take your orders, Elric, if you'll have me.'

'Willingly,' said Elric.

'There is no dispute, it seems,' said Erekosë to the remaining four who had elected to join him. 'All this is doubtless preordained. Our destinies have been linked from the first.'

'Such philosophy can lead to unhealthy fatalism,' said Terndrik of Hasghan. 'Best believe our fates are our own, even if the evidence denies it.'

'You must think as you wish,' said Erekosë. 'I have led many lives, though all, save one, are remembered but faintly.' He shrugged. 'Yet I deceive myself, I suppose, in that I work for a time when I shall find this Tanelorn and perhaps be reunited with the one I seek. That ambition is what gives me energy, Terndrik.'

Elric smiled. 'I fight, I think, because I relish the comradeship of battle. That, in itself, is a melancholy condition in which to find oneself, is it not?'

'Aye.' Erekosë glanced at the floor. 'Well, we must try to rest now.'

Chapter Four

THE OUTLINES OF the coast were dim. They waded through white water and white mist, their swords held above their heads. Swords were their only weapons. Each of the Four possessed a blade of unusual size and design, but none bore a sword which occasionally murmured to itself as did Elric's Stormbringer. Glancing back, Elric saw the Captain standing at the rail, his blind face turned towards the island, his pale lips moving as if he spoke to himself. Now the water was waist-deep and the sand beneath Elric's feet hardened and became smooth rock. He waded on, wary and ready to carry any attack to those who might be defending the island. But now the mist grew thinner, as if it could gain no hold on the land, and there were no obvious signs of defenders.

Tucked into his belt, each man had a brand, its end wrapped in oiled cloth so that it should not be wet when the time came to light it. Similarly, each was equipped with a handful of smouldering tinder in a little firebox in a pouch attached to his belt, so that the brands could be instantly ignited.

'Only fire will destroy this enemy for ever,' the Captain had said again as he handed them their brands and their tinderboxes.

As the mist cleared, it revealed a landscape of dense shadows. The shadows spread over red rock and yellow vegetation and they were shadows of all shapes and dimensions, resembling all manner of things. They seemed cast by the huge blood-coloured sun which stood at perpetual noon above the island, but what was disturbing about them was that the shadows themselves seemed without a source, as if the objects they represented were invisible or existed elsewhere than on the island itself. The sky, too, seemed full of these shadows, but whereas those on the island were still, those in the sky sometimes moved, perhaps when the clouds moved. And all the while the red sun poured down its bloody light and touched the twenty men with its unwelcome radiance just as it touched the land.

And at times, as they advanced cautiously inland, a peculiar flickering light sometimes crossed the island so that the outlines of the place became unsteady for a few seconds before returning to focus. Elric suspected his eyes and said nothing until Hown Serpent-tamer, who was having difficulty finding his land legs, remarked:

'I have rarely been ashore, it's true, but I think the quality of this land is stranger than any other I've known. It shimmers. It distorts.'

Several voices agreed with him.

'And whence come all these shadows?' Ashnar the Lynx stared around him in unashamed superstitious awe. 'Why cannot we see that which casts them?'

'It could be,' Corum said, 'that these are shadows cast by objects existing in other dimensions of the Earth. If all dimensions meet here, as has been suggested, that could be a likely explanation.' He put his silver hand to his embroidered eye-patch. 'This is not the strangest example I have witnessed of such a conjunction.'

'Likely?' Otto Blendker snorted. 'Pray let none give me an *unlikely* explanation, if you please!'

They pressed on through the shadows and the lurid light until they arrived at the outskirts of the ruins.

These ruins, thought Elric, had something in common with the ramshackle city of Ameeron, which he had visited on his quest for the Black Sword. But they were altogether more vast – more a collection of smaller cities, each one in a radically different architectural style.

'Perhaps this is Tanelorn,' said Corum, who had visited the place, 'or, rather, all the versions of Tanelorn there have ever been. For Tanelorn exists in many forms, each form depending upon the wishes of those who most desire to find her.'

'This is not the Tanelorn I expected to find,' said Hawkmoon bitterly.

'Nor I,' added Erekosë bleakly.

'Perhaps it is not Tanelorn,' said Elric. 'Perhaps it is not.'

'Or perhaps this is a graveyard,' said Corum distantly, frowning with his single eye. 'A graveyard containing all the forgotten versions of that strange city.'

They began to clamber over the ruins, their arms clattering as they moved, heading for the centre of the place. Elric could tell by the introspective expressions in the faces of many of his companions that they, like him, were wondering if this were not a dream. Why else should they find themselves in this peculiar situation, unquestioningly risking their lives – perhaps their souls – in a fight with which none of them was identified?

Erekosë moved closer to Elric as they marched. 'Have you noticed,' said he, 'that the shadows now represent something?'

Elric nodded. 'You can tell from the ruins what some of the buildings looked like when they were whole. The shadows are the shadows of those buildings – the original buildings before they became ruined.'

'Just so,' said Erekosë. Together, they shuddered.

At last they approached the likely centre of the place and here was a building which was not ruined. It stood in a cleared space, all curves and ribbons of metal and glowing tubes.

'It resembles a machine more than a building,' said Hawkmoon.

'And a musical instrument more than a machine,' Corum mused.

The party came to a halt, each group of four gathering about its leader. There was no question but that they had arrived at their goal.

Now that Elric looked carefully at the building he could see that it was in fact two buildings – both absolutely identical and joined at various points by curling systems of pipes which might be connecting corridors, though it was difficult to imagine what manner of being could utilise them.

'Two buildings,' said Erekosë. 'We were not prepared for this. Shall we split up and attack both?'

Instinctively Elric felt that this action would be unwise. He shook his head. 'I think we should go together into one, else our strength will be weakened.'

'I agree,' said Hawkmoon, and the rest nodded.

Thus, there being no cover to speak of, they marched boldly towards the nearest building to a point near the ground where a black opening of irregular proportions could be discerned. Ominously, there was still no sign of defenders. The buildings pulsed and glowed and occasionally whispered, but that was all.

Elric and his party were the first to enter, finding themselves in a damp, warm passage which curved almost immediately to the right. They were followed by the others until all stood in this passage warily glaring ahead, expecting to be attacked. But no attack came.

With Elric at their head, they moved on for some moments before the passage began to tremble violently and sent Hown Serpent-tamer crashing to the floor cursing. As the man in the sea-green armour scrambled up, a voice began to echo along the passage, seemingly coming from a great distance yet nonetheless loud and irritable.

'*Who? Who? Who?*' shrieked the voice.

'*Who? Who? Who invades me?*'

The passage's tremble subsided a little into a constant quivering motion. The voice became a muttering, detached and uncertain.

'*What attacks? What?*'

The twenty men glanced at one another in puzzlement. At length Elric shrugged and led the party on and soon the passage had widened out into a hall whose walls, roof and floor were damp with sticky fluid and whose air was hard to breathe. And now, somehow passing themselves through the walls of this hall, came the first of the defenders, ugly beasts who must be the servants of that mysterious brother and sister Agak and Gagak.

'*Attack!*' cried the distant voice. '*Destroy this. Destroy it!*'

The beasts were of a primitive sort, mostly gaping mouth and slithering body, but there were many of them oozing towards the twenty men, who quickly formed themselves into the four

fighting units and prepared to defend themselves. The creatures made a dreadful slushing sound as they approached and the ridges of bone which served them as teeth clashed as they reared up to snap at Elric and his companions. Elric whirled his sword and it met hardly any resistance as it sliced through several of the things at once. But now the air was thicker than ever and a stench threatened to overwhelm them as fluid drenched the floor.

'Move on through them,' Elric instructed, 'hacking a path through as you go. Head for yonder opening.' He pointed with his left hand.

And so they advanced, cutting back hundreds of the primitive beasts and thus decreasing the breathability of the air.

'The creatures are not hard to fight,' gasped Hown Serpent-tamer, 'But each one we kill robs us a little of our own chances of life.'

Elric was aware of the irony. 'Cunningly planned by our enemies, no doubt.' He coughed and slashed again at a dozen of the beasts slithering towards him. The things were fearless, but they were stupid, too. They made no attempt at strategy.

Finally Elric reached the next passage, where the air was slightly purer. He sucked gratefully at the sweeter atmosphere and waved his companions on.

Sword-arms rising and falling, they gradually retreated back into the passage, followed by only a few of the beasts. The creatures seemed reluctant to enter the passage and Elric suspected that somewhere within it there must lie a danger which even they feared. There was nothing for it, however, but to press on and he was only grateful that all twenty had survived this initial ordeal.

Gasping, they rested for a moment, leaning against the trembling walls of the passage, listening to the tones of that distant voice, now muffled and indistinct.

'I like not this castle at all,' growled Brut of Lashmar, inspecting a rent in his cloak where a creature had seized it. 'High sorcery commands it.'

'It is only what we knew,' Ashnar the Lynx reminded him, and Ashnar was plainly hard put to control his terror. The finger-bones in his braids kept time with the trembling of the walls and the huge barbarian looked almost pathetic as he steeled himself to go on.

'They are cowards, these sorcerers,' Otto Blendker said. 'They do not show themselves.' He raised his voice. 'Is their aspect so loathsome that they are afraid lest we look upon them?' It was a challenge not taken up. As they pushed on through the passages there was no sign either of Agak or his sister Gagak. It became gloomier and brighter in turns. Sometimes the passages narrowed so that it was difficult to squeeze their bodies through, sometimes they widened into what were almost halls. Most of the time they appeared to be climbing higher into the building.

Elric tried to guess the nature of the building's inhabitants. There were no steps in the castle, no artefacts he could recognise. For no particular reason he developed an image of Agak and Gagak as reptilian in form, for reptiles would prefer gently rising passages to steps and doubtless would have little need of conventional furniture. There again it was possible that they could change their shape at will, assuming human form when it suited them. He was becoming impatient to face either one or both of the sorcerers.

Ashnar the Lynx had other reasons – or so he said – for his own lack of patience.

'They said there'd be treasure here,' he muttered. 'I thought to stake my life against a fair reward, but there's nought here of value.' He put a horny hand against the damp material of the wall. 'Not even stone or brick. What are these walls made of, Elric?'

Elric shook his head. 'That has puzzled me, also, Ashnar.'

Then Elric saw large, fierce eyes peering out of the gloom ahead. He heard a rattling noise, a rushing noise, and the eyes grew larger and larger. He saw a red mouth, yellow fangs, orange fur. Then the growling sounded and the beast sprang at him even as he raised Stormbringer to defend himself and shouted a warning to the others. The creature was a baboon, but huge, and there were at least a dozen others following the first. Elric drove his body forward behind his sword, taking the beast in its groin.

Claws reached out and dug into his shoulder and waist. He groaned as he felt at least one set of claws draw blood. His arms were trapped and he could not pull Stormbringer free. All he could do was twist the sword in the wound he had already made. With all his might, he turned the hilt. The great ape shouted, its bloodshot eyes blazing, and it bared its yellow fangs as its muzzle shot towards Elric's throat. The teeth closed on his neck, the stinking breath threatened to choke him. Again he twisted the blade. Again the beast yelled in pain.

The fangs were pressing into the metal of Elric's gorget, the only thing saving him from immediate death. He struggled to free at least one arm, twisting the sword for the third time, then tugging it sideways to widen the wound in the groin. The growls and groans of the baboon grew more intense and the teeth tightened their hold on his neck, but now, mingled with the noises of the ape, he began to hear a murmuring and he felt Stormbringer pulse in his hand. He knew that the sword was drawing power from the ape even as the ape sought to destroy him. Some of that power began to flow into his body.

Desperately Elric put all his remaining strength into dragging the sword across the ape's body, slitting its belly wide so that its blood and entrails spilled over him as he was suddenly free and staggering backwards, wrenching the sword out in the same movement. The ape, too, was staggering back, staring down in stupefied awe at its own horrible wound before it fell to the floor of the passage.

Elric turned, ready to give aid to his nearest comrade, and he was in time to see Terndrik of Hasghan die, kicking in the clutches of an even larger ape, his head bitten clean from his shoulders and his red blood gouting.

Elric drove Stormbringer cleanly between the shoulders of Terndrik's slayer, taking the ape in the heart. Beast and human victim fell together. Two others were dead and several bore bad wounds, but the remaining warriors fought on, swords and armour smeared with crimson. The narrow passage stank of ape, of sweat and of blood. Elric pressed into the fight, chopping at the skull of an ape which grappled with Hown Serpent-tamer, who had lost his sword. Hown darted a look of thanks at Elric as he bent to retrieve his blade and together they set upon the largest of all the baboons. This creature stood much taller than Elric and had Erekosë pressed against the wall, Erekosë's sword through its shoulder.

From two sides, Hown and Elric stabbed and the baboon snarled and screamed, turning to face the new attackers, Erekosë's blade quivering in its shoulder. It rushed upon them and they stabbed again together, taking the monster in its heart and its lung so that when it roared at them blood vomited from its mouth. It fell to its knees, its eyes dimming, then sank slowly down.

And now there was silence in the passage and death lay all about them.

Terndrik of Hasghan was dead. Two of Corum's party were dead. All of Erekosë's surviving men bore major wounds. One of Hawkmoon's men was dead, but the remaining three were virtually unscathed. Brut of Lashmar's helm was dented, but he was otherwise unwounded and Ashnar the Lynx was dishevelled, nothing more. Ashnar had taken two of the baboons during the fight. But now the barbarian's eyes rolled as he leaned, panting, against the wall.

'I begin to suspect this venture of being uneconomical,' he said with a half-grin. He rallied himself, stepping over a baboon's corpse to join Elric. 'The less time we take over it, the better. What think you, Elric?'

'I would agree.' Elric returned his grin. 'Come.' And he led the way through the passage and into a chamber whose walls gave off a pinkish light. He had not walked far before he felt something catch at his ankle and he stared down in horror to see a long, thin snake winding itself about his leg. It was too late to use his sword; instead he seized the reptile behind its head and dragged it partially free of his leg before hacking the head from the body. The others were now stamping and shouting warnings to each other. The snakes did not appear to be venomous, but there were thousands of them, appearing, it seemed, from out of the floor itself.

They were flesh-coloured and had no eyes, more closely resembling earthworms than ordinary reptiles, but they were strong enough.

Hown Serpent-tamer sang a strange song now, with many liquid, hissing notes, and this seemed to have a calming effect upon the creatures. One by one at first and then in increasing numbers, they dropped back to the floor, apparently sleeping. Hown grinned at his success.

Elric said, 'Now I understand how you came by your surname.'

'I was not sure the song would work on these,' Hown told him, 'for they are unlike any serpents I have ever seen in the seas of my own world.'

They waded on through mounds of sleeping serpents, noticing that the next passage rose sharply. At times they were forced to use their hands to steady themselves as they climbed the peculiar, slippery material of the floor.

It was much hotter in this passage and they were all sweating, pausing several times to rest and mop their brows. The passage seemed to extend upwards for ever, turning occasionally, but never levelling out for more than a few feet. At times it narrowed to little more than a tube through which they had to squirm on their stomachs and at other times the roof disappeared into the gloom over their heads. Elric had long since given up trying to relate their position to what he had seen of the outside of the castle. From time to time small, shapeless creatures rushed towards them in shoals apparently with the intention of attacking them, but these were rarely more than an irritation and were soon all but ignored by the party as it continued its climb.

For a while they had not heard the strange voice which had greeted them upon their entering, but now it began to whisper again, its tones more urgent than before.

'Where? Where? Oh, the pain!'

They paused, trying to locate the source of the voice, but it seemed to come from everywhere at once.

Grim-faced, they continued, plagued by thousands of little creatures which bit at their exposed flesh like so many gnats, yet the creatures were not insects. Elric had seen nothing like them before. They were shapeless, primitive and all but colourless. They battered at his face as he moved; they were like a wind. Half-blinded, choked, sweating, he felt his strength leaving him. The air was so thick now, so hot, so salty, it was as if he moved through liquid. The others were as badly affected as was he; some were staggering and two men fell, to be helped up again by comrades almost as exhausted. Elric was tempted to strip off his armour, but he knew this would leave more of his flesh to the mercy of the little flying creatures.

Still they climbed and now more of the serpentine things they had seen earlier began to writhe around their feet, hampering them further, for all that Hown sang his sleeping song until he was hoarse.

'We can survive this only a little longer,' said Ashnar the Lynx, moving close to Elric. 'We shall be in no condition to meet the sorcerer if we ever find him or his sister.'

Elric nodded a gloomy head. 'My thoughts, too, yet what else may we do, Ashnar?'

'Nothing,' said Ashnar in a low voice. 'Nothing.'

'*Where? Where? Where?*' The word rustled all about them. Many of the party were becoming openly nervous.

Chapter Five

THEY HAD REACHED the top of the passage. The querulous voice was much louder now, but it quavered more. They saw an archway and beyond the archway a lighted chamber.

'Agak's room, without doubt,' said Ashnar, taking a better grip on his sword.

'Possibly,' said Elric. He felt detached from his body. Perhaps it was the heat and the exhaustion, or his growing sense of disquiet, but something made him withdraw into himself and hesitate before entering the chamber.

The place was octagonal and each of its eight sloping sides was of a different colour and each colour changed constantly. Occasionally the walls became semi-transparent, revealing a complete view of the ruined city (or collection of cities) far below, and also a view of the twin castle to this one, still connected by tubes and wires.

It was the large pool in the centre of the chamber which attracted most of their attention. It seemed deep and was full of evil-smelling, viscous stuff. It bubbled. Shapes formed in it. Grotesque and strange, beautiful and familiar, the shapes seemed always upon the brink of taking permanent form before falling back into the stuff of the pool. And the voice was still louder and there was no question now that it came from the pool.

'WHAT? WHAT? WHO INVADES?'

Elric forced himself closer to the pool and for a moment saw his own face staring out at him before it melted.

'WHO INVADES? AH! I AM TOO WEAK!'

Elric spoke to the pool. 'We are of those you would destroy,' he said. 'We are those on whom you would feed.'

'AH! AGAK! AGAK! I AM SICK! WHERE ARE YOU?'

Ashnar and Brut joined Elric. The faces of the warriors were filled with disgust.

'Agak,' growled Ashnar the Lynx, his eyes narrowing. 'At last some sign that the sorcerer is here!'

The others had all crowded in, to stand as far away from the pool as possible, but all stared, fascinated by the variety of the shapes forming and disintegrating in the viscous liquid.

'I WEAKEN... MY ENERGY NEEDS TO BE REPLENISHED... WE MUST BEGIN NOW, AGAK... IT TOOK US SO LONG TO REACH THIS PLACE. I THOUGHT I COULD REST. BUT THERE IS DISEASE HERE. IT FILLS MY BODY. AGAK. AWAKEN, AGAK. AWAKEN!'

'Some servant of Agak's, charged with the defence of the chamber?' suggested Hown Serpent-tamer in a small voice.

But Elric continued to stare into the pool as he began, he thought, to realise the truth.

'Will Agak wake?' Brut said. 'Will he come?' He glanced nervously around him.

'Agak!' called Ashnar the Lynx. 'Coward!'

'Agak!' cried many of the other warriors, brandishing their swords.

But Elric said nothing and he noted, too, that Hawkmoon and Corum and Erekosë all remained silent. He guessed that they must be filled with the same dawning understanding.

He looked at them. In Erekosë's eyes he saw an agony, a pity both for himself and his comrades.

'We are the Four Who Are One,' said Erekosë. His voice shook.

Elric was seized by an alien impulse, an impulse which disgusted and terrified him. 'No...' He attempted to sheathe Stormbringer, but the sword refused to enter its scabbard.

'AGAK! QUICKLY!' said the voice from the pool.

'If we do not do this thing,' said Erekosë, 'they will eat all our worlds. Nothing will remain.'

Elric put his free hand to his head. He swayed upon the edge of that frightful pool. He moaned.

'We must do it, then.' Corum's voice was an echo.

'I will not,' said Elric. 'I am myself.'

'And I!' said Hawkmoon.

But Corum Jhaelen Irsei said, 'It is the only way for us, for the single thing that we are. Do you not see that? We are the only creatures of our worlds who possess the means of slaying the sorcerers – in the only manner in which they can be slain!'

Elric looked at Corum, at Hawkmoon, at Erekosë, and again he saw something of himself in all of them.

'We are the Four Who Are One,' said Erekosë. 'Our united strength is greater than the sum. We must come together, brothers. We must conquer here before we can hope to conquer Agak.'

'No...' Elric moved away, but somehow he found himself standing at a corner of the bubbling, noxious pool from which the voice still murmured and complained, in which shapes still formed, re-formed and faded. And at each of the other three corners stood one of his companions. All had a set, fatalistic look to them.

The warriors who had accompanied the four drew back to the walls. Otto Blendker and Brut of Lashmar stood near the doorway, listening for anything which might come up the passage to the chamber. Ashnar the Lynx fingered the brand at his belt, a look of pure horror on his rugged features.

Elric felt his arm begin to rise, drawn upward by his sword, and he saw that his three companions were also lifting their swords. The swords reached out across the pool and their tips met above the exact centre.

Elric yelled as something entered his being. Again he tried to break free, but the power was too strong. Other voices spoke in his head.

'I understand...' This was Corum's distant murmur. *'It is the only way.'*

'Oh, no, no...' And this was Hawkmoon, but the words came from Elric's lips.

'AGAK!' cried the pool. The stuff became more agitated, more alarmed. *'AGAK! QUICKLY! WAKE!'*

Elric's body began to shake, but his hand kept a firm hold upon the sword. The atoms of his body flew apart and then united again into a single flowing entity which travelled up the blade of the sword towards the apex. And Elric was still Elric, shouting with the terror of it, sighing with the ecstasy of it.

Elric was still Elric when he drew away from the pool and looked upon himself for a single moment, seeing himself wholly joined with his three other selves.

A being hovered over the pool. On each side of its head was a face and each face belonged to one of the companions. Serene and terrible, the eyes did not blink. It had eight arms and the arms were still; it squatted over the pool on eight legs, and its armour and accoutrements were of all colours blending and at the same time separate.

The being clutched a single great sword in all eight hands and both he and the sword glowed with a ghastly golden light.

Then Elric had rejoined this body and had become a different thing – himself and three others and something else which was the sum of that union.

The Four Who Were One reversed its monstrous sword so that the point was directed downward at the frenetically boiling stuff in the pool below. The stuff feared the sword. It mewled.

'Agak, Agak...'

The being of whom Elric was a part gathered its great strength and began to plunge the sword down.

Shapeless waves appeared on the surface of the pool. Its whole colour changed from sickly yellow to an unhealthy green. *'Agak, I die...'*

Inexorably the sword moved down. It touched the surface.

The pool swept back and forth; it tried to ooze over the sides and onto the floor. The sword bit deeper and the Four Who Were One felt new strength flow up the blade. There came a moan; slowly the pool quieted. It became silent. It became still. It became grey.

Then the Four Who Were One descended into the pool to be absorbed.

*

It could see clearly now. It tested its body. It controlled every limb, every function. It had triumphed; it had revitalised the pool. Through its single octagonal eye it looked in all directions at the same time over the wide ruins of the city; then it focused all its attention upon its twin.

Agak had awakened too late, but he was awakening at last, roused by the dying cries of his sister Gagak, whose body the mortals had first invaded and whose intelligence they had overwhelmed, whose eye they now used and whose powers they would soon attempt to utilise.

Agak did not need to turn his head to look upon the being he still saw as his sister. Like hers, his intelligence was contained within the huge eight-sided eye.

'Did you call me, sister?'

'I spoke your name, that is all, brother.' There were enough vestiges of Gagak's life-force in the Four Who Were One for it to imitate her manner of speaking.

'You cried out?'

'A dream.' The Four paused and then it spoke again: *'A disease. I dreamed that there was something upon this island which made me unwell.'*

'Is that possible? We do not know sufficient about these dimensions or the creatures inhabiting them. Yet none is as powerful as Agak and Gagak. Fear not, sister. We must begin our work soon.'

'It is nothing. Now I am awake.'

Agak was puzzled. *'You speak oddly.'*

'The dream...' answered the creature which had entered Gagak's body and destroyed her.

'We must begin,' said Agak. *'The dimensions turn and the time has come. Ah, feel it. It waits for us to take it. So much rich energy. How we shall conquer when we go home!'*

'I feel it,' replied the Four, and it did. It felt its whole universe, dimension upon dimension, swirling all about it. Stars and planets and moons through plane upon plane, all full of the energy upon which Agak and Gagak had desired to feed. And there was enough of Gagak still within the Four to make the Four experience a deep,

anticipatory hunger which, now that the dimensions attained the right conjunction, would soon be satisfied.

The Four was tempted to join with Agak and feast, though it knew if it did so it would rob its own universe of every shred of energy. Stars would fade, worlds would die. Even the Lords of Law and Chaos would perish, for they were part of the same universe. Yet to possess such power it might be worth committing such a tremendous crime... It controlled this desire and gathered itself for its attack before Agak became too wary.

'Shall we feast, sister?'

The Four realised that the ship had brought it to the island at exactly the proper moment. Indeed, they had almost come too late.

'Sister?' Agak was again puzzled. *'What...?'*

The Four knew it must disconnect from Agak. The tubes and wires fell away from his body and were withdrawn into Gagak's.

'What's this?' Agak's strange body trembled for a moment. *'Sister?'*

The Four prepared itself. For all that it had absorbed Gagak's memories and instincts, it was still not confident that it would be able to attack Agak in her chosen form. And since the sorceress had possessed the power to change her form, the Four began to change, groaning greatly, experiencing dreadful pain, drawing all the materials of its stolen being together so that what had appeared to be a building now became pulpy, unformed flesh. And Agak, stunned, looked on.

'Sister? Your sanity...'

The building, the creature that was Gagak, threshed, melted and erupted. It screamed in agony.

It attained its form.

It laughed.

Four faces laughed upon a gigantic head. Eight arms waved in triumph, eight legs began to move. And over that head it waved a single, massive sword.

And it was running.

It ran upon Agak while the alien sorcerer was still in his static form. Its sword was whirling and shards of ghastly golden light fell away from it as it moved, lashing the shadowed landscape. The Four was as large as Agak. And at this moment it was as strong.

But Agak, realising his danger, began to suck. No longer would this be a pleasurable ritual shared with his sister. He must suck at the energy of this universe if he were to find the strength to defend himself, to gain what he needed to destroy his attacker, the slayer of his sister. Worlds died as Agak sucked.

But not enough. Agak tried cunning.

'This is the centre of your universe. All its dimensions intersect here. Come, you can share the power. My sister is dead. I accept her death. You shall be my partner now. With this power we shall conquer a universe far richer than this!'

'No!' said the Four, still advancing.

'Very well, but be assured of your defeat.'

The Four swung its sword. The sword fell upon the faceted eye within which Agak's intelligence-pool bubbled, just as his sister's had once bubbled. But Agak was stronger already and healed himself at once.

Agak's tendrils emerged and lashed at the Four and the Four cut at the tendrils as it sought his body. And Agak sucked more energy to himself. His body, which the mortals had mistaken for a building, began to glow burning scarlet and to radiate an impossible heat.

The sword roared and flared so that black light mingled with the gold and flowed against the scarlet. And all the while the Four could sense its own universe shrinking and dying.

'Give back, Agak, what you have stolen!' said the Four.

Planes and angles and curves, wires and tubes, flickered with deep red heat and Agak sighed. The universe whimpered.

'I am stronger than you,' said Agak. *'Now.'*

And Agak sucked again.

The Four knew that Agak's attention was diverted for just that short while as he fed. And the Four knew that it, too, must draw energy from its own universe if Agak were to be defeated. So the sword was raised.

The sword was flung back, its blade slicing through tens of thousands of dimensions and drawing their power to it. Then it began to swing back. It swung and black light bellowed from its blade. It swung and Agak became aware of it. His body began to alter. Down towards the sorcerer's great eye, down towards Agak's intelligence-pool swept the black blade.

Agak's many tendrils rose to defend the sorcerer against the sword, but the sword cut through them as if they were not there and it struck the eight-sided chamber which was Agak's eyes and it plunged on down into Agak's intelligence-pool, deep into the stuff of the sorcerer's sensibility, drawing up Agak's energy into itself and thence into its master, the Four Who Were One. And something screamed through the universe and something sent a tremor through the universe. And the universe was dead, even as Agak began to die.

The Four did not dare wait to see if Agak were completely vanquished. It swept the sword out, back through the dimensions, and everywhere the blade touched the energy was restored. The sword rang round and round, round and round, dispersing the energy. And the sword sang its triumph and its glee.

And little shreds of black and golden light whispered away and were reabsorbed.

For a moment the universe had been dead. Now it lived and Agak's energy had been added to it.

Agak lived, too, but he was frozen. He had attempted to change his shape. Now he still half-resembled the building Elric had seen when he first came to the island, but part of him resembled the Four Who Were One – here was part of Corum's face, here a leg, there a fragment of sword blade – as if Agak had believed, at the end, that the Four could only be defeated if its own form were assumed, just as the Four had assumed Gagak's form.

'*We had waited so long...*' Agak sighed and then he was dead.

And the Four sheathed its sword.

Then there came a howling through the ruins of the many cities and a strong wind blustered against the body of the Four so that it was forced to kneel on its eight legs and bow its four-faced head before the gale. Then, gradually, it reassumed the shape of Gagak, the sorceress, and then it lay within Gagak's stagnating intelligence-pool and then it rose over it, hovered for a moment, withdrew its sword from the pool. The four beings fled apart and Elric and Hawkmoon and Erekosë and Corum stood with sword blades touching over the centre of the dead brain.

The four men sheathed their swords. They stared for a second into each other's eyes and all saw terror and awe there. Elric turned away.

He could find neither thoughts nor emotions in him which would relate to what had happened. There were no words he could use. He stood looking dumbly at Ashnar the Lynx and he wondered why Ashnar giggled and chewed at his beard and scraped at the flesh of his own face with his fingernails, his sword forgotten upon the floor of the grey chamber.

'*Now I have flesh again. Now I have flesh,*' Ashnar kept saying.

Elric wondered why Hown Serpent-tamer lay curled in a ball at Ashnar's feet, and why when Brut of Lashmar emerged from the passage he fell down and lay stretched upon the floor, stirring a little and moaning as if in disturbed slumber. Otto Blendker came into the chamber. His sword was in its scabbard. His eyes were tight shut and he hugged at himself, shivering.

Elric thought to himself: *I must forget all this or sanity will disappear for ever.*

He went to Brut and helped the blond warrior to his feet. 'What did you see?'

'More than I deserved, for all my sins. We were trapped – trapped in that skull...' Then Brut began to weep as a small child might weep and Elric took the tall warrior in his own arms and stroked his head and could not find words or sounds with which to comfort him.

'We must go,' said Erekosë. His eyes were glazed. He staggered as he walked.

Thus, dragging those who had fainted, leading those who had gone mad, leaving those who had died behind, they fled through the dead passages of Gagak's body, no longer plagued by the things she had created in her attempt to rid that body of those she had experienced as an invading disease. The passages and chambers were cold and brittle and the men were glad when they stood outside and saw the ruins, the sourceless shadows, the red, static sun.

Otto Blendker was the only one of the warriors who seemed to retain his sanity through the ordeal, when they had been absorbed, unknowingly, into the body of the Four Who Were One. He dragged his brand from his belt and he took out his tinder and ignited it. Soon the brand was flaming and the others lighted theirs from his. Elric trudged to where Agak's remains still lay and he shuddered as he recognised in a monstrous stone face part of his own features. He felt that the stuff could not possibly burn, but it did. Behind him Gagak's body blazed, too. They were swiftly consumed and pillars of growling fire jutted into the sky, sending up a smoke of white and crimson which for a little while obscured the red disc of the sun.

The men watched the corpses burn.

'I wonder,' said Corum, 'if the Captain knew why he sent us here?'

'Or if he suspected what would happen?' said Hawkmoon. Hawkmoon's tone was near to resentful.

'Only we – only that being – could battle Agak and Gagak in anything resembling their own terms,' said Erekosë. 'Other means would not have been successful, no other creature could have the particular qualities, the enormous power needed to slay such strange sorcerers.'

'So it seems,' said Elric, and he would talk no more of it.

'Hopefully,' said Corum, 'you will forget this experience as you forgot – or will forget – the other.'

Elric offered him a hard stare. 'Hopefully, brother,' he said.

Erekosë's chuckle was ironic. 'Who could recall that?' And he, too, said no more.

Ashnar the Lynx, who had ceased his gigglings as he watched the fire, shrieked suddenly and broke away from the main party. He ran towards the flickering column and then veered away, disappearing among the ruins and the shadows.

Otto Blendker gave Elric a questioning stare, but Elric shook his head. 'Why follow him? What can we do for him?' He looked down at Hown Serpent-tamer. He had particularly liked the man in the sea-green armour. He shrugged.

When they moved on, they left the curled body of Hown Serpent-tamer where it lay, helping only Brut of Lashmar across the rubble and down to the shore.

Soon they saw the white mist ahead and knew they neared the sea, though the ship was not in sight.

At the edge of the mist both Hawkmoon and Erekosë paused.

'I will not rejoin the ship,' said Hawkmoon. 'I feel I've served my passage now. If I can find Tanelorn, this, I suspect, is where I must look.'

'My own feelings.' Erekosë nodded his head.

Elric looked at Corum. Corum smiled. 'I have already found Tanelorn. I go back to the ship in the hope that soon it will deposit me upon a more familiar shore.'

'That is my hope,' said Elric. His arm still supported Brut of Lashmar.

Brut whispered, 'What was it? What happened to us?'

Elric increased his grip upon the warrior's shoulder. 'Nothing,' he said.

Then, as Elric tried to lead Brut into the mist, the blond warrior stepped back, breaking free. 'I will stay,' he said. He moved away from Elric. 'I am sorry.'

Elric was puzzled. 'Brut?'

'I am sorry,' Brut said again. 'I fear you. I fear that ship.'

Elric made to follow the warrior, but Corum put a hard silver hand upon his shoulder. 'Comrade, let us be gone from this place.' His smile was bleak. 'It is what is back there that I fear more than the ship.'

They stared over the ruins. In the distance they could see the remains of the fire and there were two shadows there now, the shadows of Gagak and Agak as they had first appeared to them.

Elric drew a cold breath of air. 'With that I agree,' he told Corum.

Otto Blendker was the only warrior who chose to return to the ship with them. 'If that is Tanelorn, it is not, after all, the place I sought,' he said.

Soon they were waist-deep in the water. They saw again the outlines of the Dark Ship; they saw the Captain leaning on the rail, his arm raised as if in salute to someone or something upon the island.

'Captain,' called Corum, 'we come aboard.'

'You are welcome,' said the Captain. 'Yes, you are welcome.' The blind face turned towards them as Elric reached out for the rope ladder. 'Would you care to sail for a while into the silent places, the restful places?'

'I think so,' said Elric. He paused, halfway up the ladder, and he touched his head. 'I have many wounds.'

He reached the rail and with his own cool hands the Captain helped him over. 'They will heal, Elric.'

Elric moved closer to the mast. He leaned against it and watched the silent crew as they unfurled the sail. Corum and Otto Blendker came aboard. Elric listened to the sharp sound of the anchor as it was drawn up. The ship swayed a little.

Otto Blendker looked at Elric, then at the Captain, then he turned and went into his cabin, saying nothing at all as he closed the door.

The sail filled, the ship began to move. The Captain reached out and found Elric's arm. He took Corum's arm, too, and led them towards his cabin. 'The wine,' he said. 'It will heal all the wounds.'

At the door of the Captain's cabin Elric paused. 'And does the wine have other properties?' he asked. 'Does it cloud a man's reason? Was it that which made me accept your commission, Captain?'

The Captain shrugged. 'What is reason?'

The ship was gathering speed. The white mist was thicker and a cold wind blew at the rags of cloth and metal Elric wore. He sniffed, thinking for a moment that he smelled smoke upon that wind.

He put his two hands to his face and touched his flesh. His face was cold. He let his hands fall to his sides and he followed the Captain into the warmth of the cabin.

The Captain poured wine into silver cups from his silver jug. He stretched out a hand to offer a cup to Elric and to Corum. They drank.

A little later the Captain said, 'How do you feel?'

Elric said, 'I feel nothing.'

And that night he dreamed only of shadows and in the morning he could not understand his dream at all.

Book Two

Sailing to the Present

Chapter One

HIS BONE-WHITE, LONG-FINGERED hand upon a carved demon's head in black-brown hardwood (one of the few such decorations to be found anywhere about the vessel), the tall man stood alone in the ship's fo'c'sle and stared through large, slanting crimson eyes at the mist into which they moved with a speed and sureness to make any mortal mariner marvel and become incredulous.

There were sounds in the distance, incongruous with the sounds of even this nameless, timeless sea: thin sounds, agonised and terrible, for all that they remained remote – yet the ship followed them, as if drawn by them; they grew louder – pain and despair were there, but terror was predominant.

Elric had heard such sounds echoing from his cousin Yyrkoon's sardonically named 'Pleasure Chambers' in the days before he had fled the responsibilities of ruling all that remained of the old Melnibonéan Empire. These were the voices of men whose very souls were under siege; men to whom death meant not mere extinction, but a continuation of existence, forever in thrall to some cruel and supernatural master. He had heard men cry so when his salvation and his nemesis, his great black battle-blade Stormbringer, drank their souls.

He did not savour the sound: he hated it, turned his back away from the source and was about to descend the ladder to the main deck when he realised that Otto Blendker had come up behind him. Now that Corum had been borne off by friends with chariots which could ride upon the surface of the water, Blendker was the last of those comrades to have fought at Elric's side against the two alien sorcerers Gagak and Agak.

Blendker's black, scarred face was troubled. The ex-scholar, turned hireling sword, covered his ears with his huge palms.

'Ach! By the Twelve Symbols of Reason, Elric, who makes that din? It's as though we sail close to the shores of hell itself!'

Prince Elric of Melniboné shrugged. 'I'd be prepared to forego an answer and leave my curiosity unsatisfied, Master Blendker, if only our ship would change course. As it is, we sail closer and closer to the source.'

Blendker grunted his agreement. 'I've no wish to encounter whatever it is that causes those poor fellows to scream so! Perhaps we should inform the Captain.'

'You think he does not know where his own ship sails?' Elric's smile had little humour.

The tall black man rubbed at the inverted V-shaped scar which ran from his forehead to his jawbones. 'I wonder if he plans to put us into battle again.'

'I'll not fight another for him.' Elric's hand moved from the carved rail to the pommel of his runesword. 'I have business of my own to attend to, once I'm back on real land.'

A wind came from nowhere. There was a sudden rent in the mist. Now Elric could see that the ship sailed through rust-coloured water. Peculiar lights gleamed in that water, just below the surface. There was an impression of creatures moving ponderously in the depths of the ocean and, for a moment, Elric thought he glimpsed a white, bloated face not dissimilar to his own – a Melnibonéan face. Impulsively he whirled, back to the rail, looking past Blendker as he strove to control the nausea in his throat.

For the first time since he had come aboard the Dark Ship he was able clearly to see the length of the vessel. Here were the two great wheels, one beside him on the foredeck, one at the far end of the ship on the reardeck, tended now as always by the steersman, the Captain's sighted twin. There was the great mast bearing the taut black sail and, fore and aft of this, the two deck cabins, one of which was entirely empty (its occupants having been killed during their last landfall) and one of which was occupied only by himself and Blendker. Elric's gaze was drawn back to the steersman and not for the first time the albino wondered how much influence the Captain's twin had over the course of the Dark Ship.

The man seemed tireless, rarely, to Elric's knowledge, going below to his quarters, which occupied the stern deck as the Captain's occupied the foredeck. Once or twice Elric or Blendker had tried to involve the steersman in conversation, but he appeared to be as dumb as his brother was blind.

The cryptographic, geometrical carvings covering all the ship's wood and most of its metal, from sternpost to figurehead, were picked out by the shreds of pale mist still clinging to them (and again Elric wondered if the ship actually generated the mist normally surrounding it) and, as he watched, the designs slowly turned to pale pink fire as the light from that red star, which forever followed them, permeated the overhead cloud.

A noise from below. The Captain, his long red-gold hair drifting in a breeze which Elric could not feel, emerged from his cabin. The Captain's circlet of blue jade, worn like a diadem, had turned to something of a violet shade in the pink light, and his buff-coloured hose and tunic reflected the hue – even the silver sandals with their silver lacing glittered with the rosy tint.

Again Elric looked upon that mysterious blind face, as unhuman, in the accepted sense, as his own, and puzzled upon the origin of the one who would allow himself to be called nothing but 'Captain'.

As if at the Captain's summons, the mist drew itself about the ship again, as a woman might draw a froth of furs about her body. The red star's light faded, but the distant screams continued.

Did the Captain notice the screams now for the first time, or was this a pantomime of surprise? His blind head tilted, a hand went to his ear. He murmured in a tone of satisfaction, 'Aha!' The head lifted. 'Elric?'

'Here,' said the albino. 'Above you.'

'We are almost there, Elric.'

The apparently fragile hand found the rail of the companionway. The Captain began to climb.

Elric faced him at the top of the ladder. 'If it's a battle...'

The Captain's smile was enigmatic, bitter. 'It was a fight – or shall be one.'

'... we'll have no part of it,' concluded the albino firmly.

'It is not one of the battles in which my ship is directly involved,' the blind man reassured him. 'Those whom you can hear are the vanquished – lost in some future which I think you will experience close to the end of your present incarnation.'

Elric waved a dismissive hand. 'I'll be glad, Captain, if you would cease such vapid mystification. I'm weary of it.'

'I'm sorry it offends you. I answer literally, according to my instincts.'

The Captain, going past Elric and Otto Blendker so that he could stand at the rail, seemed to be apologising. He said nothing for a while, but listened to the disturbing and confused babble from the mist. Then he nodded, apparently satisfied.

'We'll sight land shortly. If you would disembark and seek your own world, I should advise you to do so now. This is the closest we shall ever come again to your plane.'

Elric let his anger show. He cursed, invoking Arioch's name, and put a hand upon the blind man's shoulder. 'What? You cannot return me directly to my own plane?'

'It is too late.' The Captain's dismay was apparently genuine. 'The ship sails on. We near the end of our long voyage.'

'But how shall I find my world? I have no sorcery great enough to move me between the spheres! And demonic assistance is denied me here.'

'There is one gateway to your world,' the Captain told him. 'That is why I suggest you disembark. Elsewhere there is none at all. Your sphere and this one intersect directly.'

'But you say this lies in my future.'

'Be sure – you will return to your own time. Here you are timeless. It is why your memory is so poor. It is why you remember so little of what befalls you. Seek for the gateway – it is crimson and it emerges from the sea off the coast of the island.'

'Which island?'

'The one we approach.'

Elric hesitated. 'And where shall you go, when I have landed?'

'To Tanelorn,' said the Captain. 'There is something I must do

J. CAWTHORN-79

there. My brother and I must complete our destiny. We carry cargo as well as men. Many will try to stop us now, for they fear our cargo. We might perish, but yet we must do all we can to reach Tanelorn.'

'Was that not, then, Tanelorn, where we fought Agak and Gagak?'

'That was nothing more than a broken dream of Tanelorn, Elric.'

The Melnibonéan knew that he would receive no more information from the Captain.

'You offer me a poor choice – to sail with you into danger and never see my own world again, or to risk landing on yonder island inhabited, by the sound of it, by the damned and those which prey upon the damned!'

The Captain's blind eyes moved in Elric's direction. 'I know,' he said softly. 'But it is the best I can offer you, nonetheless.'

The screams, the imploring, terrified shouts, were closer now, but there were fewer of them. Glancing over the side, Elric thought he saw a pair of armoured hands rising from the water; there was foam, red-flecked and noxious, and there was yellowish scum in which pieces of frightful flotsam drifted; there were broken timbers, scraps of canvas, tatters of flags and clothing, fragments of weapons and, increasingly, there were floating corpses.

'But where was the battle?' Blendker whispered, fascinated and horrified by the sight.

'Not on this plane,' the Captain told him. 'You see only the wreckage which has drifted over from one world to another.'

'Then it was a supernatural battle?'

The Captain smiled again. 'I am not omniscient. But, yes, I believe there were supernatural agencies involved. The warriors of half a world fought in the sea-battle – to decide the fate of the multiverse. It is – or will be – one of the decisive battles to determine the fate of Mankind, to fix Man's destiny for the coming Cycle.'

'Who were the participants?' asked Elric, voicing the question in spite of his resolve. 'What were the issues as they understood them?'

'You will know in time, I think.' The Captain's head faced the sea again.

Blendker sniffed the air. 'Ach! It's foul!'

Elric, too, found the odour increasingly unpleasant. Here and there now the water was lighted by guttering fires which revealed the faces of the drowning, some of whom still managed to cling to pieces of blackened driftwood. Not all the faces were human, though they had the appearance of having once been human; things with the snouts of pigs and of bulls raised twisted hands to the Dark Ship and grunted plaintively for succour, but the Captain ignored them and the steersman held his course.

Fires spluttered and water hissed; smoke mingled with the mist. Elric had his sleeve over his mouth and nose and was glad that the smoke and mist between them helped obscure the sights, for as the wreckage grew thicker not a few of the corpses he saw reminded him more of reptiles than of men, their pale, lizard bellies spilling something other than blood.

'If that is my future,' Elric told the Captain, 'I've a mind to remain on board, after all.'

'You have a duty, as have I,' said the Captain quietly. 'The future must be served, as much as the past and the present.'

Elric shook his head. 'I fled the duties of an empire because I sought freedom,' the albino told him. 'And freedom I must have.'

'No,' murmured the Captain. 'There is no such thing. Not yet. Not for us. We must go through much more before we can even begin to guess what freedom is. The price for the knowledge alone is probably higher than any you would care to pay at this stage of your life. Indeed, life itself is often the price.'

'I also sought release from metaphysics when I left Melniboné,' said Elric. 'I'll get the rest of my gear and take the land that's offered. With luck this Crimson Gate will be quickly found and I'll be back among dangers and torments which will, at least, be familiar.'

'It is the only decision you could have made.' The Captain's blind head turned towards Blendker. 'And you, Otto Blendker? What shall you do?'

'Elric's world is not mine and I like not the sound of those screams. What can you promise me, sir, if I sail on with you?'

'Nothing but a good death.' There was regret in the Captain's voice.

'Death is the promise we're all born with, sir. A good death is better than a poor one. I'll sail on with you.'

'As you like. I think you're wise.' The Captain sighed. 'I'll say farewell to you, then, Elric of Melniboné. You fought well in my service and I thank you.'

'Fought for what?' Elric asked.

'Oh, call it Mankind. Call if Fate. Call it a dream or an ideal, if you wish.'

'Shall I never have a clearer answer?'

'Not from me. I do not think there is one.'

'You allow a man little faith.' Elric began to descend the companionway.

'There are two kinds of faith, Elric. Like freedom, there is a kind which is easily kept but proves not worth the keeping, and there is a kind which is hard-won. I agree, I offer little of the former.'

Elric strode towards his cabin. He laughed, feeling genuine affection for the blind man at that moment. 'I thought I had a penchant for such ambiguities, but I have met my match in you, Captain.'

He noticed that the steersman had left his place at the wheel and was swinging out a boat on its davits, preparatory to lowering it.

'Is that for me?'

The steersman nodded.

Elric ducked into his cabin. He was leaving the ship with nothing but that which he had brought aboard, only his clothing and his armour were in a poorer state of repair than they had been, and his mind was in a considerably greater state of confusion.

Without hesitation he gathered up his things, drawing his heavy cloak about him, pulling on his gauntlets, fastening buckles and thongs, then he left the cabin and returned to the deck. The Captain was pointing through the mist at the dark outlines of a coast. 'Can you see land, Elric?'

'I can.'

'You must go quickly, then.'

'Willingly.'

Elric swung himself over the rail and into the boat. The boat struck the side of the ship several times, so that the hull boomed like the beating of some huge funeral drum. Otherwise there was silence now upon the misty waters and no sign of wreckage.

Blendker saluted him. 'I wish you luck, comrade.'

'You, too, Master Blendker.'

The boat began to sink towards the flat surface of the sea, the pulleys of the davits creaking. Elric clung to the rope, letting go as the boat hit the water. He stumbled and sat down heavily upon the seat, releasing the ropes so that the boat drifted at once away from the Dark Ship. He got out the oars and fitted them into their rowlocks.

As he pulled towards the shore he heard the Captain's voice calling to him, but the words were muffled by the mist and he would never know, now, if the blind man's last communication had been a warning or merely some formal pleasantry. He did not care. The boat moved smoothly through the water; the mist began to thin, but so, too, did the light fade.

Suddenly he was under a twilight sky, the sun already gone and stars appearing. Before he had reached the shore it was already completely dark, with the moon not yet risen, and it was with difficulty that he beached the boat on what seemed flat rocks, and stumbled inland until he judged himself safe enough from any inrushing tide.

Then, with a sigh, he lay down, thinking just to order his thoughts before moving on; but, almost instantly, he was asleep.

Chapter Two

ELRIC DREAMED.

He dreamed not merely of the end of his world but of the end of an entire cycle in the history of the cosmos. He dreamed that he was not only Elric of Melniboné but that he was other men, too – men who were pledged to some numinous cause which even they could not describe. And he dreamed that he had dreamed of the Dark Ship and Tanelorn and Agak and Gagak while he lay exhausted upon a beach somewhere beyond the borders of Pikarayd; and when he woke up he was smiling sardonically, congratulating himself for the possession of a grandiose imagination. But he could not clear his head entirely of the impression left by that dream.

This shore was not the same, so plainly something had befallen him – perhaps he had been drugged by slavers, then later abandoned when they found him not what they expected... But, no, the explanation would not do. If he could discover his whereabouts, he might also recall the true facts.

It was dawn, for certain. He sat up and looked about him.

He was sprawled upon a dark, sea-washed limestone pavement, cracked in a hundred places, the cracks so deep that the small streams of foaming salt water rushing through these many narrow channels made raucous what would otherwise have been a very still morning.

Elric climbed to his feet, using his scabbarded runesword to steady himself. His bone-white lids closed for a moment over his crimson eyes as he sought, again, to recollect the events which had brought him here.

He recalled his flight from Pikarayd, his panic, his falling into a coma of hopelessness, his dreams. And, because he was evidently neither dead nor a prisoner, he could at least conclude that his pursuers had, after all, given up the chase, for if they had found him they would have killed him.

Opening his eyes and casting about him, he marked the peculiar blue quality of the light, doubtless a trick of the sun behind the grey clouds, which made the landscape ghastly and gave the sea a dull, metallic look.

The limestone terraces which rose from the sea and stretched above him shone intermittently, like polished lead. On an impulse he held his hand to the light and inspected it. The normally lustreless white of his skin was now tinged with a faint, bluish luminosity. He found it pleasing and smiled as a child might smile, in innocent wonder.

He had expected to be tired, but he now realised that he felt unusually refreshed, as if he had slept long after a good meal, and, deciding not to question the fact of this fortunate (and unlikely) gift, he determined to climb the cliffs in the hope that he might get some idea of his bearings before he decided which direction he would take.

Limestone could be a little treacherous, but it made easy climbing, for there was almost always somewhere that one terrace met another.

He climbed carefully and steadily, finding many footholds, and seemed to gain considerable height quite quickly, yet it was noon before he had reached the top and found himself standing at the edge of a broad, rocky plateau which fell away sharply to form a close horizon. Beyond the plateau was only the sky. Save for sparse, brownish grass, little grew here and there were no signs at all of human habitation. It was now, for the first time, that Elric realised the absence of any form of wildlife. Not a single seabird flew in the air, not an insect crept through the grass. Instead, there was an enormous silence hanging over the brown plain.

Elric was still remarkably untired, so he decided to make the best use he could of his energy and reach the edge of the plateau in the hope that, from there, he would sight a town or a village. He pressed on, feeling no lack of food and water, and his stride was singularly energetic, still; but he had misjudged his distance and the sun had begun to set well before his journey to the edge was completed. The sky on all sides turned a deep, velvety blue and the few clouds that there were in it were also tinged blue, and now, for the first time, Elric realised that the sun itself was not its normal shade, that it burned blackish purple, and he wondered again if he still dreamed.

The ground began to rise sharply and it was with some effort that he walked, but before the light had completely faded he was on the steep flank of a hill, descending towards a wide valley which, though bereft of trees, contained a river which wound through rocks and russet turf and bracken.

After a short rest, Elric decided to press on, although night had fallen, and see if he could reach the river where he might at least drink and, possibly, in the morning find fish to eat.

Again, no moon appeared to aid his progress and he walked for two or three hours in a darkness which was almost total, stumbling occasionally into large rocks, until the ground levelled and he felt sure he had reached the floor of the valley.

He had developed a strong thirst by now and was feeling somewhat hungry, but decided that it might be best to wait until morning before seeking the river when, rounding a particularly tall rock, he saw, with some astonishment, the light of a campfire.

Hopefully this would be the fire of a company of merchants, a trading caravan on its way to some civilised country which would allow him to travel with it, perhaps in return for his services as a mercenary swordsman (it would not be the first time, since he had left Melniboné, that he had earned his bread in such a way).

Yet Elric's old instincts did not desert him; he approached the fire cautiously and let no-one see him. Beneath an overhang of rock, made shadowy by the flame's light, he stood and observed the group of fifteen or sixteen men who sat or lay close to the fire, playing some kind of game involving dice and slivers of numbered ivory.

Gold, bronze and silver gleamed in the firelight as the men staked large sums on the fall of a dice and the turn of a slip of ivory.

Elric guessed that if they had not been so intent on their game, these men must certainly have detected his approach, for they were not, after all, merchants. By the evidence, they were warriors, wearing scarred leather and dented metal, their weapons ready to hand, yet they belonged to no army – unless it be an army of bandits – for they were of all races and, oddly, seemed to be from various periods in the history of the Young Kingdoms.

It was as if they had looted some scholar's collection of relics. An axeman of the later Lormyrian Republic, which had come to an end some two hundred years ago, lay with his shoulder rubbing the elbow of a Chalalite bowman, from a period roughly contemporary with Elric's own. Close to the Chalalite sat a short Ilmioran infantryman of a century past. Next to him was a Filkharian in the barbaric dress of that nation's earliest times. Tarkeshites, Shazaarians, Vilmirians all mingled and the only thing they had in common, by the look of them, was a villainous, hungry cast to their features.

In other circumstances Elric might have skirted this encampment and moved on, but he was so glad to find human beings of any sort that he ignored the disturbing incongruities of the group; yet he remained content to watch them.

One of the men, less unwholesome than the others, was a bulky, black-bearded, bald-headed sea-warrior clad in the casual leathers and silks of the people of the Purple Towns. It was when this man produced a large gold Melnibonéan wheel – a coin not minted, as most coins, but carved by craftsmen to a design both ancient and intricate – that Elric's caution was fully conquered by his curiosity.

Very few of those coins existed in Melniboné and none, that Elric had heard of, outside; for the coins were not used for trade with the Young Kingdoms. They were prized, even by the nobility of Melniboné.

It seemed to Elric that the bald-headed man could only have acquired the coin from another Melnibonéan traveller – and Elric knew of no other Melnibonéans who shared his penchant for exploration. His wariness dismissed, he stepped into the circle.

If he had not been completely obsessed by the thought of the Melnibonéan wheel he might have taken some satisfaction in the sudden scuffle to arms which resulted. Within seconds, the majority of the men were on their feet, their weapons drawn.

For a moment, the gold wheel was forgotten. His hand upon his runesword's pommel, he presented the other in a placatory gesture.

'Forgive the interruption, gentlemen. I am but one tired fellow soldier who seeks to join you. I would beg some information and purchase some food, if you have it to spare.'

On foot, the warriors had an even more ruffianly appearance. They grinned among themselves, entertained by Elric's courtesy but not impressed by it.

One, in the feathered helmet of a Pan Tangian sea-chief, with features to match – swarthy, sinister – pushed his head forward on its long neck and said banteringly:

'We've company enough, Whiteface. And few here are over-fond of the man-demons of Melniboné. You must be rich.'

Elric recalled the animosity with which Melnibonéans were regarded in the Young Kingdoms, particularly by those from Pan Tang who envied the Dragon Isle her power and her wisdom and, of late, had begun crudely to imitate Melniboné.

Increasingly on his guard, he said evenly, 'I have a little money.'

'Then we'll take it, demon.' The Pan Tangian presented a dirty palm just below Elric's nose as he growled, 'Give it over and be on your way.'

Elric's smile was polite and fastidious, as if he had been told a poor joke.

The Pan Tangian evidently thought the joke better than did Elric, for he laughed heartily and looked to his nearest fellows for approval.

Coarse laughter infected the night and only the bald-headed, black-bearded man did not join in the jest, but took a step or two back, while all the others pressed forward.

The Pan Tangian's face was close to Elric's own; his breath was foul and Elric saw that his beard and hair were alive with lice, yet he kept his head, replying in the same equable tone:

'Give me some decent food, a flask of water – some wine, if you have it – and I'll gladly give you the money I have.'

The laughter rose and fell again as Elric continued:

'But if you would take my money and leave me with nought – then I must defend myself. I have a good sword.'

The Pan Tangian strove to imitate Elric's irony. 'But you will note, Sir Demon, that we outnumber you. Considerably.'

Softly the albino spoke: 'I've noticed that fact, but I'm not disturbed by it,' and he had drawn the black blade even as he finished speaking, for they had come at him with a rush.

And the Pan Tangian was the first to die, sliced through the side, his vertebrae sheared, and Stormbringer, having taken its first soul, began to sing.

A Chalalite died next, leaping with stabbing javelin poised, on the point of the runesword, and Stormbringer murmured with pleasure.

But it was not until it had sliced the head clean off a Filkharian pike-master that the sword began to croon and come fully to life, black fire flickering up and down its length, its strange runes glowing.

Now the warriors knew they battled sorcery and became more cautious, yet they scarcely paused in their attack, and Elric, thrusting and parrying, hacking and slicing, needed all of the fresh, dark energy the sword passed on to him.

Lance, sword, axe and dirk were blocked, wounds were given and received, but the dead had not yet outnumbered the living when Elric found himself with his back against the rock and nigh a dozen sharp weapons seeking his vitals.

It was at this point, when Elric had become somewhat less than confident that he could best so many, that the bald-headed warrior, axe in one gloved hand, sword in the other, came swiftly into the firelight and set upon those of his fellows closest to him.

'I thank you, sir!' Elric was able to shout, during the short respite this sudden turn produced. His morale improved, he resumed the attack.

The Lormyrian was cloven from hip to thigh as he dodged a feint; a Filkharian, who should have been dead four hundred years before, fell with the blood bubbling from lips and nostrils, and the corpses began to pile one upon the other. Still Stormbringer sang its sinister battle-song and still the runesword passed its power to its master so that with every death Elric found strength to slay more of the soldiers.

Those who remained now began to express their regret for their hasty attack. Where oaths and threats had issued from their mouths, now came plaintive petitions for mercy and those who had laughed with such bold braggadocio now wept like young girls, but Elric, full of his old battle-joy, spared none.

Meanwhile the man from the Purple Towns, unaided by sorcery, put axe and sword to good work and dealt with three more of his one-time comrades, exulting in his work as if he had nursed a taste for it for some time.

'Yoi! But this is worthwhile slaughter!' cried the black-bearded one.

And then that busy butchery was suddenly done and Elric realised that none was left save himself and his new ally, who stood leaning on his axe, panting and grinning like a hound at the kill, replacing a steel skull-cap upon his pate from where it had fallen during the fight and wiping a bloody sleeve over the sweat glistening on his brow, and saying, in a deep, good-humoured tone:

'Well, now, it is we who are wealthy, of a sudden.'

Elric sheathed a Stormbringer still reluctant to return to its scabbard. 'You desire their gold. Is that why you aided me?'

The black-bearded soldier laughed. 'I owed them a debt and had been biding my time, waiting to pay. These rascals are all that were left of a pirate crew which slew everyone aboard my own ship when we wandered into strange waters – they would have slain me had I not told them I wished to join them. Now I am revenged. Not that I am above taking the gold, since much of it belongs to me and my dead brothers. It will go to their wives and their children when I return to the Purple Towns.'

'How did you convince them not to kill you, too?' Elric sought among the ruins of the fire for something to eat. He found some cheese and began to chew upon it.

'They had no captain or navigator, it seemed. None were real sailors at all, but coast-huggers, based upon this island. They were stranded here, you see, and had taken to piracy as a last resort, but were too terrified to risk the open sea. Besides, after the fight, they had no ship. We had managed to sink that as we fought. We sailed mine to this shore, but provisions were already low and they had no stomach for setting sail without full holds, so I pretended that I knew this coast (may the gods take my soul if I ever see it again after this business) and offered to lead them inland to a village they might loot. They had heard of no such village, but believed me when I said it lay in a hidden valley. That way I prolonged my life while I waited for the opportunity to be revenged upon them. It was a foolish hope, I know. Yet –' grinning – 'as it happened, it was well-founded after all! Eh?'

The black-bearded man glanced a little warily at Elric, uncertain of what the albino might say, hoping, however, for comradeship, though it was well known how haughty Melnibonéans were. Elric could tell that all these thoughts went through his new acquaintance's mind; he had seen many others make similar calculations. So he smiled openly and slapped the man on the shoulder.

'You saved my life, also, my friend. We are both fortunate.'

The man sighed in relief and slung his axe upon his back. 'Aye – lucky's the word. But shall our luck hold, I wonder?'

'You do not know the island at all?'

'Nor the waters, either. How we came to them I'll never guess. Enchanted waters, though, without question. You've seen the colour of the sun?'

'I have.'

'Well –' the seaman bent to remove a pendant from around the Pan Tangian's throat – 'you'd know more about enchantments and sorceries than I. How came you here, Sir Melnibonéan?'

'I know not. I fled from some who hunted me. I came to a shore and could flee no further. Then I dreamed a great deal. When next I awoke I was on the shore again, but of this island.'

'Spirits of some sort – maybe friendly to you – took you to safety, away from your enemies.'

'That's just possible,' Elric agreed, 'for we have many allies among the elementals. I am called Elric and I am self-exiled from Melniboné. I travel because I believe I have something to learn from the folk of the Young Kingdoms. I have no power, save what you see...'

The black-bearded man's eyes narrowed in appraisal as he pointed at himself with his thumb. 'I'm Smiorgan Baldhead, once a sea-lord of the Purple Towns. I commanded a fleet of merchantmen. Perhaps I still do. I shall not know until I return – if I ever do return.'

'Then let us pool our knowledge and our resources, Smiorgan Baldhead, and make plans to leave this island as soon as we can.'

Elric walked back to where he saw traces of the abandoned game, trampled into the mud and the blood. From among the dice and the ivory slips, the silver and the bronze coins, he found the gold Melnibonéan wheel. He picked it up and held it in his outstretched palm. The wheel almost covered the whole palm. In the old days, it had been the currency of kings.

'This was yours, friend?' he asked Smiorgan.

Smiorgan Baldhead looked up from where he was still searching the Pan Tangian for his stolen possessions. He nodded.

'Aye. Would you keep it as part of your share?'

Elric shrugged. 'I'd rather know whence it came. Who gave it you?'

'It was not stolen. It's Melnibonéan, then?'

'Yes.'

'I guessed it.'

'From whom did you obtain it?'

Smiorgan straightened up, having completed his search. He scratched at a slight wound on his forearm. 'It was used to buy passage on our ship – before we were lost – before the raiders attacked us.'

'Passage? By a Melnibonéan?'

'Maybe,' said Smiorgan. He seemed reluctant to speculate.

'Was he a warrior?'

Smiorgan smiled in his beard. 'No. It was a woman gave that to me.'

'How came she to take passage?'

Smiorgan began to pick up the rest of the money. 'It's a long tale and, in part, a familiar one to most merchant sailors. We were seeking new markets for our goods and had equipped a good-sized fleet, which I commanded as the largest shareholder.' He seated himself casually upon the big corpse of the Chalalite and began to count the money. 'Would you hear the tale or do I bore you already?'

'I'd be glad to listen.'

Reaching behind him, Smiorgan pulled a wine-flask from the belt of the corpse and offered it to Elric, who accepted it and drank sparingly of a wine which was unusually good.

Smiorgan took the flask when Elric had finished. 'That's part of our cargo,' he said. 'We were proud of it. A good vintage, eh?'

'Excellent. So you set off from the Purple Towns?'

'Aye. Going towards the Unmapped East. We sailed for a couple of weeks, sighting some of the bleakest coasts I have ever seen, and then we saw no land at all for another week. That was when we entered a stretch of water we came to call the Roaring Rocks – like the Serpent's Teeth off Shazaar's coast, but much greater in expanse, and larger, too. Huge volcanic cliffs which rose from the sea on every side and around which the waters heaved and boiled and howled with a fierceness I've rarely experienced. Well, in short, the fleet was dispersed and at least four ships were lost on those rocks. At last we were able to escape those waters and found ourselves becalmed and alone. We searched for our sister ships for a while and then decided to give ourselves another week before turning for home, for we had no liking to go back into the Roaring Rocks again. Low on provisions, we sighted land at last – grassy cliffs and hospitable beaches and, inland, some signs of cultivation, so we knew we had found civilisation again. We put into a small fishing port and satisfied the natives – who spoke no tongue used in the Young Kingdoms – that we were friendly. And that was when the woman approached us.'

'The Melnibonéan woman?'

'If Melnibonéan she was. She was a fine-looking woman, I'll say that. We were short of provisions, as I told you, and short of any means of purchasing them, for the fishermen desired little of what we had to trade. Having given up our original quest, we were content to head westward again.'

'The woman?'

'She wished to buy passage to the Young Kingdoms – and was content to go with us as far as Menii, our home port. For her passage she gave us two of those wheels. One was used to buy provisions in the town – Graghin, I think it was called – and after making repairs we set off again.'

'You never reached the Purple Towns?'

'There were more storms – strange storms. Our instruments were useless, our lodestones were of no help to us at all. We became even more completely lost than before. Some of my men argued that we had gone beyond our own world altogether. Some blamed the woman, saying she was a sorceress who had no intention of going to Menii. But I believed her. Night fell and seemed to last for ever until we sailed into a calm dawn beneath a blue sun. My men were close to panic – and it takes much to make my men panic – when we sighted the island. As we headed for it those pirates attacked us in a ship which belonged to history – it should have been on the bottom of the ocean, not on the surface. I've seen pictures of such craft in murals on a temple wall in Tarkesh. In ramming us, she stove in half her port side and was sinking even when they swarmed aboard. They were desperate, savage men, Elric – half-starved and blood-hungry. We were weary after our voyage, but fought well. During the fighting the woman disappeared, killed herself, maybe, when she saw the stamp of our conquerors. After a long fight only myself and one other, who died soon after, were left. That was when I became cunning and decided to wait for revenge.'

'The woman had a name?'

'None she would give. I have thought the matter over and suspect that, after all, we were used by her. Perhaps she did not seek Menii and the Young Kingdoms. Perhaps it was this world she sought, and, by sorcery, led us here.'

'This world? You think it different from our own?'

'If only because of the sun's strange colour. Do you not think so, too? You, with your Melnibonéan knowledge of such things, must believe it.'

'I have dreamed of such things,' Elric admitted, but he would say no more.

'Most of the pirates thought as I – they were from all the ages of the Young Kingdoms. That much I discovered. Some were from the earliest years of the era, some from our own time – and some were from the future. Adventurers, most of them, who, at some stage in their lives, sought a legendary land of great riches which lay on the other side of an ancient gateway, rising from the middle of the ocean; but they found themselves trapped here, unable to sail back through this mysterious gate. Others had been involved in sea-fights, thought themselves drowned and woken up on the shores of the island. Many, I suppose, had once had reasonable virtues, but there is little to support life on the island and they had become wolves, living off one another or any ship unfortunate enough to pass, inadvertently, through this gate of theirs.'

Elric recalled part of his dream. 'Did any call it the "Crimson Gate"?'

'Several did, aye.'

'And yet the theory is unlikely, if you'll forgive my scepticism,' Elric said. 'As one who has passed through the Shade Gate to Ameeron...'

'You know of other worlds, then?'

'I've never heard of this one. And I am versed in such matters. That is why I doubt the reasoning. And yet, there was the dream...'

'Dream?'

'Oh, it was nothing. I am used to such dreams and give them no significance.'

'The theory cannot seem surprising to a Melnibonéan, Elric!' Smiorgan grinned again. 'It's I who should be sceptical, not you.'

And Elric replied, half to himself: 'Perhaps I fear the implications more.' He lifted his head, and with the shaft of a broken spear began to poke at the fire. 'Certain ancient sorcerers of Melniboné proposed that an infinite number of worlds coexist with our own. Indeed, my dreams, of late, have hinted as much!' He forced himself to smile. 'But I cannot afford to believe such things. Thus, I reject them.'

'Wait for the dawn,' said Smiorgan Baldhead. 'The colour of the sun shall prove the theory.'

'Perhaps it will prove only that we both dream,' said Elric. The smell of death was strong in his nostrils. He pushed aside those corpses nearest to the fire and settled himself to sleep.

Smiorgan Baldhead had begun to sing a strong yet lilting song in his own dialect, which Elric could scarcely follow.

'Do you sing of your victory over your enemies?' the albino asked.

Smiorgan paused for a moment, half-amused. 'No, Sir Elric, I sing to keep the shades at bay. After all, these fellows' ghosts must still be lurking nearby, in the dark, so little time has passed since they died.'

'Fear not,' Elric told him. 'Their souls are already eaten.'

But Smiorgan sang on, and his voice was louder, his song more intense, than ever it had been before.

Just before he fell asleep, Elric thought he heard a horse whinny, and he meant to ask Smiorgan if any of the pirates had been mounted, but he fell asleep before he could do so.

Chapter Three

RECALLING LITTLE OF his voyage on the Dark Ship, Elric would never know how he came to reach the world in which he now found himself. In later years he would recall most of these experiences as dreams, and indeed they seemed dreamlike even as they occurred.

He slept uneasily, and in the morning the clouds were heavier, shining with that strange, leaden light, though the sun itself was obscured. Smiorgan Baldhead of the Purple Towns was pointing upward, already on his feet, speaking with quiet triumph:

'Will that evidence suffice to convince you, Elric of Melniboné?'

'I am convinced of a quality about the light – possibly about this terrain – which makes the sun appear blue,' Elric replied. He glanced with distaste around him at the carnage. The corpses made a wretched sight and he was filled with a nebulous misery that was neither remorse nor pity.

Smiorgan's sigh was sardonic. 'Well, Sir Sceptic, we had best retrace my steps and seek my ship. What say you?'

'I agree,' the albino told him.

'How far had you marched from the coast when you found us?'

Elric told him.

Smiorgan smiled. 'You arrived in the nick of time, then. I should have been most embarrassed by today if the sea had been reached and I could show my pirate friends no village! I shall not forget this favour you have done me, Elric. I am a count of the Purple Towns and have much influence. If there is any service I can perform for you when we return, you must let me know.'

'I thank you,' Elric said gravely. 'But first we must discover a means of escape.'

Smiorgan had gathered up a satchel of food, some water and

some wine. Elric had no stomach to make his breakfast among the dead, so he slung the satchel over his shoulder. 'I'm ready,' he said.

Smiorgan was satisfied. 'Come – we go this way.'

Elric began to follow the sea-lord over the dry, crunching turf. The steep sides of the valley loomed over them, tinged with a peculiar and unpleasant greenish hue, the result of the brown foliage being stained by the blue light from above. When they reached the river, which was narrow and ran rapidly through boulders giving easy means of crossing, they rested and ate. Both men were stiff from the previous night's fighting; both were glad to wash the dried blood and mud from their bodies in the water.

Refreshed, the pair climbed over the boulders and left the river behind, ascending the slopes, speaking little so that their breath was saved for the exertion. It was noon by the time they reached the top of the valley and observed a plain not unlike the one which Elric had first crossed. Elric now had a fair idea of the island's geography: it resembled the top of a mountain, with an indentation near the centre which was the valley. Again he became sharply aware of the absence of any wildlife and remarked on this to Count Smiorgan, who agreed that he had seen nothing – no bird, fish nor beast since he had arrived.

'It's a barren little world, friend Elric, and a misfortune for a mariner to be wrecked upon its shores.'

They moved on, until the sea could be observed meeting the horizon in the far distance.

It was Elric who first heard the sound behind them, recognising the steady thump of the hoofs of a galloping horse, but when he looked back over his shoulder he could see no sign of a rider, nor anywhere that a rider could hide. He guessed that, in his tiredness, his ears were betraying him. It had been thunder that he had heard.

Smiorgan strode implacably onward, though he, too, must have heard the sound.

Again it came. Again, Elric turned. Again he saw nothing.

'Smiorgan? Did you hear a rider?'

Smiorgan continued to walk without looking back. 'I heard,' he grunted.

'You have heard it before?'

'Many times since I arrived. The pirates heard it, too, and some believed it their nemesis – an Angel of Death seeking them out for retribution.'

'You don't know the source?'

Smiorgan paused, then stopped, and when he turned his face was grim. 'Once or twice I have caught a glimpse of a horse, I think. A tall horse – white – richly dressed – but with no man upon his back. Ignore it, Elric, as I do. We have larger mysteries with which to occupy our minds!'

'You are afraid of it, Smiorgan?'

He accepted this. 'Aye. I confess it. But neither fear nor speculation will rid us of it. Come!'

Elric was bound to see the sense of Smiorgan's statement and he accepted it; yet when the sound came again, about an hour later, he could not resist turning. Then he thought he glimpsed the outline of a large stallion, caparisoned for riding, but that might have been nothing more than an idea Smiorgan had put in his mind.

The day grew colder and in the air was a peculiar, bitter odour. Elric remarked on the smell to Count Smiorgan and learned that this, too, was familiar.

'The smell comes and goes, but it is usually here in some strength.'

'Like sulphur,' said Elric.

Count Smiorgan's laugh had much irony in it, as if Elric made reference to some private joke of Smiorgan's own. 'Oh, aye! Sulphur right enough!'

The drumming of hoofs grew louder behind them as they neared the coast and at last Elric, and Smiorgan too, turned around again, to look.

And now a horse could be seen plainly – riderless, but saddled and bridled, its dark eyes intelligent, its beautiful white head held proudly.

'Are you still convinced of the absence of sorcery here, Sir Elric?' Count Smiorgan asked with some satisfaction. 'The horse was invisible. Now it is visible.' He shrugged the battle-axe on his shoulder into a better position. 'Either that, or it moves from one world to another with ease, so that all we mainly hear are its hoofbeats.'

'If so,' said Elric sardonically, eyeing the stallion, 'it might bear us back to our own world.'

'You admit, then, that we are marooned in some limbo?'

'Very well, yes. I admit the possibility.'

'Have you no sorcery to trap the horse?'

'Sorcery does not come so easily to me, for I have no great liking for it,' the albino told him.

As they spoke, they approached the horse, but it would let them get no closer. It snorted and moved backwards, keeping the same distance between them and itself.

At last, Elric said, 'We waste time, Count Smiorgan. Let's get to your ship with speed and forget blue suns and enchanted horses as quickly as we may. Once aboard the ship I can doubtless help you with a little incantation or two, for we'll need aid of some sort if we're to sail a large ship by ourselves.'

They marched on, but the horse continued to follow them. They came to the edge of the cliffs, standing high above a narrow, rocky bay in which a battered ship lay at anchor. The ship had the high, fine lines of a Purple Towns merchantman, but its decks were piled with shreds of torn canvas, pieces of broken rope, shards of timber, torn-open bales of cloth, smashed wine jars and all manner of other refuse, while in several places her rails were smashed and two or three of her yards had splintered. It was evident that she had been through both storms and sea-fights and it was a wonder that she still floated.

'We'll have to tidy her up as best we can, using only the mains'l for motion,' mused Smiorgan. 'Hopefully we can salvage enough food to last us...'

'Look!' Elric pointed, sure that he had seen someone in the shadows near the afterdeck. 'Did the pirates leave any of their company behind?'

'None.'

'Did you see anyone on the ship, just then?'

'My eyes play filthy tricks on my mind,' Smiorgan told him. 'It is this damned blue light. There is a rat or two aboard, that's all. And that's what you saw.'

'Possibly.' Elric looked back. The horse appeared to be unaware of them as it cropped the brown grass. 'Well, let's finish the journey.'

They scrambled down the steeply sloping cliff face and were soon on the shore, wading through the shallows for the ship, clambering up the slippery ropes which still hung over the sides and, at last, setting their feet with some relief upon the deck.

'I feel more secure already,' said Smiorgan. 'This ship was my home for so long! He searched through the scattered cargo until he found an unbroken wine jar, carved off the seal and handed it to Elric. Elric lifted the heavy jar and let a little of the good wine flow into his mouth. As Count Smiorgan began to drink, Elric was sure he saw another movement near the afterdeck, and he moved closer.

Now he was certain that he heard strained, rapid breathing – like the breathing of one who sought to stifle his need for air rather than be detected. They were slight sounds, but the albino's ears, unlike his eyes, were sharp. His hand ready to draw his sword, he stalked towards the source of the sound, Smiorgan now behind him.

She emerged from her hiding place before he reached her. Her hair hung in heavy, dirty coils about her pale face; her shoulders were slumped and her soft arms hung limply at her sides, and her dress was stained and ripped.

As Elric approached, she fell on her knees before him. 'Take my life,' she said humbly, 'but I beg you – do not take me back to Saxif D'Aan, though I know you must be his servant or his kinsman.'

'It's she!' cried Smiorgan in astonishment. 'It's our passenger. She must have been in hiding all this time.'

Elric stepped forward, lifting up the girl's chin so that he could study her face. There was a Melnibonéan cast about her features,

J. CAWTHORN-79

but she was, to his mind, of the Young Kingdoms; she lacked the pride of a Melnibonéan woman, too. 'What name was that you used, girl?' he asked kindly. 'Did you speak of Saxif D'Aan? Earl Saxif D'Aan of Melniboné?'

'I did, my lord.'

'Do not fear me as his servant,' Elric told her. 'And as for being a kinsman, I suppose you could call me that, on my mother's side – or rather my great-grandmother's side. He was an ancestor. He must have been dead for two centuries, at least!'

'No,' she said. 'He lives, my lord.'

'On this island?'

'This island is not his home, but it is in this plane that he exists. I sought to escape him through the Crimson Gate. I fled through the gate in a skiff, reached the town where you found me, Count Smiorgan, but he drew me back once I was aboard your ship. He drew me back and the ship with me. For that, I have remorse – and for what befell your crew. Now I know he seeks me. I can feel his presence growing nearer.'

'Is he invisible?' Smiorgan asked suddenly. 'Does he ride a white horse?'

She gasped. 'You see! He *is* near! Why else should the horse appear on this island?'

'He rides it?' Elric asked.

'No, no! He fears the horse almost as much as I fear him. The horse pursues him!'

Elric produced the Melnibonéan gold wheel from his purse. 'Did you take this from Earl Saxif D'Aan?'

'I did.'

The albino frowned.

'Who is this man, Elric?' Count Smiorgan asked. 'You describe him as an ancestor – yet he lives in this world. What do you know of him?'

Elric weighed the large gold wheel in his hand before replacing it in his pouch. 'He was something of a legend in Melniboné. His story is part of our literature. He was a great sorcerer – one of the greatest – and he fell in love. It's rare enough for Melnibonéans to fall in love, as others understand the emotion, but rarer for one to have such feelings for a girl who was not even of our own race. She was half-Melnibonéan, so I heard, but from a land which was, in those days, a Melnibonéan possession, a western province close to Dharijor. She was bought by him in a batch of slaves he planned to use for some sorcerous experiment, but he singled her out, saving her from whatever fate it was the others suffered. He lavished his attention upon her, giving her everything. For her, he abandoned his practices, retired to live quietly away from Imrryr, and I think she showed him a certain affection, though she did not seem to love him. There was another, you see, called Carolak, as I recall, and also half-Melnibonéan, who had become a mercenary in Shazaar and risen in the favour of the Shazaarian Court. She had been pledged to this Carolak before her abduction...'

'She loved him?' Count Smiorgan asked.

'She was pledged to marry him, but let me finish my story...' Elric continued: 'Well, at length Carolak, now a man of some substance, second only to the king in Shazaar, heard of her fate and swore to rescue her. He came with raiders to Melniboné's shores and, aided by sorcery, sought out Saxif D'Aan's palace. That done, he sought the girl, finding her at last in the apartments Saxif D'Aan had set aside for her use. He told her that he had come to claim her as his bride, to rescue her from persecution. Oddly, the girl resisted, suggesting that she had been too long a slave in the Melnibonéan harem to re-adapt to the life of a princess in the Shazaarian Court. Carolak scoffed at this and seized her. He managed to escape the castle and had the girl over the saddle of his horse and was about to rejoin his men on the coast when Saxif D'Aan detected them. Carolak, I think, was slain, or else a spell was put on him, but Saxif D'Aan, in his terrible jealousy and certain that the girl had planned the escape with a lover, ordered her to die upon the Wheel of Chaos – a machine rather like that coin in design. Her limbs were broken slowly and Saxif D'Aan sat and watched, through long days, while she died. Her skin was peeled from her flesh, and Earl Saxif D'Aan observed every detail of her punishment. Soon it was evident that the drugs and sorcery used to sustain her life were failing and Saxif D'Aan ordered her taken from the Wheel of Chaos and laid upon a couch. "Well," he said, "you have been punished for betraying me and I am glad. Now you may die." And he saw that her lips, blood-caked and frightful, were moving, and he bent to hear her words.'

'Those words? Revenge? An oath?' asked Smiorgan.

'Her last gesture was an attempt to embrace him. And the words were those she had never uttered to him before, much as he had hoped that she would. Then she died.'

Smiorgan rubbed at his beard. 'Gods! What then? What did your ancestor do?'

'He knew remorse.'

'Of course!'

'Not so, for a Melnibonéan. Remorse is a rare emotion with us. Few have ever experienced it. Torn by guilt, Earl Saxif D'Aan left Melniboné, never to return. It was assumed that he had died in some remote land, trying to make amends for what he had done to the only creature he had ever loved. But now, it seems, he sought the Crimson Gate, perhaps thinking it an opening into hell.'

'But why should he plague me!' the girl cried. 'I am not she! My name is Vassliss. I am a merchant's daughter, from Jharkor. I was voyaging to visit my uncle in Vilmir when our ship was wrecked. A few of us escaped in an open boat. More storms seized us. I was flung from the boat and was drowning when –' she shuddered – 'when *his* galley found me. I was grateful, then...'

'What happened?' Elric pushed the matted hair away from her face and offered her some of their wine. She drank gratefully.

'He took me to his palace and told me that he would marry me, that I should be his empress for ever and rule beside him. But I was frightened. There was such pain in him – and such cruelty, too. I thought he must devour me, destroy me. Soon after my capture, I took the money and the boat and fled for the gateway, which he had told me about...'

'You could find this gateway for us?' Elric asked.

'I think so. I have some knowledge of seamanship, learned

from my father. But what would be the use, sir? He would find us again and drag us back. And he must be very near, even now.'

'I have a little sorcery myself,' Elric assured her, 'and will pit it against Saxif D'Aan's, if I must.' He turned to Count Smiorgan. 'Can we get a sail aloft quickly?'

'Fairly quickly.'

'Then let's hurry, Count Smiorgan Baldhead. I might have the means of getting us through this Crimson Gate and free from any further involvement in the dealings of the dead!'

Chapter Four

While Count Smiorgan and Vassliss of Jharkor watched, Elric lowered himself to the deck, panting and pale. His first attempt to work sorcery in this world had failed and had exhausted him.

'I am further convinced,' he told Smiorgan, 'that we are in another plane of existence, for I should have worked my incantations with less effort.'

'You have failed.'

Elric rose with some difficulty. 'I shall try again.'

He turned his white face skyward; he closed his eyes; he stretched out his arms and his body tensed as he began the incantation again, his voice growing louder and louder, higher and higher, so that it resembled the shrieking of a gale.

He forgot where he was; he forgot his own identity; he forgot those who were with him as his whole mind concentrated upon the Summoning. He sent his call out beyond the confines of the world, into that strange plane where the elementals dwelled – where the powerful creatures of the air could still be found – the *sylphs* of the breeze, and the *sharnahs*, who lived in the storms, and the most powerful of all, the *h'Haarshanns*, creatures of the whirlwind.

And now at last some of them began to come at his summons, ready to serve him as, by virtue of an ancient pact, the elementals had served his forefathers. And slowly the sail of the ship began to fill, and the timbers creaked, and Smiorgan raised the anchor, and the ship was sailing away from the island, through the rocky gap of the harbour, and out into the open sea, still beneath a strange blue sun.

Soon a huge wave was forming around them, lifting up the ship and carrying it across the ocean, so that Count Smiorgan and the girl marvelled at the speed of their progress, while Elric, his crimson eyes open now, but blank and unseeing, continued to croon to his unseen allies.

Thus the ship progressed across the waters of the sea, and at last the island was out of sight and the girl, checking their position against the position of the sun, was able to give Count Smiorgan sufficient information for him to steer a course.

As soon as he could, Count Smiorgan went up to Elric, who straddled the deck, still as stiff-limbed as before, and shook him.

'Elric! You will kill yourself with this effort. We need your friends no longer!'

At once the wind dropped and the wave dispersed and Elric, gasping, fell to the deck.

'It is harder here,' he said. 'It is so much harder here. It is as if I have to call across far greater gulfs than any I have known before.'

And then Elric slept.

He lay in a warm bunk in a cool cabin. Through the porthole filtered diffused blue light. He sniffed. He caught the odour of hot food and, turning his head, saw that Vassliss stood there, a bowl of broth in her hands. 'I was able to cook this,' she said. 'It will improve your health. As far as I can tell, we are nearing the Crimson Gate. The seas are always rough around the gate, so you will need your strength.'

Elric thanked her pleasantly and began to eat the broth as she watched him.

'You are very like Saxif D'Aan,' she said. 'Yet harder in a way – and gentler, too. He is so remote. I know why that girl could never tell him that she loved him.'

Elric smiled. 'Oh, it's nothing more than a folktale, probably, the story I told you. This Saxif D'Aan could be another person altogether – or an imposter, even, who has taken his name – or a sorcerer. Some sorcerers take the names of other sorcerers, for they think it gives them more power.'

There came a cry from above, but Elric could not make out the words.

The girl's expression became alarmed. Without a word to Elric, she hurried from the cabin.

Elric, rising unsteadily, followed her up the companionway.

Count Smiorgan Baldhead was at the wheel of his ship and he was pointing towards the horizon behind them. 'What do you make of that, Elric?'

Elric peered at the horizon but could see nothing. Often his eyes were weak, as now. But the girl said in a voice of quiet despair:

'It is a golden sail.'

'You recognise it?' Elric asked her.

'Oh, indeed I do. It is the galleon of Earl Saxif D'Aan. He has found us. Perhaps he was lying in wait along our route, knowing we must come this way.'

'How far are we from the gate?'

'I am not sure.'

At that moment, there came a terrible noise from below, as if something sought to stave in the timbers of the ship.

'It's in the forward hatches!' cried Smiorgan. 'See what it is, friend Elric! But take care, man!'

Cautiously Elric prised back one of the hatch covers and peered into the murky fastness of the hold. The noise of stamping and thumping continued on and, as his eyes adjusted to the light, he saw the source.

The white horse was there. It whinnied as it saw him, almost in greeting.

'How did it come aboard?' Elric asked. 'I saw nothing. I heard nothing.'

The girl was almost as white as Elric. She sank to her knees beside the hatch, burying her face in her arms.

'He has us! He has us!'

'There is still a chance we can reach the Crimson Gate in time,' Elric reassured her. 'And once in my own world, why, I can work much stronger sorcery to protect us.'

'No,' she sobbed, 'it is too late. Why else would the white horse be here? He knows that Saxif D'Aan must soon board us.'

'He'll have to fight us before he shall have you,' Elric promised her.

'You have not seen his men. Cut-throats all. Desperate and wolfish! They'll show you no mercy. You would be best advised to hand me over to Saxif D'Aan at once and save yourselves. You'll gain nothing from trying to protect me. But I'd ask you a favour.'

'What's that?'

'Find me a small knife to carry, that I may kill myself as soon as I know you two are safe.'

Elric laughed, dragging her to her feet. 'I'll have no such melodramatics from you, lass! We stand together. Perhaps we can bargain with Saxif D'Aan.'

'What have you to barter?'

'Very little. But he is not aware of that.'

'He can read your thoughts, seemingly. He has great powers!'

'I am Elric of Melniboné. I am said to possess a certain facility in the sorcerous arts, myself.'

'But you are not as single-minded as Saxif D'Aan,' she said simply. 'Only one thing obsesses him – the need to make me his consort.'

'Many girls would be flattered by the attention – glad to be an empress with a Melnibonéan emperor for a husband.' Elric was sardonic.

She ignored his tone. 'That is why I fear him so,' she said in a murmur. 'If I lost my determination for a moment, I could love him. I should be destroyed! It is what *she* must have known!'

Chapter Five

THE GLEAMING GALLEON, sails and sides all gilded so that it seemed the sun itself pursued them, moved rapidly upon them while the girl and Count Smiorgan watched aghast and Elric desperately attempted to recall his elemental allies, without success.

Through the pale blue light the golden ship sailed relentlessly in their wake. Its proportions were monstrous, its sense of power vast, its gigantic prow sending up huge, foamy waves on both sides as it sped silently towards them.

With the look of a man preparing himself to meet death, Count Smiorgan Baldhead of the Purple Towns unslung his battle-axe and loosened his sword in its scabbard, setting his little metal cap upon his bald pate. The girl made no sound, no movement at all, but she wept.

Elric shook his head and his long, milk-white hair formed a halo around his face for a moment. His moody crimson eyes began to focus on the world around him. He recognised the ship; it was of a pattern with the golden battle-barges of Melniboné – doubtless the ship in which Earl Saxif D'Aan had fled his homeland, searching for the Crimson Gate. Now Elric was convinced that this must be that same Saxif D'Aan and he knew less fear than did his companions, but considerably greater curiosity. Indeed, it was almost with nostalgia that he noted the ball of fire, like a natural comet, glowing with green light, come hissing and spluttering towards them, flung by the ship's forward catapult. He half expected to see a great dragon wheeling in the sky overhead, for it was with dragons and gilded battlecraft like these that Melniboné had once conquered the world.

The fireball fell into the sea a few inches from their bow and was evidently placed there deliberately, as a warning.

'Don't stop!' cried Vassliss. 'Let the flames slay us! It will be better!'

Smiorgan was looking upward. 'We have no choice. Look! He has banished the wind, it seems.'

They were becalmed. Elric smiled a grim smile. He knew now what the folk of the Young Kingdoms must have felt when his ancestors had used these identical tactics against them.

'Elric?' Smiorgan turned to the albino. 'Are these your people? That ship's Melnibonéan without question!'

'So are the methods,' Elric told him. 'I am of the blood royal of Melniboné. I could be emperor, even now, if I chose to claim my throne. There is some small chance that Earl Saxif D'Aan, though an ancestor, will recognise me and, therefore, recognise my authority. We are a conservative people, the folk of the Dragon Isle.'

The girl spoke through dry lips, hopelessly: 'He recognises only the authority of the Lords of Chaos, who give him aid.'

'All Melnibonéans recognise that authority,' Elric told her with a certain humour.

From the forward hatch, the sound of the stallion's stamping and snorting increased.

'We're besieged by enchantments!' Count Smiorgan's normally ruddy features had paled. 'Have you none of your own, Prince Elric, you can use to counter them?'

'None, it seems.'

The golden ship loomed over them. Elric saw that the rails, high overhead, were crowded not with Imrryrian warriors but with cut-throats equally as desperate as those he had fought on the island, and, apparently, drawn from the same variety of historical periods and nations. The galleon's long sweeps scraped the sides of the smaller vessel as they folded, like the legs of some water insect, to enable the grappling irons to be flung out. Iron claws bit into the timbers of the little ship and the brigandly crowd overhead cheered, grinning at them, menacing them with their weapons.

The girl began to run to the seaward side of the ship, but Elric caught her by the arm.

'Do not stop me, I beg you!' she cried. 'Rather, jump with me and drown!'

'You think that death will save you from Saxif D'Aan?' Elric said. 'If he has the power you say, death will only bring you more firmly into his grasp!'

'Oh!' The girl shuddered and then, as a voice called down to them from one of the tall decks of the gilded ship, she gave a moan and fainted into Elric's arms, so that, weakened as he was by his spell-working, it was all that he could do to stop himself falling with her to the deck.

The voice rose over the coarse shouts and guffaws of the crew. It was pure, lilting and sardonic. It was the voice of a Melnibonéan, though it spoke the common tongue of the Young Kingdoms, a corruption, in itself, of the speech of the Bright Empire.

'May I have the captain's permission to come aboard?'

Count Smiorgan growled back: 'You have us firm, sir! Don't try to disguise an act of piracy with a polite speech!'

'I take it I have your permission, then.' The unseen speaker's tone remained exactly the same.

Elric watched as part of the rail was drawn back to allow a gangplank, studded with golden nails to give firmer footing, to be lowered from the galleon's deck to theirs.

A tall figure appeared at the top of the gangplank. He had the fine features of a Melnibonéan nobleman, was thin, proud in his bearing, clad in voluminous robes of cloth-of-gold, an elaborate helmet in gold and ebony upon his long auburn locks. He had grey-blue eyes, pale, slightly flushed skin, and he carried, so far as Elric could see, no weapons of any kind.

With considerable dignity, Earl Saxif D'Aan began to descend, his rascals at his back. The contrast between this beautiful intellectual and those he commanded was remarkable. Where he walked with straight back, elegant and noble, they slouched, filthy, degenerate, unintelligent, grinning with pleasure at their easy victory. Not a man among them showed any sign of human dignity; each was overdressed in tattered and unclean finery, each had at least three weapons upon his person, and there was much evidence of looted jewellery, of nose-rings, earrings, bangles, necklaces, toe- and finger-rings, pendants, cloak-pins and the like.

'Gods!' murmured Smiorgan. 'I've rarely seen such a collection of scum, and I thought I'd encountered most kinds in my voyages. How can such a man bear to be in their company?'

'Perhaps it suits his sense of irony,' Elric suggested.

Earl Saxif D'Aan reached their deck and stood looking up at them to where they still positioned themselves, on the poop deck. He gave a slight bow. His features were controlled and only his eyes suggested something of the intensity of emotion dwelling within him, particularly as they fell upon the girl in Elric's arms.

'I am Earl Saxif D'Aan of Melniboné, now of the Islands beyond the Crimson Gate. You have something with you which is mine. I would claim it from you.'

'You mean the Lady Vassliss of Jharkor?' Elric said, his voice as steady as Saxif D'Aan's.

Saxif D'Aan seemed to note Elric for the first time. A slight frown crossed his brow and was quickly dismissed. 'She is mine,' he said. 'You may be assured that she will come to no harm at my hands.'

Elric, seeking some advantage, knew that he risked much when he next spoke, in the High Tongue of Melniboné, used between those of the blood royal. 'Knowledge of your history does not reassure me, Saxif D'Aan.'

Almost imperceptibly, the golden man stiffened and fire flared in his grey-blue eyes. 'Who are you, to speak the Tongue of Kings? Who are you, who claims knowledge of my past?'

'I am Elric, son of Sadric, and I am the four-hundred-and-twenty-eighth emperor of the folk of R'lin K'ren A'a, who landed upon the Dragon Isle ten thousand years ago. I am Elric, your emperor, Earl Saxif D'Aan, and I demand your fealty.' And Elric held up his right hand, upon which still gleamed a ring set with a single Actorios stone, the Ring of Kings.

Earl Saxif D'Aan now had firm control of himself again. He gave no sign that he was impressed. 'Your sovereignty does not extend beyond your own world, noble emperor, though I greet you as a fellow monarch.' He spread his arms so that his long sleeves rustled. 'This world is mine. All that exists beneath the blue sun do I rule. You trespass, therefore, in my domain. I have every right to do as I please.'

'Pirate pomp,' muttered Count Smiorgan, who had understood nothing of the conversation but had gathered something of what passed by the tone. 'Pirate braggadocio. What does he say, Elric?'

'He convinces me that he is not, in your sense, a pirate, Count Smiorgan. He claims that he is ruler of this plane. Since there is apparently no other, we must accept his claim.'

'Gods! Then let him behave like a monarch and let us sail safely out of his waters!'

'We may – if we give him the girl.'

Count Smiorgan shook his head. 'I'll not do that. She's my passenger, in my charge. I must die rather than do that. It is the code of the sea-lords of the Purple Towns.'

'You are famous for your adherence to that code,' Elric said. 'As for myself, I have taken this girl into my protection and, as hereditary emperor of Melniboné, I cannot allow myself to be browbeaten.'

They had conversed in a murmur, but, somehow, Earl Saxif D'Aan had heard them.

'I must let you know,' he said evenly, in the common tongue, 'that the girl is mine. You steal her from me. Is that the action of an emperor?'

'She is not a slave,' Elric said, 'but the daughter of a free merchant in Jharkor. You have no rights upon her.'

Earl Saxif D'Aan said, 'Then I cannot open the Crimson Gate for you. You must remain in my world for ever.'

'You have closed the gate? Is it possible?'

'To me.'

'Do you know that the girl would rather die than be captured by you, Earl Saxif D'Aan? Does it give you pleasure to instil such fear?'

The golden man looked directly into Elric's eyes as if he made some cryptic challenge. 'The gift of pain has ever been a favourite gift among our folk, has it not? Yet it is another gift I offer her. She calls herself Vassliss of Jharkor, but she does not know herself. I know her. She is Gratyesha, Princess of Fwem-Omeyo, and I would make her my bride.'

'How can it be that she does not know her own name?'

'She is reincarnated – soul and flesh are identical – that is how I know. And I have waited, Emperor of Melniboné, for many scores of years for her. Now I shall not be cheated of her.'

'As you cheated yourself, two centuries past, in Melniboné?'

'You risk much with your directness of language, brother monarch!' There was a hint of a warning in Saxif D'Aan's tone, a warning much fiercer than any implied by the words.

'Well –' Elric shrugged – 'you have more power than we do. My sorcery works poorly in your world. Your ruffians outnumber us. It should not be difficult for you to take her from us.'

'You must give her to me. Then you may go free, back to your own world and your own time.'

Elric smiled. 'There is sorcery here. She is no reincarnation. You'd bring your lost love's spirit from the netherworld to inhabit this girl's body. Am I not right? That is why she must be given freely, or your sorcery will rebound upon you – or might – and you would not take the risk.'

Earl Saxif D'Aan turned his head away so that Elric might not see his eyes. 'She is the girl,' he said, in the High Tongue. 'I know that she is. I mean her soul no harm. I would merely give it back its memory.'

'Then it is stalemate,' said Elric.

'Have you no loyalty to a brother of the royal blood?' Saxif D'Aan murmured, still refusing to look at Elric.

'You claimed no such loyalty, as I recall, Earl Saxif D'Aan. If you accept me as your emperor, then you must accept my decisions. I keep the girl in my custody. Or you must take her by force.'

'I am too proud.'

'Such pride shall ever destroy love,' said Elric, almost in sympathy. 'What now, King of Limbo? What shall you do with us?'

Earl Saxif D'Aan lifted his noble head, about to reply, when from the hold the stamping and the snorting began again. His eyes widened. He looked questioningly at Elric, and there was something close to terror in his face.

'What's that? What have you in the hold?'

'A mount, my lord, that is all,' said Elric equably.

'A horse? An ordinary horse?'

'A white one. A stallion, with bridle and saddle. It has no rider.'

At once Saxif D'Aan's voice rose as he shouted orders for his men. 'Take those three aboard our ship. This one shall be sunk directly. Hurry! Hurry!'

Elric and Smiorgan shook off the hands which sought to seize them and they moved towards the gangplank, carrying the girl between them, while Smiorgan muttered, 'At least we are not slain, Elric. But what becomes of us now?'

Elric shook his head. 'We must hope that we can continue to use Earl Saxif D'Aan's pride against him, to our advantage, though the gods alone know how we shall resolve the dilemma.'

Earl Saxif D'Aan was already hurrying up the gangplank ahead of them.

'Quickly,' he shouted. 'Raise the plank!'

They stood upon the decks of the golden battle-barge and watched as the gangplank was drawn up, the length of rail replaced.

'Bring up the catapults,' Saxif D'Aan commanded. 'Use lead. Sink that vessel at once!'

The noise from the forward hold increased. The horse's voice echoed over ships and water. Hoofs smashed at timber and then, suddenly, it came crashing through the hatch covers, scrambling for purchase on the deck with its front hoofs, and then standing there, pawing at the planks, its neck arching, its nostrils dilating, and its eyes glaring, as if ready to do battle.

Now Saxif D'Aan made no attempt to hide the terror on his face. His voice rose to a scream as he threatened his rascals with every sort of horror if they did not obey him with utmost speed. The catapults were dragged up and huge globes of lead were lobbed onto the decks of Smiorgan's ship, smashing through the planks like arrows through parchment so that almost immediately the ship began to sink.

'Cut the grappling hooks!' cried Saxif D'Aan, wrenching a blade from the hand of one of his men and sawing at the nearest rope. 'Cast loose – quickly!'

Even as Smiorgan's ship groaned and roared like a drowning beast, the ropes were cut. The ship keeled over at once, and the horse disappeared.

'Turn about!' shouted Saxif D'Aan. 'Back to Fhaligarn and swiftly, or your souls shall feed my fiercest demons!'

There came a peculiar, high-pitched neighing from the foaming water, as Smiorgan's ship, stern uppermost, gasped and was swallowed. Elric caught a glimpse of the white stallion, swimming strongly.

'Go below!' Saxif D'Aan ordered, indicating a hatchway. 'The horse can smell the girl and thus is doubly difficult to lose.'

'Why do you fear it?' Elric asked. 'It is only a horse. It cannot harm you.'

Saxif D'Aan uttered a laugh of profound bitterness. 'Can it not, brother monarch? Can it not?'

As they carried the girl below, Elric was frowning, remembering a little more of the legend of Saxif D'Aan, of the girl he had punished so cruelly, and of her lover, Prince Carolak. The last he heard of Saxif D'Aan was the sorcerer crying:

'More sail! More sail!'

And then the hatches had closed behind them and they found themselves in an opulent Melnibonéan day-cabin, full of rich hangings, precious metal, decorations of exquisite beauty and, to Count Smiorgan, disturbing decadence. But it was Elric, as he lowered the girl to a couch, who noticed the smell.

'Augh! It's the smell of a tomb – of damp and mould. Yet nothing rots. It is passing peculiar, friend Smiorgan, is it not?'

'I scarcely noticed, Elric.' Smiorgan's voice was hollow. 'But I would agree with you on one thing. We are entombed. I doubt we'll live to escape this world now.'

Chapter Six

An hour had passed since they had been forced aboard. The doors had been locked behind them, and it seemed Saxif D'Aan was too preoccupied with escaping the white stallion to bother with them. Peering through the lattice of a porthole, Elric could look back to where their ship had been sunk. They were many leagues distant already; yet he still thought, from time to time, that he saw the head and shoulders of the stallion above the waves.

Vassliss had recovered and sat pale and shivering upon the couch.

'What more do you know of that horse?' Elric asked her. 'It would be helpful to me if you could recall anything you have heard.'

She shook her head. 'Saxif D'Aan spoke little of it, but I gather he fears the rider more than he does the horse.'

'Ah!' Elric frowned. 'I suspected it! Have you ever seen the rider?'

'Never. I think that Saxif D'Aan has never seen him, either. I think he believes himself doomed if that rider should ever sit upon the white stallion.'

Elric smiled to himself.

'Why do you ask so much about the horse?' Smiorgan wished to know.

Elric shook his head. 'I have an instinct, that is all. Half a memory. But I'll say nothing and think as little as I may, for there is no doubt Saxif D'Aan, as Vassliss suggests, has some power of reading the mind.'

They heard a footfall above, descending to their doors.

A bolt was drawn and Saxif D'Aan, his composure fully restored, stood in the opening, his hands in his golden sleeves.

'You will forgive, I hope, the peremptory way in which I sent you here. There was danger which had to be averted at all costs. As a result, my manners were not all that they should have been.'

'Danger to us?' Elric asked. 'Or to you, Earl Saxif D'Aan?'

'In the circumstances, to all of us, I assure you.'

'Who rides the horse?' Smiorgan asked bluntly. 'And why do you fear him?'

Earl Saxif D'Aan was master of himself again, so there was no sign of a reaction. 'That is very much my private concern,' he said softly. 'Will you dine with me now?'

The girl made a noise in her throat and Earl Saxif D'Aan turned piercing eyes upon her. 'Gratyesha, you will want to cleanse yourself and make yourself beautiful again. I will see that facilities are placed at your disposal.'

'I am not Gratyesha,' she said. 'I am Vassliss, the merchant's daughter.'

'You will remember,' he said. 'In time, you will remember.' There was such certainty, such obsessive power, in his voice that even Elric experienced a frisson of awe. 'The things will be brought to you, and you may use this cabin as your own until we return to my palace on Fhaligarn. My lords...' He indicated that they should leave.

Elric said, 'I'll not leave her, Saxif D'Aan. She is too afraid.'

'She fears only the truth, brother.'

'She fears you and your madness.'

Saxif D'Aan shrugged insouciantly. 'I shall leave first, then. If you would accompany me, my lords...' He strode from the cabin and they followed.

Elric said, over his shoulder, 'Vassliss, you may depend upon my protection.' And he closed the cabin doors behind him.

Earl Saxif D'Aan was standing upon the deck, exposing his noble face to the spray which was flung up by the ship as it moved with supernatural speed through the sea.

'You called me mad, Prince Elric? Yet you must be versed in sorcery, yourself.'

'Of course. I am of the blood royal. I am reckoned knowledgeable in my own world.'

'But here? How well does your sorcery work?'

'Poorly, I'll admit. The spaces between the planes seem greater.'

'Exactly. But I have bridged them. I have had time to learn how to bridge them.'

'You are saying that you are more powerful than am I?'

'It is a fact, is it not?'

'It is. But I did not think we were about to indulge in sorcerous battles, Earl Saxif D'Aan.'

'Of course. Yet, if you were to think of besting me by sorcery, you would think twice, eh?'

'I should be foolish to contemplate such a thing at all. It could cost me my soul. My life, at least.'

'True. You are a realist, I see.'

'I suppose so.'

'Then we can progress on simpler lines, to settle the dispute between us.'

'You propose a duel?' Elric was surprised.

Earl Saxif D'Aan's laughter was light. 'Of course not – against your sword? That has power in all worlds, though the magnitude varies.'

'I'm glad that you are aware of that,' Elric said significantly.

'Besides,' added Earl Saxif D'Aan, his golden robes rustling as he moved a little nearer to the rail, 'you would not kill me – for only I have the means of your escaping this world.'

'Perhaps we'd elect to remain,' said Elric.

'Then you would be my subjects. But, no – you would not like it here. I am self-exiled. I could not return to my own world now, even if I wished to do so. It has cost me much, my knowledge. But I would found a dynasty here, beneath the blue sun. I must have my wife, Prince Elric. I must have Gratyesha.'

'Her name is Vassliss,' said Elric obstinately.

'She thinks it is.'

'Then it is. I have sworn to protect her, as has Count Smiorgan. Protect her we shall. You will have to kill us all.'

'Exactly,' said Earl Saxif D'Aan with the air of a man who has been coaching a poor student towards the correct answer to a problem. 'Exactly. I shall have to kill you all. You leave me with little alternative, Prince Elric.'

'Would that benefit you?'

'It would. It would put a certain powerful demon at my service for a few hours.'

'We should resist.'

'I have many men. I do not value them. Eventually, they would overwhelm you. Would they not?'

Elric remained silent.

'My men would be aided by sorcery,' added Saxif D'Aan. 'Some would die, but not too many, I think.'

Elric was looking beyond Saxif D'Aan, staring out to sea. He was sure that the horse still followed. He was sure that Saxif D'Aan knew, also.

'And if we gave up the girl?'

'I should open the Crimson Gate for you. You would be honoured guests. I should see that you were borne safely through, even taken safely to some hospitable land in your own world, for even if you passed through the gate there would be danger. The storms.'

Elric appeared to deliberate.

'You have only a little time to make your decision, Prince Elric. I had hoped to reach my palace, Fhaligarn, by now. I shall not allow you very much longer. Come, make your decision. You know I speak the truth.'

'You know that I can work some sorcery in your world, do you not?'

'You summoned a few friendly elementals to your aid, I know. But at what cost? Would you challenge me directly?'

'It would be unwise of me,' said Elric.

Smiorgan was tugging at his sleeve. 'Stop this useless talk. He knows that we have given our word to the girl and that we *must* fight him!'

Earl Saxif D'Aan sighed. There seemed to be genuine sorrow in his voice. 'If you are determined to lose your lives...' he began.

'I should like to know why you set such importance upon the

speed with which we make up our minds,' Elric said. 'Why cannot we wait until we reach Fhaligarn?'

Earl Saxif D'Aan's expression was calculating, and again he looked full into Elric's crimson eyes. 'I think you know,' he said, almost inaudibly.

But Elric shook his head. 'I think you give me too much credit for intelligence.'

'Perhaps.'

Elric knew that Saxif D'Aan was attempting to read his thoughts; he deliberately blanked his mind, and suspected that he sensed frustration in the sorcerer's demeanour.

And then the albino had sprung at his kinsman, his hand chopping at Saxif D'Aan's throat. The earl was taken completely off guard. He tried to call out, but his vocal cords were numbed. Another blow, and he fell to the deck, senseless.

'Quickly, Smiorgan,' Elric shouted, and he had leaped into the rigging, climbing swiftly upward to the top yards. Smiorgan, bewildered, followed, and Elric had drawn his sword, even as he reached the crow's nest, driving upward through the rail so that the lookout was taken in the groin scarcely before he realised it.

Next, Elric was hacking at the ropes holding the mainsail to the yard. Already a number of Saxif D'Aan's ruffians were climbing after them.

The heavy golden sail came loose, falling to envelop the pirates and take several of them down with it.

Elric climbed into the crow's nest and pitched the dead man over the rail in the wake of his comrades. Then he had raised his sword over his head, holding it in his two hands, his eyes blank again, his head raised to the blue sun, and Smiorgan, clinging to the mast below, shuddered as he heard a peculiar crooning come from the albino's throat.

More of the cut-throats were ascending, and Smiorgan hacked at the rigging, having the satisfaction of seeing half a score go flying down to break their bones on the deck below, or be swallowed by the waves.

Earl Saxif D'Aan was beginning to recover, but he was still stunned.

'Fool!' he was crying. 'Fool!' But it was not possible to tell if he referred to Elric or to himself.

Elric's voice became a wail, rhythmical and chilling, as he chanted his incantation, and the strength from the man he had killed flowed into him and sustained him. His crimson eyes seemed to flicker with fires of another, nameless colour, and his whole body shook as the strange runes shaped themselves in a throat which had never been made to speak such sounds.

His voice became a vibrant groan as the incantation continued, and Smiorgan, watching as more of the crew made efforts to climb the mainmast, felt an unearthly coldness creep through him.

Earl Saxif D'Aan screamed from below:

'You would not dare!'

The sorcerer began to make passes in the air, his own incantation tumbling from his lips, and Smiorgan gasped as a creature made of smoke took shape only a few feet below him. The creature smacked its lips and grinned and stretched a paw, which became flesh even as it moved, towards Smiorgan. He hacked at the paw with his sword, whimpering.

'Elric!' cried Count Smiorgan, clambering higher so that he grasped the rail of the crow's nest. 'Elric! He sends demons against us now!'

But Elric ignored him. His whole mind was in another world, a darker, bleaker world even than this one. Through grey mists, he saw a figure, and he cried a name. 'Come!' he called in the ancient tongue of his ancestors. 'Come!'

Count Smiorgan cursed as the demon became increasingly substantial. Red fangs clashed and green eyes glared at him. A claw stroked his boot and no matter how much he struck with his sword, the demon did not appear to notice the blows.

There was no room for Smiorgan in the crow's nest, but he stood on the outer rim, shouting with terror, desperate for aid. Still Elric continued to chant.

'Elric! I am doomed!'

The demon's paw grasped Smiorgan by his ankle.

'Elric!'

Thunder rolled out at sea; a bolt of lightning appeared for a second and then was gone. From nowhere there came the sound of a horse's hoofs pounding, and a human voice shouting in triumph.

Elric sank back against the rail, opening his eyes in time to see Smiorgan being dragged slowly downward. With the last of his strength he flung himself forward, leaning far out to stab downwards with Stormbringer. The runesword sank cleanly into the demon's right eye. It roared, letting go of Smiorgan, striking at the blade which drew its energy from it and, as that energy passed into the blade and thence to Elric, the albino grinned a frightful grin so that, for a second, Smiorgan became more frightened of his friend that he had been of the demon. The demon began to dematerialise, its only means of escape from the sword which drank its life-force, but more of Saxif D'Aan's rogues were behind it, and their blades rattled as they sought the pair.

Elric swung himself back over the rail, balanced precariously on the yard as he slashed at their attackers, yelling the old battle-cries of his people. Smiorgan could do little but watch. He noted that Saxif D'Aan was no longer on deck and he shouted urgently to Elric:

'Elric! Saxif D'Aan. He seeks out the girl.'

Elric now took the attack to the pirates, and they were more than anxious to avoid the moaning runesword, some even leaping into the sea rather than encounter it. Swiftly the two leaped from yard to yard until they were again upon the deck.

'What does he fear? Why does he not use more sorcery?' panted Count Smiorgan, as they ran towards the cabin.

'I have summoned the one who rides the horse,' Elric told him. 'I had so little time – and I could tell you nothing of it, knowing that Saxif D'Aan would read my intention in your mind, if he could not in mine!'

The cabin doors were firmly secured from the inside. Elric began to hack at them with the Black Sword.

But the doors resisted as they should not have resisted. 'Sealed by sorcery and I've no means of unsealing it,' said the albino.

'Will he kill her?'

'I don't know. He might try to take her into some other plane. We must –'

Hoofs clattered on the deck and the white stallion reared behind them, only now it had a rider, clad in bright purple-and-yellow armour. He was bareheaded and youthful, though there were several old scars upon his face. His hair was thick and curly and blond and his eyes were a deep blue.

He drew tightly upon his reins, steadying the horse. He looked piercingly at Elric. 'Was it you, Melnibonéan, who opened the pathway for me?'

'It was.'

'Then I thank you, though I cannot repay you.'

'You have repaid me,' Elric told him, then drew Smiorgan aside as the rider leaned forward and spurred his horse directly at the closed doors, smashing through as though they were rotted cotton.

There came a terrible cry from within and then Earl Saxif D'Aan, hampered by his complicated robes of gold, rushed from the cabin, seizing a sword from the hand of the nearest corpse, darting Elric a look not so much of hatred but of bewildered agony as he turned to face the blond rider.

The rider had dismounted now and came from the cabin, one arm around the shivering girl, Vassliss, one hand upon the reins of his horse, and he said, sorrowfully:

'You did me a great wrong, Earl Saxif D'Aan, but you did Gratyesha an infinitely more terrible one. Now you must pay.'

Saxif D'Aan paused, drawing a deep breath, and when he looked up again, his eyes were steady, his dignity had returned.

'Must I pay in full?' he said.

'In full.'

'It is all I deserve,' said Saxif D'Aan. 'I escaped my doom for many years, but I could not escape the knowledge of my crime. She loved me, you know. Not you.'

J.CAWTHORN.79

'She loved us both, I think. But the love she gave you was her entire soul and I should not want that from any woman.'

'You are the loser, then.'

'You never knew how much she loved you.'

'Only – only afterwards...'

'I pity you, Earl Saxif D'Aan.' The young man gave the reins of his horse to the girl, and he drew his sword. 'We are strange rivals, are we not?'

'You have been all these years in limbo, where I banished you – in that garden on Melniboné?'

'All these years. Only my horse could follow you. The horse of Tendric, my father, also of Melniboné, and also a sorcerer.'

'If I had known that, then, I'd have slain you cleanly and sent the horse to limbo.'

'Jealousy weakened you, Earl Saxif D'Aan. But now we fight as we should have fought then – man to man, with steel, for the hand of the one who loves us both. It is more than you deserve.'

'Much more,' agreed the sorcerer. And he brought up his sword to lunge at the young man who, Smiorgan guessed, could only be Prince Carolak himself.

The fight was predetermined. Saxif D'Aan knew that, if Carolak did not. Saxif D'Aan's skill in arms was up to the standard of any Melnibonéan nobleman, but it could not match the skill of a professional soldier, who had fought for his life time after time.

Back and forth across the deck, while Saxif D'Aan's rascals looked on in open-mouthed astonishment, the rivals fought a duel which should have been fought and resolved two centuries before, while the girl they both plainly thought was the reincarnation of Gratyesha watched them with as much concern as might her original have watched when Saxif D'Aan first encountered Prince Carolak in the gardens of his palace, so long ago.

Saxif D'Aan fought well, and Carolak fought nobly, for on many occasions he avoided an obvious advantage, but at length Saxif D'Aan threw away his sword, crying: 'Enough. I'll give you your vengeance, Prince Carolak. I'll let you take the girl. But you'll not give me your damned mercy – you'll not take my pride.'

And Carolak nodded, stepped forward, and struck straight for Saxif D'Aan's heart.

The blade entered clean and Earl Saxif D'Aan should have died, but he did not. He crawled along the deck until he reached the base of the mast, and he rested his back against it, while the blood pumped from the wounded heart. And he smiled.

'It appears,' he said faintly, 'that I cannot die, so long have I sustained my life by sorcery. I am no longer a man.'

He did not seem pleased by this thought, but Prince Carolak, stepping forward and leaning over him, reassured him. 'You will die,' he promised, 'soon.'

'What will you do with her – with Gratyesha?'

'Her name is Vassliss,' said Count Smiorgan insistently. 'She is a merchant's daughter, from Jharkor.'

'She must make up her own mind,' Carolak said, ignoring Smiorgan.

Earl Saxif D'Aan turned glazed eyes on Elric. 'I must thank you,' he said. 'You brought me the one who could bring me peace, though I feared him.'

'Is that why, I wonder, your sorcery was so weak against me?' Elric said. 'Because you wished Carolak to come and release you from your guilt?'

'Possibly, Elric. You are wiser in some matters, it seems, than am I.'

'What of the Crimson Gate?' Smiorgan growled. 'Can that be opened? Have you still the power, Earl Saxif D'Aan?'

'I think so.' From the folds of his bloodstained garments of gold, the sorcerer produced a large crystal which shone with the deep colours of a ruby. 'This will not only lead you to the gate, it will enable you to pass through, only I must warn you...' Saxif D'Aan began to cough. 'The ship –' he gasped, 'the ship – like my body – has been sustained by means of sorcery – therefore...' His head slumped forward. He raised it with a huge effort and stared beyond them at the girl who still held the reins of the white stallion. 'Farewell, Gratyesha, Princess of Fwem-Omeyo. I loved you.' The eyes remained fixed upon her, but they were dead eyes now.

Carolak turned back to look at the girl. 'How do you call yourself, Gratyesha?'

'They call me Vassliss,' she told him. She smiled up into his youthful, battle-scarred face. 'That is what they call me, Prince Carolak.'

'You know who I am?'

'I know you now.'

'Will you come with me, Gratyesha? Will you be my bride, at last, in the strange new lands I have found, beyond the world?'

'I will come,' she said.

He helped her up into the saddle of his white stallion and climbed so that he sat behind her. He bowed to Elric of Melniboné. 'I thank you again, Sir Sorcerer, though I never thought to be helped by one of the royal blood of Melniboné.

Elric's expression was not without humour. 'In Melniboné,' he said, 'I'm told it's tainted blood.'

'Tainted with mercy, perhaps.'

'Perhaps.'

Prince Carolak saluted them. 'I hope you find peace, Prince Elric, as I have found it.'

'I fear my peace will more resemble that which Saxif D'Aan found,' Elric said grimly. 'Nonetheless, I thank you for your good words, Prince Carolak.'

Then Carolak, laughing, had ridden his horse for the rail, leaped it, and vanished.

There was a silence upon the ship. The remaining ruffians looked uncertainly from one to the other. Elric addressed them:

'Know you this – I have the key to the Crimson Gate – and only I have the knowledge to use it. Help me sail the ship, and you'll have freedom from this world! What say you?'

'Give us our orders, captain,' said a toothless individual, and he cackled with mirth. 'It's the best offer we've had in a hundred years or more!'

Chapter Seven

It was Smiorgan who first saw the Crimson Gate. He held the great red gem in his hand and pointed ahead.

'There! There, Elric! Saxif D'Aan has not betrayed us!'

The sea had begun to heave with huge, turbulent waves, and with the mainsail still tangled upon the deck, it was all that the crew could do to control the ship, but the chance of escape from the world of the blue sun made them work with every ounce of energy and, slowly, the golden battle-barge neared the towering crimson pillars.

The pillars rose from the grey, roaring water, casting a peculiar light upon the crests of the waves. They appeared to have little substance, and yet stood firm against the battering of the tons of water lashing around them.

'Let us hope they are wider apart than they look,' said Elric. 'It would be a hard enough task steering through them in calm waters, let alone this kind of sea.'

'I'd best take the wheel, I think,' said Count Smiorgan, handing Elric the gem, and he strode back up the tilting deck, climbing to the covered wheelhouse and relieving the frightened man who stood there.

There was nothing Elric could do but watch as Smiorgan turned the huge vessel into the waves, riding the tops as best he could, but sometimes descending with a rush which made Elric's heart rise to his mouth. All around them, then, the cliffs of water threatened, but the ship was taking another wave before the main force of water could crash onto her decks. For all this, Elric was quickly soaked through and, though sense told him he would be best below, he clung to the rail, watching as Smiorgan steered the ship with uncanny sureness towards the Crimson Gate.

And then the deck was flooded with red light and Elric was half blinded. Grey water flew everywhere; there came a dreadful scraping sound, then a snapping as oars broke against the pillars. The ship shuddered and began to turn, sideways to the wind, but Smiorgan forced her around and suddenly the quality of the light changed subtly, though the sea remained as turbulent as ever and Elric knew, deep within him, that overhead, beyond the heavy clouds, a yellow sun was burning again.

But now there came a creaking and a crashing from within the bowels of the battle-barge. The smell of mould, which Elric had noted earlier, became stronger, almost overpowering.

Smiorgan came hurrying back, having handed over the wheel. His face was pale again. 'She's breaking up, Elric,' he called out, over the noise of the wind and the waves. He staggered as a huge wall of water struck the ship and snatched away several planks from the deck. 'She's falling apart, man!'

'Saxif D'Aan tried to warn us of this!' Elric shouted back. 'As he was kept alive by sorcery, so was his ship. She was old before he sailed her to that world. While there, the sorcery which sustained her remained strong – but on this plane it has no power at all. Look!' And he pulled at a piece of the rail, crumbling the rotten wood with his fingers. 'We must find a length of timber which is still good.'

At that moment a yard came crashing from the mast and struck the deck, bouncing, then rolling towards them.

Elric crawled up the sloping deck until he could grasp the spar and test it. 'This one's still good. Use your belt or whatever else you can and tie yourself to it!'

The wind wailed through the disintegrating rigging of the ship; the sea smashed at the sides, driving great holes below the waterline.

The ruffians who had crewed her were in a state of complete panic, some trying to unship small boats which crumbled even as they swung them out, others lying flat against the rotted decks and praying to whatever gods they still worshipped.

Elric strapped himself to the broken yard as firmly as he could and Smiorgan followed his example. The next wave to hit the ship full on lifted them with it, cleanly over what remained of the rail and into the chilling, shouting waters of that terrible sea.

Elric kept his mouth tight shut against the water and reflected on the irony of his situation. It seemed that, having escaped so much, he was to die a very ordinary death, by drowning.

It was not long before his senses left him and he gave himself up to the swirling and somehow friendly waters of the ocean.

He awoke, struggling.

There were hands upon him. He strove to fight them off, but he was too weak. Someone laughed, a rough, good-humoured sound.

The water no longer roared and crashed around him. The wind no longer howled. Instead there was a gentler movement. He heard waves lapping against timber. He was aboard another ship.

He opened his eyes, blinking in warm, yellow sunlight. Red-cheeked Vilmirian sailors grinned down at him. 'You're a lucky man – if man you be!' said one.

'My friend?' Elric sought for Smiorgan.

'He was in better shape than were you. He's down in Duke Avan's cabin now.'

'Duke Avan?' Elric knew the name, but in his dazed condition could remember nothing to help him place the man. 'You saved us?'

'Aye. We found you both drifting, tied to a broken yard carved with the strangest designs I've ever seen. A Melnibonéan craft, was she?'

'Yes, but rather old.'

They helped him to his feet. They had stripped him of his clothes and wrapped him in woollen blankets. The sun was already drying his hair. He was very weak. He said:

'My sword?'

'Duke Avan has it, below.'

'Tell him to be careful of it.'

'We're sure he will.'

'This way,' said another. 'The duke awaits you.'

Book Three

Sailing to the Past

Chapter One

ELRIC SAT BACK in the comfortable, well-padded chair and accepted the wine-cup handed him by his host. While Smiorgan ate his fill of the hot food provided for them, Elric and Duke Avan appraised one another.

Duke Avan was a man of about forty, with a square, handsome face. He was dressed in a gilded silver breastplate, over which was arranged a white cloak. His breeches, tucked into black knee-length boots, were of cream-coloured doeskin. On a small sea-table at his elbow rested his helmet crested with scarlet feathers.

'I am honoured, sir, to have you as my guest,' said Duke Avan. 'I know you to be Elric of Melniboné. I have been seeking you for several months, ever since news came to me that you had left your homeland (and your power) behind and were wandering, as it were, incognito in the Young Kingdoms.'

'You know much, sir.'

'I, too, am a traveller by choice. I almost caught up with you in Pikarayd, but I gather there was some sort of trouble there. You left quickly and then I lost your trail altogether. I was about to give up looking for your aid when, by the greatest of good fortune, I found you floating in the water!' Duke Avan laughed.

'You have the advantage of me,' said Elric, smiling. 'You raise many questions.'

'He's Avan Astran of Old Hrolmar,' grunted Count Smiorgan from the other side of a huge ham bone. 'He's well known as an adventurer – explorer – trader. His reputation's the best. We can trust him, Elric.'

'I recall the name now,' Elric told the duke. 'But why should you seek my aid?'

The smell of the food from the table had at last impinged and

Elric got up. 'Would you mind if I ate something while you explained, Duke Avan?'

'Eat your fill, Prince Elric. I am honoured to have you as a guest.'

'You have saved my life, sir. I have never had it saved so courteously!'

Duke Avan smiled. 'I have never before had the pleasure of, let us say, catching so courteous a fish. If I were a superstitious man, Prince Elric, I should guess that some other force threw us together in this way.'

'I prefer to think of it as coincidence,' said the albino, beginning to eat. 'Now, sir, tell me how I can aid you.'

'I shall not hold you to any bargain, merely because I have been lucky enough to save your life,' said Duke Avan Astran, 'please bear that in mind.'

'I shall, sir.'

Duke Avan stroked the feathers of his helmet. 'I have explored most of the world, as Count Smiorgan rightly says. I have been to your own Melniboné and I have even ventured east, to Elwher and the Unmapped East. I have been to Myyrrhn, where the Winged Folk live. I have travelled as far as World's Edge and hope one day to go beyond. But I have never crossed the Boiling Sea and I know only a small stretch of coast along the Western Continent – the continent that has no name. Have you been there, Elric, in your travels?'

The albino shook his head. 'I seek experience of other cultures, other civilisations – that is why I travel. There has been nothing, so far, to take me there. The continent is inhabited only by savages, is it not?'

'So we are told.'

'You have other intelligence?'

'You know that there is some evidence,' said Duke Avan in a deliberate tone, 'that your own ancestors came originally from that mainland?'

'Evidence?' Elric pretended lack of interest. 'A few legends, that is all.'

'One of those legends speaks of a city older than dreaming Imrryr. A city that still exists in the deep jungles of the West.'

Elric recalled his conversation with Earl Saxif D'Aan, and he smiled to himself. 'You mean R'lin K'ren A'a?'

'Aye. A strange name.' Duke Avan Astran leaned forward, his eyes alight with delighted curiosity. 'You pronounce it more fluently than could I. You speak the secret tongue, the High Tongue, the Speech of Kings...'

'Of course.'

'You are forbidden to teach it to any but your own children, are you not?'

'You appear conversant with the customs of Melniboné, Duke Avan,' Elric said, his lids falling so that they half covered his eyes. He leaned back in his seat as he bit into a piece of fresh bread with relish. 'Do you know what the words mean?'

'I have been told that they mean simply "Where the High Ones Meet" in the ancient speech of Melniboné,' Duke Avan Astran told him.

Elric inclined his head. 'That is so. Doubtless only a small town, in reality. Where local chiefs gathered, perhaps once a year, to discuss the price of grain.'

'You believe that, Prince Elric?'

Elric inspected a covered dish. He helped himself to veal in a rich, sweet sauce. 'No,' he said.

'You believe, then, that there was an ancient civilisation even before your own, from which your own culture sprang? You believe that R'lin K'ren A'a is still there, somewhere in the jungles of the West?'

Elric waited until he had swallowed. He shook his head.

'No,' he said. 'I believe that it does not exist at all.'

'You are not curious about your ancestors?'

'Should I be?'

'They were said to be different in character from those who founded Melniboné. Gentler...' Duke Avan Astran looked deep into Elric's face.

Elric laughed. 'You are an intelligent man, Duke Avan of Old

Hrolmar. You are a perceptive man. Oh, and indeed you are a cunning man, sir!'

Duke Avan grinned at the compliment. 'And you know much more of the legends than you are admitting, if I am not mistaken.'

'Possibly.' Elric sighed as the food warmed him. 'We are known as a secretive people, we of Melniboné.'

'Yet,' said Duke Avan, 'you seem untypical. Who else would desert an empire to travel in lands where his very race was hated?'

'An emperor rules better, Duke Avan Astran, if he has close knowledge of the world in which he rules.'

'Melniboné rules the Young Kingdoms no longer.'

'Her power is still great. But that, anyway, was not what I meant. I am of the opinion that the Young Kingdoms offer something which Melniboné has lost.'

'Vitality?'

'Perhaps.'

'Humanity!' grunted Count Smiorgan Baldhead. 'That is what your race has lost, Prince Elric. I say nothing of you – but look at Earl Saxif D'Aan. How can one so wise be such a simpleton? He lost everything – pride, love, power – because he had no humanity. And what humanity he had – why, it destroyed him.'

'Some say it will destroy me,' said Elric, 'but perhaps "humanity" is, indeed, what I seek to bring to Melniboné, Count Smiorgan.'

'Then you will destroy your kingdom!' said Smiorgan bluntly. 'It is too late to save Melniboné.'

'Perhaps I can help you find what you seek, Prince Elric,' said Duke Avan Astran quietly. 'Perhaps there is time to save Melniboné, if you feel such a mighty nation is in danger.'

'From within,' said Elric. 'But I speak too freely.'

'For a Melnibonéan, that is true.'

'How did you come to hear of this city?' Elric wished to know. 'No other man I have met in the Young Kingdoms has heard of R'lin K'ren A'a.'

'It is marked on a map I have.'

Deliberately, Elric chewed his meat and swallowed it. 'The map is doubtless a forgery.'

'Perhaps. Do you recall anything else of the legend of R'lin K'ren A'a?'

'There is the story of the Creature Doomed to Live.' Elric pushed the food aside and poured wine for himself. 'The city is said to have received its name because the Lords of the Higher Worlds once met there to decide the rules of the Cosmic Struggle. They were overheard by the one inhabitant of the city who had not flown when they came. When they discovered him, they doomed him to remain alive for ever, carrying the frightful knowledge in his head...'

'I have heard that story, too. But the one that interests me is that the inhabitants of R'lin K'ren A'a never returned to their city. Instead they struck northwards and crossed the sea. Some reached an island we now call Sorcerer's Isle while others went further – blown by a great storm – and came at length to a large island inhabited by dragons whose venom caused all it touched to burn... to Melniboné, in fact.'

'And you wish to test the truth of that story. Your interest is that of a scholar?'

Duke Avan laughed. 'Partly. But my main interest in R'lin K'ren A'a is more materialistic. For your ancestors left a great treasure behind them when they fled their city. Particularly they abandoned an image of Arioch, the Lord of Chaos – a monstrous image, carved in jade, whose eyes were two huge, identical gems of a kind unknown anywhere else in all the lands of the Earth. Jewels from another plane of existence. Jewels which could reveal all the secrets of the Higher Worlds, of the past and the future, of the myriad planes of the cosmos...'

'All cultures have similar legends. Wishful thinking, Duke Avan, that is all...'

'But the Melnibonéans had a culture unlike any others. The Melnibonéans are not true men, as you well know. Their powers are superior, their knowledge far greater...'

'It was once thus,' Elric said. 'But that great power and knowledge is not mine. I have only a fragment of it...'

'I did not seek you in Bakshaan and later in Jadmar because

I believed you could verify what I have heard. I did not cross the sea to Filkhar, then to Argimiliar and at last to Pikarayd because I thought you would instantly confirm all that I have spoken of – I sought you because I think you the only man who would wish to accompany me on a voyage which would give us the truth or falsehood to these legends once and for all.'

Elric tilted his head and drained his wine-cup.

'Cannot you do that for yourself? Why should you desire my company on the expedition? From what I have heard of you, Duke Avan, you are not one who needs support in his venturings...'

Duke Avan laughed. 'I went alone to Elwher when my men deserted me in the Weeping Waste. It is not in my nature to know physical fear. But I have survived my travels this long because I have shown proper foresight and caution before setting off. Now it seems I must face dangers I cannot anticipate – sorcery, perhaps. It struck me, therefore, that I needed an ally who had some experience of fighting sorcery. And since I would have no truck with the ordinary kind of wizard such as Pan Tang spawns, you were my only choice. You seek knowledge, Prince Elric, just as I do. Indeed, it could be said that if it had not been for your yearning for knowledge, your cousin would never have attempted to usurp the Ruby Throne of Melniboné...'

'Enough of that,' Elric said bitterly. 'Let's talk of this expedition. Where is the map?'

'You will accompany me?'

'Show me the map.'

Duke Avan drew a scroll from his pouch. 'Here it is.'

'Where did you find it?'

'On Melniboné.'

'You have been there recently?' Elric felt anger rise in him.

Duke Avan raised a hand. 'I went there with a group of traders and I gave much for a particular casket which had been sealed, it seemed, for an eternity. Within that casket was this map.' He spread out the scroll on the table. Elric recognised the style and the script – the old High Speech of Melniboné. It was a map of part of the Western Continent – more than he had ever seen on any other map. It showed a great river winding into the interior for a hundred miles or more. The river appeared to flow through a jungle and then divide into two rivers which later rejoined. The 'island' of land thus formed had a black circle marked on it. Against this circle, in the involved writing of ancient Melniboné, was the name R'lin K'ren A'a. Elric inspected the scroll carefully. It did not seem to be a forgery.

'Is this all you found?' he asked.

'The scroll was sealed and this was embedded in the seal,' Duke Avan said, handing something to Elric.

Elric held the object in his palm. It was a tiny ruby of a red so deep as to seem black at first, but when he turned it into the light he saw an image at the centre of the ruby and he recognised that image. He frowned, then he said, 'I will agree to your proposal, Duke Avan. Will you let me keep this?'

'Do you know what it is?'

'No. But I should like to find out. There is a memory somewhere in my head...'

'Very well, take it. I will keep the map.'

'When did you have it in mind to set off?'

Duke Avan's smile was sardonic. 'We are already sailing around the southern coast to the Boiling Sea.'

'There are few who have returned from that ocean,' Elric murmured bitterly. He glanced across the table and saw that Smiorgan was imploring with his eyes for Elric not to have any part of Duke Avan's scheme. Elric smiled at his friend. 'The adventure is to my taste.'

Miserably, Smiorgan shrugged. 'It seems it will be a little longer before I return to the Purple Towns.'

Chapter Two

THE COAST OF Lormyr had disappeared in warm mist and Duke Avan Astran's schooner dipped its graceful prow towards the West and the Boiling Sea.

The Vilmirian crew of the schooner were used to a less demanding climate and more casual work than this and they went about their tasks, it seemed to Elric, with something of an aggrieved air.

Standing beside Elric on the ship's poop deck, Count Smiorgan Baldhead wiped sweat from his pate and growled: 'Vilmirians are a lazy lot, Prince Elric. Duke Avan needs real sailors for a voyage of this kind. I could have picked him a crew, given the chance...'

Elric smiled. 'Neither of us was given the chance, Count Smiorgan. It was a fait accompli. He's a clever man, Duke Astran.'

'It is not a cleverness I entirely respect, for he offered us no real choice. A free man is a better companion than a slave, says the old aphorism.'

'Why did you not disembark when you had the chance, then, Count Smiorgan?'

'Because of the promise of treasure,' said the black-bearded man frankly. 'I would return with honour to the Purple Towns. Forget you not that I commanded the fleet that was lost...'

Elric understood.

'My motives are straightforward,' said Smiorgan. 'Yours are much more complicated. You seem to desire danger as other men desire love-making or drinking – as if in danger you find forgetfulness.'

'Is that not true of many professional soldiers?'

'You are not a mere professional soldier, Elric. That you know as well as I.'

'Yet few of the dangers I have faced have helped me forget,' Elric pointed out. 'Rather they have strengthened the reminder of what I am – of the dilemma I face. My own instincts war against the traditions of my race.' Elric drew a deep, melancholy breath. 'I go where danger is because I think that an answer might lie there – some reason for all this tragedy and paradox. Yet I know I shall never find it.'

'But it is why you sail to R'lin K'ren A'a, eh? You hope that your remote ancestors had the answer you need?'

'R'lin K'ren A'a is a myth. Even should the map prove genuine what shall we find but a few ruins? Imrryr has stood for ten thousand years and she was built at least two centuries after my people settled on Melniboné. Time will have taken R'lin K'ren A'a away.'

'And this statue, this Jade Man, Avan spoke of?'

'If the statue ever existed, it could have been looted at any time in the past hundred centuries.'

'And the Creature Doomed to Live?'

'A myth.'

'But you hope, do you not, that it is all as Duke Avan says...?' Count Smiorgan put a hand on Elric's arm. 'Do you not?'

Elric stared ahead, into the writhing steam which rose from the sea. He shook his head.

'No, Count Smiorgan. I *fear* that it is all as Duke Avan says.'

The wind blew whimsically and the schooner's passage was slow as the heat grew greater and the crew sweated still more and murmured fearfully. And upon each face, now, was a stricken look.

Only Duke Avan seemed to retain his confidence. He called to them all to take heart; he told them that they should all be rich soon; and he gave orders for the oars to be unshipped, for the wind could no longer be trusted. They grumbled at this, stripping off their shirts to reveal skins as red as cooked lobsters. Duke Avan made a joke of that. But the Vilmirians no longer laughed at his jokes as they had done in the milder seas of their home waters.

Around the ship the sea bubbled and roared, and they navigated by their few instruments, for the steam obscured everything.

Once a green thing erupted from the sea and glared at them before disappearing.

They ate and slept little and Elric rarely left the poop deck. Count Smiorgan bore the heat silently and Duke Avan, seemingly oblivious to any discomfort, went cheerfully about the ship, calling encouragement to his men.

Count Smiorgan was fascinated by the waters. He had heard of them, but never crossed them. 'These are only the outer reaches of this sea, Elric,' he said in some wonder. 'Think what it must be like at the middle.'

Elric grinned. 'I would rather not. As it is, I fear I'll be boiled to death before another day has passed.'

Passing by, Duke Avan heard him and clapped him on the shoulder. 'Nonsense, Prince Elric! The steam is good for you! There is nothing healthier!' Seemingly with pleasure, Duke Avan stretched his limbs. 'It cleans all the poisons from the system.'

Count Smiorgan offered him a glowering look and Duke Avan laughed. 'Be of better cheer, Count Smiorgan. According to my charts – such as they are – a couple of days will see us nearing the coasts of the Western Continent.'

'The thought fails to raise my spirits very greatly,' said Count Smiorgan, but he smiled, infected by Avan's good humour.

But shortly thereafter the sea grew slowly less frenetic and the steam began to disperse until the heat became more tolerable.

At last they emerged into a calm ocean beneath a shimmering blue sky in which hung a red-gold sun.

But three of the Vilmirian crew had died to cross the Boiling Sea, and four more had a sickness in them which made them cough a great deal, and shiver, and cry out in the night.

For a while they were becalmed, but at last a soft wind began to blow and fill the schooner's sails and soon they had sighted their first land – a little yellow island where they found fruit and a spring of fresh water. Here, too, they buried the three men who had succumbed to the sickness of the Boiling Sea, for the Vilmirians had refused to have them buried in the ocean on the grounds that the bodies would be 'stewed like meat in a pot'.

While the schooner lay at anchor, just off the island, Duke

Avan called Elric to his cabin and showed him, for a second time, that ancient map.

Pale golden sunlight filtered through the cabin's ports and fell upon the old parchment, beaten from the skin of a beast long since extinct, as Elric and Duke Avan Astran of Old Hrolmar bent over it.

'See,' Duke Avan said, pointing. 'This island's marked. The map's scale seems reasonably accurate. Another three days and we shall be at the mouth of the river.'

Elric nodded. 'But it would be wise to rest here for a while until our strength is fully restored and the morale of the crew is raised higher. There are reasons, after all, why men have avoided the jungles of the West over the centuries.'

'Certainly there are savages there – some say they are not even human – but I'm confident we can deal with those dangers. I have much experience of strange territories, Prince Elric.'

'But you said yourself you feared other dangers.'

'True. Very well, we'll do as you suggest.'

On the fourth day a strong wind began to blow from the east and they raised anchor. The schooner leaped over the waves under only half her canvas and the crew saw this as a good omen.

'They are mindless fools,' Smiorgan said as they stood clinging to the rigging in the prow. 'The time will come when they will wish they were suffering the cleaner hardships of the Boiling Sea. This journey, Elric, could benefit none of us, even if the riches of R'lin K'ren A'a are still there.'

But Elric did not answer. He was lost in strange thoughts, unusual thoughts for him, for he was remembering his childhood and his father who had been the last true ruler of the Bright Empire – proud, insouciant, cruel. His father had expected him – perhaps because of his strange albinism – to restore the glories of Melniboné. Instead Elric threatened to destroy what was left of that glory. Like himself, his father had had no real place in this new age of the Young Kingdoms, but had refused to acknowledge it. This journey to the Western Continent, to the land of his ancestors, had a peculiar attraction for him. Here no new nations had emerged. The continent had, as far as he knew, remained the same since R'lin K'ren A'a had been abandoned. The jungles would be the jungles his folk had known, the land would be the land that had given birth to his peculiar race, moulded the character of its people with their sombre pleasures, their melancholy arts and their dark delights. Had his ancestors felt this agony of knowledge, this impotence in the face of the understanding that existence had no point, no purpose, no hope? Was this why they had built their civilisation in that particular pattern, why they had disdained the more placid, spiritual values of mankind's philosophers? He knew that many of the intellectuals of the Young Kingdoms pitied the powerful folk of Melniboné as mad. But if they had been mad and if they had imposed a madness upon the world that had lasted a hundred centuries, what had made them so? Perhaps the secret did lie in R'lin K'ren A'a – not in any tangible form but in the ambiance created by the dark jungles and the deep, old rivers. Perhaps here, at last, he would be able to feel at one with himself.

He ran his fingers through his milk-white hair and there was a kind of innocent anguish in his crimson eyes. He might be the last of his kind and yet he was unlike his kind. Smiorgan had been wrong. Elric knew that everything that existed had its opposite. In danger he might find peace. And yet, of course, in peace there was danger. Being an imperfect creature in an imperfect world he would always know paradox. And that was why in paradox there was always a kind of truth. That was why philosophers and soothsayers flourished. In a perfect world there would be no place for them. In an imperfect world the mysteries were always without solution and that was why there was always a great choice of solutions.

It was on the morning of the third day that the coast was sighted and the schooner steered her way through the sandbanks of the great delta and anchored, at last, at the mouth of the dark and nameless river.

Chapter Three

Evening came and the sun began to set over the black outlines of the massive trees. A rich, ancient smell came from the jungle and through the twilight echoed the cries of strange birds and beasts. Elric was impatient to begin the quest up the river. Sleep – never welcome – was now impossible to achieve. He stood unmoving on the deck, his eyes hardly blinking, his brain barely active, as if expecting something to happen to him. The rays of the sun stained his face and threw black shadows over the deck and then it was dark and still under the moon and the stars. He wanted the jungle to absorb him. He wanted to be one with the trees and the shrubs and the creeping beasts. He wanted thought to disappear. He drew the heavily scented air into his lungs as if that alone would make him become what at that moment he desired to be. The drone of insects became a murmuring voice that called him into the heart of the old, old forest. And yet he could not move – could not answer. And at length Count Smiorgan came up on deck and touched his shoulder and said something and passively he went below to his bunk and wrapped himself in his cloak and lay there, still listening to the voice of the jungle.

Even Duke Avan seemed more introspective than usual when they upped anchor the next morning and began to row against the sluggish current. There were few gaps in the foliage above their heads and they had the impression that they were entering a huge, gloomy tunnel, leaving the sunlight behind with the sea. Bright plants twined among the vines that hung from the leafy canopy and caught in the ship's masts as they moved. Ratlike animals with long arms swung through the branches and peered at them with bright, knowing eyes. The river turned and the sea was no longer in sight. Shafts of sunlight filtered down to the deck and the light had a greenish tinge to it. Elric became more alert than he had ever been since he agreed to accompany Duke Avan. He took a keen interest in every detail of the jungle and the black river over which moved schools of insects like agitated clouds of mist and in which blossoms drifted like drops of blood in ink. Everywhere were rustlings, sudden squawks, barks and wet noises made by fish or river animals as they hunted the prey disturbed by the ship's oars which cut into the great clumps of weed and sent the things that hid there scurrying. The others began to complain of insect bites, but Elric was not troubled by them, perhaps because no insect could desire his deficient blood.

Duke Avan passed him on the deck. The Vilmirian slapped at his forehead. 'You seem more cheerful, Prince Elric.'

Elric smiled absently. 'Perhaps I am.'

'I must admit I personally find all this a bit oppressive. I'll be glad when we reach the city.'

'You are still convinced you'll find it?'

'I'll be convinced otherwise when I've explored every inch of the island we're bound for.'

So absorbed had he become in the atmosphere of the jungle that Elric was hardly aware of the ship or his companions. The ship beat very slowly up the river, moving at little more than walking speed.

A few days passed, but Elric scarcely noticed, for the jungle did not change – and then the river widened and the canopy parted and the wide, hot sky was suddenly full of huge birds crowding upwards as the ship disturbed them. All but Elric were pleased to be under the open sky again and spirits rose. Elric went below.

The attack on the ship came almost immediately. There was a whistling noise and a scream and a sailor writhed and fell over clutching at a grey, thin semicircle of something which had buried itself in his stomach. An upper yard came crashing to the deck, bringing sail and rigging with it. A headless body took four paces towards the poop deck before collapsing, the blood pumping from the obscene hole that was its neck. And everywhere was the thin whistling noise. Elric heard the sounds from below and came back instantly, buckling on his sword. The first face he saw was Smiorgan's. The bald-pated man looked perturbed as he crouched against a rail on the starboard side. Elric had the impression of grey blurs whistling past, slashing into flesh and rigging, wood and canvas. Some fell to the deck and he saw that they were thin discs of crystalline rock, about a foot in diameter. They were being hurled from both banks of the river and there was no protection against them.

He tried to see who was throwing the discs and glimpsed something moving in the trees along the right bank. Then the discs ceased suddenly and there was a pause before some of the sailors dashed across the deck to seek better cover. Duke Avan suddenly appeared in the stern. He had unsheathed his sword.

'Get below. Get your bucklers and any armour you can find. Bring bows. Arm yourselves, men, or you're finished.'

And as he spoke their attackers broke from the trees and began to wade into the water. No more discs came and it seemed likely they had exhausted their supply.

'By Chardros!' Avan gasped. 'Are these real creatures or some sorcerer's conjurings?'

The things were essentially reptilian but with feathery crests and neck wattles, though their faces were almost human. Their forelegs were like the arms and hands of men, but their hind legs were incredibly long and storklike. Balanced on these legs, their bodies towered over the water. They carried great clubs in which slits had been cut and doubtless these were what they used to hurl the crystalline discs. Staring at their faces, Elric was horrified. In some subtle way they reminded him of the characteristic faces of his own folk – the folk of Melniboné. Were these creatures his cousins? Or were they a species from which his people had evolved? He stopped asking the questions as an intense hatred for the creatures filled him. They were obscene: sight of them brought bile into his throat. Without thinking, he drew Stormbringer from its sheath.

The Black Sword began to howl and the familiar black radiance

spilled from it. The runes carved into its blade pulsed a vivid scarlet which turned slowly to a deep purple and then to black once more.

The creatures were wading through the water on their stiltlike legs and they paused when they saw the sword, glancing at one another. And they were not the only ones unnerved by the sight, for Duke Avan and his men paled, too.

'Gods!' Avan yelled. 'I know not which I prefer the look of – those who attack us or that which defends us!'

'Stay well away from that sword,' Smiorgan warned. 'I hear it has the habit of killing more than its master chooses.'

And now the reptilian savages were upon them, clutching at the ship's rails as the armed sailors rushed back on deck to meet the attack.

Clubs came at Elric from all sides, but Stormbringer shrieked and parried each blow. He held the sword in both hands, whirling it this way and that, ploughing great gashes in the scaly bodies.

The creatures hissed and opened red mouths in agony and rage while their thick, black blood sank into the waters of the river. Although from the legs upward they were only slightly larger than a tall, well-built man, they had more vitality than any human and the deepest cuts hardly seemed to affect them, even when administered by Stormbringer. Elric was astonished at this resistance to the sword's power. Often a nick was enough for the sword to draw a man's soul from him. These things seemed immune. Perhaps they had no souls...

He fought on, his hatred giving him strength.

But elsewhere on the ship the sailors were being routed. Rails were torn off and the great clubs crushed planks and brought down more rigging. The savages were intent on destroying the ship as well as the crew. And there was little doubt, now, that they would be successful.

Avan shouted to Elric. 'By the names of all the gods, Prince Elric, can you not summon some further sorcery? We are doomed else!'

Elric knew Avan spoke truth. All around him the ship was being gradually pulled apart by the hissing reptilian creatures.

Most of them had sustained horrible wounds from the defenders, but only one or two had collapsed. Elric began to suspect that they did, in fact, fight supernatural enemies.

He backed away and sought shelter beneath a half-crushed doorway as he tried to concentrate on a method of calling upon supernatural aid.

He was panting with exhaustion and he clung to a beam as the ship rocked back and forth in the water. He fought to clear his head.

And then the incantation came to him. He was not sure if it was appropriate, but it was the only one he could recall. His ancestors had made pacts, thousands of years before, with all the elementals who controlled the animal world. In the past he had summoned help from various of these spirits but never from the one he now sought to call. From his mouth began to issue the ancient, beautiful and convoluted words of Melniboné's High Speech.

'King with Wings! Lord of all that work and are not seen, upon whose labours all else depends! Nnuuurrrr'c'c of the Insect Folk, I summon thee!'

Save for the motion of the ship, Elric ceased to be aware of all else happening around him. The sounds of the fight dimmed and were heard no more as he sent his voice out beyond his plane of the Earth into another – the plane dominated by King Nnuuurrrr'c'c of the Insects, paramount lord of his people.

In his ears now Elric heard a buzzing and gradually the buzzing formed itself in words.

'Who art thou, mortal? What right hast thee to summon me?'

'I am Elric, ruler of Melniboné. My ancestors aided thee, Nnuuurrrr'c'c.'

'Aye – but long ago.'

'And it is long ago that they last called on thee for thine aid!'

'True. What aid dost thou now require, Elric of Melniboné?'

'Look upon my plane. Thou wilt see that I am in danger. Canst thou abolish this danger, friend of the Insects?'

Now a filmy shape formed and could be seen as if through several layers of cloudy silk. Elric tried to keep his eyes upon it, but it kept leaving his field of vision and then returning for a few moments. He knew that he looked into another plane of the Earth.

'Canst thou help me, Nnuuurrrr'c'c?'

'Hast thou no patron of thine own species? Some Lord of Chaos who can aid thee?'

'My patron is Arioch and he is a temperamental demon at best. These days he aids me little.'

'Then I must send thee allies, mortal. But call upon me no more when this is done.'

'I shall not summon thee again, Nnuuurrrr'c'c.'

The layers of film disappeared and with them the shape.

The noise of the battle crashed once again on Elric's consciousness and he heard with sharper clarity than before the screams of the sailors and the hissing of the reptilian savages and when he looked out from his shelter he saw that at least half the crew was dead.

As he came on deck Smiorgan ran up. 'I thought you slain, Elric! What became of you?' He was plainly relieved to see his friend still lived.

'I sought aid from another plane – but it does not seem to have materialised.'

'I'm thinking we're doomed and had best try to swim downstream away from here and seek a hiding place in the jungle,' Smiorgan said.

'What of Duke Avan? Is he dead?'

'He lives. But those creatures are all but impervious to our weapons. This ship will sink ere long.' Smiorgan lurched as the deck tilted and he reached out to grab a trailing rope, letting his long sword dangle by its wrist-thong. 'They are not attacking the stern at present. We can slip into the water there...'

'I made a bargain with Duke Avan,' Elric reminded the islander. 'I cannot desert him.'

'Then we'll all perish!'

'What's that?' Elric bent his head, listening intently.

'I hear nothing.'

It was a whine which deepened in tone until it became a drone. Now Smiorgan heard it also and looked about him, seeking the source of the sound. And suddenly he gasped, pointing upward. 'Is that the aid you sought?'

There was a vast cloud of them, black against the blue of the sky. Every so often the sun would flash on a dazzling colour – a rich blue, green or red. They came spiralling down towards the ship and now both sides fell silent, staring skyward.

The flying things were like huge dragonflies and the brightness and richness of their colouring was breathtaking. It was their wings which made the droning sound which now began to increase in loudness and heighten in pitch as the huge insects sped nearer.

Realising that they were the object of the attack the reptile men stumbled backwards on their long legs, trying to reach the shore before the gigantic insects were upon them.

But it was too late for flight.

The dragonflies settled on the savages. Soon nothing could be seen of the bodies. The hissing increased and sounded almost pitiful as the insects bore their victims down to the surface and then inflicted on them whatever terrible death it was. Perhaps they stung with their tails – it was not possible for the watchers to see.

Sometimes a storklike leg would emerge from the water and thrash in the air for a moment. But soon, just as the reptiles were covered by the insect bodies, so were their cries drowned by the strange and blood-chilling humming that arose on all sides.

A sweating Duke Avan, sword still in hand, ran up the deck. 'Is this your doing, Prince Elric?'

Elric looked on with satisfaction, but the others were plainly disgusted. 'It was,' he said.

'Then I thank you for your aid. This ship is holed in a dozen places and is letting in water at a terrible rate. It's a wonder we have not yet sunk. I've given orders to begin rowing and I hope we make it to the island in time.' He pointed upstream. 'There, you can just see it.'

'What if there are more of those savages there?' Smiorgan asked.

Avan smiled grimly, indicating the further shore. 'Look.' On their peculiar legs a dozen or more of the reptiles were fleeing into the jungle, having witnessed the fate of their comrades. 'They'll be reluctant to attack us again, I think.'

Now the huge dragonflies were rising into the air again and Avan turned away as he glimpsed what they had left behind. 'By the gods, you work fierce sorcery, Prince Elric! Ugh!'

Elric smiled and shrugged. 'It is effective, Duke Avan.' He sheathed his runesword. It seemed reluctant to enter the scabbard and it moaned as if in resentment.

Smiorgan glanced at it. 'That blade looks as if it will want to feast soon, Elric, whether you desire it or not.'

'Doubtless it will find something to feed on in the forest,' said the albino. He stepped over a piece of broken mast and went below.

Count Smiorgan Baldhead looked at the new scum on the surface of the water and he shuddered.

Chapter Four

The wrecked schooner was almost awash when the crew clambered overboard with lines and began the task of dragging it up the mud that formed the banks of the island. Before them was a wall of foliage that seemed impenetrable. Smiorgan followed Elric, lowering himself into the shallows. They began to wade ashore.

As they left the water and set foot on the hard, baked earth, Smiorgan stared at the forest. No wind moved the trees and a peculiar silence had descended. No birds called from the trees, no insects buzzed, there were none of the barks and cries of animals they had heard on their journey upriver.

'Those supernatural friends of yours seem to have frightened more than the savages away,' the black-bearded man murmured. 'This place seems lifeless.'

Elric nodded. 'It is strange.'

Duke Avan joined them. He had discarded his finery – ruined in the fight, anyway – and now wore a padded leather jerkin and doeskin breeches. His sword was at his side. 'We'll have to leave most of our men behind with the ship,' he said regretfully. 'They'll make what repairs they can while we press on to find R'lin K'ren A'a.' He tugged his light cloak about him. 'Is it my imagination, or is there an odd atmosphere?'

'We have already remarked on it,' Smiorgan said. 'Life seems to have fled the island.'

Duke Avan grinned. 'If all we face is as timid, we have nothing further to fear. I must admit, Prince Elric, that had I wished you harm and then seen you conjure those monsters from thin air, I'd think twice about getting too close to you! Thank you, by the way, for what you did. We should have perished by now if it had not been for you.'

'It was for my aid that you asked me to accompany you,' Elric said wearily. 'Let's eat and rest and then continue with our expedition.'

A shadow passed over Duke Avan's face then. Something in Elric's manner had disturbed him.

Entering the jungle was no easy matter. Armed with axes the six members of the crew (all that could be spared) began to hack at the undergrowth. And still the unnatural silence prevailed...

By nightfall they were less than half a mile into the forest and completely exhausted. The forest was so thick that there was barely room to pitch their tent. The only light in the camp came from the small, sputtering fire outside the tent. The crewmen slept where they could in the open.

Elric could not sleep, but now it was not the jungle which kept him awake. He was puzzled by the silence, for he was sure that it was not their presence which had driven all life away. There was not a single small rodent, bird or insect anywhere to be seen. There were no traces of animal life. The island had been deserted by all but vegetation for a long while – perhaps for centuries or tens of centuries. He remembered another part of the old legend of R'lin K'ren A'a. It had been said that when the gods came to meet there not only the citizens fled, but also all the wildlife. Nothing had dared see the High Lords or listen to their conversation. Elric shivered, turning his white head this way and that on the rolled cloak that supported it, his crimson eyes tortured. If there were dangers on this island, they would be subtler dangers than those they had faced on the river.

The noise of their passage through the forest was the only sound to be heard on the island as they forced their way on the next morning.

With lodestone in one hand and map in the other, Duke Avan Astran sought to guide them, directing his men where to cut their path. But the going became even slower and it was obvious that no creatures had come this way for many ages.

By the fourth day they had reached a natural clearing of flat volcanic rock and found a spring there. Gratefully they made camp. Elric began to wash his face in the cool water when he heard a yell behind him. He sprang up. One of the crewmen was reaching for an arrow and fitting it to his bow.

'What is it?' Duke Avan called.

'I saw something, my lord!'

'Nonsense, there are no –'

'Look!' The man drew back the string and let fly into the upper terraces of the forest. Something did seem to stir then and Elric thought he saw a flash of grey among the trees.

'Did you see what kind of creature it was?' Smiorgan asked the man.

'No, master. I feared at first it was those reptiles again.'

'They're too frightened to follow us onto this island,' Duke Avan reassured him.

'I hope you're right,' Smiorgan said nervously.

'Then what could it have been?' Elric wondered.

'I – I thought it was a man, master,' the crewman stuttered.

Elric stared thoughtfully into the trees. 'A man?'

Smiorgan asked, 'You were hoping for this, Elric?'

'I am not sure...'

Duke Avan shrugged. 'More likely the shadow of a cloud passing over the trees. According to my calculations we should have reached the city by now.'

'You think, after all, that it does not exist?' Elric said.

'I am beginning not to care, Prince Elric.' The duke leaned against the bole of a huge tree, brushing aside a vine which touched his face. 'Still there's nought else to do. The ship won't be ready to sail yet.' He looked up into the branches. 'I did not think I should miss those damned insects that plagued us on our way here...'

The crewman who had shot the arrow suddenly shouted again. 'There! I saw him! It is a man!'

While the others stared but failed to discern anything Duke Avan continued to lean against the tree. 'You saw nothing. There is nothing here to see.'

Elric turned towards him. 'Give me the map and the lodestone, Duke Avan. I have a feeling I can find the way.'

The Vilmirian shrugged, an expression of doubt on his square, handsome face. He handed the things over to Elric.

They rested the night and in the morning they continued, with Elric leading the way.

And at noon they broke out of the forest and saw the ruins of R'lin K'ren A'a.

Chapter Five

NOTHING GREW AMONG the ruins of the city. The streets were broken and the walls of the houses had fallen, but there were no weeds flowering in the cracks and it seemed that the city had but recently been brought down by an earthquake. Only one thing still stood intact, towering over the ruins. It was a gigantic statue of white, grey and green jade – the statue of a naked youth with a face of almost feminine beauty that turned sightless eyes towards the north.

'The eyes!' Duke Avan Astran said. 'They're gone!'

The others said nothing as they stared at the statue and the ruins surrounding it. The area was relatively small and the buildings had had little decoration. The inhabitants seemed to have been a simple, well-to-do folk – totally unlike the Melnibonéans of the Bright Empire. Elric could not believe that the people of R'lin K'ren A'a had been his ancestors. They had been too sane.

'The statue's already been looted,' Duke Avan continued. 'Our damned journey's been in vain!'

Elric laughed. 'Did you really think you would be able to prise the Jade Man's eyes from their sockets, my lord?'

The statue was as tall as any tower of the Dreaming City and the head alone must have been the size of a reasonably large building. Duke Avan pursed his lips and refused to listen to Elric's mocking voice. 'We may yet find the journey worth our while,' he said. 'There were other treasures in R'lin K'ren A'a. Come...'

He led the way into the city.

Very few of the buildings were even partially standing, but they were nonetheless fascinating if only for the peculiar nature of their building materials, which were of a kind the travellers had never seen before.

The colours were many, but faded by time – soft reds and

yellows and blues – and they flowed together to make almost infinite combinations.

Elric reached out to touch one wall and was surprised at the cool feel of the smooth material. It was neither stone nor wood nor metal. Perhaps it had been brought here from another plane?

He tried to visualise the city as it had been before it was deserted. The streets had been wide, there had been no surrounding wall, the houses had been low and built around large courtyards. If this was, indeed, the original home of his people, what had happened to change them from the peaceful citizens of R'lin K'ren A'a to the insane builders of Imrryr's bizarre and dreaming towers? Elric had thought he might find a solution to a mystery here, but instead he had found another mystery. It was his fate, he thought, shrugging to himself.

And then the first crystal disc hummed past his head and smashed against a collapsing wall.

The next disc split the skull of a crewman and a third nicked Smiorgan's ear before they had thrown themselves flat amongst the rubble.

'They're vengeful, those creatures,' Avan said with a hard smile. 'They'll risk much to pay us back for their comrades' deaths!'

Terror was on the face of each surviving crewman and fear had begun to creep into Avan's eyes.

More discs clattered nearby, but it was plain that the party was temporarily out of sight of the reptiles. Smiorgan coughed as white dust rose from the rubble and caught in his throat.

'You'd best summon those monstrous allies of yours again, Elric.'

Elric shook his head. 'I cannot. My ally said he would not serve me a second time.' He looked to his left where the four walls of a small house still stood. There seemed to be no door, only a window.

'Then call something,' Count Smiorgan said urgently. 'Anything.'

'I am not sure...'

Then Elric rolled over and sprang for the shelter, flinging himself through the window to land on a pile of masonry that grazed his hands and knees.

He staggered upright. In the distance he could see the huge blind statue of the god dominating the city. This was said to be an image of Arioch – though it resembled no image of Arioch Elric remembered. Did that image protect R'lin K'ren A'a – or did it threaten it? Someone screamed. He glanced through the opening and saw that a disc had chopped through a man's forearm.

He drew Stormbringer and raised it, facing the jade statue.

'Arioch!' he cried. 'Arioch – aid me!'

Black light burst from the blade and it began to sing, as if joining in Elric's incantation.

'Arioch!'

Would the demon come? Often the patron of the kings of Melniboné refused to materialise, claiming that more urgent business called him – business concerning the eternal struggle between Law and Chaos.

'Arioch!'

Sword and man were now wreathed in a palpitating black mist and Elric's white face was flung back, seeming to writhe as the mist writhed.

'Arioch! I beg thee to aid me! It is Elric who calls thee!'

And then a voice reached his ears. It was a soft, purring, reasonable voice. It was a tender voice.

'Elric, I am fondest of thee. I love thee more than any other mortal – but aid thee I cannot – not yet.'

Elric cried desperately: 'Then we are doomed to perish here!'

'Thou canst escape this danger. Flee alone into the forest. Leave the others while thou hast time. Thou hast a destiny to fulfil elsewhere and elsewhen...'

'I will not desert them.'

'Thou art foolish, sweet Elric.'

'Arioch – since Melniboné's founding thou hast aided her kings. Aid her last king this day!'

'I cannot dissipate my energies. A great struggle looms. And it would cost me much to return to R'lin K'ren A'a. Flee now. Thou shalt be saved. Only the others will die.'

And then the Duke of Hell had gone. Elric sensed the passing of his presence. He frowned, fingering his belt pouch, trying to recall something he had once heard. Slowly, he resheathed the reluctant sword. Then there was a thump and Smiorgan stood panting before him.

'Well, is aid on the way?'

'I fear not.' Elric shook his head in despair. 'Once again Arioch refuses me. Once again he speaks of a greater destiny – a need to conserve his strength.'

'Your ancestors could have picked a more tractable demon as their patron. Our reptilian friends are closing in. Look...' Smiorgan pointed to the outskirts of the city. A band of about a dozen stilt-legged creatures were advancing, their huge clubs at the ready.

There was a scuffling noise from the rubble on the other side of the wall and Avan appeared, leading his men through the opening. He was cursing.

'No extra aid is coming, I fear,' Elric told him.

The Vilmirian smiled grimly. 'Then the monsters out there knew more than did we!'

'It seems so.'

'We'll have to try to hide from them,' Smiorgan said without much conviction. 'We'd not survive a fight.'

The little party left the ruined house and began to inch its way through what cover it could find, moving gradually nearer to the centre of the city and the statue of the Jade Man.

A sharp hiss from behind them told them that the reptile warriors had sighted them again and another Vilmirian fell with a crystal disc protruding from his back. They broke into a panicky run.

Ahead now was a red building of several storeys which still had its roof.

'In there!' Duke Avan shouted.

With some relief they dashed unhesitatingly up worn steps and through a series of dusty passages until they paused to catch their breath in a great, gloomy hall.

The hall was completely empty and a little light filtered through cracks in the wall.

'This place has lasted better than the others,' Duke Avan said. 'I wonder what its function was. A fortress, perhaps.'

'They seem not to have been a warlike race,' Smiorgan pointed out. 'I suspect the building had some other function.'

The three surviving crewmen were looking fearfully about them. They looked as if they would have preferred to have faced the reptile warriors outside.

Elric began to cross the floor and then paused as he saw something painted on the far wall.

Smiorgan saw it too. 'What's that, friend Elric?'

Elric recognised the symbols as the written High Speech of old Melniboné, but it was subtly different and it took him a short time to decipher its meaning.

'Know you what it says, Elric?' Duke Avan murmured, joining them.

'Aye – but it's cryptic enough. It says: "If thou hast come to slay me, then thou art welcome. If thou hast come without the means to awaken the Jade Man, then begone..."'

'Is it addressed to us, I wonder,' Avan mused, 'or has it been there for a long while?'

Elric shrugged. 'It could have been inscribed at any time during the past ten thousand years...'

Smiorgan walked up to the wall and reached out to touch it. 'I would say it was fairly recent,' he said. 'The paint still being wet.'

Elric frowned. 'Then there are inhabitants here still. Why do they not reveal themselves?'

'Could those reptiles out there be the denizens of R'lin K'ren A'a?' Avan said. 'There is nothing in the legends that says they were humans who fled this place...'

Elric's face clouded and he was about to make an angry reply when Smiorgan interrupted.

'Perhaps there is just one inhabitant. Is that what you are thinking, Elric? The Creature Doomed to Live? Those sentiments could be his...'

Elric put his hands to his face and made no reply.

'Come,' Avan said. 'We've no time to debate on legends.' He

strode across the floor and entered another doorway, beginning to descend steps. As he reached the bottom they heard him gasp.

The others joined him and saw that he stood on the threshold of another hall. But this one was ankle-deep in fragments of stuff that had been thin leaves of a metallic material which had the flexibility of parchment. Around the walls were thousands of small holes, rank upon rank, each with a character painted over it.

'What is it?' Smiorgan asked.

Elric stooped and picked up one of the fragments. This had half a Melnibonéan character engraved on it. There had even been an attempt to obliterate this.

'It was a library,' he said softly. 'The library of my ancestors. Someone has tried to destroy it. These scrolls must have been virtually indestructible, yet a great deal of effort has gone into making them indecipherable.' He kicked at the fragments. 'Plainly our friend – or friends – is a consistent hater of learning.'

'Plainly,' Avan said bitterly. 'Oh, the *value* of those scrolls to the scholar! All destroyed!'

Elric shrugged. 'To limbo with the scholar – their value to me was quite considerable!'

Smiorgan put a hand on his friend's arm and Elric shrugged it off. 'I had hoped...'

Smiorgan cocked his bald head. 'Those reptiles have followed us into the building, by the sound of it.'

They heard the distant sound of strange footsteps in the passages behind them.

The little band of men moved as silently as they could through the ruined scrolls and crossed the hall until they entered another corridor which led sharply upward.

Then, suddenly, daylight was visible.

Elric peered ahead. 'The corridor has collapsed ahead of us and is blocked, by the look of it. The roof has caved in and we may be able to escape through the hole.'

They clambered upward over the fallen stones, glancing warily behind them for signs of their pursuers.

At last they emerged in the central square of the city. On the far sides of this square were placed the feet of the great statue, which now towered high above their heads.

Directly before them were two peculiar constructions which, unlike the rest of the buildings, were completely whole. They were domed and faceted and were made of some glasslike substance which diffracted the rays of the sun.

From below they heard the reptile men advancing down the corridor.

'We'll seek shelter in the nearest of those domes,' Elric said. He broke into a trot, leading the way.

The others followed him through the irregularly shaped opening at the base of the dome.

Once inside, however, they hesitated, shielding their eyes and blinking heavily as they tried to discern their way.

'It's like a maze of mirrors!' Smiorgan gasped. 'By the gods, I've never seen a better. Was that its function, I wonder?'

Corridors seemed to go off in all directions – yet they might be nothing more than reflections of the passage they were in. Cautiously Elric began to continue further into the maze, the five others following him.

'This smells of sorcery to me,' Smiorgan muttered as they advanced. 'Have we been forced into a trap, I wonder?'

Elric drew his sword. It murmured softly – almost querulously.

Everything shifted suddenly and the shapes of his companions grew dim.

'Smiorgan! Duke Avan!'

He heard voices murmuring, but they were not the voices of his friends.

'Count Smiorgan!'

But then the burly sea-lord faded away altogether and Elric was alone.

Chapter Six

HE TURNED AND a wall of red brilliance struck his eyes and blinded him.

He called out and his voice was turned into a dismal wail which mocked him.

He tried to move, but he could not tell whether he remained in the same spot or walked a dozen miles.

Now there was someone standing a few yards away, seemingly obscured by a screen of multicoloured transparent gems. He stepped forward and made to dash away the screen, but it vanished and he stopped suddenly.

He looked on a face of infinite sorrow.

And the face was his own face, save that the man's colouring was normal and his hair was black.

'What are you?' Elric said thickly.

'I have had many names. One is Erekosë. I have been many men. Perhaps I am all men.'

'But you are like me!'

'I am you.'

'No!'

The phantom's eyes held tears as it stared in pity at Elric.

'Do not weep for me!' Elric roared. 'I need no sympathy from you!'

'Perhaps I weep for myself, for I know our fate.'

'And what is that?'

'You would not understand.'

'Tell me.'

'Ask your gods.'

Elric raised his sword. Fiercely he said, 'No – I'll have my answer from you!'

And the phantom faded away.

Elric shivered. Now the corridor was populated by a thousand such phantoms. Each murmured a different name. Each wore different clothes. But each had his face, if not his colouring.

'Begone!' he screamed. 'Oh, gods, what is this place?'

And at his command they disappeared.

'Elric?'

The albino whirled, sword ready. But it was Duke Avan Astran of Old Hrolmar. He touched his own face with trembling fingers, but said levelly, 'I must tell you that I believe I am losing my sanity, Prince Elric...'

'What have you seen?'

'Many things. I cannot describe them.'

'Where are Smiorgan and the others?'

'Doubtless each went his separate way, as we did.'

Elric raised Stormbringer and brought the blade crashing against a crystal wall. The Black Sword moaned, but the wall merely changed its position.

But through a gap now Elric saw ordinary daylight. 'Come, Duke Avan – there is escape!'

Avan, dazed, followed him and they stepped out of the crystal and found themselves in the central square of R'lin K'ren A'a.

But there were noises. Carts and chariots moved about the square. Stalls were erected on one side. People moved peacefully about. And the Jade Man did not dominate the sky above the city. Here, there was no Jade Man at all.

Elric looked at the faces. They were the eldritch features of the folk of Melniboné. Yet these had a different cast to them which he could not at first define. Then he recognised what they had. It was tranquillity. He reached out his hand to touch one of the people.

'Tell me, friend, what year...?'

But the man did not hear him. He walked by.

Elric tried to stop several of the passers-by, but not one could see or hear him.

'How did they lose this peace?' Duke Avan asked wonderingly. 'How did they become like you, Prince Elric?'

Elric almost snarled as he turned sharply to face the Vilmirian. 'Be silent!'

Duke Avan shrugged. 'Perhaps this is merely an illusion.'

'Perhaps,' Elric said sadly. 'But I am sure this is how they lived – until the coming of the High Ones.'

'You blame the gods, then?'

'I blame the despair that the gods brought.'

Duke Avan nodded gravely. 'I understand.'

He turned back towards the great crystal and then stood listening. 'Do you hear that voice, Prince Elric? What is it saying?'

Elric heard the voice. It seemed to be coming from the crystal. It was speaking the old tongue of Melniboné, but with a strange accent. 'This way,' it said. 'This way.'

Elric paused. 'I have no liking to return there.'

Avan said, 'What choice have we?'

They stepped together through the entrance.

Again they were in the maze that could be one corridor or many, and the voice was clearer. 'Take two paces to your right,' it instructed.

Avan glanced at Elric. 'What was that?'

Elric told him.

'Shall we obey?' Avan asked.

'Aye.' There was resignation in the albino's voice.

They took two paces to their right.

'Now four to your left,' said the voice.

They took four paces to their left.

'Now one forward.'

They emerged into the ruined square of R'lin K'ren A'a.

Smiorgan and one Vilmirian crewman stood there.

'Where are the others?' Avan demanded.

'Ask him,' Smiorgan said wearily, gesturing with the sword in his right hand.

They stared at the man who was either an albino or a leper. He was completely naked and he bore a distinct likeness to Elric. At first Elric thought this was another phantom, but then he saw that there were also several differences in their faces. There was something sticking from the man's side, just above the third rib. With a shock, Elric recognised it as the broken shaft of a Vilmirian arrow.

The naked man nodded. 'Aye – the arrow found its mark. But it could not slay me, for I am J'osui C'reln Reyr...'

'You believe yourself to be the Creature Doomed to Live,' Elric murmured.

'I am he.' The man gave a bitter smile. 'Do you think I try to deceive you?'

Elric glanced at the arrow shaft and then shook his head.

'You are ten thousand years old?' Avan stared at him.

'What does he say?' asked J'osui C'reln Reyr of Elric. Elric translated.

'Is that all it has been?' The man sighed. Then he looked intently at Elric. 'You are of my race?'

'It seems so.'

'Of what family?'

'Of the royal line.'

'Then you have come at last. I, too, am of that line.'

'I believe you.'

'I notice that the Olab seek you.'

'The Olab?'

'Those primitives with the clubs.'

'Aye. We encountered them on our journey upriver.'

'I will lead you to safety. Come.'

Elric allowed J'osui C'reln Reyr to take them across the square to where part of a tottering wall still stood. The man then lifted a flagstone and showed them steps leading down into darkness. They followed him, descending cautiously as he caused the flagstone to lower itself above their heads. And then they found themselves in a room lit by crude oil lamps. Save for a bed of dried grasses the room was empty.

'You live sparely,' Elric said.

'I have need for nothing else. My head is sufficiently furnished...'

'Where do the Olab come from?' Elric asked.

'They are but recently arrived in these parts. Scarcely a thousand years ago – or perhaps half that time – they came from further upriver after some quarrel with another tribe. They do not usually come to the island. You must have killed many of them for them to wish you such harm.'

'We killed many.'

J'osui C'reln Reyr gestured at the others who were staring at him in some discomfort. 'And these? Primitives, also, eh? They are not of our folk.'

'There are few of our folk left.'

'What does he say?' Duke Avan asked.

'He says that those reptile warriors are called the Olab,' Elric told him.

'And was it these Olab who stole the Jade Man's eyes?'

When Elric translated the question the Creature Doomed to Live was astonished. 'Did you not know, then?'

'Know what?'

'Why, you have been *in* the Jade Man's eyes! Those great crystals in which you wandered – that is what they are!'

Chapter Seven

When Elric offered this information to Duke Avan, the Vilmirian burst into laughter. He flung his head back and roared with mirth while the others looked gloomily on. The cloud that had fallen across his features of late suddenly cleared and he became again the man whom Elric had first met.

Smiorgan was the next to smile and even Elric acknowledged the irony of what had happened to them.

'Those crystals fell from his face like tears soon after the High Ones departed,' continued J'osui C'reln Reyr.

'So the High Ones did come here.'

'Aye – the Jade Man brought the message and all the folk departed, having made their bargain with him.'

'The Jade Man was not built by your people?'

'The Jade Man is Duke Arioch of Hell. He strode from the forest one day and stood in the square and told the people what was to come about – that our city lay at the centre of some particular configuration and that it was only there that the Lords of the Higher Worlds could meet.'

'And the bargain?'

'In return for their city, our royal line might in the future increase their power with Arioch as their patron. He would give them great knowledge and the means to build a new city elsewhere.'

'And they accepted this bargain without question?'

'There was little choice, kinsman.'

Elric lowered his eyes to regard the dusty floor. 'And thus they were corrupted,' he murmured.

'Only I refused to accept the pact, I did not wish to leave this city and I mistrusted Arioch. When all others set off down the river, I remained here – where we are now – and I heard the Lords of the Higher Worlds arrive and I heard them speak, laying down the rules under which Law and Chaos would fight thereafter. When they had gone, I emerged. But Arioch – the Jade Man – was still here. He looked down on me through his crystal eyes and he cursed me. When that was done the crystals fell and landed where you now see them. Arioch's spirit departed, but his jade image was left behind.'

'And you still retain all memory of what transpired between the Lords of Law and Chaos?'

'That is my doom.'

'Perhaps your fate was less harsh than that which befell those who left,' Elric said quietly. 'I am the last inheritor of that particular doom...'

J'osui C'reln Reyr looked puzzled and then he stared into Elric's eyes and an expression of pity crossed his face. 'I had not thought there was a worse fate – but now I believe there might be...'

Elric said urgently, 'Ease my soul, at least. I must know what passed between the High Lords in those days. I must understand the nature of my existence – as you, at least, understand yours. Tell me, I beg you!'

J'osui C'reln Reyr frowned and he stared deeply into Elric's eyes. 'Do you not know all my story, then?'

'Is there more?'

'I can only *remember* what passed between the High Lords – but when I try to tell my knowledge aloud or try to write it down, I cannot...'

Elric grasped the man's shoulder. 'You must try! You must try!'

'I know that I cannot.'

Seeing the torture in Elric's face, Smiorgan came up to him. 'What is it, Elric?'

Elric's hand clutched his head. 'Our journey has been useless.' Unconsciously he used the old Melnibonéan tongue.

'It need not be,' said J'osui C'reln Reyr. 'For me, at least.' He paused. 'Tell me, how did you find this city? Was there a map?'

Elric produced the map. 'This one.'

'Aye, that is the one. Many centuries ago I put it into a casket which I placed in a small trunk. I launched the trunk into the river, hoping that it would follow my people and they would know what it was.'

'The casket was found in Melniboné, but no-one had bothered to open it,' Elric explained. 'That will give you an idea of what happened to the folk who left here...'

The strange man nodded gravely. 'And was there still a seal upon the map?'

'There was. I have it.'

'An image of one of the manifestations of Arioch, embedded in a small ruby?'

'Aye. I thought I recognised the image, but I could not place it.'

'The Image in the Gem,' murmured J'osui C'reln Reyr. 'As I prayed, it has returned – borne by one of the royal line!'

'What is its significance?'

Smiorgan interrupted. 'Will this fellow help us to escape, Elric? We are becoming somewhat impatient...'

'Wait,' the albino said. 'I will tell you everything later.'

'The Image in the Gem could be the instrument of my release,' said the Creature Doomed to Live. 'If he who possesses it is of the royal line, then he can command the Jade Man.'

'But why did you not use it?'

'Because of the curse that was put on me. I had the power to command, but not to summon the demon. It was a joke, I understand, of the High Lords.'

Elric saw bitter sadness in the eyes of J'osui C'reln Reyr. He looked at the white, naked flesh and the white hair and the body that was neither old nor young, at the shaft of the arrow sticking out above the third rib on the left side.

'What must I do?' he asked.

'You must summon Arioch and then you must command him to enter his body again and recover his eyes so that he may see to walk away from R'lin K'ren A'a.'

'And when he walks away?'

'The curse goes with him.'

Elric was thoughtful. If he did summon Arioch – who was plainly reluctant to come – and then commanded him to do something he did not wish to do, he stood the chance of making an enemy of that powerful, if unpredictable, entity. Yet they were trapped here by the Olab warriors, with no means of escaping them. If the Jade Man walked, the Olab would almost certainly flee and there would be time to get back to the ship and reach the sea. He explained everything to his companions. Both Smiorgan and Avan looked dubious and the remaining Vilmirian crewman looked positively terrified.

'I must do it,' Elric decided, 'for the sake of this man. I must call Arioch and lift the doom that is on R'lin K'ren A'a.'

'And bring a greater doom to us!' Duke Avan said, putting his hand automatically upon his sword hilt. 'No. I think we should take our chances with the Olab. Leave this man – he is mad – he raves. Let's be on our way.'

'Go if you choose,' Elric said. 'But I will stay with the Creature Doomed to Live.'

'Then you will stay here for ever. You cannot believe his story!'

'But I do believe it.'

'You must come with us. Your sword will help. Without it, the Olab will certainly destroy us.'

'You saw that Stormbringer has little effect against the Olab.'

'And yet it has some. Do not desert me, Elric!'

'I am not deserting you. I must summon Arioch. That summoning will be to your benefit, if not to mine.

'I am unconvinced.'

'It was my sorcery you wanted on this venture. Now you shall have my sorcery.'

Avan backed away. He seemed to fear something more than the Olab, more than the Summoning. He seemed to read a threat in Elric's face of which even Elric was unaware.

'We must go outside,' said J'osui C'reln Reyr. 'We must stand beneath the Jade Man.'

'And when this is done,' Elric asked suddenly, 'how will we leave R'lin K'ren A'a?'

'There is a boat. It has no provisions, but much of the city's treasure is on it. It lies at the west end of the island.'

'That is some comfort,' Elric said. 'And you could not use it yourself?'

'I could not leave.'

'Is that part of the curse?'

'Aye – the curse of my timidity.'

'Timidity has kept you here ten thousand years?'

'Aye...'

They left the chamber and went out into the square. Night had fallen and a huge moon was in the sky. From where Elric stood it seemed to frame the Jade Man's sightless head like a halo. It was completely silent. Elric took the Image in the Gem from his pouch and held it between the forefinger and thumb of his left hand. With his right he drew Stormbringer. Avan, Smiorgan and the Vilmirian crewman fell back.

He stared up at the huge jade legs, the genitals, the torso, the arms, the head, and he raised his sword in both hands and screamed:

'ARIOCH!'

Stormbringer's voice almost drowned his. It pulled in his hands; it threatened to leave his grasp altogether as it howled.

'ARIOCH!'

All the watchers saw now was the throbbing, radiant sword, the white face and hands of the albino and his crimson eyes glaring through the blackness.

'ARIOCH!'

And then a voice which was not Arioch's came to Elric's ears and it seemed that the sword itself spoke.

'*Elric – Arioch must have blood and souls. Blood and souls, my lord...*'

'No. These are my friends and the Olab cannot be harmed by Stormbringer. Arioch must come without the blood, without the souls.'

'Only those can summon him for certain!' said a voice, more clearly now. It was sardonic and it seemed to come from behind him. He turned, but there was nothing there.

He saw Duke Avan's nervous face, and as his eyes fixed on the Vilmirian's countenance, the sword swung around, twisting against Elric's grip and plunging towards the duke.

'No!' cried Elric. 'Stop!'

But Stormbringer would not stop until it had plunged deep into Duke Avan's heart and quenched its thirst. The crewman stood transfixed as he watched his master die.

Duke Avan writhed. 'Elric! What treachery do you...?' He screamed. 'Ah, no!'

He jerked. 'Please...'

He quivered. 'My soul...'

He died.

Elric withdrew the sword and cut the crewman down as he ran to his master's aid. The action had been without thought.

'Now Arioch has his blood and his souls,' he said coldly. 'Let Arioch come!'

Smiorgan and the Creature Doomed to Live had retreated, staring at the possessed Elric in horror. The albino's face was cruel.

'LET ARIOCH COME!'

'I am here, Elric.'

Elric whirled and saw that something stood in the shadow of the statue's legs – a shadow within a shadow.

'Arioch – thou must return to this manifestation and make it leave R'lin K'ren A'a forever.'

'I do not choose to, Elric.'

'Then I must command thee, Duke Arioch.'

'Command? Only he who possesses the Image in the Gem may command Arioch – and then only once.'

'I have the Image in the Gem.' Elric held up the tiny object. 'See.'

The shadow within a shadow swirled for a moment as if in anger.

'If I obey your command, you will set in motion a chain of events which you might not desire,' Arioch said, speaking suddenly in Low Melnibonéan as if to give extra gravity to his words.

'Then let it be. I command you to enter the Jade Man and pick up its eyes so that it might walk again. Then I command you to leave here and take the curse of the High Ones with you.'

Arioch replied, 'When the Jade Man ceases to guard the place where the High Ones meet, then the great struggle of the Upper Worlds begins on this plane.'

'I command thee, Arioch. Go into the Jade Man!'

'You are an obstinate creature, Elric.'

'Go!' Elric raised Stormbringer. It seemed to sing in monstrous glee and it seemed at that moment to be more powerful than Arioch himself, more powerful than all the Lords of the Higher Worlds.

The ground shook. Fire suddenly blazed around the form of the great statue. The shadow within a shadow disappeared.

And the Jade Man stooped.

Its great bulk bent over Elric and its hands reached past him and it groped for the two crystals that lay on the ground. Then it found them and took one in each hand, straightening its back.

Elric stumbled towards the far corner of the square where Smiorgan and J'osui C'reln Reyr already crouched in terror.

A fierce light now blazed from the Jade Man's eyes and the jade lips parted.

'It is done, Elric!' said a huge voice.

J'osui C'reln Reyr began to sob.

'Then go, Arioch.'

'I go. The curse is lifted from R'lin K'ren A'a and from J'osui C'reln Reyr – but a greater curse now lies upon your whole plane.'

'What is this, Arioch? Explain yourself!' Elric cried.

'Soon you will have your explanation. Farewell!'

The enormous legs of jade moved suddenly and in a single step had cleared the ruins and had begun to crash through the jungle. In a moment the Jade Man had disappeared.

Then the Creature Doomed to Live laughed. It was a strange joy that he voiced. Smiorgan blocked his ears.

'And now!' shouted J'osui C'reln Reyr. 'Now your blade must take my life. I can die at last!'

Elric passed his hand across his face. He had hardly been aware of any of the recent events. 'No,' he said in a dazed tone. 'I cannot...'

And Stormbringer flew from his hand – flew to the body of the Creature Doomed to Live and buried itself in its chest.

And as he died, J'osui C'reln Reyr laughed. He fell to the ground and his lips moved. A whisper came from them. Elric stepped nearer to hear.

'The sword has my knowledge now. My burden has left me.'

The eyes closed.

J'osui C'reln Reyr's ten-thousand-year life-span had ended.

Weakly, Elric withdrew Stormbringer and sheathed it. He stared down at the body of the Creature Doomed to Live and then he looked up, questioningly, at Smiorgan.

The burly sea-lord turned away.

The sun began to rise. Grey dawn came. Elric watched the corpse of J'osui C'reln Reyr turn to powder that was stirred by the wind and mixed with the dust of the ruins. He walked back across the square to where Duke Avan's twisted body lay and he fell to his knees beside it.

'You were warned, Duke Avan Astran of Old Hrolmar, that ill befell those who linked their fortunes with Elric of Melniboné. But you thought otherwise. Now you know.' With a sigh he got to his feet.

Smiorgan stood beside him. The sun was now touching the taller parts of the ruins. Smiorgan reached out and gripped his friend's shoulder.

'The Olab have vanished. I think they've had their fill of sorcery.'

'Another man has been destroyed by me, Smiorgan. Am I forever to be tied to this cursed sword? I must discover a way to rid myself of it or my heavy conscience will bear me down so that I cannot rise at all.'

Smiorgan cleared his throat, but was otherwise silent.

'I will lay Duke Avan to rest,' Elric said. 'You go back to where we left the ship and tell the men that we come.'

Smiorgan began to stride across the square towards the east.

Elric tenderly picked up the body of Duke Avan and went towards the opposite side of the square, to the underground room where the Creature Doomed to Live had lived out his life for ten thousand years.

It seemed so unreal to Elric now, but he knew that it had not been a dream, for the Jade Man had gone. His tracks could be seen through the jungle. Whole clumps of trees had been flattened.

He reached the place and descended the stairs and laid Duke Avan down on the bed of dried grasses. Then he took the duke's dagger and, for want of anything else, dipped it in the duke's blood and wrote on the wall above the corpse:

This was Duke Avan Astran of Old Hrolmar. He explored the world and brought much knowledge and treasure back to Vilmir, his land. He dreamed and became lost in the dream of another and so died. He enriched the Young Kingdoms – and thus encouraged another dream. He died so that the Creature Doomed to Live might die, as he desired...

Elric paused. Then he threw down the dagger. He could not justify his own feelings of guilt by composing a high-sounding epitaph for the man he had slain.

He stood there, breathing heavily, then once again picked up the dagger.

He died because Elric of Melniboné desired a peace and a knowledge he could never find. He died by the Black Sword.

Outside in the middle of the square, at noon, still lay the lonely body of the last Vilmirian crewman. Nobody had known his name. Nobody felt grief for him or tried to compose an epitaph for him. The dead Vilmirian had died for no high purpose, followed no fabulous dream. Even in death his body would fulfil no function. On this island there was no carrion-eater to feed. In the dust of the city there was no earth to fertilise.

Elric came back into the square and saw the body. For a moment, to Elric, it symbolised everything that had transpired here and would transpire later.

'There is no purpose,' he murmured.

Perhaps his remote ancestors had, after all, realised that, but had not cared. It had taken the Jade Man to make them care and then go mad in their anguish. The knowledge had caused them to close their minds to much.

'Elric!'

It was Smiorgan returning. Elric looked up.

'I met the only survivor on the trail. Before he died he told me the Olab had dealt with the crew and the ship before they came after us. They're all slain. The boat is destroyed.'

Elric remembered something the Creature Doomed to Live had told him. 'There is a boat,' he said. 'It lies at the west end of the island.'

It took them the rest of the day and all of that night to discover where J'osui C'reln Reyr had hidden his boat. They pulled it down to the water in the diffused light of the morning and they inspected it.

'It's a sturdy boat,' said Count Smiorgan approvingly. 'By the look of it, it's made of that same strange material we saw in the library of R'lin K'ren A'a.' He climbed in and searched through the lockers.

Elric was staring back at the city, thinking of a man who might have become his friend, just as Count Smiorgan had become his friend. He had no friends, save Cymoril, in Melniboné. He sighed.

Smiorgan had opened several lockers and was grinning at what he saw there. 'Pray the gods I return safe to the Purple Towns – we have what I sought! Look, Elric! Treasure! We have benefited from this venture, after all!'

'Aye...' Elric's mind was on other things. He forced himself to think of more practical matters. 'But the jewels will not feed us, Count Smiorgan,' he said. 'It will be a long journey home.'

'Home?' Count Smiorgan straightened his great back, a bunch of necklaces in either fist. 'Melniboné?'

'The Young Kingdoms. You offered to guest me in your house, as I recall.'

'For the rest of your life, if you wish. You saved my life, friend Elric – now you have helped me save my honour.'

'These past events have not disturbed you? You saw what my blade can do – to friends as well as enemies.'

'We do not brood, we of the Purple Towns,' said Count Smiorgan seriously. 'And we are not fickle in our friendships. You know an anguish, Prince Elric, that I'll never feel – never understand –

but I have already given you my trust. Why should I take it away again? That is not how we are taught to behave in the Purple Towns.' Count Smiorgan brushed at his black beard and he winked. 'There must be a few cases of provisions among the wreckage of Avan's schooner. We'll sail around the island and pick them up.'

Elric tried to shake the black mood from himself, but it was hard, for he had slain a man who had trusted him, and Smiorgan's talk of trust only made the guilt heavier.

Together they launched the boat into the weed-thick water and Elric looked back once more at the silent forest and a shiver passed through him. He thought of all the hopes he had entertained on the journey upriver and he cursed himself for a fool.

He tried to think back, to work out how he had come to be in this place, but too much of the past was confused with those singularly graphic dreams to which he was prone. Had Saxif D'Aan and the world of the blue sun been real? Even now, it faded. Was this place real? There was something dreamlike about it. It seemed to him he had sailed on many fateful seas since he had fled from Pikarayd. Now the promise of the peace of the Purple Towns was very dear to him.

Soon the time must come when he must return to Cymoril and the Dreaming City, to decide if he was ready to take up the responsibilities of the Bright Empire of Melniboné, but until that moment he would guest with his new friend, Smiorgan, and learn the ways of the simpler, more direct folk of Menii.

As they raised the sail and began to move with the current, Elric said to Smiorgan suddenly, 'You trust me, then, Count Smiorgan?'

The sea-lord was a little surprised by the directness of the question. He fingered his beard. 'Aye,' he said at length, 'as a man. But we live in cynical times, Prince Elric. Even the gods have lost their innocence, have they not?'

Elric was puzzled. 'Do you think that I shall ever betray you – as – as I betrayed Avan, back there?'

Smiorgan shook his head. 'It's not in my nature to speculate upon such matters. You are loyal, Prince Elric. You feign cynicism, yet I think I've rarely met a man so much in need of a little real cynicism.' He smiled. 'Your sword betrayed you, did it not?'

'To serve me, I suppose.'

'Aye. There's the irony of it. Man may trust man, Prince Elric, but perhaps we'll never have a truly sane world until men learn to trust mankind. That would mean the death of magic, I think.'

And it seemed to Elric, then, that his runesword trembled at his side, and moaned very faintly, as if it were disturbed by Count Smiorgan's words.

The Dreaming City

Introduction

FOR TEN THOUSAND years did the Bright Empire of Melniboné flourish – ruling the world. Ten thousand years before history was recorded – or ten thousand years after history had ceased to be chronicled. For that span of time, reckon it how you will, the Bright Empire had thrived. Be hopeful, if you like, and think of the dreadful past the Earth has known, or brood upon the future. But if you would believe the unholy truth – then Time is an agony of Now, and so it will always be.

Ravaged, at last, by the formless terror called Time, Melniboné fell and newer nations succeeded her: Ilmiora, Sheegoth, Maidahk, S'aaleem. Then memory began: Ur, India, China, Egypt, Assyria, Persia, Greece, and Rome – all these came after Melniboné. But none lasted ten thousand years.

And none dealt in the terrible mysteries, the secret sorceries of old Melniboné. None used such power or knew how. Only Melniboné ruled the Earth for one hundred centuries – and then she, shaken by the casting of frightful runes, attacked by powers greater than men; powers who decided that Melniboné's span of ruling had been overlong – then she crumbled and her sons were scattered. They became wanderers across an Earth which hated and feared them, siring few offspring, slowly dying, slowly forgetting the secrets of their mighty ancestors. Such a one was the cynical, laughing Elric, a man of bitter brooding and gusty humour, proud prince of ruins, lord of a lost and humbled people; last son of Melniboné's sundered line of kings.

Elric, the moody-eyed wanderer – a lonely man who fought a world, living by his wits and his runesword Stormbringer. Elric, last lord of Melniboné, last worshipper of its grotesque and beautiful gods – reckless reaver and cynical slayer – torn by great griefs and with knowledge locked in his skull which would turn lesser men to babbling idiots. Elric, moulder of madnesses, dabbler in wild delights...

Chapter One

'WHAT'S THE HOUR?' The black-bearded man wrenched off his gilded helmet and flung it from him, careless of where it fell. He drew off his leathern gauntlets and moved closer to the roaring fire, letting the heat soak into his frozen bones.

'Midnight is long past,' growled one of the other armoured men who gathered around the blaze. 'Are you still sure he'll come?'

'It's said that he's a man of his word, if that comforts you.'

It was a tall, pale-faced youth who spoke. His thin lips formed the words and spat them out maliciously. He grinned a wolf-grin and stared the new arrival in the eyes, mocking him.

The newcomer turned away with a shrug. 'That's so – for all your irony, Yaris. He'll come.' He spoke as a man does when he wishes to reassure himself.

There were six men, now, around the fire. The sixth was Smiorgan – Count Smiorgan Baldhead of the Purple Towns. He was a short, stocky man of fifty years with a scarred face partially covered with a thick, black growth of hair. His morose eyes smouldered and his lumpy fingers plucked nervously at his rich-hilted longsword. His pate was hairless, giving him his name, and over his ornate, gilded armour hung a loose woollen cloak, dyed purple.

Smiorgan said thickly, 'He has no love for his cousin. He has become bitter. Yyrkoon sits on the Ruby Throne in his place and has proclaimed him an outlaw and a traitor. Elric needs us if he would take his throne and his bride back. We can trust him.'

'You're full of trust tonight, count,' Yaris smiled thinly, 'a rare thing to find in these troubled times. I say this –' He paused and took a long breath, staring at his comrades, summing them up. His gaze flicked from lean-faced Dharmit of Jharkor to Fadan of Lormyr who pursed his podgy lips and looked into the fire.

'Speak up, Yaris,' petulantly urged the patrician-featured Vilmirian, Naclon. 'Let's hear what you have to say, lad, if it's worth hearing.'

Yaris looked towards Jiku the dandy, who yawned impolitely and scratched his long nose.

'Well!' Smiorgan was impatient. 'What d'you say, Yaris?'

'I say that we should start now and waste no more time waiting on Elric's pleasure! He's laughing at us in some tavern a hundred miles from here – or else plotting with the Dragon Princes to trap us. For years we have planned this raid. We have little time in which to strike – our fleet is too big, too noticeable. Even if Elric has not betrayed us, then spies will soon be running eastwards to warn the Dragons that there is a fleet massed against them. We stand to win a fantastic fortune – to vanquish the greatest merchant city in the world – to reap immeasurable riches – or horrible death at the hands of the Dragon Princes, if we wait overlong. Let's bide our time no more and set sail before our prize hears of our plan and brings up reinforcements!'

'You always were too ready to mistrust a man, Yaris.' King Naclon of Vilmir spoke slowly, carefully – distastefully eyeing the taut-featured youth. 'We could not reach Imrryr without Elric's knowledge of the maze-channels which lead to its secret ports. If Elric will not join us – then our endeavour will be fruitless – hopeless. We need him. We must wait for him – or else give up our plans and return to our homelands.'

'At least I'm willing to take a risk,' yelled Yaris, anger lancing from his slanting eyes. 'You're getting old – all of you. Treasures are not won by care and forethought but by swift slaying and reckless attack.'

'Fool!' Dharmit's voice rumbled around the fire-flooded hall. He laughed wearily. 'I spoke thus in my youth – and lost a fine fleet soon after. Cunning and Elric's knowledge will win us Imrryr – that and the mightiest fleet to sail the Dragon Sea since Melniboné's banners fluttered over all the nations of the Earth. Here we are – the most powerful sea-lords in the world, masters, every one of us, of more than a hundred swift vessels. Our names are feared and famous – our fleets ravage the coasts of a score of lesser nations. We hold *power*!' He clenched his great fist and shook it in Yaris's face. His tone became more level and he smiled viciously, glaring at the youth and choosing his words with precision.

'But all this is worthless – meaningless – without the power which Elric has. That is the power of knowledge – of dream-learned sorcery, if I must use the cursed word. His fathers knew of the maze which guards Imrryr from sea-attack. And his fathers passed that secret on to him. Imrryr, the Dreaming City, dreams in peace – and will continue to do so unless we have a guide to help us steer a course through the treacherous waterways which lead to her harbours. We *need* Elric – we know it, and he knows it. That's the truth!'

'Such confidence, gentlemen, is warming to the heart.' There was irony in the heavy voice which came from the entrance to the hall. The heads of the six sea-lords jerked towards the doorway.

Yaris's confidence fled from him as he met the eyes of Elric of Melniboné. They were old eyes in a fine featured, youthful face. Yaris shuddered, turned his back on Elric, preferring to look into the bright glare of the fire.

Elric smiled warmly as Count Smiorgan gripped his shoulder. There was a certain friendship between the two. He nodded condescendingly to the other four and walked with lithe grace towards the fire. Yaris stood aside and let him pass. Elric was tall, broad-shouldered and slim-hipped. He wore his long hair bunched and pinned at the nape of his neck and, for an obscure reason, affected the dress of a Southern barbarian. He had long, knee-length boots of soft doe-leather, a breastplate of strangely wrought silver, a jerkin of chequered blue-and-white linen, britches of scarlet wool and a cloak of rustling green velvet. At his hip rested his runesword of black iron – the feared Stormbringer, forged by ancient and alien sorcery.

His bizarre dress was tasteless and gaudy, and did not match his sensitive face and long-fingered, almost delicate hands, yet he flaunted it since it emphasised the fact that he did not belong in any company – that he was an outsider and an outcast. But, in reality, he had little need to wear such outlandish gear – for his eyes and skin were enough to mark him.

Elric, last lord of Melniboné, was a pure albino who drew his power from a secret and terrible source.

Smiorgan sighed. 'Well, Elric, when do we raid Imrryr?'

Elric shrugged. 'As soon as you like; I care not. Give me a little time in which to do certain things.'

'Tomorrow? Shall we sail tomorrow?' Yaris said hesitantly, conscious of the strange power dormant in the man he had earlier accused of treachery.

Elric smiled, dismissing the youth's statement. 'Three days' time,' he said, 'Three – or more.'

'Three days! But Imrryr will be warned of our presence by then!' Fat, cautious Fadan spoke.

'I'll see that your fleet's not found,' Elric promised. 'I have to go to Imrryr first – and return.'

'You won't do the journey in three days – the fastest ship could not make it.' Smiorgan gaped.

'I'll be in the Dreaming City in less than a day,' Elric said softly, with finality.

Smiorgan shrugged. 'If you say so, I'll believe it – but why this necessity to visit the city ahead of the raid?'

'I have my own compunctions, Count Smiorgan. But worry not – I shan't betray you. I'll lead the raid myself, be sure of that.' His dead-white face was lighted eerily by the fire and his red eyes smouldered. One lean hand firmly gripped the hilt of his runesword and he appeared to breathe more heavily. 'Imrryr fell, in spirit, five hundred years ago – she will fall completely soon – for ever! I have a little debt to settle. This is my sole reason for aiding you. As you know I have made only a few conditions – that you raze the city to the ground and a certain man and woman are not harmed. I refer to my cousin Yyrkoon and his sister Cymoril...'

Yaris's thin lips felt uncomfortably dry. Much of his blustering manner resulted from the early death of his father. The old sea-king had died – leaving the youthful Yaris as the new ruler of his lands and his fleets. Yaris was not at all certain that he was capable of commanding such a vast kingdom – and tried to appear more confident than he actually felt. Now he said: 'How shall we hide the fleet, Lord Elric?'

The Melnibonéan acknowledged the question. 'I'll hide it for you,' he promised. 'I go now to do this – but make sure all your men are off the ships first – will you see to it, Smiorgan?'

'Aye,' rumbled the stocky count.

He and Elric departed from the hall together, leaving five men behind; five men who sensed an air of icy doom hanging about the overheated hall.

'How could he hide such a mighty fleet when we, who know this fjord better than any, found nowhere?' Dharmit of Jharkor said bewilderedly.

None answered him.

They waited, tensed and nervous, while the fire flickered and died untended. Eventually Smiorgan returned, stamping noisily on the boarded floor. There was a haunted haze of fear surrounding him; an almost tangible aura, and he was shivering, terribly. Tremendous, racking undulations swept up his body and his breath came short.

'Well? Did Elric hide the fleet – all at once? What did he do?' Dharmit spoke impatiently, choosing not to heed Smiorgan's ominous condition.

'He has hidden it.' That was all Smiorgan said, and his voice was thin, like that of a sick man, weak from fever.

Yaris went to the entrance and tried to stare beyond the fjord slopes where many campfires burned, tried to make out the outlines of ships' masts and rigging, but he could see nothing.

'The night mist's too thick,' he murmured, 'I can't tell whether our ships are anchored in the fjord or not.' Then he gasped involuntarily as a white face loomed out of the clinging fog. 'Greetings, Lord Elric,' he stuttered, noting the sweat on the Melnibonéan's strained features.

Elric staggered past him, into the hall. 'Wine,' he mumbled, 'I've done what's needed and it's cost me hard.'

Dharmit fetched a jug of strong Cadsandrian wine and with a shaking hand poured some into a carved wooden goblet. Wordlessly he passed the cup to Elric who quickly drained it. 'Now I will sleep,' he said, stretching himself into a chair and wrapping his green cloak around him. He closed his disconcerting crimson eyes and fell into a slumber born of utter weariness.

Fadan scurried to the door, closed it and pulled the heavy iron bar down.

None of the six slept much that night and, in the morning, the door was unbarred and Elric was missing from the chair. When they went outside, the mist was so heavy that they soon lost sight of one another, though scarcely two feet separated any of them.

Elric stood with his legs astride on the shingle of the narrow beach. He looked back at the entrance to the fjord and saw, with satisfaction, that the mist was still thickening, though it lay only over the fjord itself, hiding the mighty fleet. Elsewhere, the weather was clear and overhead a pale winter sun shone sharply on the black rocks of the rugged cliffs which dominated the coastline. Ahead of him the sea rose and fell monotonously, like the chest of a sleeping water-giant, grey and pure, glinting in the cold sunlight. Elric fingered the raised runes on the hilt of his black broadsword and a steady north wind blew into the voluminous folds of his dark green cloak, swirling it around his tall, lean frame.

The albino felt fitter than he had done on the previous night when he had expended all his strength in conjuring the mist. He was well-versed in the arts of nature-wizardry, but he did not have the reserves of power which the Sorcerer Emperors of Melniboné had possessed when they had ruled the world. His ancestors had passed their knowledge down to him – but not their mystic vitality and many of the spells and secrets that he had were unusable, since he did not have the reservoir of strength, either of soul or of body, to work them. But for all that, Elric knew of only one other man who matched his knowledge – his cousin Yyrkoon. His hand gripped the hilt tighter as he thought of the cousin who had twice betrayed his trust, and he forced himself to concentrate on his present task – the speaking of spells to aid him on his voyage to the Isle of the Dragon Masters whose only city, Imrryr the Beautiful, was the object of the sea-lords' massing.

Drawn up on the beach, a tiny sailing-boat lay. Elric's own small craft, sturdy, oddly wrought and far stronger, far older, than it appeared. The brooding sea flung surf around its timbers as the tide withdrew, and Elric realised that he had little time in which to work his helpful sorcery.

His body tensed and he blanked his conscious mind, summoning secrets from the dark depths of his dreaming soul. Swaying, his eyes staring unseeingly, his arms jerking out ahead of him and making unholy signs in the air, he began to speak in a sibilant monotone. Slowly the pitch of his voice rose, resembling the scarcely heard shriek of a distant gale as it comes closer – then, quite suddenly, the voice rose higher until it was howling wildly to the skies and the air began to tremble and quiver. Shadow-shapes began slowly to form and they were never still but darted around Elric's body as, stiff-legged, he started forward towards his boat.

His voice was inhuman as it howled insistently, summoning the wind elementals – the *sylphs* of the breeze; the *sharnahs*, makers of gales; the *h'Haarshanns*, builders of whirlwinds – hazy and formless, they eddied around him as he summoned their aid with the alien words of his forefathers who had, in dream-quests taken ages before, made impossible, unthinkable pacts with the elementals in order to procure their services.

Still stiff-limbed, Elric entered the boat and, like an automaton, ran his fingers up the sail and set its ropes, binding himself to his tiller. Then a great wave erupted out of the placid sea, rising higher and higher until it towered over the vessel. With a surging crash, the water smashed down on the boat, lifted it and bore it out to sea. Sitting blank-eyed in the stern, Elric still crooned his hideous song of sorcery as the spirits of the air plucked at the sail and sent the boat flying over the water faster than any mortal ship could speed. And all the while, the deafening, unholy shriek of the released elementals filled the air about the boat as the shore vanished and open sea was all that was visible.

Chapter Two

So it was, with wind-demons for shipmates, that Elric, last prince of the royal line of Melniboné, returned to the last city still ruled by his own race – the last city and the final remnant of extant Melnibonéan architecture. All the other great cities lay in ruins, abandoned save for hermits and solitaries. The cloudy pink and subtle yellow tints of the old city's nearer towers came into sight within a few hours of Elric's leaving the fjord and just offshore of the Isle of the Dragon Masters the elementals left the boat and fled back to their secret haunts among the peaks of the highest mountains in the world. Elric awoke, then, from his trance, and regarded with fresh wonder the beauty of his own birthplace's delicate towers which were visible even so far away, guarded still by the formidable sea wall with its great gate, the five-doored maze and the twisting, high-walled channels, of which only one led to the inner harbour of Imrryr.

Elric knew that he dare not risk entering the harbour by the maze, though he understood the route perfectly. He decided, instead, to land the boat further up the coast in a small inlet of which he had knowledge. With sure, capable hands, he guided the little craft towards the hidden inlet which was obscured by a growth of shrubs loaded with ghastly blue berries of a type decidedly poisonous to men since their juice first turned one blind and then slowly mad. This berry, the *noidel*, grew only on Melniboné, as did other rare and deadly plants whose mixture sustained the frail prince.

Light, low-hanging cloud wisps streamed slowly across the sun-painted sky, like fine cobwebs caught by a sudden breeze. All the world seemed blue and gold and green and white, and Elric, pulling his boat up on the beach, breathed the clean, sharp air of winter and savoured the scent of decaying leaves and rotting undergrowth. Somewhere a bitch-fox barked her pleasure to her mate and Elric regretted the fact that his depleted race no longer appreciated natural beauty, preferring to stay close to their city and spend many of their days in drugged slumber; in study. It was not the city which dreamed, but its overcivilised inhabitants. Or had they become one and the same? Elric, smelling the rich, clean winter-scents, was wholly glad that he had renounced his birthright and no longer ruled the city as he had been born to do.

Instead, Yyrkoon, his cousin, sprawled on the Ruby Throne of Imrryr the Beautiful and hated Elric because he knew that the albino, for all his disgust with crowns and rulership, was still the rightful king of the Dragon Isle and that he, Yyrkoon, was an usurper, not elected by Elric to the throne, as Melnibonéan tradition demanded.

But Elric had better reasons for hating his cousin. For those reasons the ancient capital would fall in all its magnificent splendour and the last fragment of a glorious empire would be obliterated as the pink, the yellow, the purple and white towers crumbled – if Elric had his vengeful way and the sea-lords were successful.

On foot, Elric strode inland, towards Imrryr, and as he covered the miles of soft turf, the sun cast an ochre pall over the land and sank, giving way to a dark and moonless night, brooding and full of evil portent.

At last he came to the city. It stood out in stark black silhouette, a city of fantastic magnificence, in conception and in execution. It was the oldest city in the world, built by artists and conceived as a work of art rather than a functional dwelling-place, but Elric knew that squalor lurked in many narrow streets and that the lords of Imrryr left many of the towers empty and uninhabited rather than let the bastard population of the city dwell therein. There were few Dragon Masters left; few who would claim Melnibonéan blood.

Built to follow the shape of the ground, the city had an organic appearance, with winding lanes spiralling to the crest of the hill where stood the castle, tall and proud and many-spired, the final, crowning masterpiece of the ancient, forgotten artist who had built it. But there was no life-sound emanating from Imrryr

the Beautiful, only a sense of soporific desolation. The city slept – and the Dragon Masters and their ladies and their special slaves dreamed drug-induced dreams of grandeur and incredible horror, learning unusable skills, while the rest of the population, ordered by curfew, tossed on straw-strewn stone and tried not to dream at all.

Elric, his hand ever near his sword hilt, slipped through an unguarded gate in the city wall and began to walk cautiously through the ill-lit streets, moving upwards, through the winding lanes, towards Yyrkoon's great palace.

Wind sighed through the empty rooms of the Dragon towers and sometimes Elric would have to withdraw into places where the shadows were deeper when he heard the tramp of feet and a group of guards would pass, their duty being to see that the curfew was rigidly obeyed. Often he would hear wild laughter echoing from one of the towers, still ablaze with bright torchlight which flung strange, disturbing shadows on the walls; often, too, he would hear a chilling scream and a frenzied, idiot's yell as some wretch of a slave died in obscene agony to please his master.

Elric was not appalled by the sounds and the dim sights. He appreciated them. He was still a Melnibonéan – their rightful leader if he chose to regain his powers of kingship – and though he had an obscure urge to wander and sample the less sophisticated pleasures of the outside world, ten thousand years of a cruel, brilliant and malicious culture were behind him, its wisdom gained as he slept, and the pulse of his ancestry beat strongly in his deficient veins.

Elric knocked impatiently upon the heavy, blackwood door. He had reached the palace and now stood by a small back entrance, glancing cautiously around him, for he knew that Yyrkoon had given the guards orders to slay him if he entered Imrryr.

A bolt squealed on the other side of the door and it moved silently inwards. A thin, seamed face confronted Elric.

'Is it the king?' whispered the man, peering out into the night. He was a tall, extremely thin individual with long, gnarled limbs which shifted awkwardly as he moved nearer, straining his beady eyes to get a glimpse of Elric.

'It's Prince Elric,' the albino said. 'But you forget, Tanglebones, my friend, that a new king sits on the Ruby Throne.'

Doctor Tanglebones shook his head and his sparse hair fell over his face. With a jerking movement he brushed it back and stood aside for Elric to enter. 'The Dragon Isle has but one king – and his name is Elric, whatever usurper would have it otherwise.'

Elric ignored this statement, but he smiled thinly and waited for the man to push the bolt back into place.

'She still sleeps, sire,' Tanglebones murmured as he climbed unlit stairs, Elric behind him.

'I guessed that,' Elric said. 'I do not underestimate my good cousin's powers of sorcery.'

Upwards, now, in silence, the two men climbed until at last they reached a corridor which was aflare with dancing torchlight. The marble walls reflected the flames and showed Elric, crouching with Tanglebones behind a pillar, that the room in which he was interested was guarded by a massive archer – a eunuch by the look of him – who was alert and wakeful. The man was hairless and fat, his blue-black gleaming armour tight on his flesh, but his fingers were curled round the string of his short, bone bow and there was a slim arrow resting on the string. Elric guessed that this man was one of the crack eunuch archers, a member of the Silent Guard, Imrryr's finest company of warriors.

Tanglebones, who had taught the young Elric the arts of fencing and archery, had known of the guard's presence and had prepared for it. Earlier he had placed a bow behind the pillar. Silently he picked it up and, bending it against his knee, strung it. He fitted an arrow to the string, aimed it at the right eye of the guard and let fly – just as the eunuch turned to face him. The shaft missed. It clattered against the man's helmet and fell harmlessly to the reed-strewn stones of the floor.

So Elric acted swiftly, leaping forward, his runesword drawn and its alien power surging through him. It howled in a searing arc of black steel and cut through the bone bow which the eunuch had hoped would deflect it. The guard was panting and his thick lips were wet as he drew breath to yell. As he opened his mouth, Elric saw what he had expected, the man was tongueless and was a mute. His own shortsword came out and he just managed to parry Elric's next thrust. Sparks flew from the iron and Stormbringer bit into the eunuch's finely edged blade; he staggered and fell back before the nigromantic sword which appeared to be endowed with a life of its own. The clatter of metal echoed loudly up and down the short corridor and Elric cursed the fate which had made the man turn at the crucial moment. Grimly, silently, he broke down the eunuch's clumsy guard.

The eunuch saw only a dim glimpse of his opponent behind the black, whirling blade which appeared to be so light and which was twice the length of his own stabbing sword. He wondered, frenziedly, who his attacker could be and he thought he recognised the face. Then a scarlet eruption obscured his vision, he felt searing agony at his face and then, philosophically, for eunuchs are necessarily given to a certain fatalism, he realised that he was to die.

Elric stood over the eunuch's bloated body and tugged his sword from the corpse's skull, wiping the mixture of blood and brains on his late opponent's cloak. Tanglebones had wisely vanished. Elric could hear the clatter of sandalled feet rushing up the stairs. He pushed the door open and entered the room which was lit by two small candles placed at either end of a wide, richly tapestried bed. He went to the bed and looked down at the raven-haired girl who lay there.

Elric's mouth twitched and bright tears leapt into his strange red eyes. He was trembling as he turned back to the door, sheathed his sword and pulled the bolts into place. He returned to the bedside and knelt down beside the sleeping girl. Her features were as delicate and of a similar mould as Elric's own, but she had an added, exquisite beauty. She was breathing shallowly, in a sleep induced not by natural weariness but by her own brother's evil sorcery.

Elric reached out and tenderly took one fine-fingered hand in his. He put it to his lips and kissed it.

'Cymoril,' he murmured, and an agony of longing throbbed in that name. 'Cymoril – wake up.'

The girl did not stir, her breathing remained shallow and her eyes remained shut. Elric's white features twisted and his red eyes blazed as he shook in terrible and passionate rage. He gripped the hand, so limp and nerveless, like the hand of a corpse; gripped it until he had to stop himself for fear that he would crush the delicate fingers.

A shouting soldier began to beat at the door.

Elric replaced the hand on the girl's breast and stood up. He glanced uncomprehendingly at the door.

A sharper, colder voice interrupted the soldier's yelling.

'What is happening? Who disturbs my poor sleeping sister?'

'Yyrkoon, the black hellspawn,' said Elric to himself.

Confused babblings from the soldier and Yyrkoon's voice raised as he shouted through the door. 'Whoever is in there – you will be destroyed a thousand times when you are caught. You cannot escape. If my good sister is harmed in any way – then you will never die, I promise you that. But you will pray to your gods that you could!'

'Yyrkoon, you paltry bombast – you cannot threaten one who is your equal in the dark arts. It is I, Elric – your rightful master. Return to your rabbit hole before I call down every power upon, above, and under the earth to blast you!'

Yyrkoon laughed hesitantly. 'So you have returned again to try to waken my sister. Any such attempt will not only slay her – it will send her soul into the deepest hell – where you may join it, willingly!'

'You offspring of a festering worm, Yyrkoon. You'll have cause to repent this vile spell before your time is run! And by Arnara's six breasts – you it will be who samples the thousand deaths before long.'

'Enough of this.' Yyrkoon raised his voice. 'Soldiers – I command you to break this door down – and take that traitor alive. Elric – there are two things you will never again have – my sister's love and the Ruby Throne. Make what you can of the little time available to you, for soon you will be grovelling to me and praying for release from your soul's agony!'

Elric ignored Yyrkoon's threats and looked at the narrow window to the room. It was just large enough for a man's body to pass through. He bent down and kissed Cymoril upon the lips, then he went to the door and silently withdrew the bolts.

There came a crash as a soldier flung his weight against the door. It swung open, pitching the man forward to stumble and fall on his face. Elric drew his sword, lifted it high and chopped at the warrior's neck. The head sprang from its shoulders and Elric yelled loudly in a deep, rolling voice.

'*Arioch! Arioch!* I give you blood and souls – only aid me now! This man I give you, mighty Duke of Hell – aid your servant, Elric of Melniboné!'

Three soldiers entered the room in a bunch. Elric struck at one and sheared off half his face. The man screamed horribly.

'Arioch, Lord of the Darks – I give you blood and souls. Aid me, great one!'

In the far corner of the gloomy room, a blacker mist began, slowly, to form. But the soldiers pressed closer and Elric was hard put to hold them back.

He was screaming the name of Arioch, Lord of the Higher Hell, incessantly, almost unconsciously as he was pressed back further by the weight of the warriors' numbers. Behind them, Yyrkoon mouthed in rage and frustration, urging his men, still, to take Elric alive. This gave Elric some small advantage. The runesword was glowing with a strange black light and its shrill howling grated in the ears of those who heard it. Two more corpses now littered the carpeted floor of the chamber, their blood soaking into the fine fabric.

'*Blood and souls for my lord Arioch!*'

The dark mist heaved and began to take shape, Elric spared a look towards the corner and shuddered despite his inurement to hell-born horror. The warriors now had their backs to the thing in the corner and Elric was by the window. The amorphous mass, that was a less than pleasant manifestation of Elric's fickle patron god, heaved again and Elric made out its intolerably alien shape. Bile flooded into his mouth and, as he drove the soldiers towards the thing which was sinuously flooding forward, he fought against madness.

Suddenly, the soldiers seemed to sense that there was something behind them. They turned, four of them, and each screamed insanely as the black horror made one final rush to engulf them. Arioch crouched over them, sucking out their souls. Then, slowly, their bones began to give and snap and still shrieking bestially the men flopped like obnoxious invertebrates upon the floor: their spines broken, they still lived. Elric turned away, thankful for once that Cymoril slept, and leapt to the window ledge. He looked down and realised with despair that he was not going to escape by that route after all. Several hundred feet lay between him and the ground. He rushed to the door where Yyrkoon, his eyes wide with fear, was trying to drive Arioch back. Arioch was already fading.

Elric pushed past his cousin, spared a final glance at Cymoril, then ran the way he had come, his feet slipping on blood. Tanglebones met him at the head of the dark stairway.

'What has happened, King Elric – what's in there?'

Elric seized Tanglebones by his lean shoulder and made him descend the stairs. 'No time,' he panted, 'but we must hurry while Yyrkoon is still engaged with his current problem. In five days' time Imrryr will experience a new phase in her history – perhaps the last. I want you to make sure that Cymoril is safe. Is that clear?'

'Aye, Lord, but...'

They reached the door and Tanglebones shot the bolts and opened it.

'There is no time for me to say anything else. I must escape while I can. I will return in five days – with companions. You will realise what I mean when that time comes. Take Cymoril to the Tower of D'a'rputna – and await me there.'

Then Elric was gone, soft-footed, running into the night with the shrieks of the dying still ringing through the blackness after him.

Chapter Three

ELRIC STOOD UNSMILING in the prow of Count Smiorgan's flagship. Since his return to the fjord and the fleet's subsequent sailing for open sea, he had spoken only orders, and those in the tersest of terms. The sea-lords muttered that a great hate lay in him, that it festered his soul and made him a dangerous man to have as comrade or enemy; and even Count Smiorgan avoided the moody albino.

The reaver prows struck eastward and the sea was black with light ships dancing on the bright water in all directions; they looked like the shadow of some enormous seabird flung on the water. Over half a thousand fighting ships stained the ocean – all of them of similar form, long and slim and built for speed rather than battle, since they were for coast-raiding and trading. Sails were caught by the pale sun; bright colours of fresh canvas – orange, blue, black, purple, red, yellow, light green or white. And every ship had sixteen or more rowers – each rower a fighting man. The crews of the ships were also the warriors who would attack Imrryr – there was no wastage of good manpower since the sea-nations were underpopulated, losing hundreds of men each year in their regular raids.

In the centre of the great fleet, certain larger vessels sailed. These carried massive catapults on their decks and were to be used for storming the sea wall of Imrryr. Count Smiorgan and the other lords looked at their ships with pride, but Elric only stared ahead of him, never sleeping, rarely moving, his white face lashed by salt spray and wind, his white hand tight upon his sword hilt.

The reaver ships ploughed steadily eastwards – forging towards the Dragon Isle and fantastic wealth – or hellish horror. Relentlessly, doom-driven, they beat onwards, their oars splashing in unison, their sails bellying taut with a good wind.

Onwards they sailed, towards Imrryr the Beautiful, to rape and plunder the world's oldest city.

Two days after the fleet had set sail, the coastline of the Dragon Isle was sighted and the rattle of arms replaced the sound of oars as the mighty fleet hove to and prepared to accomplish what sane men thought impossible.

Orders were bellowed from ship to ship and the fleet began to mass into battle formation, then the oars creaked in their grooves and ponderously, with sails now furled, the fleet moved forward again.

It was a clear day, cold and fresh, and there was a tense excitement about all the men, from sea-lord to galley-hand, as they considered the immediate future and what it might bring. Serpent prows bent towards the great stone wall which blocked off the first entrance to the harbour. It was nearly a hundred feet high and towers were built upon it – more functional than the lacelike spires of the city which shimmered in the distance, behind them. The ships of Imrryr were the only vessels allowed to pass through the great gate in the centre of the wall, and the route through the maze – the exact entrance even – was a well-kept secret from outsiders.

On the sea wall, which now loomed tall above the fleet, amazed guards scrambled frantically to their posts. To them, threat of attack was well-nigh unthinkable, yet here it was – a great fleet, the greatest they had ever seen – come against Imrryr the Beautiful! They took to their posts, their yellow cloaks and kilts rustling, their bronze armour rattling, but they moved with bewildered reluctance as if refusing to accept what they saw. And they went to their posts with desperate fatalism, knowing that even if the ships never entered the maze itself, they would not be alive to witness the reavers' failure.

Dyvim Tarkan, Commander of the Wall, was a sensitive man who loved life and its pleasures. He was high-browed and handsome, with a thin wisp of beard and a tiny moustache. He looked well in the bronze armour and high-plumed helmet; he did not want to die. He issued terse orders to his men and, with well-ordered precision, they obeyed him. He listened with concern to the distant shouts from the ships and he wondered what the first move of the reavers would be. He did not wait long for his answer.

A catapult on one of the leading vessels twanged throatily and its throwing arm rushed up, releasing a great rock which sailed, with every appearance of leisurely grace, towards the wall. It fell short and splashed into the sea which frothed against the stones of the wall.

Swallowing hard and trying to control the shake in his voice, Dyvim Tarkan ordered his own catapult to discharge. With a thudding crash the release rope was cut and a retaliatory iron ball went hurtling towards the enemy fleet. So tight-packed were the ships that the ball could not miss – it struck full on the deck of the flagship of Dharmit of Jharkor and crushed the timbers in. Within seconds, accompanied by the cries of maimed and drowning men, the ship had sunk and Dharmit with it. Some of the crew were taken aboard other vessels but the wounded were left to drown.

Another catapult sounded and this time a tower full of archers was squarely hit. Masonry erupted outwards and those who still lived fell sickeningly to die in the foam-tipped sea lashing the wall. This time, angered by the deaths of their comrades, Imrryrian archers sent back a stream of slim arrows into the enemy's midst. Reavers howled as red-fletched shafts buried themselves thirstily in flesh. But reavers returned the arrows liberally and soon only a handful of men were left on the wall as further catapult rocks smashed into towers and men, destroying their only war machine and part of the wall besides.

Dyvim Tarkan still lived, though red blood stained his yellow tunic and an arrow shaft protruded from his left shoulder. He still lived when the first ram-ship moved intractably towards the great wooden gate and smashed against it, weakening it. A second ship sailed in beside it and, between them, they stove in the gate and glided through the entrance. Perhaps it was outraged horror that tradition had been broken which caused poor Dyvim Tarkan to lose his footing at the edge of the wall and fall screaming down to break his neck on the deck of Count Smiorgan's flagship as it sailed triumphantly through the gate.

Now the ram-ships made way for Count Smiorgan's craft, for Elric had to lead the way through the maze. Ahead of them loomed five tall entrances, black gaping maws all alike in shape and size. Elric pointed to the second from the left and with short strokes the oarsmen began to paddle the ship into the dark mouth of the entrance. For some minutes, they sailed in darkness.

'Flares!' shouted Elric. 'Light the flares!'

Torches had already been prepared and these were now lighted. The men saw that they were in a vast tunnel hewn out of natural rock which twisted in all directions.

'Keep close,' Elric ordered and his voice was magnified a score of times in the echoing cavern. Torchlight blazed and Elric's face was a mask of shadow and frisking light as the torches threw up long tongues of flame to the bleak roof. Behind him, men could be heard muttering in awe and, as more craft entered the maze and lit their own torches, Elric could see some torches waver as their bearers trembled in superstitious fear. Elric felt some discomfort as he glanced through the flickering shadows and his eyes, caught by torchflare, gleamed fever-bright.

With dreadful monotony, the oars splashed onwards as the tunnel widened and several more cave mouths came into sight. 'The middle entrance,' Elric ordered. The steersman in the stern nodded and guided the ship towards the entrance Elric had indicated. Apart from the muted murmur of some men and the splash of oars, there was a grim and ominous silence in the towering cavern.

Elric stared down at the cold, dark water and shuddered.

Eventually they moved once again into bright sunlight and the men looked upwards, marvelling at the height of the great walls above them. Upon those walls squatted more yellow-clad, bronze-armoured archers and as Count Smiorgan's vessel led the way out of the black caverns, the torches still burning in the cool winter air, arrows began to hurtle down into the narrow canyon, biting into throats and limbs.

'Faster!' howled Elric. 'Row faster – speed is our only weapon now.'

With frantic energy the oarsmen bent to their sweeps and the ships began to pick up speed even though Imrryrian arrows took heavy toll of the reaver crewmen. Now the high-walled channel ran straight and Elric saw the quays of Imrryr ahead of him.

'Faster! Faster! Our prize is in sight!'

Then, suddenly, the ship broke past the walls and was in the calm waters of the harbour, facing the warriors drawn up on the quay. The ship halted, waiting for reinforcements to plunge out of the channel and join them. When twenty ships were through, Elric gave the command to attack the quay and now Stormbringer howled from its scabbard. The flagship's port side thudded against the quay as arrows rained down upon it. Shafts whistled all around Elric but, miraculously, he was unscathed as he led a bunch of yelling reavers onto land. Imrryrian axemen bunched forward and confronted the reavers, but it was plain that they had little spirit for the fight – they were too disconcerted by the course which events had taken.

Elric's black blade struck with frenzied force at the throat of the leading axeman and sheared off his head. Howling demoniacally now that it had again tasted blood, the sword began to writhe in Elric's grasp, seeking fresh flesh in which to bite. There was a hard, grim smile on the albino's colourless lips and his eyes were narrowed as he struck without discrimination at the warriors.

He planned to leave the fighting to those he had led to Imrryr, for he had other things to do – and quickly. Behind the yellow-garbed soldiers, the tall towers of Imrryr rose, beautiful in their soft and scintillating colours of coral pink and powdery blue, of gold and pale yellow, white and subtle green. One such tower was Elric's objective – the tower of D'a'rputna where he had ordered Tanglebones to take Cymoril, knowing that in the confusion this would be possible.

Elric hacked a blood-drenched path through those who attempted to halt him and men fell back, screaming horribly as the runesword drank their souls.

Now Elric was past them, leaving them to the bright blades of the reavers who poured onto the quayside, and was running up through the twisting streets, his sword slaying anyone who attempted to stop him. Like a white-faced ghoul he was, his clothing tattered and bloody, his armour chipped and scratched, but he ran speedily over the cobblestones of the twisting streets and came at last to the slender tower of hazy blue and soft gold – the Tower of D'a'rputna. Its door was open, showing that someone was inside, and Elric rushed through it and entered the large ground-floor chamber. No-one greeted him.

'Tanglebones!' he yelled, his voice roaring loudly even in his own ears. 'Tanglebones – are you here?' He leapt up the stairs in great bounds, calling his servant's name. On the third floor he stopped suddenly, hearing a low groan from one of the rooms. 'Tanglebones – is that you?' Elric strode towards the room, hearing a strangled gasping. He pushed open the door and his stomach seemed to twist within him as he saw the old man lying upon the bare floor of the chamber, striving vainly to stop the flow of blood which gouted from a great wound in his side.

'What's happened man – where's Cymoril?'

Tanglebones's old face twisted in pain and grief. 'She – I – I brought her here, master, as you ordered. But...' he coughed and blood dribbled down his wizened chin, 'but – Prince Yyrkoon – he – he apprehended me – must have followed us here. He – struck me down and took Cymoril back with him – said she'd be – safe in the Tower of B'aal'nezbett. Master – I'm sorry...'

'So you should be,' Elric retorted savagely. Then his tone softened. 'Do not worry, old friend – I'll avenge you and myself. I can still reach Cymoril now I know where Yyrkoon has taken her. Thank you for trying, Tanglebones – may your long journey down the last river be uneventful.'

He turned abruptly on his heel and left the chamber, running down the stairs and out into the street again.

The Tower of B'aal'nezbett was the highest tower in the Royal Palace. Elric knew it well, for it was there that his ancestors had studied their dark sorceries and conducted frightful experiments.

He shuddered as he thought what Yyrkoon might be doing to his own sister.

The streets of the city seemed hushed and strangely deserted, but Elric had no time to ponder why this should be so. Instead he dashed towards the palace, found the main gate unguarded and the main entrance to the building deserted. This too was unique, but it constituted luck for Elric as he made his way upwards, climbing familiar ways towards the topmost tower.

Finally, he reached a door of shimmering black crystal which had no bolt or handle to it. Frenziedly, Elric struck at the crystal with his sorcerous blade but the crystal appeared only to flow and re-form. His blows had no effect.

Elric racked his mind, seeking to remember the single alien word which would make the door open. He dared not put himself in the trance which would have, in time, brought the word to his lips, instead he had to dredge his subconscious and bring the word forth. It was dangerous but there was little else he could do. His whole frame trembled as his face twisted and his brain began to shake. The word was coming as his vocal cords jerked in his throat and his chest heaved.

He ripped the word from his throat and his whole mind and body ached with the strain. Then he cried:

'I command thee – open!'

He knew that once the door opened, his cousin would be aware of his presence, but he had to risk it. The crystal expanded, pulsating and seething, and then began to flow *out*. It flowed into nothingness, into something beyond the physical universe, beyond time. Elric breathed thankfully and passed into the Tower of B'aal'nezbett. But now an eery fire, chilling and mind-shattering, was licking around Elric as he struggled up the steps towards the central chamber. There was a strange music surrounding him, uncanny music which throbbed and sobbed and pounded in his head.

Above him he saw a leering Yyrkoon, a black runesword also in his hand, the mate of the one in Elric's own grasp.

'Hellspawn!' Elric said thickly, weakly, 'I see you have recovered

Mournblade – well, test its powers against its brother if you dare. I have come to destroy you, cousin.'

Stormbringer was giving forth a peculiar moaning sound which sighed over the shrieking, unearthly music accompanying the licking, chilling fire. The runesword writhed in Elric's fist and he had difficulty in controlling it. Summoning all his strength he plunged up the last few steps and aimed a wild blow at Yyrkoon. Beyond the eery fire bubbled yellow-green lava, on all sides, above and beneath. The two men were surrounded only by the misty fire and the lava which lurked beyond it – they were outside the Earth and facing one another for a final battle. The lava seethed and began to ooze inwards, dispersing the fire.

The two blades met and a terrible shrieking roar went up. Elric felt his whole arm go numb and it tingled sickeningly. Elric felt like a puppet. He was no longer his own master – the blade was deciding his actions for him. The blade, with Elric behind it, roared past its brother sword and cut a deep wound in Yyrkoon's left arm. He howled and his eyes widened in agony. Mournblade struck back at Stormbringer, catching Elric in the very place he had wounded his cousin. He sobbed in pain, but continued to move upwards, now wounding Yyrkoon in the right side with a blow strong enough to have killed any other man. Yyrkoon laughed then – laughed like a gibbering demon from the foulest depths of hell. His sanity had broken at last and Elric now had the advantage. But the great sorcery which his cousin had conjured was still in evidence and Elric felt as if a giant had grasped him, was crushing him as he pressed his advantage, Yyrkoon's blood spouting from the wound and covering Elric, also. The lava was slowly withdrawing and now Elric saw the entrance to the central chamber. Behind his cousin another form moved. Elric gasped. Cymoril had awakened and, with horror on her face, was shrieking at him.

The sword still swung in a black arc, cutting down Yyrkoon's brother blade and breaking the usurper's guard.

'Elric!' cried Cymoril desperately. 'Save me – save me now, else we are doomed for eternity.'

Elric was puzzled by the girl's words. He could not understand the sense of them. Savagely he drove Yyrkoon upwards towards the chamber.

'Elric – put Stormbringer away. Sheathe your sword or we shall part again.'

But even if he could have controlled the whistling blade, Elric would not have sheathed it. Hate dominated his being and he would sheathe it in his cousin's evil heart before he put it aside.

Cymoril was weeping, now, pleading with him. But Elric could do nothing. The drooling, idiot thing which had been Yyrkoon of Imrryr turned at its sister's cries and stared leeringly at her. It cackled and reached out one shaking hand to seize the girl by her shoulder. She struggled to escape, but Yyrkoon still had his evil strength. Taking advantage of his opponent's distraction Elric cut deep through his body, almost severing the trunk from the waist.

And yet, incredibly, Yyrkoon remained alive, drawing his vitality from the blade which still clashed against Elric's own runecarved sword. With a final push he flung Cymoril forward and she died screaming on the point of Stormbringer.

Then Yyrkoon laughed one final cackling shriek and his black soul went howling down to hell.

The tower resumed its former proportions, all fire and lava gone. Elric was dazed – unable to marshal his thoughts. He looked down at the dead bodies of the brother and the sister. He saw them, at first, only as corpses – a man's and a woman's.

Dark truth dawned on his clearing brain and he moaned in grief, like an animal. He had slain the girl he loved. The runesword fell from his grasp, stained by Cymoril's lifeblood, and clattered unheeded down the stairs. Sobbing now, Elric dropped beside the dead girl and lifted her in his arms.

'Cymoril,' he moaned, his whole body throbbing. 'Cymoril – I have slain you.'

Chapter Four

ELRIC LOOKED BACK at the roaring, crumbling, tumbling, flame-spewing ruins of Imrryr and drove his sweating oarsmen faster. The ship, sail still unfurled, bucked as a contrary current of wind caught it and Elric was forced to cling to the ship's side lest he be tossed overboard. He looked back at Imrryr and felt a tightness in his throat as he realised that he was truly rootless, now; a renegade and a womanslayer, though involuntarily the latter. He had lost the only woman he had loved in his blind lust for revenge. Now it was finished – everything was finished. He could envisage no future, for his future had been bound up with his past and now, effectively, that past was flaming in ruins behind him. Dry sobs eddied in his chest and he gripped the ship's rail yet more firmly.

His mind reluctantly brooded on Cymoril. He had laid her corpse upon a couch and had set fire to the tower. Then he had gone back to find the reavers successful, straggling back to their ships loaded with loot and girl-slaves, jubilantly firing the tall and beautiful buildings as they went.

He had caused to be destroyed the last tangible sign that the grandiose, magnificent Bright Empire had ever existed. He felt that most of himself was gone with it.

Elric looked back at Imrryr and suddenly a greater sadness overwhelmed him as a tower, as delicate and as beautiful as fine lace, cracked and toppled with flames leaping about it.

He had shattered the last great monument to the earlier race – his own race. Men might have learned again, one day, to build strong, slender towers like those of Imrryr, but now the knowledge was dying with the thundering chaos of the fall of the Dreaming City and the fast-diminishing race of Melniboné.

But what of the Dragon Masters? Neither they nor their golden

ships had met the attacking reavers – only their foot soldiers had been there to defend the city. Had they hidden their ships in some secret waterway and fled inland when the reavers overran the city? They had put up too short a fight to be truly beaten. It had been far too easy. Now that the ships were retreating, were they planning some sudden retaliation? Elric felt that they might have such a plan – perhaps a plan concerning dragons. He shuddered. He had told the others nothing of the beasts which Melnibonéans had controlled for centuries. Even now, someone might be unlocking the gates of the underground Dragon Caves. He turned his mind away from the unnerving prospect.

As the fleet headed towards open sea, Elric's eyes were still looking sadly towards Imrryr as he paid silent homage to the city of his forefathers and the dead Cymoril. He felt hot bitterness sweep over him again as the memory of her death upon his own sword point came sharply to him. He recalled her warning, when he had left her to go adventuring in the Young Kingdoms, that by putting Yyrkoon on the Ruby Throne as regent, by relinquishing his power for a year, he doomed them both. He cursed himself. Then a muttering, like a roll of distant thunder, spread through the fleet and he wheeled sharply, intent on discovering the cause of the consternation.

Thirty golden-sailed Melnibonéan battle-barges had appeared on both sides of the harbour, issuing from two mouths of the maze. Elric realised that they must have hidden in the other channels, waiting to attack the fleet when they returned, satiated and depleted. Great war-galleys they were, the last ships of Melniboné and the secret of their building was unknown. They had a sense of age and slumbering might about them as they rowed swiftly, each with four or five banks of great sweeping oars, to encircle the raven ships.

Elric's fleet seemed to shrink before his eyes as though it were a bobbing collection of wood-shavings against the towering splendour of the shimmering battle-barges. They were well-equipped and fresh for a fight, whereas the weary reavers were intensely battle-tired. There was only one way to save a small part of the fleet, Elric knew. He would have to conjure a witch-wind for sail-power. Most of the flagships were around him and he now occupied that of Yaris, for the youth had got himself wildly drunk and had died by the knife of a Melnibonéan slave wench. Next to Elric's ship was Count Smiorgan's and the stocky sea-lord was frowning, knowing full well that he and his ships, for all their superior numbers, would not stand up to a sea-fight.

But the conjuring of winds great enough to move many vessels was a dangerous thing, for it released colossal power and the elementals who controlled the winds were apt to turn upon the sorcerer himself if he was not more than careful. But it was the only chance, otherwise the rams which sent ripples from the golden prows would smash the reaver ships to driftwood.

Steeling himself, Elric began to speak the ancient and terrible, many-vowelled names of the beings who existed in the air. Again, he could not risk the trance-state, for he had to watch for signs of the elementals turning upon him. He called to them in a speech that was sometimes high like the cry of a gannet, sometimes rolling like the roar of shorebound surf, and the dim shapes of the Powers of the Wind began to flit before his blurred gaze. His heart throbbed horribly in his ribs and his legs felt weak. He summoned all his strength and conjured a wind which shrieked wildly and chaotically about him, rocking even the huge Melnibonéan ships back and forth. Then he directed the wind and sent it into the sails of some forty of the reaver ships. Many he could not save for they lay outside even his wide range.

But forty of the craft escaped the smashing rams and, amidst the sound of howling wind and sundered timbers, leapt on the waves, their masts creaking as the wind cracked into their sails. Oars were torn from the hands of the rowers, leaving a wake of broken wood on the white salt trail which boiled behind each of the reaver ships.

Quite suddenly, they were beyond the slowly closing circle of Melnibonéan ships and careering madly across the open sea, while all the crews sensed a difference in the air and caught glimpses of strange, soft-shaped forms around them. There was a discomforting sense of evil about the beings which aided them, an awesome alienness.

Smiorgan waved to Elric and grinned thankfully.

'We're safe, thanks to you, Elric!' he yelled across the water. 'I knew you'd bring us luck!'

Elric ignored him.

Now the Dragon Lords, vengeance-bent, gave chase. Almost as fast as the magic-aided reaver fleet were the golden barges of Imrryr, and some reaver galleys, whose masts cracked and split beneath the force of the wind driving them, were caught.

Elric saw mighty grappling hooks of dully gleaming metal swing out from the decks of the Imrryrian galleys and thud with a moan of wrenched timber into those of the fleet which lay broken and powerless behind him. Fire leapt from catapults upon the Dragon Lords' ships and careered towards many a fleeing reaver craft. Searing, foul-stinking flame hissed like lava across the decks and ate into planks like vitriol into paper. Men shrieked, beating vainly at brightly burning clothes, some leaping into water which would not extinguish the fire. Some sank beneath the sea and it was possible to trace their descent as, flaming even below the surface, men and ships fluttered to the bottom like blazing, tired moths.

Reaver decks, untouched by fire, ran red with reaver blood as the enraged Imrryrian warriors swung down the grappling ropes and dropped among the raiders, wielding great swords and battle-axes and wreaking terrible havoc amongst the sea-ravens. Imrryrian arrows and Imrryrian javelins swooped from the towering decks of Imrryrian galleys and tore into the panicky men on the smaller ships.

All this Elric saw as he and his vessels began slowly to overhaul the leading Imrryrian ship, flag-galley of Admiral Magum Colim, commander of the Melnibonéan fleet.

Now Elric spared a word for Count Smiorgan. 'We've outrun them!' he shouted above the howling wind to the next ship where Smiorgan stood staring wide-eyed at the sky. 'But keep your ships heading westwards or we're finished!'

Smiorgan did not reply. He still looked skyward and there was horror in his eyes; in the eyes of a man who, before this, had never known the quivering bite of fear. Uneasily, Elric let his own eyes follow the gaze of Smiorgan. Then he saw them.

They were dragons, without doubt! The great reptiles were some miles away, but Elric knew the stamp of the huge flying beasts. The average wingspan of these near-extinct monsters was some thirty feet across. Their snakelike bodies, beginning in a narrow-snouted head and terminating in a dreadful whip of a tail, were forty feet long and although they did not breathe the legendary fire and smoke, Elric knew that their venom was combustible and could set fire to wood or fabric on contact.

Imrryrian warriors rode the dragon backs. Armed with long, spearlike goads, they blew strangely shaped horns which sang out curious notes over the turbulent sea and calm blue sky. Nearing the golden fleet, now half a league away, the leading dragon sailed down and circled towards the huge golden flag-galley, its wings making a sound like the crack of lightning as they beat through the air.

The grey-green, scaled monster hovered over the golden ship as it heaved in the white-foamed turbulent sea. Framed against the cloudless sky, the dragon was in sharp perspective and it was possible for Elric to get a clear view of it. The goad which the Dragon Master waved to Admiral Magum Colim was a long, slim spear upon which the strange pennant of black-and-yellow zigzag lines was, even at this distance, noticeable. Elric recognised the insignia on the pennant.

Dyvim Tvar, friend of Elric's youth, Lord of the Dragon Caves, was leading his charges to claim vengeance for Imrryr the Beautiful.

Elric howled across the water to Smiorgan. 'These are your main danger, now. Do what you can to stave them off!' There was a rattle of iron as the men prepared, near-hopelessly, to repel the new menace. Witch-wind would give little advantage over the fast-flying dragons. Now Dyvim Tvar had evidently conferred with Magum Colim and his goad lashed out at the dragon throat.

The huge reptile jerked upwards and began to gain altitude. Eleven other dragons were behind it, joining it now.

With seeming slowness, the dragons began to beat relentlessly towards the reaver fleet as the crewmen prayed to their own gods for a miracle.

They were doomed. There was no escaping the fact. Every reaver ship was doomed and the raid had been fruitless.

Elric could see the despair in the faces of the men as the masts of the reaver ships continued to bend under the strain of the shrieking witch-wind. They could do nothing, now, but die...

Elric fought to rid his mind of the swirling uncertainty which filled it. He drew his sword and felt the pulsating, evil power which lurked in runecarved Stormbringer. But he hated that power now – for it had caused him to kill the only human he had cherished. He realised how much of his strength he owed to the black-iron sword of his fathers and how weak he might be without it. He was an albino and that meant that he lacked the vitality of a normal human being. Savagely, futilely, as the mist in his mind was replaced by red fear, he cursed the pretensions of revenge he had held, cursed the day when he had agreed to lead the raid on Imrryr and most of all he bitterly vilified dead Yyrkoon and his twisted envy which had been the cause of the whole doom-ridden course of events.

But it was too late now for curses of any kind. The loud slapping of beating dragon wings filled the air and the monsters loomed over the fleeing reaver craft. He had to make some kind of decision – though he had no love for life, he refused to die by the hands of his own people. When he died, he promised himself, it would be by his hand. He made his decision, hating himself.

He called off the witch-wind as the dragon venom seared down and struck the last ship in line.

He put all his powers into sending a stronger wind into the sails of his own boat while his bewildered comrades in the suddenly becalmed ships called over the water, enquiring desperately the reason for his act. Elric's ship was moving fast, now, and might just escape the dragons. He hoped so.

He deserted the man who had trusted him, Count Smiorgan, and watched as venom poured from the sky and engulfed him in blazing green-and-scarlet flame. Elric fled, keeping his mind from thoughts of the future, and sobbed aloud, that proud prince of ruins; and he cursed the malevolent gods for the black day when idly, for their amusement, they had spawned sentient creatures like himself.

Behind him, the last reaver ships flared into sudden appalling brightness and, although half-thankful that they had escaped the fate of their comrades, the crew looked at Elric accusingly. He sobbed on, not heeding them, great griefs racking his soul.

A night later, off the coast of an island called Pan Tang, when the ship was safe from the dreadful recriminations of the Dragon Masters and their beasts, Elric stood brooding in the stern while the men eyed him with fear and hatred, muttering of betrayal and heartless cowardice. They appeared to have forgotten their own fear and subsequent safety.

Elric brooded and he held the black runesword in his two hands. Stormbringer was more than an ordinary battle-blade, this he had known for years, but now he realised that it was possessed of more sentience than he had imagined. Yet he was horribly dependent upon it; he realised this with soul-rending certainty. But he feared and resented the sword's power – hated it bitterly for the chaos it had wrought in his brain and spirit. In an agony of uncertainty he held the blade in his hands and forced himself to weigh the factors involved. Without the sinister sword, he would lose pride – perhaps even life – but he might know the soothing tranquillity of pure rest; with it he would have power and strength – but the sword would guide him into a doom-racked future. He would savour power – but never peace.

He drew a great, sobbing breath and, blind misgiving influencing him, threw the sword into the moon-drenched sea.

Incredibly, it did not sink. It did not even float on the water. It fell point forwards into the sea and *stuck* there, quivering as if it were embedded in timber. It remained throbbing in the water, six inches of its blade immersed, and began to give off a weird devil-scream – a howl of horrible malevolence.

With a choking curse Elric stretched out his slim, white, gleaming hand, trying to recover the sentient hellblade. He stretched further, leaning far out over the rail. He could not grasp it – it lay some feet from him, still. Gasping, a sickening sense of defeat overwhelming him, he dropped over the side and plunged into the bone-chilling water, striking out with strained, grotesque strokes, towards the hovering sword. He was beaten – the sword had won.

He reached it and put his fingers around the hilt. At once it settled in his hand and Elric felt strength seep slowly back into his aching body. Then he realised that he and the sword were interdependent, for though he needed the blade, Stormbringer, parasitic, required a user – without a man to wield it, the blade was also powerless.

'We must be bound to one another then,' Elric murmured despairingly. 'Bound by hell-forged chains and fate-haunted circumstance. Well, then – let it be thus so – and men will have cause to tremble and flee when they hear the names of Elric of Melniboné and Stormbringer, his sword. We are two of a kind – produced by an age which has deserted us. Let us give this age *cause* to hate us!'

Strong again, Elric sheathed Stormbringer and the sword settled against his side; then, with powerful strokes, he began to swim towards the island while the men he left on the ship breathed with relief and speculated whether he would live or perish in the bleak waters of that strange and nameless sea...

A Portrait in Ivory

Chapter One

An Encounter with a Lady

ELRIC, WHO HAD slept well and revived himself with fresh-brewed herbs, was in improved humour as he mixed honey and water into his glass of green breakfast wine. Typically, his night had been filled with distressing dreams, but any observer would see only a tall, insouciant 'silverskin' with high cheekbones, slightly sloping eyes and tapering ears, revealing nothing of his inner thoughts.

He had found a quiet hostelry away from the noisy centre of Séred-Öma, this city of tall palms. Here, merchants from all over the Young Kingdoms gathered to trade their goods in return for the region's most valuable produce. This was not the dates or livestock, on which Séred-Öma's original wealth had been founded, but the extraordinary creations of artists famed everywhere in the lands bordering the Sighing Desert. Their carvings, especially of animals and human portraits, were coveted by kings and princes. It was the reputation of these works of art which brought the crimson-eyed albino out of his way to see them for himself. Even in Melniboné, where barbarian art for the most part was regarded with distaste, the sculptors of Séred-Öma had been admired.

Though Elric had left the scabbarded runesword and black armour of his new calling in his chamber and wore the simple chequered clothing of a regional traveller, his fellow guests tended to keep a certain distance from him. Those who had heard little of Melniboné's fall had celebrated the Bright Empire's destruction with great glee until the implications of that sudden defeat were understood. Certainly, Melniboné no longer controlled the world's trade and could no longer demand ransom from the Young Kingdoms, but the world was these days in confusion as upstart nations vied to seize the power for themselves. And meanwhile, Melnibonéan mercenaries found employment in the armies of rival countries. Without being certain of his identity, they could tell at once that Elric was one of those misplaced unhuman warriors, infamous for their cold good manners and edgy pride.

Rather than find themselves in a quarrel with him, the customers of the Rolling Pig kept their distance. The haughty albino too seemed indisposed to open a conversation. Instead, he sat at his corner table staring into his morning wine, brooding on what could not be forgotten. His history was written on handsome features which would have been youthful were it not for his thoughts. He reflected on an unsettled past and an uneasy future. Even had someone dared approach him, however sympathetically, to ask what concerned him, he would have answered lightly and coldly, for, save in his nightmares, he refused to confront most of those concerns. Thus, he did not look up when a woman, wearing the conical russet hat and dark veil of her caste, approached him through the crowd of busy dealers.

'Sir?' Her voice was a dying melody. 'Master Melnibonéan, could you tolerate my presence at your table?' Falling rose petals, sweet and brittle from the sun.

'Lady,' said Elric, in the courteous tone his people reserved for their own high-born kin, 'I am at my breakfast. But I will gladly order more wine...'

'Thank you, sir. I did not come here to share your hospitality. I came to ask a favour.' Behind the veil her eyes were grey-green. Her skin had the golden bloom of the Na'äne, who had once ruled here and were said to be a race as ancient as Elric's own. 'A favour you have every reason to refuse.'

The albino seemed almost amused, perhaps because, as he looked into her eyes, he detected beauty behind the veil, an unexpected intelligence he had not encountered since he had left Imrryr's burning ruins behind him. How he had longed to hear the swift wit of his own people, the eloquent argument, the careless insults. All that and more had been denied him for too long. To himself he had become sluggish, almost as dull as the conniving princelings and self-important merchants to whom he sold his sword. Now, there was something in the music of her speech, something in the lilt of irony colouring each phrase she uttered, that spoke to his own sleeping intellect. 'You know me too well, lady. Clearly, my fate is in your hands, for you're able to anticipate my every attitude and response. I have good reason not to grant you a favour, yet you still come to ask one, so either you are prescient or I am already your servant.'

'I would serve you, sir,' she said gently. Her half-hidden lips curved in a narrow smile. She shrugged. 'And, in so doing, serve myself.'

'I thought my curiosity atrophied,' he answered. 'My imagination a petrified knot. Here you pick at threads to bring it back to life. This loosening is unlikely to be pleasant. Should I fear you?' He lifted a dented pewter cup to his lips and tasted the remains of his wine. 'You are a witch, perhaps? Do you seek to revive the dead? I am not sure...'

'I am not sure, either,' she told him. 'Will you trust me enough to come with me to my house?'

'I regret madam, I am only lately bereaved –'

'I'm no sensation-seeker, sir, but an honest woman with an honest ambition. I do not tempt you with the pleasures of the flesh, but of the soul. Something which might engage you for a while, even ease your mind a little. I can more readily convince you of this if you come to my house. I live there alone, save for servants. You may bring your sword, if you wish. Indeed, if you have fellows, bring them also. Thus I offer you every advantage.'

The albino rose slowly from his bench and placed the empty goblet carefully on the well-worn wood. His own smile reflected hers. He bowed. 'Lead on, madam.' And he followed her through a crowd which parted like corn before the reaper, leaving a momentary silence behind him.

Chapter Two

The Material

SHE HAD BROUGHT him to the depth of the city's oldest quarter, where artists of every skill, she told him, were licensed to work unhindered by landlord or, save in the gravest cases, the law. This ancient sanctuary was created by time-honoured tradition and the granting of certain guarantees by the clerics whose great university had once been the centre of the settlement. These guarantees had been strengthened during the reign of the great King Alo'ofd, an accomplished player of the nine-stringed *murmerlan*, who loved all the arts and struggled with a desire to throw off the burdens of his office and become a musician. King Alo'ofd's decrees had been law for the past millennium and his successors had never dared challenge them.

'Thus, this quarter harbours not only artists of great talent,' she told him, 'but many who have only the minimum of talent. Enough to allow them to live according to our ancient freedoms. Sadly, sir, there is as much forgery practised here, of every kind, as there is originality.'

'Yours is not the only such quarter.' He spoke absently, his eyes inspecting the colourful paintings, sculptures and manuscripts displayed on every side. They were of varied quality, but only a few showed genuine inspiration and beauty. Yet the accomplishment was generally higher than Elric had usually observed in the Young Kingdoms. 'Even in Melniboné we had these districts. Two of my cousins, for instance, were calligraphers. Another composed for the flute.'

'I have heard of Melnibonéan arts,' she said. 'But we are too distant from your island home to have seen many examples. There are stories, of course.' She smiled. 'Some of them are decidedly sinister...'

'Oh, they are doubtless true. We had no trouble if audiences, for instance, died for an artist's work. Many great composers would experiment, for instance, with the human voice.' His eyes again clouded, remembering not a crime but his lost passion.

It seemed she misinterpreted him. 'I feel for you, sir. I am not one of those who celebrated the fall of the Dreaming City.'

'You could not know its influence, so far away,' he murmured, picking up a remarkable little pot and studying its design. 'But those who were our neighbours were glad to see us humiliated. I do not blame them. Our time was over.' His expression was again one of cultivated insouciance. She turned her own gaze towards a house which leaned like an amiable drunkard on the buttressed walls of two neighbours, giving the impression that if it fell, then all would fall together. The house was of wood and sandy brick, of many floors, each at an angle to the rest, covered by a waved roof.

'This is the residence,' she told him, 'where my forefathers and myself have lived and worked. It is the House of the Th'ee and I am Rai-u Th'ee, last of my line. It is my ambition to leave a single great work of art behind, carved in a material which has been in our possession for centuries, yet until now always considered too valuable to use. It is a rare material, at least to us, and possessed of a number of qualities, some of which our ancestors only hinted at.'

'My curiosity grows,' said Elric, though now he found himself wishing that he had accepted her offer and brought his sword. 'What is this material?'

'It is a kind of ivory,' she said, leading him into the ramshackle house which, for all its age and decrepitude, had clearly once been rich. Even the wall hangings, now in rags, revealed traces of their former quality. There were paintings from floor to ceiling which, Elric knew, would have commanded magnificent prices at any market. The furniture was carved by genuine artists and showed the passing of a hundred fashions, from the plain, somewhat austere style of the city's secular period, to the ornate enrichments of her pagan age. Some were inset with jewels, as were the many mirrors, framed with exquisite and elaborate ornament. Elric was surprised, given what she had told him of the quarter, that the House of Th'ee had never been robbed.

Apparently reading his thoughts, she said: 'This place has been afforded certain protections down the years.' She led him into a tall studio, lit by a single, unpapered window through which a great deal of light entered, illuminating the scrolls and boxed books lining the walls. Crowded on tables and shelves stood sculptures in every conceivable material. They were in bone and granite and hardwood and limestone. They were in clay and bronze, in iron and sea-green basalt. Bright, glinting whites, deep, swirling blacks. Colours of every possible shade from darkest blue to the lightest pinks and yellows. There was gold, silver and delicate porphyry. There were heads and torsos and reclining figures, beasts of every kind, some believed extinct. There were representations of the Lords and Ladies of Chaos and of Law, every supernatural aristocrat who had ever ruled in heaven, hell or limbo. Elementals. Animal-bodied men, birds in flight, leaping deer, men and women at rest, historical subjects, group subjects and half-finished subjects which hinted at something still to be discovered in the stone. They were the work of genius, decided the albino, and his respect for this bold woman grew.

'Yes.' Again she anticipated a question, speaking with firm pride. 'They are all mine. I love to work. Many of these are taken from life...'

He thought it impolitic to ask which.

'But you will note,' she added, 'that I have never had the pleasure of sculpting the head of a Melnibonéan. This could be my only opportunity.'

'Ah,' he began regretfully, but with great grace she silenced him, drawing him to a table on which sat a tall, shrouded object. She took away the cloth. 'This is the material we have owned down the generations but for which we had never yet found an appropriate subject.'

He recognised the material. He reached to run his hand over its warm smoothness. He had seen more than one of these in the old caves of the Phoorn, the dragons to whom his folk were related. He had seen them in living creatures who even now slept in Melniboné, wearied by their work of destruction, their old master made an exile, with no-one to care for them save a few mad old men who knew how to do nothing else.

'Yes,' she whispered, 'it is what you know it is. It cost my forefathers a great fortune for, as you can imagine, your folk were not readily forthcoming with such things. It was smuggled from Melniboné and traded through many nations before it reached us, some two and a half centuries ago.'

Elric found himself almost singing to the thing as he caressed it. He felt a mixture of nostalgia and deep sadness.

'It is dragon ivory, of course.' Her hand joined his on the hard, brilliant surface of the great curved tusk. Few Phoorn had owned such fangs. Only the greatest of the patriarchs, legendary creatures of astonishing ferocity and wisdom, who had come from their old world to this, following their kin, the humanlike folk of Melniboné. The Phoorn, too, had not been native to this world, but had fled another. They, too, had always been alien and cruel, impossibly beautiful, impossibly strange. Elric felt kinship even now for this piece of bone. It was perhaps all that remained of the first generation to settle on this plane.

'It is a holy thing.' His voice was growing cold again. Inexplicable pain forced him to withdraw from her. 'It is my own kin. Blood for blood, the Phoorn and the folk of Melniboné are one. It was our power. It was our strength. It was our continuity. This is ancestral bone. Stolen bone. It would be sacrilege...'

'No, Prince Elric, in my hands it would be a unification. A resolution. A completion. You know why I have brought you here.'

'Yes.' His hand fell to his side. He swayed, as if faint. He felt a need for the herbs he carried with him. 'But it is still sacrilege...'

'Not if I am the one to give it life.' Her veil was drawn back now and he saw how impossibly young she was, what beauty she had: a beauty mirrored in all the things she had carved and moulded. Her desire was, he was sure, an honest one. Two very different emotions warred within him. Part of him felt she was right, that she could unite the two kinsfolk in a single image and bring honour to all his ancestors, a kind of resolution to their mutual history. Part of him feared what she might create. In honouring his past, would she be destroying the future? Then some fundamental part of him made him gather himself up and turn to her. She gasped at what she saw burning in those terrible, ruby eyes.

'Life?'

'Yes,' she said. 'A new life honouring the old. Will you sit for me?' She too was caught up in his mood, for she too was endangering everything she valued, possibly her own soul, to make what might be her very last great work. 'Will you allow me to create your memorial? Will you help me redeem that destruction whose burden is so heavy upon you? A symbol for everything that was Melniboné?'

He let go of his caution but felt no responsive glee. The fire dulled in his eyes. His mask returned. 'I will need you to help me brew certain herbs, madam. They will sustain me while I sit for you.'

Her step was light as she led him into a room where she had lit a stove and on which water already boiled, but his own face still resembled the stone of her carvings. His gaze was turned inward, his eyes alternately flared and faded like a dying candle. His chest moved with deep, almost dying breaths as he gave himself up to her art.

Chapter Three

The Sitting

How many hours did he sit, still and silent in the chair? At one time she remarked on the fact that he scarcely moved. He said that he had developed the habit over several hundred years and, when she voiced surprise, permitted himself a smile. 'You have not heard of Melniboné's dream couches? They are doubtless destroyed with the rest. It is how we learn so much when young. The couches let us dream for a year, even centuries, while the time passing for those awake was but minutes. I appear to you as a relatively young man, lady. But actually I have lived for centuries. It took me that time to pursue my dream-quests, which in turn taught me my craft and prepared me for...' And then he stopped speaking, his pale lids falling over his troubled, unlikely eyes.

She drew breath, as if to ask a further question, then thought better of it. She brewed him cup after cup of invigorating herbs and she continued to work, her delicate chisels fashioning an extraordinary likeness. She had genius in her hands. Every line of the albino's head was rapidly reproduced. And Elric, almost dreaming again, stared into the middle distance. His thoughts were far away and in the past, where he had left the corpse of his beloved Cymoril to burn on the pyre he had made of his own ancient home, the great and beautiful Imrryr, the Dreaming City, the Dreamers' City, which many had considered indestructible, had believed to be more conjuring than reality, created by the Melnibonéan Sorcerer Kings into a delicate reality, whose towers, so tall they disappeared amongst clouds, were actually the result of supernatural will rather than the creation of architects and masons.

Yet Elric had proven such theories false when Melniboné burned. Now all knew him for a traitor and none trusted him, even those whose ambition he had served. They said he was twice a traitor, once to his own folk, second to those he had led on the raid which had razed Imrryr and upon whom he had turned. But in his own mind he was thrice a traitor, for he had slain his beloved Cymoril, beautiful sister of cousin Yyrkoon, who had tricked Elric into killing her with that terrible black blade whose energy both sustained and drained him.

It was for Cymoril, more than Imrryr, that Elric mourned. But he showed none of this to the world and never spoke of it. Only in his dreams, those terrible, troubled dreams, did he see her again, which is why he almost always slept alone and presented a carefully cultivated air of insouciance to the world at large.

Had he agreed to the sculptress's request because she reminded him of his cousin?

Hour upon tireless hour she worked with her exquisitely made instruments until at last she had finished. She sighed and it seemed her breath was a gentle witch-wind, filling the head with vitality. She turned the portrait for his inspection.

It was as if he stared into a mirror. For a moment he thought he saw movement in the bust, as if his own essence had been absorbed by it. Save for the blank eyes, the carving might have been himself. Even the hair had been carved to add to the portrait's lifelike qualities.

She looked to him for his approval and received the faintest of smiles. 'You have made the likeness of a monster,' he murmured. 'I congratulate you. Now history will know the face of the man they call Elric Kinslayer.'

'Ah,' she said, 'you curse yourself too much, my lord. Do you look into the face of one who bears a guilt-weighted conscience?'

And of course, he did. She had captured exactly that quality of melancholy and self-hatred behind the mask of insouciance which characterised the albino in repose.

'Whoever looks on this will not say you were careless of your crimes.' Her voice was so soft it was almost a whisper now.

At this he rose suddenly, putting down his cup. 'I need no sentimental forgiveness,' he said coldly. 'There is no forgiveness, no understanding, of that crime. History will be right to curse me for a coward, a traitor, a killer of women and of his own blood. You have done well, madam, to brew me those herbs, for I now feel strong enough to put all this and your city behind me!'

She watched him leave, walking a little unsteadily like a man carrying a heavy burden, through the busy night, back to the inn where he had left his sword and armour. She knew that by morning he would be gone, riding out of Séred-Öma, never to return. Her hands caressed the likeness she had made, the blind, staring eyes, the mouth which was set in a grimace of self-mocking carelessness.

And she knew he would always wonder, even as he put a thousand leagues between them, if he had not left at least a little of his yearning, desperate soul behind him.

While the Gods Laugh

I, while the gods laugh, the world's vortex am;
Maelstrom of passions in that hidden sea
Whose waves of all-time lap the coasts of me,
And in small compass the dark waters cram.

– Mervyn Peake,
'Shapes and Sounds', 1941

Chapter One

ONE NIGHT, AS Elric sat moodily drinking alone in a tavern – ever the best places for discovering news – a wingless woman of Myyrrhn came gliding out of the storm and rested her lithe body against him.

Her face was thin and frail-boned, almost as white as Elric's own albino skin, and she wore flimsy pale green robes which contrasted well with her dark red hair.

The tavern was ablaze with candle-flame and alive with droning argument and gusty laughter, but the words of the woman of Myyrrhn came clear and liquid, carrying over the zesty din.

'I have sought you twenty days,' she said to Elric who regarded her insolently through hooded crimson eyes and lazed in a high-backed chair, a silver wine-cup in his long-fingered right hand and his left on the pommel of his sorcerous runesword Stormbringer.

'Twenty days,' murmured the Melnibonéan softly, speaking as if to himself, mockingly rude. 'A long time for a beautiful and lonely woman to be wandering the world.' He opened his eyes a trifle wider and spoke to her directly: 'I am Elric of Melniboné, as you evidently know. I grant no favours and ask none. Bearing this in mind, tell me why you have sought me for twenty days.'

Equably, the woman replied, undaunted by the albino's supercilious tone. 'You are a bitter man, Elric; I know this also – and you are grief-haunted for reasons which are already legend. I ask you no favours – but bring you myself and a proposition. What do you desire most in the world?'

'Peace,' Elric told her simply. Then he smiled ironically and said: 'I am an evil man, lady, and my destiny is hell-doomed, but I am not unwise, nor unfair. Let me remind you a little of the truth. Call this legend if you prefer – I do not care.

'A woman died a year ago, on the blade of my trusty sword.' He patted the blade sharply and his eyes were suddenly hard and self-mocking. 'Since then I have courted no woman and desired none. Why should I break such secure habits? If asked, I grant you that I could speak poetry to you, and that you have a grace and beauty which moves me to interesting speculation, but I would not load any part of my dark burden upon one as exquisite as you. Any relationship between us, other than formal, would necessitate my unwilling shifting of part of that burden.' He paused for an instant and then said slowly: 'I should admit that I scream in my sleep sometimes and am often tortured by incommunicable self-loathing. Go while you can, lady, and forget Elric for he can bring only grief to your soul.'

With a quick movement he turned his gaze from her and lifted the silver wine-cup, draining it and replenishing it from a jug at his side.

'No,' said the wingless woman of Myyrrhn calmly, 'I will not. Come with me.'

She rose and gently took Elric's hand. Without knowing why, Elric allowed himself to be led from the tavern and out into the wild, rainless storm which howled around the Filkharian city of Raschil. A protective and cynical smile hovered about his mouth as she drew him towards the sea-lashed quayside where she told him her name. Shaarilla of the Dancing Mist, wingless daughter of a dead necromancer – a cripple in her own strange land, and an outcast.

Elric felt uncomfortably drawn to this calm-eyed woman who wasted few words. He felt a great surge of emotion well within him, emotion he had never thought to experience again, and he wanted to take her finely moulded shoulders and press her slim body to his. But he quelled the urge and studied her marble delicacy and her wild hair which flowed in the wind about her head.

Silence rested comfortably between them while the chaotic wind howled mournfully over the sea. Here, Elric could ignore the warm stink of the city and he felt almost relaxed. At last, looking away from him towards the swirling sea, her green robe curling in the wind, she said: 'You have heard, of course, of the Dead Gods' Book?'

Elric nodded. He was interested, despite the need he felt to dissociate himself as much as possible from his fellows. The mythical book was believed to contain knowledge which could solve many problems that had plagued men for centuries – it held a holy and mighty wisdom which every sorcerer desired to sample. But it was believed destroyed, hurled into the sun when the Old Gods were dying in the cosmic wastes which lay beyond the outer reaches of the solar system. Another legend, apparently of later origin, spoke vaguely of the dark ones who had interrupted the Book's sunward coursing and had stolen it before it could be destroyed. Most scholars discounted this legend, arguing that, by this time, the Book would have come to light if it did still exist.

Elric made himself speak flatly so that he appeared to be uninterested when he answered Shaarilla. 'Why do you mention the Book?'

'I know that it exists,' Shaarilla replied intensely, 'and I know where it is. My father acquired the knowledge just before he died. Myself – and the Book – you may have if you will help me get it.'

Could the secret of peace be contained in the Book? Elric wondered. Would he, if he found it, be able to dispense with Stormbringer?

'If you want it so badly that you seek my help,' he said eventually, 'why do you not wish to keep it?'

'Because I would be afraid to have such a thing perpetually in my custody – it is not a book for an ordinary mortal to own, but you are possibly the last mighty nigromancer left in the world and it is fitting that you should have it. Besides, you might kill me to obtain it – I would never be safe with such a volume in my hands. I need only one small part of its wisdom.'

'What is that?' Elric enquired, studying her patrician beauty with a new pulse stirring within him.

Her mouth set and the lids fell over her eyes. 'When we have the Book in our hands – then you will have your answer. Not before.'

'This answer is good enough,' Elric remarked quickly, seeing that he would gain no more information at that stage. 'And the answer appeals to me.' Then, half before he realised it, he seized her shoulders in his slim, pale hands and pressed his colourless lips to her scarlet mouth.

Elric and Shaarilla rode westwards, towards the Silent Land, across the lush plains of Shazaar where their ship had berthed two days earlier. The border country between Shazaar and the Silent Land was a lonely stretch of territory, unoccupied even by peasant dwellings; a no man's land, though fertile and rich in natural wealth. The inhabitants of Shazaar had deliberately refrained from extending their borders further, for though the dwellers in the Silent Land rarely ventured beyond the Marshes of the Mist, the natural borderline between the two lands, the inhabitants of Shazaar held their unknown neighbours in almost superstitious fear.

The journey had been clean and swift, though ominous, with several persons who should have known nothing of their purpose warning the travellers of nearing danger. Elric brooded, recognising the signs of doom but choosing to ignore them and communicate nothing to Shaarilla who, for her part, seemed content with Elric's silence. They spoke little in the day and so saved their breath for the wild love-play of the night.

The thud of the two horses' hoofs on the soft turf, the muted creak and clatter of Elric's harness and sword, were the only sounds to break the stillness of the clear winter day as the pair rode steadily, nearing the quaking, treacherous trails of the Marshes of the Mist.

One gloomy night, they reached the borders of the Silent Land, marked by the marsh, and they halted and made camp, pitching their silk tent on a hill overlooking the mist-shrouded wastes.

Banked like black pillows against the horizon, the clouds were ominous. The moon lurked behind them, sometimes piercing them sufficiently to send a pale tentative beam down onto the glistening marsh or its ragged, grassy frontiers. Once, a moonbeam glanced off silver, illuminating the dark silhouette of Elric, but, as if repelled by the sight of a living creature on that bleak hill, the moon once again slunk behind its cloud-shield, leaving Elric thinking deeply. Leaving Elric in the darkness he desired.

Thunder rumbled over distant mountains, sounding like the laughter of far-off gods. Elric shivered, pulled his blue cloak more tightly about him, and continued to stare over the misted lowlands.

Shaarilla came to him soon, and she stood beside him, swathed in a thick woollen cloak which could not keep out all the damp chill in the air.

'The Silent Land,' she murmured. 'Are all the stories true, Elric? Did they teach you of it in old Melniboné?'

Elric frowned, annoyed that she had disturbed his thoughts. He turned abruptly to look at her, staring blankly out of crimson-irised eyes for a moment and then saying flatly:

'The inhabitants are unhuman and feared. This I know. Few men ventured into their territory, ever. None has returned, to my knowledge. Even in the days when Melniboné was a powerful empire, this was one nation my ancestors never ruled – nor did they desire to do so. Nor did they make a treaty. The denizens of the Silent Land are said to be a dying race, far more selfish than my ancestors ever were, who enjoyed dominion over the Earth long before Melnibonéans gained any sort of power. They rarely venture beyond the confines of their territory, nowadays, encompassed as it is by marshland and mountains.'

Shaarilla laughed, then, with little humour. 'So they are unhuman are they, Elric? Then what of my people, who are related to them? What of me, Elric?'

'You're unhuman enough for me,' replied Elric insouciantly, looking her in the eyes. She smiled.

'A compliment? I'll take it for one – until your glib tongue finds a better.'

That night they slept restlessly and, as he had predicted, Elric screamed agonisingly in his turbulent, terror-filled sleep and he called a name which made Shaarilla's eyes fill with pain and jealousy. Wide-eyed in his grim sleep, Elric seemed to be staring at the one he named, speaking other words in a sibilant language which made Shaarilla block her ears and shudder.

The next morning, as they broke camp, folding the rustling fabric of the yellow silk tent between them, Shaarilla avoided looking at Elric directly but later, since he made no move to speak, she asked him, in a voice which shook somewhat, a question.

It was a question which she needed to ask, but one which came hard to her lips. 'Why do you desire the Dead Gods' Book, Elric? What do you believe you will find in it?'

Elric shrugged, dismissing the question, but she repeated her words less slowly, with more insistence.

'Very well then,' he said eventually. 'But it is not easy to answer you in a few sentences. I desire, if you like, to know one of two things.'

'And what is that, Elric?'

The tall albino dropped the folded tent to the grass and sighed. His fingers played nervously with the pommel of his runesword. 'Can an ultimate god exist – or not? That is what I need to know, Shaarilla, if my life is to have any direction at all.

'The Lords of Law and Chaos now govern our lives. But is there some being greater than them?'

Shaarilla put a hand on Elric's arm. 'Why must you know?' she said.

'Despairingly, sometimes, I seek the comfort of a benign god, Shaarilla. My mind goes out, lying awake at night, searching through black barrenness for something – anything – which will take me to it, warm me, protect me, tell me that there is order in the chaotic tumble of the universe; that it is consistent, this precision of the planets, not simply a brief, bright spark of sanity in an eternity of malevolent anarchy.'

Elric sighed and his quiet tones were tinged with hopelessness. 'Without some confirmation of the order of things, my only comfort is to accept anarchy. This way, I can revel in chaos and know, without fear, that we are all doomed from the start – that our brief existence is both meaningless and damned. I can accept, then, that we are more than forsaken, because there was never anything there to forsake us. I have weighed the proof, Shaarilla, and must believe that anarchy prevails, in spite of all the laws which seemingly govern our actions, our sorcery, our logic. I see only chaos in the world. If the book we seek tells me otherwise, then I shall gladly believe it. Until then, I will put my trust only in my sword and myself.'

Shaarilla stared at Elric strangely. 'Could not this philosophy of yours have been influenced by recent events in your past? Do you fear the consequences of your murder and treachery? Is it not more comforting for you to believe in deserts which are rarely just?'

Elric turned on her, crimson eyes blazing in anger, but even as he made to speak, the anger fled him and he dropped his eyes towards the ground, hooding them from her gaze.

'Perhaps,' he said lamely. 'I do not know. That is the only *real* truth, Shaarilla. *I do not know.*'

Shaarilla nodded, her face lit by an enigmatic sympathy; but Elric did not see the look she gave him, for his own eyes were full of crystal tears which flowed down his lean, white face and took his strength and will momentarily from him.

'I am a man possessed,' he groaned, 'and without this devil-blade I carry I would not be a man at all.'

Chapter Two

THEY MOUNTED THEIR swift, black horses and spurred them with abandoned savagery down the hillside towards the marsh, their cloaks whipping behind them as the wind caught them, lashing them high into the air. Both rode with set, hard faces, refusing to acknowledge the aching uncertainty which lurked within them.

And the horses' hoofs had splashed into quaking bogland before they could halt.

Cursing, Elric tugged hard on his reins, pulling his horse back onto firm ground. Shaarilla, too, fought her own panicky stallion and guided the beast to the safety of the turf.

'How do we cross?' Elric asked her impatiently.

'There was a map –' Shaarilla began hesitantly.

'*Where is it?*'

'It – it was lost. I lost it. But I tried hard to memorise it. I think I'll be able to get us safely across.'

'How did you lose it – and why didn't you tell me of this before?' Elric stormed.

'I'm sorry, Elric – but for a whole day, just before I found you in that tavern, my memory was gone. Somehow, I lived through a day without knowing it – and when I awoke, the map was missing.'

Elric frowned. 'There is some force working against us, I am sure,' he muttered, 'but what it is, I do not know.' He raised his voice and said to her: 'Let us hope that your memory is not too faulty, now. These marshes are infamous the world over, but by all accounts, only natural hazards wait for us.' He grimaced and put his fingers around the hilt of his runesword. 'Best go first, Shaarilla, but stay close. Lead the way.'

She nodded, dumbly, and turned her horse's head towards the north, galloping along the bank until she came to a place where a great, tapering rock loomed. Here, a grassy path, four feet or so across, led out into the misty marsh. They could only see a little distance ahead, because of the clinging mist, but it seemed that the trail remained firm for some way. Shaarilla walked her horse onto the path and jolted forward at a slow trot, Elric following immediately behind her.

Through the swirling, heavy mist which shone whitely, the horses moved hesitantly and their riders had to keep them on short, tight rein. The mist padded the marsh with silence and the gleaming, watery fens around them stank with foul putrescence. No animal scurried, no bird shrieked above them. Everywhere was a haunting, fear-laden silence which made both horses and riders uneasy.

With panic in their throats, Elric and Shaarilla rode on, deeper and deeper into the unnatural Marshes of the Mist, their eyes wary and even their nostrils quivering for scent of danger in the stinking morass.

Hours later, when the sun was long past its zenith, Shaarilla's horse reared, screaming and whinnying. She shouted for Elric, her exquisite features twisted in fear as she stared into the mist. He spurred his own bucking horse forwards and joined her.

Something moved, slowly, menacingly in the clinging whiteness. Elric's right hand whipped over to his left side and grasped the hilt of Stormbringer.

The blade shrieked out of its scabbard, a black fire gleaming along its length and alien power flowing from it into Elric's arm and through his body. A weird, unholy light leapt into Elric's crimson eyes and his mouth was wrenched into a hideous grin as he forced the frightened horse further into the skulking mist.

'Arioch, Lord of the Seven Darks, be with me now!' Elric yelled as he made out the shifting shape ahead of him. It was white, like the mist, yet somehow *darker*. It stretched high above Elric's head. It was nearly ten feet tall and almost as broad. But it was still only an outline, seeming to have no face or limbs – only movement: darting, malevolent movement! But Arioch, his patron god, chose not to hear.

Elric could feel his horse's great heart beating between his legs as the beast plunged forward under its rider's iron control. Shaarilla was screaming something behind him, but he could not hear the words. Elric hacked at the white shape, but his sword met only mist and it howled angrily. The fear-crazed horse would go no further and Elric was forced to dismount.

'Keep hold of the steed,' he shouted behind him to Shaarilla and moved on light feet towards the darting shape which hovered ahead of him, blocking his path.

Now he could make out some of its saliencies. Two eyes, the colour of thin, yellow wine, were set high in the thing's body, though it had no separate head. A mouthing, obscene slit, filled with fangs, lay just beneath the eyes. It had no nose or ears that Elric could see. Four appendages sprang from its upper parts and its lower body slithered along the ground, unsupported by any limbs. Elric's eyes ached as he looked at it. It was incredibly disgusting to behold and its amorphous body gave off a stench of death and decay. Fighting down his fear, the albino inched forward warily, his sword held high to parry any thrust the thing might make with its arms. Elric recognised it from a description in one of his grimoires. It was a Mist Giant – possibly the only Mist Giant, Bellbane. Even the wisest wizards were uncertain how many existed – one or many. It was a ghoul of the swamplands which fed off the souls and the blood of men and beasts. But the Marshes of this Mist were far to the east of Bellbane's reputed haunts.

Elric ceased to wonder why so few animals inhabited that stretch of the swamp. Overhead the sky was beginning to darken.

Stormbringer throbbed in Elric's grasp as he called the names of the ancient demon-gods of his people. The nauseous ghoul obviously recognised the names. For an instant, it wavered backwards. Elric made his legs move towards the thing. Now he saw that the ghoul was not white at all. But it had no colour to it that Elric could recognise. There was a suggestion of orangeness dashed with sickening greenish yellow, but he did not see the colours with his eyes – he only *sensed* the alien, unholy tinctures.

Then Elric rushed towards the thing, shouting the names

which now had no meaning to his surface consciousness. *'Balaan – Marthim! Aesma! Alastor! Saebos! Verdelet! Nizilfkm! Haborym!* Haborym of the Fires Which Destroy!' His whole mind was torn in two. Part of him wanted to run, to hide, but he had no control over the power which now gripped him and pushed him to meet the horror. His sword blade hacked and slashed at the shape. It was like trying to cut through water – sentient, pulsating water. But Stormbringer had effect. The whole shape of the ghoul quivered as if in dreadful pain. Elric felt himself plucked into the air and his vision went. He could see nothing – do nothing but hack and cut at the thing which now held him.

Sweat poured from him as, blindly, he fought on.

Pain which was hardly physical – a deeper, horrifying pain – filled his being as he howled now in agony and struck continually at the yielding bulk which embraced him and was pulling him slowly towards its gaping maw. He struggled and writhed in the obscene grasp of the thing. With powerful arms, it was holding him, almost lasciviously, drawing him closer as a rough lover would draw a girl. Even the mighty power intrinsic in the runesword did not seem enough to kill the monster. Though its efforts were somewhat weaker than earlier, it still drew Elric nearer to the gnashing, slavering mouth-slit.

Elric cried the names again, while Stormbringer danced and sang an evil song in his right hand. In agony, Elric writhed, praying, begging and promising, but still he was drawn inch by inch towards the grinning maw.

Savagely, grimly, he fought and again he screamed for Arioch. A mind touched his – sardonic, powerful, evil – and he knew Arioch responded at last! Almost imperceptibly, the Mist Giant weakened. Elric pressed his advantage and the knowledge that the ghoul was losing its strength gave him more power. Blindly, agony piercing every nerve of his body, he struck and struck.

Then, quite suddenly, he was falling.

He seemed to fall for hours, slowly, weightlessly until he landed upon a surface which yielded beneath him. He began to sink.

Far off, beyond time and space, he heard a distant voice calling to him. He did not want to hear it; he was content to lie where he was as the cold, comforting stuff in which he lay dragged him slowly into itself.

Then some sixth sense made him realise that it was Shaarilla's voice calling him and he forced himself to make sense out of her words.

'Elric – the marsh! You're in the marsh. Don't move!'

He smiled to himself. Why should he move? Down he was sinking, slowly, calmly – down into the welcoming marsh... *Had there been another time like this; another marsh?*

With a mental jolt, full awareness of the situation came back to him and he jerked his eyes open. Above him was mist. To one side a pool of unnameable colouring was slowly evaporating, giving off a foul odour. On the other side he could just make out a human form, gesticulating wildly. Beyond the human form were the barely discernible shapes of two horses. Shaarilla was there. Beneath him –

Beneath him was the marsh.

Thick, stinking slime was sucking him downwards as he lay spreadeagled upon it, half-submerged already. Stormbringer was still in his right hand. He could just see it if he turned his head. Carefully, he tried to lift the top half of his body from the sucking morass. He succeeded, only to feel his legs sink deeper. Sitting upright, he shouted to the girl.

'Shaarilla! Quickly – a rope!'

'There is no rope, Elric!' She was ripping off her top garment, frantically tearing it into strips.

Still Elric sank, his feet finding no purchase beneath them.

Shaarilla hastily knotted the strips of cloth. She flung the make-shift rope inexpertly towards the sinking albino. It fell short. Fumbling in her haste, she threw it again. This time his groping left hand found it. The girl began to haul on the fabric. Elric felt himself rise a little and then stop.

'It's no good, Elric – I haven't the strength.'

Cursing her, Elric shouted: 'The horse – tie it to the horse!'

She ran towards one of the horses and looped the cloth around the pommel of the saddle. Then she tugged at the beast's reins and began to walk it away.

Swiftly, Elric was dragged from the sucking bog and, still gripping Stormbringer, was pulled to the inadequate safety of the strip of turf.

Gasping, he tried to stand, but found his legs incredibly weak beneath him. He rose, staggered, and fell. Shaarilla knelt down beside him.

'Are you hurt?'

Elric smiled in spite of his weakness. 'I don't think so.'

'It was dreadful. I couldn't see properly what was happening. You seemed to disappear and then – then you screamed that – that name!' She was trembling, her face pale and taut.

'What name?' Elric was genuinely puzzled. 'What name did I scream?'

She shook her head. 'It doesn't matter – but whatever it was – it saved you. You reappeared soon afterwards and fell into the marsh...'

Stormbringer's power was still flowing into the albino. He already felt stronger.

With an effort, he got up and stumbled unsteadily towards his horse.

'I'm sure that the Mist Giant does not usually haunt this marsh – it was sent here. By what – or whom – I don't know, but we must get to firmer ground while we can.'

Shaarilla said: 'Which way – back or forward?'

Elric frowned. 'Why, forward, of course. Why do you ask?'

She swallowed and shook her head. 'Let's hurry, then,' she said.

They mounted their horses and rode with little caution until the marsh and its cloak of mist was behind them.

Now the journey took on a new urgency as Elric realised that some force was attempting to put obstacles in their way. They rested little and savagely rode their powerful horses to a virtual standstill.

On the fifth day they were riding through barren, rocky country and a light rain was falling.

The hard ground was slippery so that they were forced to ride more slowly, huddled over the sodden necks of their horses, muffled in cloaks which only inadequately kept out the drizzling rain. They had ridden in silence for some time before they heard a ghastly cackling baying ahead of them and the rattle of hoofs.

Elric motioned towards a large rock looming to their right. 'Shelter there,' he said. 'Something comes towards us – possibly more enemies. With luck, they'll pass us.' Shaarilla mutely obeyed him and together they waited as the hideous baying grew nearer.

'One rider – several other beasts,' Elric said, listening intently. 'The beasts either follow or pursue the rider.'

Then they were in sight – racing through the rain. A man frantically spurring an equally frightened horse – and behind him, the distance decreasing, a pack of what at first appeared to be dogs. But these were not dogs – they were half-dog and half-bird, with the lean, shaggy bodies and legs of dogs but possessing birdlike talons in place of paws and savagely curved beaks which snapped where muzzles should have been.

'The hunting dogs of the Dharzi!' gasped Shaarilla. 'I thought that they, like their masters, were long extinct!'

'I, also,' Elric said. 'What are they doing in these parts? There was never contact between the Dharzi and the dwellers of this land.'

'Brought here – by *something*,' Shaarilla whispered. 'Those devil-dogs will scent us to be sure.'

Elric reached for his runesword. 'Then we can lose nothing by aiding their quarry,' he said, urging his mount forward. 'Wait here, Shaarilla.'

By this time, the devil-pack and the man they pursued were rushing past the sheltering rock, speeding down a narrow defile. Elric spurred his horse down the slope.

'Ho there!' he shouted to the frantic rider. 'Turn and stand, my friend – I'm here to aid you!'

His moaning runesword lifted high, Elric thundered towards the snapping, howling devil-dogs and his horse's hoofs struck one with an impact which broke the unnatural beast's spine. There

were some five or six of the weird dogs left. The rider turned his horse and drew a long sabre from a scabbard at his waist. He was a small man, with a broad ugly mouth. He grinned in relief.

'A lucky chance, this meeting, good master.'

This was all he had time to remark before two of the dogs were leaping at him and he was forced to give his whole attention to defending himself from their slashing talons and snapping beaks.

The other three dogs concentrated their vicious attention upon Elric. One leapt high, its beak aimed at Elric's throat. He felt foul breath on his face and hastily brought Stormbringer round in an arc which chopped the dog in two. Filthy blood spattered Elric and his horse and the scent of it seemed to increase the fury of the other dogs' attack. But the blood made the dancing black runes-word sing an almost ecstatic tune and Elric felt it writhe in his grasp and stab at another of the hideous dogs. The point caught the beast just below its breastbone as it reared up at the albino. It screamed in terrible agony and turned its beak to seize the blade. As the beak connected with the lambent black metal of the sword, a foul stench, akin to the smell of burning, struck Elric's nostrils and the beast's scream broke off sharply.

Engaged with the remaining devil-dog, Elric caught a fleeting glimpse of the charred corpse. His horse was rearing high, lashing at the last alien animal with flailing hoofs. The dog avoided the horse's attack and came at Elric's unguarded left side. The albino swung in the saddle and brought his sword hurtling down to slice into the dog's skull and spill brains and blood on the wet and gleaming ground. Still somehow alive, the dog snapped feebly at Elric, but the Melnibonéan ignored its futile attack and turned his attention to the little man who had dispensed with one of his adversaries, but was having difficulty with the second. The dog had grasped the sabre with its beak, gripping the sword near the hilt.

Talons raked towards the little man's throat as he strove to shake the dog's grip. Elric charged forward, his runesword aimed like a lance to where the devil-dog dangled in mid-air, its talons slashing, trying to reach the flesh of its former quarry. Stormbringer caught the beast in its lower abdomen and ripped upwards, slitting the thing's underparts from crutch to throat. It released its hold on the small man's sabre and fell writhing to the ground. Elric's horse trampled it into the rocky ground. Breathing heavily, the albino sheathed Stormbringer and warily regarded the man he had saved. He disliked unnecessary contact with anyone and did not wish to be embarrassed by a display of emotion on the little man's part.

He was not disappointed, for the wide, ugly mouth split into a cheerful grin and the man bowed in the saddle as he returned his own curved blade to its scabbard.

'Thanks, good sir,' he said lightly. 'Without your help, the battle might have lasted longer. You deprived me of good sport, but you meant well. Moonglum is my name.'

'Elric of Melniboné, I,' replied the albino, but saw no reaction on the little man's face. This was strange, for the name of Elric was now infamous throughout most of the world. The story of his treachery and the slaying of his cousin Cymoril had been told and elaborated upon in taverns throughout the Young Kingdoms. Much as he hated it, he was used to receiving some indication of recognition from those he met. His albinism was enough to mark him.

Intrigued by Moonglum's ignorance, and feeling strangely drawn towards the cocky little rider, Elric studied him in an effort to discover from what land he came. Moonglum wore no armour and his clothes were of faded blue material, travel-stained and worn. A stout leather belt carried the sabre, a dirk and a woollen purse. Upon his feet, Moonglum wore ankle-length boots of cracked leather. His horse furniture was much used but of obviously good quality. The man himself, seated high in the saddle, was barely more than five feet tall, with legs too long in proportion to the rest of his slight body. His nose was short and uptilted, beneath grey-green eyes, large and innocent-seeming. A mop of vivid red hair fell over his forehead and down his neck, unrestrained. He sat his horse comfortably, still grinning but looking now behind Elric to where Shaarilla rode to join them.

Moonglum bowed elaborately as the girl pulled her horse to a halt.

Elric said coldly, 'The Lady Shaarilla – Master Moonglum of –?'

'Of Elwher,' Moonglum supplied, 'The mercantile capital of the East – the finest city in the world.'

Elric recognised the name. 'So you are from Elwher, Master Moonglum. I have heard of the place. A new city, is it not? Some few centuries old. You have ridden far.'

'Indeed I have, sir. Without knowledge of the language used in these parts, the journey would have been harder, but luckily the slave who inspired me with tales of his homeland taught me the speech thoroughly.'

'But why do you travel these parts – have you not heard the legends?' Shaarilla spoke incredulously.

'Those very legends were what brought me hence – and I'd begun to discount them, until those unpleasant pups set upon me. For what reason they decided to give chase, I will not know, for I gave them no cause to take a dislike to me. This is, indeed, a barbarous land.'

Elric was uncomfortable. Light talk of the kind which Moonglum seemed to enjoy was contrary to his own brooding nature. But in spite of this, he found that he was liking the man more and more.

It was Moonglum who suggested that they travel together for a while. Shaarilla objected, giving Elric a warning glance, but he ignored it.

'Very well then, friend Moonglum, since three are stronger than two, we'd appreciate your company. We ride towards the mountains.' Elric, himself, was feeling in a more cheerful mood.

'And what do you seek there?' Moonglum enquired.

'A secret,' Elric said, and his new-found companion was discreet enough to drop the question.

Chapter Three

So they rode, while the rainfall increased and splashed and sang among the rocks with a sky like dull steel above them and the wind crooning a dirge about their ears. Three small figures riding swiftly towards the black mountain barrier which rose over the world like a brooding god. And perhaps it was a god that laughed sometimes as they neared the foothills of the range, or perhaps it was the wind whistling through the dark mystery of canyons and precipices and the tumble of basalt and granite which climbed towards lonely peaks. Thunderclouds formed around those peaks and lightning smashed downwards like a monster finger searching the earth for grubs. Thunder rattled over the range and Shaarilla spoke her thoughts at last to Elric; spoke them as the mountains came in sight.

'Elric – let us go back, I beg you. Forget the Book – there are too many forces working against us. Take heed of the signs, Elric, or we are doomed!'

But Elric was grimly silent, for he had long been aware that the girl was losing her enthusiasm for the quest she had started.

'Elric – please. We will never reach the Book. Elric, turn back.'

She rode beside him, pulling at his garments until impatiently he shrugged himself clear of her grasp and said:

'I am intrigued too much to stop now. Either continue to lead the way – or tell me what you know and stay here. You desired to sample the Book's wisdom once – but now a few minor pitfalls on our journey have frightened you. What was it you needed to learn, Shaarilla?'

She did not answer him, but said instead: 'And what was it you desired, Elric? Peace, you told me. Well, I warn you, you'll find no peace in those grim mountains – if we reach them at all.'

'You have not been frank with me, Shaarilla,' Elric said coldly, still looking ahead of him at the black peaks. 'You know something of the forces seeking to stop us.'

She shrugged. 'It matters not – I know little. My father spoke a few vague warnings before he died, that is all.'

'What did he say?'

'He said that He who guards the Book would use all his power to stop mankind from using its wisdom.'

'What else?'

'Nothing else. But it is enough, now that I see that my father's warning was truly spoken. It was this guardian who killed him, Elric – or one of the guardian's minions. I do not wish to suffer that fate, in spite of what the Book might do for me. I had thought you powerful enough to aid me – but now I doubt it.'

'I have protected you so far,' Elric said simply. 'Now tell me what you seek from the Book?'

'I am too ashamed.'

Elric did not press the question, but eventually she spoke softly, almost whispering. 'I sought my wings,' she said.

'Your wings – you mean the Book might give you a spell so that you could grow wings!' Elric smiled ironically. 'And that is why you seek the vessel of the world's mightiest wisdom!'

'If you were thought deformed in your own land – it would seem important enough to you,' she shouted defiantly.

Elric turned his face towards her, his crimson-irised eyes burning with a strange emotion. He put a hand to his dead white skin and a crooked smile twisted his lips. 'I, too, have felt as you do,' he said quietly. That was all he said and Shaarilla dropped behind him again, shamed.

They rode on in silence until Moonglum, who had been riding discreetly ahead, cocked his overlarge skull on one side and suddenly drew rein.

Elric joined him. 'What is it, Moonglum?'

'I hear horses coming this way,' the little man said. 'And voices which are disturbingly familiar. More of those devil-dogs, Elric – and this time accompanied by riders!'

Elric, too, heard the sounds, now, and shouted a warning to Shaarilla.

'Perhaps you were right,' he called. 'More trouble comes towards us.'

'What now?' Moonglum said, frowning.

'Ride for the mountains,' Elric replied, 'and we may yet outdistance them.'

They spurred their steeds into a fast gallop and sped towards the hills.

But their flight was hopeless. Soon a black pack was visible on the horizon and the sharp birdlike baying of the devil-dogs drew nearer. Elric stared backward at their pursuers. Night was beginning to fall, and visibility was decreasing with every passing moment but he had a vague impression of the riders who raced behind the pack. They were swathed in dark cloaks and carried long spears. Their faces were invisible, lost in the shadow of the hoods which covered their heads.

Now Elric and his companions were forcing their horses up a steep incline, seeking the shelter of the rocks which lay above.

'We'll halt here,' Elric ordered, 'and try to hold them off. In the open they could easily surround us.'

Moonglum nodded affirmatively, agreeing with the good sense contained in Elric's words. They pulled their sweating steeds to a standstill and prepared to join battle with the howling pack and their dark-cloaked masters.

Soon the first of the devil-dogs were rushing up the incline, their beak-jaws slavering and their talons rattling on stone. Standing between two rocks, blocking the way between with their bodies, Elric and Moonglum met the first attack and quickly dispatched three of the animals. Several more took the place of the dead and the first of the riders was visible behind them as night crept closer.

'Arioch!' swore Elric, suddenly recognising the riders. 'These are the Lords of Dharzi – dead these ten centuries. We're fighting dead men, Moonglum, and the too-tangible ghosts of their dogs.

Unless I can think of a sorcerous means to defeat them, we're doomed!'

The zombie-men appeared to have no intention of taking part in the attack for the moment. They waited, their dead eyes eerily luminous, as the devil-dogs attempted to break through the swinging network of steel with which Elric and his companion defended themselves. Elric was racking his brains – trying to dredge a spoken spell from his memory which would dismiss these living dead. Then it came to him, and hoping that the forces he had to invoke would decide to aid him, he began to chant:

'Let the Laws which govern all things
Not so lightly be dismissed;
Let the Ones who flaunt the Earth Kings
With a fresher death be kissed.'

Nothing happened. 'I've failed.' Elric muttered hopelessly as he met the attack of a snapping devil-dog and spitted the thing on his sword.

But then – the ground rocked and seemed to *seethe* beneath the feet of the horses upon whose backs the dead men sat. The tremor lasted a few seconds and then subsided.

'The spell was not powerful enough,' Elric sighed.

The earth trembled again and small craters formed in the ground of the hillside upon which the dead Lords of Dharzi impassively waited. Stones crumbled and the horses stamped nervously. Then the earth rumbled.

'Back!' yelled Elric warningly. 'Back – or we'll go with them!' They retreated – backing towards Shaarilla and their waiting horses as the ground sagged beneath their feet. The Dharzi mounts were rearing and snorting and the remaining dogs turned nervously to regard their masters with puzzled, uncertain eyes. A low moan was coming from the lips of the living dead. Suddenly, a whole area of the surrounding hillside split into cracks, and yawning crannies appeared in the surface. Elric and his companions swung themselves onto their horses as, with a frightful multivoiced scream, the dead lords were swallowed by the earth, returning to the depths from which they had been summoned.

A deep unholy chuckle arose from the shattered pit. It was the mocking laughter of the earth elemental King Grome, taking his rightful subjects back into his keeping. Whining, the devil-dogs slunk towards the edge of the pit, sniffing around it. Then, with one accord, the black pack hurled itself down into the chasm, following its masters to whatever unholy doom awaited it.

Moonglum shuddered. 'You are on familiar terms with the strangest people, friend Elric,' he said shakily and turned his horse towards the mountains again.

They reached the black mountains on the following day and nervously Shaarilla led them along the rocky route she had memorised. She no longer pleaded with Elric to return – she was resigned to whatever fate awaited them. Elric's obsession was burning within him and he was filled with impatience – certain that he would find, at last, the ultimate truth of existence in the Dead Gods' Book. Moonglum was cheerfully sceptical, while Shaarilla was consumed with foreboding.

Rain still fell and the storm growled and crackled above them. But, as the driving rainfall increased with fresh insistence, they came, at last, to the black, gaping mouth of a huge cave.

'I can lead you no further,' Shaarilla said wearily. 'The Book lies somewhere beyond the entrance to this cave.'

Elric and Moonglum looked uncertainly at one another, neither of them sure what move to make next. To have reached their goal seemed somehow anticlimactic – for nothing blocked the cave entrance – and nothing appeared to guard it.

'It is inconceivable,' said Elric, 'that the dangers which beset us were not engineered by something, yet here we are – and no-one seeks to stop us entering. Are you sure that this is the *right* cave, Shaarilla?'

The girl pointed upwards to the rock above the entrance. Engraved in it was a curious symbol which Elric instantly recognised.

'The Sign of Chaos!' Elric exclaimed. 'Perhaps I should have guessed.'

'What does it mean, Elric?' Moonglum asked.

'That is the symbol of everlasting disruption and anarchy,' Elric told him. 'We are standing in territory presided over by the Lords of Entropy or one of their minions. So that is who our enemy is! This can only mean one thing – the Book is of extreme importance to the order of things on this plane – possibly all the myriad planes of the multiverse. It was why Arioch was reluctant to aid me – he, too, is a Lord of Chaos!'

Moonglum stared at him in puzzlement. 'What do you mean, Elric?'

'Know you not that two forces govern the world – fighting an eternal battle?' Elric replied. 'Law and Chaos. The upholders of Chaos state that in such a world as they rule, all things are possible. Opponents of Chaos – those who ally themselves with the forces of Law – say that without Law *nothing* material is possible.

'Some stand apart, believing that a balance between the two is the proper state of things, but we cannot. We have become embroiled in a dispute between the two forces. The Book is valuable to either faction, obviously, and I could guess that the minions of Entropy are worried what power we might release if we obtain this book. Law and Chaos rarely interfere directly in Men's lives – that is why only adepts are fully aware of their presence. Now perhaps, I will discover at last the answer to the one question which concerns me – does an ultimate force rule over the opposing factions of Law and Chaos?'

Elric stepped through the cave entrance, peering into the gloom while the others hesitantly followed him.

'The cave stretches back a long way. All we can do is press on until we find its far wall,' Elric said.

'Let's hope that its far wall lies not *downwards*,' Moonglum said ironically as he motioned Elric to lead on.

They stumbled forward as the cave grew darker and darker. Their voices were magnified and hollow to their own ears as the floor of the cave slanted sharply down.

'This is no cave,' Elric whispered, 'it's a *tunnel* – but I cannot guess where it leads.'

For several hours they pressed onwards in pitch-darkness, clinging to one another as they reeled forward, uncertain of their footing and still aware that they were moving down a gradual incline. They lost all sense of time and Elric began to feel as if he were living through a dream. Events seemed to have become so unpredictable and beyond his control that he could no longer cope with thinking about them in ordinary terms. The tunnel was long and dark and wide and cold. It offered no comfort and the floor eventually became the only thing which had any reality. It was firmly beneath his feet. He began to feel that possibly he was not moving – that the floor, after all, was moving and he was remaining stationary. His companions clung to him but he was not aware of them. He was lost and his brain was numb. Sometimes he swayed and felt that he was on the edge of a precipice. Sometimes he fell and his groaning body met hard stone, disproving the proximity of the gulf down which he half-expected to fall.

All the while he made his legs perform walking motions, even though he was not at all sure whether he was actually moving forward. And time meant nothing – became a meaningless concept with relation to nothing.

Until, at last, he was aware of a faint, blue glow ahead of him and he knew that he had been moving forward. He began to run down the incline, but found that he was going too fast and had to check his speed. There was a scent of alien strangeness in the cool air of the cave tunnel and fear was a fluid force which surged over him, something separate from himself.

The others obviously felt it, too, for though they said nothing, Elric could sense it. Slowly they moved downward, drawn like automata towards the pale blue glow below them.

And then they were out of the tunnel, staring awestruck at the unearthly vision which confronted them. Above them, the very air seemed of the strange blue colour which had originally attracted them. They were standing on a jutting slab of rock and, although it was still somehow *dark*, the eery blue glow illuminated a stretch of glinting silver beach beneath them. And the beach was lapped by a surging dark sea which moved restlessly like a liquid giant in disturbed slumber. Scattered along the silver beach were the dim shapes of wrecks – the bones of peculiarly designed boats, each of a different pattern from the rest. The sea surged away into darkness and there was no horizon – only blackness. Behind them, they could see a sheer cliff which was also lost in darkness beyond a certain point. And it was cold – bitterly cold, with an unbelievable sharpness. For though the sea threshed beneath them, there was no dampness in the air – no smell of salt. It was a bleak and awesome sight and, apart from the sea, they were the only things that moved – the only things to make sound, for the sea was horribly silent in its restless movement.

'What now, Elric?' whispered Moonglum, shivering.

Elric shook his head and they continued to stand there for a long time until the albino – his white face and hands ghastly in the alien light said: 'Since it is impracticable to return – we shall venture over the sea.'

His voice was hollow and he spoke as one who was unaware of his words.

Steps, cut into the living rock, led down towards the beach and now Elric began to descend them. Staring around them, their eyes lit by a terrible fascination, the others allowed him to lead them.

Chapter Four

THEIR FEET PROFANED the silence as they reached the silver beach of crystalline stones and crunched across it. Elric's crimson eyes fixed upon one of the objects littering the beach and he smiled. He shook his head savagely from side to side, as if to clear it. Trembling, he pointed to one of the boats, and the pair saw that it was intact, unlike the others. It was yellow and red – vulgarly gay in this environment and nearing it they observed that it was made of wood, yet unlike any wood they had seen. Moonglum ran his stubby fingers along its length.

'Hard as iron,' he breathed. 'No wonder it has not rotted as the others have.' He peered inside and shuddered. 'Well the owner won't argue if we take it,' he said wryly.

Elric and Shaarilla understood him when they saw the unnaturally twisted skeleton which lay at the bottom of the boat. Elric reached inside and pulled the thing out, hurling it on the stones. It rattled and rolled over the gleaming shingle, disintegrating as it did so, scattering bones over a wide area. The skull came to rest by the edge of the beach, seeming to stare sightlessly out over the disturbing ocean.

As Elric and Moonglum strove to push and pull the boat down the beach towards the sea, Shaarilla moved ahead of them and squatted down, putting her hand into the wetness. She stood up sharply, shaking the stuff from her hand.

'This is not water as I know it,' she said. They heard her, but said nothing.

'We'll need a sail,' Elric murmured. The cold breeze was moving out over the ocean. 'A cloak should serve.' He stripped off his cloak and knotted it to the mast of the vessel. 'Two of us will have to hold this at either edge,' he said. 'That way we'll have some slight control over the direction the boat takes. It's makeshift – but the best we can manage.'

They shoved off, taking care not to get their feet in the sea.

The wind caught the sail and pushed the boat out over the ocean, moving at a faster pace than Elric had at first reckoned. The boat began to hurtle forward as if possessed of its own volition and Elric's and Moonglum's muscles ached as they clung to the bottom ends of the sail.

Soon the silver beach was out of sight and they could see little – the pale blue light above them scarcely penetrating the blackness. It was then that they heard the dry flap of wings over their heads and looked up.

Silently descending were three massive apelike creatures, borne on great leathery wings. Shaarilla recognised them and gasped.

'Clakars!'

Moonglum shrugged as he hurriedly drew his sword – 'A name only – what are they?' But he received no answer for the leading winged ape descended with a rush, mouthing and gibbering, showing long fangs in a slavering snout. Moonglum dropped his portion of the sail and slashed at the beast but it veered away, its huge wings beating, and sailed upwards again.

Elric unsheathed Stormbringer – and was astounded. The blade remained silent, its familiar howl of glee muted. The blade shuddered in his hand and instead of the rush of power which usually flowed up his arm, he felt only a slight tingling. He was panic-stricken for a moment – without the sword, he would soon lose all vitality. Grimly fighting down his fear, he used the sword to protect himself from the rushing attack of one of the winged apes.

The ape gripped the blade, bowling Elric over, but it yelled in pain as the blade cut through one knotted hand, severing fingers which lay twitching and bloody on the narrow deck. Elric held tight to the side of the boat and hauled himself upright once more. Shrilling its agony, the winged ape attacked again, but this time with more caution. Elric summoned all his strength and swung the heavy sword in a two-handed grip, ripping off one of the leathery wings so that the mutilated beast flopped about the deck. Judging the place where its heart should be, Elric drove the blade in under the breastbone. The ape's movements subsided.

Moonglum was lashing wildly at two of the winged apes which were attacking him from both sides. He was down on one knee, vainly hacking at random. He had opened up the whole side of a beast's head but, though in pain, it still came at him. Elric hurled Stormbringer through the darkness and it struck the wounded beast in the throat, point first. The ape clutched with clawing fingers at the steel and fell overboard. Its corpse floated on the liquid but slowly began to sink. Elric grabbed with frantic fingers at the hilt of his sword, reaching far over the side of the boat. Incredibly, the blade was sinking with the beast; knowing Stormbringer's properties as he did, Elric was amazed. Now it was being dragged beneath the surface as any ordinary blade would be dragged. He gripped the hilt and hauled the sword out of the winged ape's carcass.

His strength was seeping swiftly from him. It was incredible. What alien laws governed this cavern world? He could not guess – and all he was concerned with was regaining his waning strength. Without the runesword's power, that was impossible!

Moonglum's curved blade had disembowelled the remaining beast and the little man was busily tossing the dead thing over the side. He turned, grinning triumphantly, to Elric.

'A good fight,' he said.

Elric shook his head. 'We must cross this sea speedily,' he replied, 'else we're lost – finished. My power is gone.'

'How? Why?'

'I know not – unless the forces of Entropy rule more strongly here. Make haste – there is no time for speculation.'

Moonglum's eyes were disturbed. He could do nothing but act as Elric said.

Elric was trembling in his weakness, holding the billowing sail with draining strength. Shaarilla moved to help him, her thin hands close to his, her deep-set eyes bright with sympathy.

'What *were* those things?' Moonglum gasped, his teeth naked and white beneath his back-drawn lips, his breath coming short.

'Clakars,' Shaarilla replied. 'They are the primeval ancestors of my people, older in origin than recorded time. My people are thought the oldest inhabitants of this planet.'

'Whoever seeks to stop us in this quest of yours had best find some – original means.' Moonglum grinned. 'The old methods don't work.' But the other two did not smile, for Elric was half-fainting and the woman was concerned only with his plight. Moonglum shrugged, staring ahead.

When he spoke again, sometime later, his voice was excited. 'We're nearing land!'

Land it was, and they were travelling fast towards it. Too fast. Elric heaved himself upright and spoke heavily and with difficulty. 'Drop the sail!' Moonglum obeyed him. The boat sped on, struck another stretch of silver beach and ground up it, the prow ploughing a dark scar through the glinting shingle. It stopped suddenly, tilting violently to one side so that the three were tumbled against the boat's rail.

Shaarilla and Moonglum pulled themselves upright and dragged the limp and nerveless albino onto the beach. Carrying him between them, they struggled up the beach until the crystalline shingle gave way to thick, fluffy moss, padding their footfalls. They laid the albino down and stared at him worriedly, uncertain of their next actions.

Elric strained to rise, but was unable to do so. 'Give me time,' he gasped. 'I won't die – but already my eyesight is fading. I can only hope that the blade's power will return on dry land.'

With a mighty effort, he pulled Stormbringer from its scabbard and he smiled in relief as the evil runesword moaned faintly and then, slowly, its song increased in power as black flame flickered along its length. Already the power was flowing into Elric's body, giving him renewed vitality. But even as strength returned, Elric's crimson eyes flared with terrible misery.

'Without this black blade,' he groaned, 'I am nothing, as you see. But what is it making of me? Am I to be bound to it for ever?'

The others did not answer him and they were both moved by

an emotion they could not define – an emotion blended of fear, hate and pity – linked with something else...

Eventually, Elric rose, trembling, and silently led them up the mossy hillside towards a more natural light which filtered from above. They could see that it came from a wide chimney, leading apparently to the upper air. By means of the light, they could soon make out a dark, irregular shape which towered in the shadow of the gap.

As they neared the shape, they saw that it was a castle of black stone – a sprawling pile covered with dark green crawling lichen which curled over its ancient bulk with an almost sentient protectiveness. Towers appeared to spring at random from it and it covered a vast area. There seemed to be no windows in any part of it and the only orifice was a rearing doorway blocked by thick bars of a metal which glowed with dull redness, but without heat. Above this gate, in flaring amber, was the Sign of the Lords of Entropy, representing eight arrows radiating from a central hub in all directions. It appeared to hang in the air without touching the black, lichen-covered stone.

'I think our quest ends here,' Elric said grimly. 'Here, or nowhere.'

'Before I go further, Elric, I'd like to know what it is you seek,' Moonglum murmured. 'I think I've earned the right.'

'A book,' Elric said carelessly. 'The Dead Gods' Book. It lies within those castle walls – of that I'm certain. We have reached the end of our journey.'

Moonglum shrugged. 'I might not have asked,' he smiled, 'for all your words mean to me. I hope that I will be allowed some small share of whatever treasure it represents.'

Elric grinned, in spite of the coldness which gripped his bowels, but he did not answer Moonglum.

'We need to enter the castle, first,' he said instead.

As if the gates had heard him, the metal bars flared to a pale green and then their glow faded back to red and finally dulled into non-existence. The entrance was unbarred and their way apparently clear.

'I like not *that*,' growled Moonglum. 'Too easy. A trap awaits us – are we to spring it at the pleasure of whoever dwells within the castle confines?'

'What else can we do?' Elric spoke quietly.

'Go back – or forward. Avoid the castle – do not tempt He who guards the Book!' Shaarilla was gripping the albino's right arm, her whole face moving with fear, her eyes pleading. 'Forget the Book, Elric!'

'*Now?*' Elric laughed humourlessly. 'Now – after this journey? No, Shaarilla, not when the truth is so close. Better to die than never to have tried to secure the wisdom in the Book when it lies so near.'

Shaarilla's clutching fingers relaxed their grip and her shoulders slumped in hopelessness. 'We cannot do battle with the minions of Entropy...'

'Perhaps we will not have to.' Elric did not believe his own words but his mouth was twisted with some dark emotion, intense and terrible. Moonglum glanced at Shaarilla.

'Shaarilla is right,' he said with conviction. 'You'll find nothing but bitterness, possibly death, inside those castle walls. Let us, instead, climb yonder steps and attempt to reach the surface.' He pointed to some twisting steps which led towards the yawning rent in the cavern roof.

Elric shook his head. 'No. You go if you like.'

Moonglum grimaced in perplexity. 'You're a stubborn one, friend Elric. Well, if it's all or nothing – then I'm with you. But personally, I have always preferred compromise.'

Elric began to walk slowly forward towards the dark entrance of the bleak and towering castle.

In a wide, shadowy courtyard a tall figure, wreathed in scarlet fire, stood awaiting them.

Elric marched on, passing the gateway. Moonglum and Shaarilla nervously followed.

Gusty laughter roared from the mouth of the giant and the scarlet fire fluttered about him. He was naked and unarmed, but the power which flowed from him almost forced the three back. His skin was scaly and of smoky purple colouring. His massive body was alive with rippling muscle as he rested lightly on the balls of his feet. His skull was long, slanting sharply backwards at the forehead and his eyes were like slivers of blue steel, showing no pupil. His whole body shook with mighty, malicious joy.

'Greetings to you, Lord Elric of Melniboné – I congratulate you for your remarkable tenacity!'

'Who are you?' Elric growled, his hand on his sword.

'My name is Orunlu the Keeper and this is a stronghold of the Lords of Entropy.' The giant smiled cynically. *'You need not finger your puny blade so nervously, for you should know that I cannot harm you now. I gained power to remain in your realm only by making a vow.'*

Elric's voice betrayed his mounting excitement. 'You cannot stop us?'

'I do not dare to – since my oblique efforts have failed. But your foolish endeavours perplex me somewhat, I'll admit. The Book is of importance to us – but what can it mean to you? I have guarded it for three hundred centuries and have never been curious enough to seek to discover why my Masters place so much importance upon it – why they bothered to rescue it on its sunward course and incarcerate it on this boring ball of earth populated by the capering, briefly lived clowns called Men.'

'I seek in it the Truth,' Elric said guardedly.

'There is no Truth but that of Eternal struggle,' the scarlet-flamed giant said with conviction.

'What rules above the forces of Law and Chaos?' Elric asked. 'What controls your destinies as it controls mine?'

The giant frowned.

'That question, I cannot answer. I do not know. There is only the Balance.'

'Then perhaps the Book will tell us who holds it.' Elric said purposely. 'Let me pass – tell me where it lies.'

The giant moved back, smiling ironically. *'It lies in a small chamber in the central tower. I have sworn never to venture there, otherwise I might even lead the way. Go if you like – my duty is over.'*

Elric, Moonglum and Shaarilla stepped towards the entrance of the castle, but before they entered, the giant spoke warningly from behind them.

'I have been told that the knowledge contained in the Book could swing the Balance on the side of the forces of Law. This disturbs me – but, it appears, there is another possibility which disturbs me even more.'

'What is that?' Elric said.

'It could create such a tremendous impact on the multiverse that complete entropy would result. My Masters do not desire that – for it could mean the destruction of all matter in the end. We exist only to fight – not to win, but to preserve the eternal struggle.'

'I care not,' Elric told him. 'I have little to lose, Orunlu the Keeper.'

'*Then go.*' The giant strode across the courtyard into blackness.

Inside the tower, light of a pale quality illuminated winding steps leading upwards. Elric began to climb them in silence, moved by his own doom-filled purpose. Hesitantly, Moonglum and Shaarilla followed in his path, their faces set in hopeless acceptance.

On and upward the steps mounted, twisting tortuously towards their goal, until at last they came to the chamber, full of blinding light, many-coloured and scintillating, which did not penetrate outwards at all but remained confined to the room which housed it.

Blinking, shielding his red eyes with his arm, Elric pressed forward, and through slitted pupils saw the source of the light lying on a small stone dais in the centre of the room.

Equally troubled by the bright light, Shaarilla and Moonglum followed him into the room and stood in awe at what they saw.

It was a huge book – the Dead Gods' Book, its covers encrusted with alien gems from which the light sprang. It gleamed, it *throbbed* with light and brilliant colour.

'At last,' Elric breathed. 'At last – the Truth!'

He stumbled forward like a man made stupid with drink, his pale hands reaching for the thing he had sought with such savage bitterness. His hands touched the pulsating cover of the Book and, trembling, turned it back.

'Now, I shall learn,' he said, half-gloatingly.

With a crash, the cover fell to the floor, sending the bright gems skipping and dancing over the paving stones.

Beneath Elric's twitching hands lay nothing but a pile of yellowish dust.

'No!' His scream was anguished, unbelieving. 'No!' Tears flowed down his contorted face as he ran his hands through the fine dust. With a groan which racked his whole being, he fell forward, his face hitting the disintegrated parchment. Time had destroyed the Book – untouched, possibly forgotten, for three hundred centuries. Even the wise and powerful gods who had created it had perished – and now its knowledge followed them into oblivion.

They stood on the slopes of the high mountain, staring down into the green valleys below them. The sun shone and the sky was clear and blue. Behind them lay the gaping hole which led into the stronghold of the Lords of Entropy.

Elric looked with sad eyes across the world and his head was lowered beneath a weight of weariness and dark despair. He had not spoken since his companions had dragged him sobbing from the chamber of the Book. Now he raised his pale face and spoke in a voice tinged with self-mockery, sharp with bitterness – a lonely voice: the calling of hungry seabirds circling cold skies above bleak shores.

'Now,' he said, 'I will live my life without ever knowing why I live it – whether it has purpose or not. Perhaps the Book could have told me. But would I have believed it, even then? I am the eternal sceptic – never *sure* that my actions are my own, never certain that an ultimate entity is not guiding me.

'I envy those who know. All I can do now is to continue my quest and hope, without hope, that before my span is ended, the truth will be presented to me.'

Shaarilla took his limp hands in hers and her eyes were wet.

'Elric – let me comfort you.'

The albino sneered bitterly. 'Would that we'd never met, Shaarilla of the Dancing Mist. For a while, you gave me hope – I had thought to be at last at peace with myself. But, because of you, I am left more hopeless than before. There is no salvation in this world – only malevolent doom. Goodbye.'

He took his hands away from her grasp and set off down the mountainside.

Moonglum darted a glance at Shaarilla and then at Elric. He took something from his purse and put it in the girl's hand.

'Good luck,' he said, and then he was running after Elric until he caught him up.

Still striding, Elric turned at Moonglum's approach and despite his brooding misery said: 'What is it, friend Moonglum? Why do you follow me?'

'I've followed you thus far, Master Elric, and I see no reason to stop,' grinned the little man. 'Besides, unlike yourself, I'm a materialist. We'll need to eat, you know.'

Elric frowned, feeling a warmth growing within him. 'What do you mean, Moonglum?'

Moonglum chuckled. 'I take advantage of situations of any kind, where I may,' he answered. He reached into his purse and displayed something on his outstretched hand which shone with a dazzling brilliancy. It was one of the jewels from the cover of the Book. 'There are more in my purse,' he said, 'And each one worth a fortune.' He took Elric's arm.

'Come Elric – what new lands shall we visit so that we may change these baubles into wine and pleasant company?'

Behind them, standing stock-still on the hillside, Shaarilla stared miserably after them until they were no longer visible. The jewel Moonglum had given her dropped from her fingers and fell, bouncing and bright, until it was lost amongst the heather. Then she turned – and the dark mouth of the cavern yawned before her.

The Singing Citadel

Chapter One

THE TURQUOISE SEA was peaceful in the golden light of early evening, and the two men at the rail of the ship stood in silence, looking north to the misty horizon. One was tall and slim, wrapped in a heavy black cloak, its cowl flung back to reveal his long, milk-white hair; the other was short and red-headed.

'She was a fine woman and she loved you,' said the short man at length. 'Why did you leave her so abruptly?'

'She was a fine woman,' the tall one replied, 'but she would have loved me to her cost. Let her seek her own land and stay there. I have already slain one woman whom I loved, Moonglum. I would not slay another.'

Moonglum shrugged. 'I sometimes wonder, Elric, if this grim destiny of yours is the figment of your own guilt-ridden mood.'

'Perhaps,' Elric replied carelessly. 'But I do not care to test the theory. Let's speak no more of this.'

The sea foamed and rushed by as the oars disrupted the surface, driving the ship swiftly towards the port of Dhakos, capital of Jharkor, one of the most powerful of the Young Kingdoms. Less than two years previously Jharkor's king, Dharmit, had died in the ill-fated raid on Imrryr, and Elric had heard that the men of Jharkor blamed him for the king's death, though this was not the case. He cared little whether they blamed him or not, for he was still disdainful of the greater part of mankind.

'Another hour will see nightfall, and it's unlikely we'll sail at night,' Moonglum said. 'I'll to bed, I think.'

Elric was about to reply when he was interrupted by a high-pitched shout from the crow's nest.

'Sail on larboard stern!'

The lookout must have been half asleep, for the ship bearing down on them could easily be made out from the deck. Elric stepped aside as the captain, a dark-faced Tarkeshite, came running along the deck.

'What's the ship, captain?' called Moonglum.

'A Pan Tang trireme – a warship. They're on ramming course.' The captain ran on, yelling orders to the helm to turn the ship aside.

Elric and Moonglum crossed the deck to see the trireme better. She was a black-sailed ship, painted black and heavily gilded, with three rowers to an oar as against their two. She was big and yet elegant, with a high curving stern and a low prow. Now they could see the waters broken by her big, brass-sheathed ram. She had two lateen-rigged sails, and the wind was in her favour.

The rowers were in a panic as they sweated to turn the ship according to the helmsman's orders. Oars rose and fell in confusion and Moonglum turned to Elric with a half-smile.

'They'll never do it. Best ready your blade, friend.'

Pan Tang was an isle of sorcerers, fully human, who sought to emulate the old power of Melniboné. Their fleets were among the best in the Young Kingdoms and raided with little discrimination. The Theocrat of Pan Tang, chief of the priest-aristocracy, was Jagreen Lern, who was reputed to have a pact with the powers of Chaos and a plan to rule the world.

Elric regarded the men of Pan Tang as upstarts who could never hope to mirror the glory of his ancestors, but even he had to admit that this ship was impressive and would easily win a fight with the Tarkeshite galley.

Soon the great trireme was bearing down on them and captain and helmsman fell silent as they realised they could not evade the ram. With a harsh sound of crushed timbers, the ram connected with the stern, holing the galley beneath the waterline.

Elric stood immobile, watching as the trireme's grappling irons hurtled towards their galley's deck. Somewhat half-heartedly, knowing they were no match for the well-trained and well-armoured Pan Tang crew, the Tarkeshites ran towards the stern, preparing to resist the boarders.

Moonglum cried urgently: 'Elric – we must help!'

Reluctantly Elric nodded. He was loathe to draw the runesword from its scabbard at his side. Of late its power seemed to have increased.

Now the scarlet-armoured warriors were swinging towards the waiting Tarkeshites. The first wave, armed with broadswords and battle-axes, hit the sailors, driving them back.

Now Elric's hand fell to the hilt of Stormbringer. As he gripped it and drew it, the blade gave an odd, disturbing moan, as if of anticipation, and a weird black radiance flickered along its length. Now it throbbed in Elric's hand like something alive as the albino ran forward to aid the Tarkeshite sailors.

Already half the defenders had been hewed down and as the rest retreated, Elric, with Moonglum at his heels, moved forward. The scarlet-armoured warriors' expressions changed from grim triumph to startlement as Elric's great black blade shrieked up and down and clove through a man's armour from shoulder to lower ribs.

Evidently they recognised him and the sword, for both were legendary. Though Moonglum was a skilled swordsman, they all but ignored him as they realised that they must concentrate all their strength on bringing Elric down if they were to survive.

The old, wild killing-lust of his ancestors now dominated Elric as the blade reaped souls. He and the sword became one and it was the sword, not Elric, that was in control. Men fell on all sides, screaming more in horror than in pain as they realised what the sword had drawn from them. Four came at him with axes whistling. He sliced off one's head, cut a deep gash in another's midriff, lopped off an arm and drove the blade point first into the heart of the last. Now the Tarkeshites were cheering, following after Elric and Moonglum as they cleared the sinking galley's decks of attackers.

Howling like a wolf, Elric grabbed a rope – part of the black-and-golden trireme's rigging – and swung towards the enemy's decks.

'Follow him!' Moonglum yelled. 'This is our only chance – this ship's doomed!'

The trireme had raised decks fore and aft. On the foredeck stood the captain, splendid in scarlet and blue, his face aghast at this turn of events. He had expected to get his prize effortlessly; now it seemed *he* was to be the prize!

Stormbringer sang a wailing song as Elric pressed towards the foredeck, a song that was at once triumphant and ecstatic. The remaining warriors no longer rushed at him, and concentrated on Moonglum, who was leading the Tarkeshite crew, leaving Elric's path to the captain clear.

The captain, a member of the theocracy, would be harder to vanquish than his men. As Elric moved towards him, he noted that the man's armour had a peculiar glow to it – it had been sorcerously treated.

The captain was typical of his kind – stocky, heavily bearded, with malicious black eyes over a strong, hooked nose. His lips were thick and red and he was smiling a little as, with axe in one hand and sword in the other, he prepared to meet Elric, who was running up the steps.

Elric gripped Stormbringer in both hands and lunged for the captain's stomach, but the man stepped sideways and parried with his sword, swinging the axe left-handed at Elric's unprotected head. The albino had to sway to one side, staggered and fell to the deck, rolling as the broadsword thudded into the deck, just missing his shoulder. Stormbringer seemed to rise of its own accord to block a further axe blow and then chopped upwards to shear off the head near the handle. The captain cursed and discarded the handle, gripped his broadsword in both hands and raised it. Again Stormbringer acted a fraction sooner than Elric's own reactions. He drove the blade up towards the man's heart. The magic-treated armour stopped it for a second; but then Stormbringer shrilled a chilling, wailing song, shuddered as if summoning more strength, slipped on the armour again. And then the magic armour split like a nutshell, leaving Elric's opponent bare-chested, his arms still raised for the strike. His eyes widened. He backed away, his sword forgotten, his gaze fixed on the evil runeblade as it struck him under the breastbone and drove in. He grimaced, whimpered, and dropped his sword, clutching instead at the blade, which was sucking out his soul.

'By Chardros – not – not – aahhh!'

He died knowing that even his soul was not safe from the hell-blade borne by the wolf-faced albino.

Elric wrenched Stormbringer from the corpse, feeling his own vitality increase as the sword passed on its stolen energy, refusing to consider the knowledge that the more he used the sword, the more he needed it.

On the deck of the trireme, only the galley-slaves were left alive. But the deck was tilting badly, for the trireme's ram and grapples still tied it to the sinking Tarkeshite ship.

'Cut the grappling ropes and back water – quickly!' Elric yelled. Sailors, realising what was happening, leapt forward to do as he ordered. The slaves backed water, and the ram came out with a groan of split wood. The grapples were cut and the doomed galley set adrift.

Elric counted the survivors. Less than half the crew were alive, and their captain had died in the first onslaught. He addressed the slaves.

'If you'd have your freedom, row well towards Dhakos,' he called. The sun was setting, but now that he was in command he decided to sail through the night by the stars.

Moonglum shouted incredulously: 'Why offer them their freedom? We could sell them in Dhakos and thus be paid for today's exertion!'

Elric shrugged. 'I offer them freedom because I choose to, Moonglum.'

The redhead sighed and turned to supervise the throwing of the dead and wounded overboard. He would never understand the albino, he decided. It was probably for the best.

And that was how Elric came to enter Dhakos in some style, when he had originally intended to slip into the city without being recognised.

Leaving Moonglum to negotiate the sale of the trireme and divide the money between the crew and himself, Elric drew his hood over his head and pushed through the crowd which had collected, making for an inn he knew of by the west gate of the city.

Chapter Two

LATER THAT NIGHT, when Moonglum had gone to bed, Elric sat in the tavern room drinking. Even the most enthusiastic of the night's roisterers had left when they had noticed with whom they shared the room; and now Elric sat alone, the only light coming from a guttering reed torch over the outside door.

Now the door opened and a richly dressed youth stood there, staring in.

'I seek the White Wolf,' he said, his head at a questioning angle. He could not see Elric clearly.

'I'm sometimes called that name in these parts,' Elric said calmly. 'Do you seek Elric of Melniboné?'

'Aye. I have a message.' The youth came in, keeping his cloak wrapped about him, for the room was cold though Elric did not notice it.

'I am Count Yolan, deputy-commander of the city guard,' the youth said arrogantly, coming up to the table at which Elric sat and studying the albino rudely. 'You are brave to come here so openly. Do you think the folk of Jharkor have such short memories they can forget that you led their king into a trap scarce two years since?'

Elric sipped his wine, then said from behind the rim of his cup: 'This is rhetoric, Count Yolan. What is your message?'

Yolan's assured manner left him; he made a rather weak gesture. 'Rhetoric to you, perhaps – but I for one feel strongly on the matter. Would not King Dharmit be here today if you had not fled from the battle that broke the power of the sea-lords and your own folk? Did you not use your sorcery to aid you in your flight, instead of using it to aid the men who thought they were your comrades?'

Elric sighed. 'I know your purpose here was not to bait me in this manner. Dharmit died on board his flagship during the first attack on Imrryr's sea-maze, not in the subsequent battle.'

'You sneer at my questions and then proffer lame lies to cover your own cowardly deed,' Yolan said bitterly. 'If I had my way you'd be fed to your hellblade there – I've heard what happened earlier.'

Elric rose slowly. 'Your taunts tire me. When you feel ready to deliver your message, give it to the innkeeper.'

He walked around the table, moving towards the stairs, but stopped as Yolan turned and plucked at his sleeve.

Elric's corpse-white face stared down at the young noble. His crimson eyes flickered with a dangerous emotion. 'I'm not used to such familiarity, young man.'

Yolan's hand fell away. 'Forgive me. I was self-indulgent and should not have let my emotions override diplomacy. I came on a matter of discretion – a message from Queen Yishana. She seeks your help.'

'I'm as disinclined to help others as I am to explain my actions,' Elric spoke impatiently. 'In the past my help has not always been to the advantage of those who've sought it. Dharmit, your queen's half-brother, discovered that.'

Yolan said sullenly: 'You echo my own warnings to the queen, sir. For all that, she desires to see you in private – tonight...' He scowled and looked away. 'I would point out that I could have you arrested should you refuse.'

'Perhaps.' Elric moved again towards the steps. 'Tell Yishana that I stay the night here and move on at dawn. She may visit me if her request is so urgent.' He climbed the stairs, leaving a gape-mouthed Yolan sitting alone in the quiet of the tavern.

Theleb K'aarna scowled. For all his skill in the black arts, he was a fool in love; and Yishana, sprawled on her fur-rich bed, knew it. It pleased her to have power over a man who could destroy her with a simple incantation if it were not for his love-weakness. Though Theleb K'aarna stood high in the hierarchy of Pan Tang, it was clear to her that she was in no danger from the sorcerer. Indeed, her intuition informed her that this man who loved to dominate others also needed to be dominated. She filled this need for him – with relish.

Theleb K'aarna continued to scowl at her. 'How can that decadent spell-singer help you where I cannot?' he muttered, sitting down on the bed and stroking her bejewelled foot.

Yishana was not a young woman, neither was she pretty. Yet there was an hypnotic quality about her tall, full body, her lush black hair and her wholly sensuous face. Few of the men she had singled out for her pleasure had been able to resist her.

Neither was she sweet-natured, just, wise, nor self-sacrificing. The historians would append no noble soubriquet to her name. Still, there was something so self-sufficient about her, something denying the usual standards by which a person was judged, that all who knew her admired her, and she was well-loved by those she ruled – loved rather as a wilful child is loved, yet loved with firm loyalty.

Now she laughed quietly, mockingly at her sorcerer lover.

'You're probably right, Theleb K'aarna, but Elric is a legend – the most spoken-of, least-known man in the world. This is my opportunity to discover what others have only speculated on – his true character.'

Theleb K'aarna made a pettish gesture. He stroked his long black beard and got up, walking to a table bearing fruit and wine. He poured wine for them both. 'If you seek to make me jealous again, you are succeeding, of course. I hold little hope for your ambition. Elric's ancestors were half-demons – his race is not human and cannot be judged by our yardsticks. To us, sorcery is learned after years of study and sacrifice – to Elric's kind, sorcery is intuitive – natural. You may not live to learn his secrets. Cymoril, his beloved cousin, died on his blade – and she was his betrothed!'

'Your concern is touching.' She lazily accepted the goblet he handed to her. 'But I'll continue with my plan, nonetheless. After all, you can hardly claim to have had much success in discovering the nature of this citadel!'

'There are subtleties I have not properly plumbed as yet!'

'Then perhaps Elric's intuition will provide answers where you fail,' she smiled. Then she got up and looked through the window where the full moon hung in a clear sky over the spires of Dhakos. 'Yolan is late. If all went properly, he should have brought Elric here by now.'

'Yolan was a mistake. You should not have sent such a close friend of Dharmit's. For all we know, he's challenged Elric and killed him!'

Again she couldn't resist laughter. 'Oh, you wish too hard – it clouds your reason. I sent Yolan because I knew he would be rude to the albino and perhaps weaken his usual insouciance – arouse his curiosity. Yolan was a kind of bait to bring Elric to us!'

'Then possibly Elric sensed this?'

'I am not overly intelligent, my love – but I think my instincts rarely betray me. We shall see soon.'

A little later there was a discreet scratch at the door and a handmaiden entered.

'Your Highness, Count Yolan has returned.'

'Only Count Yolan?' There was a smile on Theleb K'aarna's face. It was to disappear in a short while as Yishana left the room, garbed for the street.

'You are a fool!' he snarled as the door slammed. He flung down his goblet. Already he had been unsuccessful in the matter of the citadel and, if Elric displaced him, he could lose everything. He began to think very deeply, very carefully.

Chapter Three

THOUGH HE CLAIMED lack of conscience, Elric's tormented eyes belied the claim as he sat at his window, drinking strong wine and thinking on the past. Since the sack of Imrryr, he had quested the world, seeking some purpose to his existence, some meaning to his life.

He had failed to find the answer in the Dead Gods' Book. He had failed to love Shaarilla, the wingless woman of Myyrrhn, failed to forget Cymoril, who still inhabited his nightmares. And there were memories of other dreams – of a fate he dare not think upon.

Peace, he thought, was all he sought. Yet even peace in death was denied him. It was in this mood that he continued to brood until his reverie was broken by a soft scratching at the door.

Immediately his expression hardened. His crimson eyes took on a guarded look, his shoulders lifted so that when he stood up he was all cool arrogance. He placed the cup on the table and said lightly:

'Enter!'

A woman entered, swathed in a dark red cloak, unrecognisable in the gloom of the room. She closed the door behind her and stood there, motionless and unspeaking.

When at length she spoke, her voice was almost hesitant, though there was some irony in it, too.

'You sit in darkness, Lord Elric, I had thought to find you asleep...'

'Sleep, madam, is the occupation that bores me most. But I will light a torch if you find the darkness unattractive.' He went to the table and removed the cover from the small bowl of charcoal which lay there. He reached for a thin wooden spill and placed one end in the bowl, blowing gently. Soon the charcoal glowed and the taper caught, and he touched it to a reed torch that hung in a bracket on the wall above the table.

The torch flared and sent shadows skipping around the small chamber. The woman drew back her cowl and the light caught her dark, heavy features and the masses of black hair which framed them. She contrasted strongly with the slender, aesthetic albino who stood a head taller, looking at her impassively.

She was unused to impassive looks and the novelty pleased her.

'You sent for me, Lord Elric – and you see I am here.' She made a mock curtsey.

'Queen Yishana,' he acknowledged the curtsey with a slight bow. Now that she confronted him, she sensed his power – a power that perhaps attracted even more strongly than her own. And yet, he gave no hint that he responded to her. She reflected that a situation she had expected to be interesting might, ironically, become frustrating. Even this amused her.

Elric, in turn, was intrigued by this woman in spite of himself. His jaded emotions hinted that Yishana might restore their edge. This excited him and perturbed him at once.

He relaxed a little and shrugged. 'I have heard of you, Queen Yishana, in other lands than Jharkor. Sit down if you wish.' He indicated a bench and seated himself on the edge of the bed.

'You are more courteous than your summons suggested.' She smiled as she sat down, crossed her legs and folded her arms in front of her. 'Does this mean that you will listen to a proposition I have?'

He smiled back. It was a rare smile for him, a little grim, but without the usual bitterness. 'I think so. You are an unusual woman, Queen Yishana. Indeed, I would suspect that you had Melnibonéan blood if I did not know better.'

'Not all your Young Kingdom "upstarts" are quite as unsophisticated as you believe, my lord.'

'Perhaps.'

'Now that I see you at last, face to face, I find your dark legend a little hard to credit in parts – and yet, on the other hand,' she put her head on one side and regarded him frankly, 'it would seem that the legends speak of a less subtle man than the one I see before me.'

'That is the way with legends.'

'Ah,' she half-whispered, 'what a force we could be together, you and I...'

'Speculation of that sort irritates me, Queen Yishana. What is your purpose in coming here?'

'Very well, I did not expect you to listen, even.'

'I'll listen – but expect nothing more.'

'Then listen. I think the story will be appreciated, even by you.'

Elric listened and, as Yishana had suspected, the tale she told began to catch his interest...

Several months ago, Yishana told Elric, peasants in the Gharavian province of Jharkor began to talk of some mysterious riders who were carrying off young men and women from the villages.

Suspecting bandits, Yishana had sent a detachment of her White Leopards, Jharkor's finest fighting men, to the province to put down the brigands.

None of the White Leopards had returned. A second expedition had found no trace of them but, in a valley close to the town of Thokora, they had come upon a strange citadel. Descriptions of the citadel were confused. Suspecting that the White Leopards had attacked and been defeated, the officer in charge had used discretion, left a few men to watch the citadel and report anything they saw, and returned at once to Dhakos. One thing was certain – the citadel had not been in the valley a few months before.

Yishana and Theleb K'aarna had led a large force to the valley. The men left behind had disappeared but, as soon as he saw the citadel, Theleb K'aarna had warned Yishana not to attack.

'It was a marvellous sight, Lord Elric,' Yishana continued. 'The citadel scintillated with shining, rainbow colours – colours that were constantly altering, changing. The whole building looked unreal – sometimes it stood out sharply; sometimes it seemed misty, as if about to vanish. Theleb K'aarna said its nature was sorcerous, and we did not doubt him. Something from the Realm of Chaos, he said, and that seemed likely.' She got up.

She spread her hands. 'We are not used to large-scale manifestations of sorcery in these parts. Theleb K'aarna was familiar enough with sorcery – he comes from the City of Screaming Statues on Pan Tang, and such things are seen frequently – but even he was taken aback.'

'So you withdrew,' Elric prompted impatiently.

'We were about to – in fact Theleb K'aarna and myself were already riding back at the head of the army when the music came... It was sweet, beautiful, unearthly, painful – Theleb K'aarna shouted to me to ride as swiftly as I could away from it. I dallied, attracted by the music, but he slapped the rump of my horse and we rode, fast as dragons in flight, away from there. Those nearest us also escaped – but we saw the rest turn and move back towards the citadel, drawn by the music. Nearly two hundred men went back – and vanished.'

'What did you do then?' Elric asked as Yishana crossed the floor and sat down beside him. He moved to give her more room.

'Theleb K'aarna has been trying to investigate the nature of the citadel – its purpose and its controller. So far, his divinations have told him little more than he guessed: that the Realm of Chaos has sent the citadel to the Realm of Earth and is slowly extending its range. More and more of our young men and women are being abducted by the minions of Chaos.'

'And these minions?' Yishana had moved a little closer, and this time Elric did not move away.

'None who has sought to stop them has succeeded – few have lived.'

'And what do you seek of me?'

'Help.' She looked closely into his face and reached out a hand to touch him. 'You have knowledge of both Chaos and Law – old knowledge, instinctive knowledge if Theleb K'aarna is right. Why, your very gods are Lords of Chaos.'

'That is exactly true, Yishana – and because our patron gods are of Chaos, it is not in my interest to fight against any one of them.'

Now he moved towards her and he was smiling, looking into her eyes. Suddenly, he took her in his arms. 'Perhaps you will be strong enough,' he said enigmatically, just before their lips met. 'And as for the other matter – we can discuss that later.'

In the deep greenness of a dark mirror, Theleb K'aarna saw something of the scene in Elric's room and he glowered impotently. He tugged at his beard as the scene faded for the tenth time in a minute. None of his mutterings could restore it. He sat back in his chair of serpent skulls and planned vengeance. That vengeance could take time maturing, he decided; for, if Elric could be useful in the matter of the citadel, there was no point in destroying him yet...

Chapter Four

NEXT AFTERNOON, THREE riders set off for the town of Thokora. Elric and Yishana rode close together; but the third rider, Theleb K'aarna, kept a frowning distance. If Elric was at all embarrassed by this display on the part of the man he had ousted in Yishana's affections, he did not show it.

Elric, finding Yishana more than attractive in spite of himself, had agreed at least to inspect the citadel and suggest what it might be and how it might be fought. He had exchanged a few words with Moonglum before setting off.

They rode across the beautiful grasslands of Jharkor, golden beneath a hot sun. It was two days' ride to Thokora, and Elric intended to enjoy it.

Feeling less than miserable, he galloped along with Yishana, laughing with her in her enjoyment. Yet, buried deeper than it would normally have been, there was a deep foreboding in his heart as they neared the mysterious citadel, and he noted that Theleb K'aarna occasionally looked satisfied when he should have looked disgruntled.

Sometimes Elric would shout to the sorcerer. 'Ho, old spell-maker, do you feel no joyful release from the cares of the Court out here amidst the beauties of nature? Your face is long, Theleb K'aarna – breathe in the untainted air and laugh with us!' Then Theleb K'aarna would scowl and mutter, and Yishana would laugh at him and glance brightly at Elric.

So they came to Thokora and found it a smouldering pit that stank like a midden of hell.

Elric sniffed. 'This is Chaos work. You were right enough there, Theleb K'aarna. Whatever fire destroyed such a large town, it was not natural fire. Whoever is responsible for this is evidently increasing his power. As you know, sorcerer, the Lords of Law and Chaos are usually in perfect balance, neither tampering directly with our earth. Evidently the Balance has tipped a little way to one side, as it sometimes does, favouring the Lords of Disorder – allowing them access to our realm. Normally it is possible for an earthly sorcerer to summon aid from Chaos or Law for a short time, but it is rare for either side to establish itself so firmly as our friend in the citadel evidently has. What is more disturbing – for you of the Young Kingdoms, at least – is that, once such power is gained, it is possible to increase it, and the Lords of Chaos could in time conquer the Realm of Earth by gradual increase of their strength here.'

'A terrible possibility,' muttered the sorcerer, genuinely afraid. Even though he could sometimes summon help from Chaos, it was in no human being's interest to have Chaos ruling over him.

Elric climbed back into his saddle. 'We'd best make speed to the valley,' he said.

'Are you sure it is wise, after witnessing this?' Theleb K'aarna was nervous.

Elric laughed. 'What? And you a sorcerer from Pan Tang – that isle that claims to know as much of sorcery as my ancestors, the Bright Emperors! No, no – besides, I'm not in a cautious mood today!'

'Nor am I,' cried Yishana, clapping her steed's sides. 'Come, gentlemen – to the Citadel of Chaos!'

By late afternoon, they had topped the range of hills surrounding the valley and looked down at the mysterious citadel.

Yishana had described it well – but not perfectly. Elric's eyes ached as he looked at it, for it seemed to extend beyond the Realm of Earth into a different plane, perhaps several.

It shimmered and glittered and all earthly colours were there, as well as many which Elric recognised as belonging to other planes. Even the basic outline of the citadel was uncertain. In contrast, the surrounding valley was a sea of dark ash, which sometimes seemed to eddy, to undulate and send up spurting geysers of dust, as if the basic elements of nature had been disturbed and warped by the presence of the supernatural citadel.

'Well?' Theleb K'aarna tried to calm his nervous horse as it backed away from the citadel. 'Have you seen the like in the world before?'

Elric shook his head. 'Not in this world, certainly; but I've seen it before. During my final initiation into the arts of Melniboné, my father took me with him in astral form to the Realm of Chaos, there to receive the audience of my patron the Lord Arioch of the Seven Darks...'

Theleb K'aarna shuddered. 'You have been to Chaos? It is Arioch's citadel, then?'

Elric laughed in disdain. 'That! No, it is a hovel compared to the palaces of the Lords of Chaos.'

Impatiently, Yishana said: 'Then who dwells *there*?'

'As I remember, the one who dwelt in the citadel when I passed through the Chaos realm in my youth – he was no Lord of Chaos, but a kind of servant to the lords. Yet,' he frowned, 'not exactly a servant...'

'*Ach*! You speak in riddles.' Theleb K'aarna turned his horse to ride down the hills, away from the citadel. 'I know you Melnibonéans! Starving, you'd rather have a paradox than food!'

Elric and Yishana followed him some distance, then Elric stopped and pointed behind him.

'The one who dwells yonder is a paradoxical sort of fellow. He's a kind of Jester to the Court of Chaos. The Lords of Chaos respect him – perhaps fear him slightly – even though he entertains them. He delights them with cosmic riddles, with farcical satires purporting to explain the nature of the Cosmic Hand that holds Chaos and Law in balance, he juggles enigmas like baubles, laughs at what Chaos holds dear, takes seriously that which they mock at...' He paused and shrugged. 'So I have heard, at least.'

'Why should he be here?'

'Why should he be anywhere? I could guess at the motives of Chaos or Law and probably be right. But not even the Lords of the Higher Worlds can understand the motives of Balo the Jester. It is said that he is the only one allowed to move between the Realms of Chaos and Law at will, though I have never heard of him coming to the Realm of Earth before. Neither, for that matter, have I ever heard him credited with such acts of destruction as that which we've witnessed. It is a puzzle to me – one which would no doubt please him if he knew.'

'There would be one way of discovering the purpose of his visit,' Theleb K'aarna said with a faint smile. 'If someone entered the citadel...'

'Come now, sorcerer,' Elric mocked. 'I've little love for life, to be sure, but there are some things of value to me – my soul, for one!'

Theleb K'aarna began to ride on down the hill, but Elric remained thoughtfully where he was, Yishana beside him.

'You seem more troubled by this than you should be, Elric,' she said.

'It *is* disturbing. There is a hint here that, if we investigate the citadel further, we should become embroiled in some dispute between Balo and his masters – perhaps even the Lords of Law, too. To become so involved could easily mean our destruction, since the forces at work are more dangerous and powerful than anything we are familiar with on Earth.'

'But we cannot simply watch this Balo laying our cities waste, carrying off our fairest, threatening to rule Jharkor himself within a short time!'

Elric sighed, but did not reply.

'Have you no sorcery, Elric, to send Balo back to Chaos where he belongs, to seal the breach he has made in our realm?'

'Even Melnibonéans cannot match the power of the Lords of the Higher Worlds – and my forefathers knew much more of sorcery than do I. My best allies serve neither Chaos nor Law, they are elementals: Lords of Fire, Earth, Air and Water, entities with affinities with beasts and plants. Good allies in an earthly battle – but of no great use when matched against one such as Balo. I must think... At least, if I opposed Balo it would not necessarily incur the wrath of my patron lords. Something, I suppose...'

The hills rolled green and lush to the grasslands at their feet, the sun beat down from a clear sky on the infinity of grass stretching to the horizon. Above them a large predatory bird wheeled;

and Theleb K'aarna was a tiny figure, turning in the saddle to call to them in a thin voice, but his words could not be heard.

Yishana seemed dispirited. Her shoulders slightly slumped, and she did not look at Elric as she began to guide her horse slowly down towards the sorcerer of Pan Tang. Elric followed, conscious of his own indecision, yet half-careless of it. What did it matter to him if...?

The music began, faintly at first, but beginning to swell with an attractive, poignant sweetness, evoking nostalgic memories, offering peace and giving life a sharp meaning, all at once. If the music came from instruments, then they were not earthly. It produced in him a yearning to turn about and discover its source, but he resisted it. Yishana, on the other hand, was evidently not finding the music so easily resisted. She had wheeled completely round, her face radiant, her lips trembling and tears shining in her eyes.

Elric, in his wanderings in unearthly realms, had heard music like it before – it echoed many of the bizarre symphonies of old Melniboné – and it did not draw him as it drew Yishana. He recognised swiftly that she was in danger, and as she came past him, spurring her horse, he reached out to grab her bridle.

Her whip slashed at his hand and, cursing with unexpected pain, he dropped the bridle. She went past him, galloping up to the crest of the hill and vanishing over it in an instant.

'Yishana!' He shouted at her desperately, but his voice would not carry over the pulsing music. He looked back, hoping that Theleb K'aarna would lend help, but the sorcerer was riding rapidly away. Evidently, on hearing the music, he had come to a swift decision.

Elric raced after Yishana, screaming for her to turn back. His own horse reached the top of the hill and he saw her bent over her steed's neck as she goaded it towards the shining citadel.

'Yishana! You go to your doom!'

Now she had reached the outer limits of the citadel, and her horse's feet seemed to strike off shimmering waves of colour as they touched the Chaos-disturbed ground surrounding the place. Although he knew it was too late to stop her, Elric continued to speed after her, hoping to reach her before she entered the citadel itself.

But, even as he entered the rainbow swirl, he saw what appeared to be a dozen Yishanas going through a dozen gateways into the citadel. Oddly refracted light created the illusion and made it impossible to tell which was the real Yishana.

With Yishana's disappearance the music stopped and Elric thought he heard a faint whisper of laughter following it. His horse was by this time becoming increasingly difficult to control, and he did not trust himself to it. He dismounted, his legs wreathed in radiant mist, and let the horse go. It galloped off, snorting its terror.

Elric's hand moved to the hilt of his runesword, but he hesitated to draw it. Once pulled from its scabbard, the blade would demand souls before it allowed itself to be resheathed. Yet it was his only weapon. He withdrew his hand, and the blade seemed to quiver angrily at his side.

'Not yet, Stormbringer. There may be forces within who are stronger even than you!'

He began to wade through the faintly resisting light swirls. He was half-blinded by the scintillating colours around him, which sometimes shone dark blue, silver and red; sometimes gold, light green, amber. He also felt the sickening lack of any sort of orientation – distance, depth, breadth, were meaningless. He recognised what he had only experienced in an astral form – the odd, timeless, spaceless quality that marked a realm of the Higher Worlds.

He drifted, pushing his body in the direction in which he guessed Yishana had gone, for by now he had lost sight of the gateway or any of its mirage images.

He realised that, unless he was doomed to drift here until he starved, he must draw Stormbringer, for the runeblade could resist the influence of Chaos.

This time, when he gripped the sword's hilt, he felt a shock run up his arm and infuse his body with vitality. The sword came free from the scabbard. From the huge blade, carved with strange old runes, a black radiance poured, meeting the shifting colours of Chaos and dispersing them.

Now Elric shrieked the age-old battle-ululation of his folk and pressed on into the citadel, slashing at the intangible images that swirled on all sides. The gateway was ahead, and Elric knew it now, for his sword had shown him which were the mirages. It was open as Elric reached the portal. He paused for a moment, his lips moving as he remembered an invocation that he might need later. Arioch, Lord of Chaos, patron god-demon of his ancestors, was a negligent power and whimful – he could not rely on Arioch to aid him here, unless...

In slow graceful strides, a golden beast with eyes of ruby-fire was loping down the passage that led from the portal. Bright though the eyes were, they seemed blind, and its huge, doglike muzzle was closed. Yet its path could only lead it to Elric and, as it neared him, the mouth suddenly gaped showing coral fangs. In silence it came to a halt, the blind eyes never once settling on the albino, and then sprang!

Elric staggered back, raising the sword in defence. He was flung to the ground by the beast's weight and felt its body cover him. It was cold, cold, and it made no attempt to savage him – just lay on top of him and let the cold permeate his body.

Elric began to shiver as he pushed at the chilling body of the beast. Stormbringer moaned and murmured in his hand, and then it pierced some part of the beast's body, and a horrible cold strength began to fill the albino. Reinforced by the beast's own life-force, he heaved upwards. The beast continued to smother him, though now a thin, barely audible sound was coming from it. Elric guessed that Stormbringer's small wound was hurting the creature.

Desperately, for he was shaking and aching with cold, he moved the sword and stabbed again. Again the thin sound from the beast; again cold energy flooded through him, and again he heaved. This time the beast was flung off and crawled back towards the portal. Elric sprang up, raised Stormbringer high and brought the sword down on the golden creature's skull. The skull shattered as ice might shatter.

Elric ran forward into the passage and, once he was within, the place became filled with roars and shrieks that echoed and were magnified. It was as if the voice that the cold beast had lacked outside was shouting its death-agonies here.

Now the floor rose until he was running up a spiral ramp. Looking down, he shuddered, for he looked into an infinite pit of subtle, dangerous colours that swam about in such a way that he could hardly take his eyes from them. He even felt his body begin to leave the ramp and go towards the pit, but he strengthened his grip on the sword and disciplined himself to climb on.

Upwards, as he looked, was the same as downwards. Only the ramp had any kind of constancy, and this began to take on the appearance of a thinly cut jewel, through which he could see the pit and in which it was reflected.

Greens and blues and yellows predominated, but there were also traces of dark red, black and orange, and many other colours not in an ordinary human spectrum.

Elric knew he was in some province of the Higher Worlds and guessed that it would not be long before the ramp led him to new danger.

Danger did not seem to await him when at last he came to the end of the ramp and stepped onto a bridge of similar stuff, which led over the scintillating pit to an archway that shone with a steady blue light.

He crossed the bridge cautiously and as cautiously entered the arch. Everything was blue-tinged here, even himself; and he trod on, the blue becoming deeper and deeper as he progressed.

Then Stormbringer began to murmur and, either warned by the sword or by some sixth sense of his own, Elric wheeled to his right. Another archway had appeared there and from this there began to shine a light as deep red as the other was blue. Where the two met was a purple of fantastic richness and Elric stared at this, experiencing a similar hypnotic pull as he had felt when climbing the ramp. Again his mind was stronger, and he forced himself to enter the red arch. At once another arch appeared to his left, sending a beam of green light to merge with the red, and another to his left brought yellow light, one ahead brought mauve until he seemed trapped within the criss-cross of beams. He slashed at them with Stormbringer, and the black radiance reduced the beams for a moment to streamers of light, which re-formed again. Elric continued to move forward.

Now, looming through the confusion of colour, a shape appeared and Elric thought it was that of a man.

Man it was in shape – but not in size it seemed. Yet, when it drew closer, it was no giant – less than Elric's height. Still it gave the *impression* of vast proportions, rather as if it *were* a giant and Elric had grown to its size.

It blundered towards Elric and went *through* him. It was not that the man was intangible – it was Elric who felt the ghost. The creature's mass seemed of incredible density. The creature was turning, its huge hands reaching out, its face a mocking grimace. Elric struck at it with Stormbringer and was astonished as the runesword was halted, making no impression on the creature's bulk.

Yet when it grasped Elric, its hands went through him. Elric backed away, grinning now in relief. Then he saw with some terror that the light was gleaming through him. He had been right – *he* was the ghost!

The creature reached out for him again, grabbed him again, failed to hold him.

Elric, conscious that he was in no physical danger from the monster, yet also highly conscious that his sanity was about to be permanently impaired, turned and fled.

Quite suddenly he was in a hall, the walls of which were of the same unstable, shifting colours as the rest of the place. But sitting on a stool in the centre of the hall, holding in his hands some tiny creatures that seemed to be running about on his palm, was a small figure who looked up at Elric and grinned merrily.

'Welcome, King of Melniboné. And how fares the last ruler of my favourite earthly race?'

The figure was dressed in shimmering motley. On his head was a tall, spiked crown – a travesty of and a comment upon the crowns of the mighty. His face was angular and his mouth wide.

'Greetings, Lord Balo,' Elric made a mock bow. 'Strange hospitality you offer in your welcome.'

'Ahaha – it did not amuse you, eh? Men are so much harder to please than gods – you would not think it, would you?'

'Men's pleasures are rarely so elaborate. Where is Queen Yishana?'

'Allow me my pleasure also, mortal. Here she is, I think.' Balo plucked at one of the tiny creatures on his palm. Elric stepped forward and saw that Yishana was indeed there, as were many of the lost soldiers. Balo looked up at him and winked. 'They are so much easier to handle in this size.'

'I do not doubt it, though I wonder if it is not we who are larger rather than they who are smaller...'

'You are astute, mortal. But can you guess how this came to be?'

'Your creature back there – your pits and colours and archways – somehow they warp – what?'

'*Mass*, King Elric. But you would not understand such concepts. Even the Lords of Melniboné, most godlike and intelligent of mortals, only learned how to manipulate the elements in ritual invocation and spell, but never understood what they manipulated – that is where the Lords of the Higher Worlds score, whatever their differences.'

'But I survived without need for spells. I survived by disciplining my mind!'

'That helped, for certain – but you forget your greatest asset – that disturbing blade there. You use it in your petty problems to aid you, and you never realise that it is like making use of a mighty war galley to catch a sprat. That sword represents power in *any* realm, King Elric!'

'Aye, so it might. This does not interest me. Why are you here, Lord Balo?'

Balo chuckled, his laughter rich and musical. 'Oho, I am in disgrace. I quarrelled with my masters, who took exception to a joke of mine about their insignificance and egotism, about their destiny and their pride. Bad taste to them, king, is any hint of their own oblivion. I made a joke in bad taste. I fled from the Higher Worlds to Earth, where, unless invoked, the Lords of Law or

Chaos can rarely interfere. You will like my intention, Elric, as would any Melnibonéan – I intend to establish my own realm on Earth – the Realm of Paradox. A little from Law, a little from Chaos – a realm of opposites, of curiosities and jokes.'

'I'm thinking we already have such a world as you describe, Lord Balo, with no need for you to create it!'

'Earnest irony, King Elric, for an insouciant man of Melniboné.'

'Ah, that it may be. I am a boor on occasions such as these. Will you release Yishana and myself?'

'But you and I are giants – I have given you the status and appearance of a god. You and I could be partners in this enterprise of mine!'

'Unfortunately, Lord Balo, I do not possess your range of humour and am unfitted for such an exalted rôle. Besides,' Elric grinned suddenly, 'it is in my mind that the Lords of the Higher Worlds will not easily let drop the matter of your ambition, since it appears to conflict so strongly with theirs.'

Balo laughed but said nothing.

Elric also smiled, but it was an attempt to hide his racing thoughts. 'What do you intend to do if I refuse?'

'Why, Elric, you would not refuse! I can think of many subtle pranks that I could play on you...'

'Indeed? And the Black Sword?'

'Ah, yes...'

'Balo, in your mirth and obsessions you have not considered everything thoroughly. You should have exerted more effort to vanquish me before I came here.'

Now Elric's eyes gleamed hot and he lifted the sword, crying:

'Arioch! Master! I invoke thee, Lord of Chaos!'

Balo started. 'Cease that, King Elric!'

'Arioch – here is a soul for you to claim!'

'Quiet, I say!'

'Arioch! Hear me!' Elric's voice was loud and desperate.

Balo let his tiny playthings fall and rose hurriedly, skipping towards Elric.

'Your invocation is unheeded!' He laughed, reaching out for

Elric. But Stormbringer moaned and shuddered in Elric's hand and Balo withdrew his hand. His face became serious and frowning.

'Arioch of the Seven Darks – your servant calls you!'

The walls of flame trembled and began to fade. Balo's eyes widened and jerked this way and that.

'Oh, Lord Arioch – come reclaim your straying Balo!'

'You cannot!' Balo scampered across the room where one section of the flame had faded entirely, revealing darkness beyond.

'Sadly for you, little jester, he can...' The voice was sardonic and yet beautiful. From the darkness stepped a tall figure, no longer the shapeless gibbering thing that had, of late, been Arioch's favoured manifestation when visiting the Realm of Earth. Yet the great beauty of the newcomer, filled as it was with a kind of compassion mingled with pride, cruelty and sadness, showed at once that he could not be human. He was clad in doublet of pulsing scarlet, hose of ever-changing hue, a long golden sword at his hips. His eyes were large, but slanted high, his hair was long and as golden as the sword, his lips were full and his chin pointed like his ears.

'Arioch!' Balo stumbled backwards as the Lord of Chaos advanced.

'It was your mistake, Balo,' Elric said from behind the jester. 'Did you not realise only the Kings of Melniboné may invoke Arioch and bring him to the Realm of Earth? It has been their age-old privilege.'

'And much have they abused it,' said Arioch, smiling faintly as Balo grovelled. 'However, this service you have done us, Elric, will make up for past misuses. I was not amused by the matter of the Mist Giant...'

Even Elric was awed by the incredibly powerful presence of the Chaos Lord. He also felt much relieved, for he had not been sure that Arioch could be summoned in this way.

Now Arioch stretched an arm down towards Balo and lifted the jester by his collar so that he jerked and struggled in the air, his face writhing in fear and consternation.

Arioch took hold of Balo's head and squeezed it. Elric looked on in amazement as the head began to shrink. Arioch took Balo's legs and bent them in, folding Balo up and kneading him in his slender, inhuman hands until he was a small, solid ball. Arioch then popped the ball into his mouth and swallowed it.

'I have not eaten him, Elric,' he said with another faint smile. 'It is merely the easiest way of transporting him back to the realms from which he came. He has transgressed and will be punished. All this –' he waved an arm to indicate the citadel – 'is unfortunate and contradicts the plans we of Chaos have for Earth – plans which will involve you, our servant, and make you mighty.'

Elric bowed to his master. 'I'm honoured, Lord Arioch, though I seek no favours.'

Arioch's silvery voice lost some of its beauty and his face seemed to cloud for a second. 'You are pledged to serve Chaos, Elric, as were your ancestors. You *will* serve Chaos! The time draws near when both Law and Chaos will battle for the Realm of Earth – and Chaos shall win! Earth will be incorporated into our realm and you will join the hierarchy of Chaos, become immortal as we are!'

'Immortality offers little to me, my lord.'

'Ah, Elric, have the men of Melniboné become as the half-apes who now dominate Earth with their puny "civilisations"? Are you no better than those Young Kingdom upstarts? Think what we offer!'

'I shall, my lord, when the time you mention comes.' Elric's head was still lowered.

'You shall indeed,' Arioch raised his arms. 'Now to transport this toy of Balo's to its proper realm, and redress the trouble he has caused, lest some hint reaches our opponents before the proper time.'

Arioch's voice swelled like the singing of a million brazen bells and Elric sheathed his sword and clapped his hands over his ears to stop the pain.

Then Elric felt his body seem to *shred* apart, swell and stretch until it became like smoke drifting on air. Then, faster, the smoke began to be drawn together, becoming denser and denser and he seemed to be shrinking now. All around him were rolling banks of colour, flashes and indescribable noises. Then came a vast blackness and he closed his eyes against the images that seemed reflected in the blackness.

When he opened them he stood in the valley and the singing citadel was gone. Only Yishana and a few surprised-looking soldiers stood there. Yishana ran towards him.

'Elric – was it you who saved us?'

'I must claim only part of the credit,' he said.

'Not all my soldiers are here,' she said, inspecting the men. 'Where are the rest – and the villagers abducted earlier?'

'If Balo's tastes are like his masters', then I fear they now have the honour of being part of a demigod. The Lords of Chaos are not flesh-eaters, of course, being of the Higher Worlds, but there is something they savour in men which satisfies them...'

Yishana hugged her body as if in cold. 'He was huge – I cannot believe that his citadel could contain his bulk!'

'The citadel was more than a dwelling-place, that was obvious. Somehow it changed size, shape – and other things I cannot describe. Arioch of Chaos transported it and Balo back to where they belong.'

'Arioch! But he is one of the Greatest Six! How did he come to Earth?'

'An old pact with my remote ancestors. By calling him they allow him to spend a short time in our realm, and he repays them with some favour. This was done.'

'Come, Elric,' she took his arm. 'Let's away from the valley.'

Elric was weak and enfeebled by the efforts of summoning Arioch, and the experiences he had had before and since the episode. He could hardly walk; and soon it was Yishana who supported him as they made slow progress, the dazed warriors following in their wake, towards the nearest village, where they could obtain rest and horses to take them back to Dhakos.

Chapter Five

As they staggered past the blasted ruins of Thokora, Yishana pointed suddenly at the sky.

'What is that?'

A great shape was winging its way towards them. It had the appearance of a butterfly, but a butterfly with wings so huge they blotted out the sun.

'Can it be some creature of Balo's left behind?' she speculated.

'Hardly likely,' he replied. 'This has the appearance of a monster conjured by a human sorcerer.'

'Theleb K'aarna!'

'He has surpassed himself,' Elric said wryly. 'I did not think him capable.'

'It is his vengeance on us, Elric!'

'That seems reasonable. But I am weak, Yishana – and Stormbringer needs souls if it is to replenish my strength.' He turned a calculating eye on the warriors behind him who were gaping up at the creature as it came nearer. Now they could see it had a man's body, covered with hairs or feathers hued like a peacock's.

The air whistled as it descended, its fifty-foot wings dwarfing the seven feet of head and body. From its head grew two curling horns, and its arms terminated in long talons.

'We are doomed, Elric!' cried Yishana. She saw that the warriors were fleeing and she cried after them to come back. Elric stood there passively, knowing that alone he could not defeat the butterfly-creature.

'Best go with them, Yishana,' he murmured. 'I think it will be satisfied with me.'

'No!'

He ignored her and stepped towards the creature as it landed and began to glide over the ground in his direction. He drew a

quiescent Stormbringer, which felt heavy in his hand. A little strength flowed into him, but not enough. His only hope was to strike a good blow at the creature's vitals and draw some of its own life-force into himself.

The creature's voice shrilled at him, and the strange, insane face twisted as he approached. Elric realised that this was no true supernatural denizen of the netherworlds, but a once-human creature warped by Theleb K'aarna's sorcery. At least it was mortal, and he had only physical strength to contend with. In better condition it would have been easy for him – but now...

The wings beat at the air as the taloned hands grasped at him. He took Stormbringer in both hands and swung the runeblade at the thing's neck. Swiftly the wings folded in to protect its neck and Stormbringer became entangled in the strange, sticky flesh. A talon caught Elric's arm, ripping it to the bone. He yelled in pain and yanked the sword from the enfolding wing.

He tried to steady himself for another blow, but the monster grabbed his wounded arm and began drawing him towards its now lowered head – and the horns that curled from it.

He struggled, hacking at the thing's arms with the extra strength that came with the threat of death.

Then he heard a cry from behind him and saw a figure from the corner of his eye, a figure that leapt forward with two blades gleaming in either hand. The swords slashed at the talons and with a shriek the creature turned on Elric's would-be rescuer.

It was Moonglum. Elric fell backwards, breathing hard, as he watched his little red-headed friend engage the monster.

But Moonglum would not survive for long, unless aided.

Elric racked his brain for some spell that would help; but he was too weak, even if he could think of one, to raise the energy necessary to summon supernatural help.

And then it came to him! Yishana! She was not as exhausted as he. But could she do it?

He turned as the air moaned to the beating of the creature's wings. Moonglum was only just managing to hold it off, his two swords flashing rapidly as he parried every effort to grasp him.

'Yishana!' croaked the albino.

She came up to him and placed a hand on his. 'We could leave, Elric – perhaps hide from that thing.'

'No. I must help Moonglum. Listen – you realise how desperate our position is, do you not? Then keep that in mind while you recite this rune with me. Perhaps together we may succeed. There are many kinds of lizards in these parts, are there not?'

'Aye – many.'

'Then this is what you must say – and remember that we shall all perish by Theleb K'aarna's servant if you are not successful.'

In the half worlds, where dwelt the master-types of all creatures other than Man, an entity stirred, hearing its name. The entity was called Haaashaastaak; and it was scaly and cold, with no true intellect, such as men and gods possessed, but an *awareness* which served it as well if not better. It was brother, on this plane, to such entities as Meerclar, Lord of the Cats, Roofdrak, Lord of the Dogs, Nuru-ah, Lord of the Cattle, and many, many others. This was Haaashaastaak, Lord of the Lizards. It did not really hear words in the exact sense, but it heard rhythms which meant much to it, even though it did not know why. The rhythms were being repeated over and over again, but seemed too faint to be worth much attention. It stirred and yawned, but did nothing...

'Haaashaastaak, Lord of Lizards,
Your children were fathers of men,
Haaashaastaak, Prince of Reptiles,
Come aid a grandchild now!

'Haaashaastaak, Father of Scales,
Cold-blooded bringer of life...'

It was a bizarre scene, with Elric and Yishana desperately chanting the rune over and over again as Moonglum fought on, slowly losing strength.

*

Haaashaastaak quivered and became more curious. The rhythms were no stronger, yet they seemed more insistent. He would travel, he decided, to that place where those he watched over dwelt. He knew that if he answered the rhythms, he would have to obey whatever source they had. He was not, of course, aware that such decisions had been implanted into him in a far distant age – the time before the creation of Earth, when the Lords of Law and Chaos, then inhabitants of a single realm and known by another name, had watched over the forming of things and laid down the manner and logic in which things should behave, following their great edict from the voice of the Cosmic Balance – the voice which had never spoken since.

Haaashaastaak betook himself, a little slothfully, to Earth.

Elric and Yishana were still chanting hoarsely, as Haaashaastaak made his sudden appearance. He had the look of a huge iguana, and his eyes were many-coloured, many-faceted jewels, his scales seeming of gold, silver and other rich metals. A slightly hazy outline surrounded him, as if he had brought part of his own environment with him.

Yishana gasped and Elric breathed a deep sigh. As a child he had learned the languages of all animal-masters, and now he must recall the simple language of the lizard-master, Haaashaastaak.

His need fired his brain, and the words came suddenly.

'*Haaashaastaak*,' he cried pointing at the butterfly-creature, '*mokik ankkuh!*'

The lizard lord turned its jewelled eyes on the creature and its great tongue suddenly shot out towards it, curling around the monster. It shrilled in terror as it was drawn towards the lizard lord's great maw. Legs and arms kicked as the mouth closed on it. Several gulps and Haaashaastaak had swallowed Theleb K'aarna's prize creation. Then it turned its head uncertainly about for a few moments and vanished.

Pain began to throb now through Elric's torn arm as Moonglum staggered towards him, grinning in relief.

'I followed behind you at a distance as you requested,' he said, 'since you suspected treachery from Theleb K'aarna. But then

I spied the sorcerer coming this way and followed him to a cave in yonder hills,' he pointed. 'But when the deceased,' he laughed shakily, 'emerged from the cave, I decided that it would be best to chase *that*, for I had the feeling it was going in your direction.'

'I am glad you were so astute,' Elric said.

'It was your doing, really,' Moonglum replied. 'For, if you hadn't anticipated treachery from Theleb K'aarna, I might not have been here at the right moment.' Moonglum suddenly sank to the grass, leaned back, grinned and fainted.

Elric felt very dazed himself. 'I do not think we need fear anything more from your sorcerer just yet, Yishana,' he said. 'Let us rest here and refresh ourselves. Perhaps then your cowardly soldiers will have returned, and we can send them to a village to get us some horses.'

They stretched out on the grass and, lying in each other's arms, went to sleep.

Elric was astonished to wake in a bed, a soft bed. He opened his eyes and saw Yishana and Moonglum smiling down at him.

'How long have I been here?'

'More than two days. You did not wake when the horses came, so we had the warriors construct a stretcher to bear you to Dhakos. You are in my palace.'

Elric cautiously moved his stiff, bandaged arm. It was still painful. 'Are my belongings still at the inn?'

'Perhaps, if they have not been stolen. Why?'

'I have a pouch of herbs there, which will heal this arm quickly and also supply me with a little strength, which I need badly.'

'I will go and see if they are still there,' Moonglum said and walked from the chamber.

Yishana stroked Elric's milk-white hair. 'I have much to thank you for, wolf,' said she. 'You have saved my kingdom – perhaps all the Young Kingdoms. In my eyes you are redeemed for my brother's death.'

'Oh, I thank you, madam,' said Elric with a mocking tone.

She laughed. 'You are still a Melnibonéan.'

'Still that, aye.'

'A strange mixture, however. Sensitive and cruel, sardonic and loyal to your little friend Moonglum. I look forward to knowing you better, my lord.'

'As to that, I am not sure if you will have the opportunity.'

She gave him a hard look. 'Why?'

'Your résumé of my character was incomplete, Queen Yishana – you should have added "careless of the world – and yet vengeful". I wish to be revenged on your pet wizard.'

'But he is spent, surely – you said so yourself.'

'I am, as you remarked, still a Melnibonéan! My arrogant blood calls vengeance on an upstart!'

'Forget Theleb K'aarna. I will have him hunted by my White Leopards. Even his sorcery will not win against such savages as they are!'

'Forget him? Oh, no!'

'Elric, Elric – I will give you my kingdom, declare you ruler of Jharkor, if you will let me be your consort.'

He reached out and stroked her bare arm with his good hand.

'You are unrealistic, queen. To take such an action would bring wholesale rebellion in your land. To your folk, I am still the Traitor of Imrryr.'

'Not now – now you are the Hero of Jharkor.'

'How so? They did not know of their peril and thus will feel no gratitude. It were best that I settled my debt with your wizard and went on my way. The streets must already be full of rumours that you have taken your brother's murderer to your bed. Your popularity with your subjects must be at its lowest, madam.'

'I do not care.'

'You will if your nobles lead the people in insurrection and crucify you naked in the city square.'

'You are familiar with our customs.'

'We Melnibonéans are a learned folk, queen.'

'Well versed in all the arts.'

'All of them.' Again he felt his blood race as she rose and barred the door. At that moment he felt no need for the herbs which Moonglum had gone to find.

When he tiptoed from the room that night, he found Moonglum waiting patiently in the antechamber. Moonglum proffered the pouch with a wink. But Elric's mood was not light. He took bunches of herbs from the pouch and selected what he needed.

Moonglum grimaced as he watched Elric chew and swallow the stuff. Then together they stole from the palace.

Armed with Stormbringer and mounted, Elric rode slightly behind his friend as Moonglum led the way towards the hills beyond Dhakos.

'If I know the sorcerers of Pan Tang,' murmured the albino, 'then Theleb K'aarna will be more exhausted than was I. With luck we will come upon him sleeping.'

'I shall wait outside the cave in that case,' said Moonglum, for he now had some experience of Elric's vengeance-taking and did not relish watching Theleb K'aarna's slow death.

They galloped speedily until the hills were reached and Moonglum showed Elric the cave mouth.

Leaving his horse, the albino went soft-footed into the cave, his runesword ready.

Moonglum waited nervously for Theleb K'aarna's first shrieks, but none came. He waited until dawn began to bring the first faint light and then Elric, face frozen with anger, emerged from the cave.

Savagely he grasped his horse's reins and swung himself into the saddle.

'Are you satisfied?' Moonglum asked tentatively.

'Satisfied, no! The dog has vanished!'

'Gone – but...'

'He was more cunning than I thought. There are several caves and I sought him in all of them. In the farthest I discovered traces of sorcerous runes on the walls and floor. He has transported himself somewhere and I could not discover where, in spite of deciphering most of the runes! Perhaps he went to Pan Tang.'

'Ah, then our quest has been futile. Let us return to Dhakos and enjoy a little more of Yishana's hospitality.'

'No – we go to Pan Tang.'

'But, Elric, Theleb K'aarna's brother sorcerers dwell there in strength; and Jagreen Lern, the theocrat, forbids visitors!'

'No matter. I wish to finish my business with Theleb K'aarna.'

'You have no proof that he is there!'

'No matter!'

And then Elric was spurring his horse away, riding like a man possessed or fleeing from dreadful peril – and perhaps he was both possessed and fleeing. Moonglum did not follow at once but thoughtfully watched his friend gallop off. Not normally introspective, he wondered if Yishana had perhaps affected the albino more strongly than he would have wished. He did not think that vengeance on Theleb K'aarna was Elric's prime desire in refusing to return to Dhakos.

Then he shrugged and slapped his heels to his steed's flanks, racing to catch up with Elric as the cold dawn rose, wondering if they would continue towards Pan Tang once Dhakos was far enough behind.

But Elric's head contained no thoughts, only emotion flooded him – emotion he did not wish to analyse. His white hair streaming behind him, his dead-white, handsome face set, his slender hands tightly clutching the stallion's reins, he rode. And only his strange, crimson eyes reflected the misery and conflict within him.

In Dhakos that morning, other eyes held misery, but not for too long. Yishana was a pragmatic queen.

Aspects of Fantasy

(1964)

3. *Figures of Faust*

Cut is the branch that might have grown full straight,
And burnèd is Apollo's laurel-bough,
That sometime grew within this learnèd man.
Faustus is gone: regard his hellish fall,
Whose fiendful fortune may exhort the wise,
Only to wonder at unlawful things,
Whose deepness doth entice such forward wits
To practise more than heavenly power permits.

(*The Tragical History of Doctor Faustus*
by Christopher Marlowe)

A FITTING EPITAPH for the majority of hero-villains whose appearance in fantasy is the subject of this article. It helps, also, to illustrate why horror stories relying on the Christian idea of good and evil no longer convince us so much as they used to. Most modern readers can't believe in the existence of rewards and punishments for the good or evil man. Yet Faust, and heroes like him, continue to convince in spite of this. There is no denying that even to a wicked old atheist like me, the pathos and tragedy of Marlowe's closing chorus is moving (even though I suspect him of tacking it on as a sop to the Elizabethan censor).

I intend to make my 'Faust-figure' category rather a broad one, partly for reasons of space, partly because Faust is marvellously interpretable. So here the Faust theme will mean roughly the tragedy of the curious and brilliant man destroyed by his own curiosity and brilliance.

In my last article, I described the device of using natural and architectural scenes to induce a mood of terror, strangeness or sublimation. Often this device could dominate the entire novel and characters were very much in second place, not a serious defect in the terror tale or tale of wonder, but the best fantasies contain a complementary balance of marvel and characterisation. The characters need not always be subtly drawn, but they are always archetypes.

The Faustian character-type appears again and again in fantasy tales. He has appeared, in various guises, more than any other type and his development in fantasy fiction is still going on. Ignoring his ancestors (including the magician-alchemist Dr Johannes Faustus of German legend) we can begin with Marlowe's rather bitty play about him which was first published in 1604. The play is memorable for some of its passages, but is clumsily constructed and does not have the impact on present-day readers which it obviously had on its Elizabethan and Jacobean audiences.

Basically the story is of brilliant Doctor John Faustus who is a dabbler in alchemy and magic. He contacts Mephistophilis the Devil's agent, who tempts him to sell his soul. Friends and good angels urge him to desist, but he finally gives in on the following conditions:

> First, that Faustus may be a spirit in form and substance. Secondly, that Mephistophilis shall be his servant, and at his command. Thirdly, that Mephistophilis shall do for him, and bring him whatsoever [he desires] ... I, John Faustus, of Wittenburg, Doctor, by these presents, do give both body and soul to Lucifer prince of the east, and his Minister Mephistophilis; and furthermore grant unto them that, twenty-four years being expired, the articles above written inviolate, full power to fetch or carry the said John Faustus, body and soul, flesh, blood, or goods, into their habitation wheresoever.

After this businesslike document is prepared, Faustus asks Mephistophilis: 'Where is the place that men call hell?' Mephistophilis tells him that 'Hell hath no limits, nor is circumscrib'd in one self place; for where we are is hell, and where hell is, there must we ever be; and, to conclude, when all the world dissolves, and every creature shall be purified, all places shall be hell that are not heaven'. To which Faustus replies: 'Come, I think hell's a fable.'

Mephistophilis has an ominous answer: 'Aye, think so still, till experience change thy mind.'

Faustus then embarks on a series of rather disconnected adventures ranging from tragedy to farce and finally gets his comeuppance in a dramatic last scene where he repents too late. In other versions of the story Faust is saved in the nick of time by his repentance. In the Gothic tales particularly, the Faustian hero-villain has no such luck.

The basic Faust plot involves an intelligent man whose experiments lead him – and often others – to a sticky end. In religious terms this is a man who is attracted to evil, who succumbs to it and is finally ruined by it. In scientific terms it is a man who conducts a dangerous experiment which gets out of control and overcomes him.

Probably it was the influence of Goethe's more complex *Faust* and Milton's Satan of *Paradise Lost* on the German Schauer-Romantik ('Horror Romance') school of the late eighteenth century which, by *their* influence, produced the superfluity of Faustian heroes in the English Gothic novel and its progeny. Mrs Radcliffe's monk Schedoni of *The Italian* (1797) is the villain of her finest novel which concentrates on the Satanically attractive Schedoni, with his cowl which 'threw a shade over the livid paleness of his face' which 'bore the traces of many passions, which seemed to have fixed the features they no longer animated.'

M.G. Lewis was influenced by Radcliffe (though not by Schedoni) when he wrote his very readable *The Monk* (1796 – Bestseller Library, 3/6). Here, a lustful woman, Matilda, takes the place of Mephistophilis and uses sex to bring down her prey, but the pact with Satan soon follows:

> Ambrosio started, and expected the demon with terror ... The thunder ceasing to roll, a full strain of melodious music

> sounded in the air! At the same time the cloud disappeared, and he beheld a figure more beautiful than fancy's pencil ever drew. It was a youth seemingly scarce eighteen, the perfection of whose form and face was unrivalled. He was perfectly naked, a bright star sparkled on his forehead, two crimson wings extended themselves from his shoulders, and his silken locks were confined by a band of many-coloured fires, which shone with a brilliancy far surpassing that of precious stones. Circlets of diamonds were fastened around his arms and ankles, and in his right hand he bore a silver branch imitating myrtle. His form shone with dazzling glory: he was surrounded by clouds of rose-coloured light, and at the moment that he appeared a refreshing air breathed perfumes throughout the cavern. Ambrosio gazed upon the spirit with delight and wonder.

The Monk had its mysterious ruins, crypts and labyrinths and virtuous imperilled heroines, but was unusual in that the main narrative was told from the villain's viewpoint and not from the heroine's. It was also unusual for its overt eroticism. As in many other Gothic novels, the shadow of Lovelace, demon-lover of Richardson's *Clarissa Harlowe* (1748) is observed here.

In Mary Shelley's *Frankenstein* (1817) the downfall of the hero comes about because of his basically alchemical dabbling. Frankenstein continues in the Faust tradition. His evil takes on independence in the tragic monster (really the hero of the tale) and he struggles with an evil he is no longer able to control and which, in the end, is his doom. Frankenstein's monster is, of course, really an aspect of Frankenstein himself and his frantic attempts to destroy his creation, his long conversations with it, can be seen as an ever-weakening effort to control his own 'bad' self. In *Frankenstein* we see the early development of one of fantasy fiction's largest sub-genres – science fiction. Dabbling in magic is replaced by dabbling in science – but the basic theme and result is the same. Here is the first anti-science science fiction tale in which the elements of fantasy blend with an interest in scientific theory to create a theme which is today commonplace in

SF – particularly English SF in the hands of Wyndham, Ballard, Aldiss and Brunner for instance.

The last of the great Gothic hero-villains was Charles Maturin's *Melmoth the Wanderer* (University of Nebraska Press, 15/- or $1.70). Melmoth (a combination of Faust and Mephistophilis) is doomed to virtual immortality, wandering the world as an agent of the Devil, seeking to purchase another's soul in order to get his own out of pawn. One of the best Gothics, thought by some to be the form's culmination, it is spoiled by lengthy and largely boring sub-plots in the form of whole tales embedded in the main narrative – tales which don't serve any noticeable purpose in furthering the basic story. This is about Melmoth, a tragic, menacing and mysterious figure who always arrives on the scene when someone is about to suffer a nasty fate – he then tries to tempt them to barter their souls to Satan for an easier lot. He never succeeds.

The book was published in 1820 and Maturin's development of the Faust theme helped later writers to produce even subtler workings of the basic story. Technically, it relies on a mystery element involving the reader's curiosity about Melmoth's motives, which are only very gradually made clear – a device used to good effect by Wilkie Collins and more recent mystery writers, as well as authors of less sensational novels. At the end of 150 years, having failed to find one person who would agree to his proposition, Melmoth knows he must perish: 'No one has ever exchanged destinies with Melmoth the Wanderer. *I have traversed the world in the search, and no one, to gain the world, would lose his own soul!*' He then dreams of his fate:

> His last despairing reverted glance was fixed on the clock of eternity – the upraised black arm seemed to push forward the hand – it arrived at its period – he fell – he sunk – he blazed – he shrieked! The burning waves boomed over his sinking head, and the clock of eternity rung out its awful chime – 'Room for the soul of the wandered!' – and the waves of the burning ocean answered, as they lashed the adamantine rock – 'There is room for more!' – The Wanderer awoke.

Having wakened, the Wanderer discovers he has aged hideously and tells his visitors: 'I am summoned, and must obey the summons – my master has other work for me! When a meteor blazes in your atmosphere – when a comet pursues its burning path towards the sun – look up, and perhaps you may think of the spirit condemned to guide the blazing and erratic orb.'

He warns them that if they watch him leave the house 'your lives will be the forfeit of your desperate curiosity. For the same stake I risked more than life – and lost it!' He leaves and terrible shrieks are heard from the nearby cliffs overlooking the sea, indescribable sounds are heard all night over the surrounding countryside. In the morning there is only one trace of the Wanderer on the rocks above the sea – his handkerchief.

Robert Spector in his introduction to *Seven Masterpieces of Gothic Horror* (Bantam Books, 95¢) says that '*Melmoth the Wanderer* is a Faust story that begins in contemporary Ireland but re-creates the adventures of John Melmoth, who has lived since the seventeenth century through a pact with the devil. Through six episodes of terror, Maturin creates the experiences of modern anguish. Maturin combines the myths of Faust and the Wandering Jew with all the horrible episodes of the Gothic romances, and yet he never depends on blood and gore for his effects. What Maturin does is to probe the psychological depths of fear, and in doing so, he was a little ahead of his audience. Although *Melmoth* has come to be regarded by many as the masterpiece of terror fiction, it attracted little attention until psychological Gothicists like Poe and the French Romantics resurrected it some years later.'

Throughout this long book, Melmoth can also be seen as the Faceless Man of our dreams, the unknown aspect of ourselves which is symbolised, as well, in the figure of the cowled monk, his face shaded and half-seen, or the shadowy, omniscient spectre. He appears in many modern fantasy tales – Leiber's Sheelba of the Eyeless Face in the Grey Mouser yarns, Tolkien's faceless protagonist in the Rings trilogy, Anderson's Odin in *The Broken Sword* – even Bester's Burning Man in *Tiger! Tiger!* There's a link, too, perhaps, between the unknown aspect and the 'evil' aspect of ourselves in that we sense the presence of the unknown aspect and fear it, therefore judging it 'evil'.

Robert Louis Stevenson might have experienced such a process and in his *Dr Jekyll and Mr Hyde* (1886), which was inspired by fever-dreams and nightmares during a bad illness, produced a new variant on the Faust-character in Jekyll slowly becoming dominated by Hyde. We see also our bestial origins, still within us, in the frightful Mr Hyde. *Dorian Gray* (1891) for all its artificiality, is another development of the Faust theme.

The doomed hero, bound to destroy himself and those he loves, is one of the oldest character-types in literature. Byron saw himself in this rôle, to the discomfort of his friends and family, and by acting it out helped to foster it in Romantic literature. Recent hero-villains of this type have been Peake's Steerpike in the Titus Groan trilogy, Poul Anderson's Scafloc in *The Broken Sword*, T.H. White's Lancelot in *The Once and Future King*, Jane Gaskell's Zerd in *The Serpent* and my own Elric in *The Stealer of Souls*.

Bram Stoker's *Dracula* (1897) is another variation. Here, of course, vampirism is the strongest element in the story, but Count Dracula's lust for blood is almost identical with the lust for virtuous women which marked his predecessors. Faust desired to have and corrupt Margaret, just as dozens of later 'demon-lovers' like Schedoni, Ambrosio and, in real life, Byron and de Sade pursued innocence solely to destroy it. Whether witting or unwitting, the hero-villains of fantasy fiction are usually marked by their ability to destroy qualities in others, and this somehow makes *them* attractive to women readers who are fascinated by them and men readers who identify with them. There is no doubting their appeal, and they are not likely to lose it.

Byron himself wrote an early vampire tale ('A Fragment', 1819) and Goethe's contribution to vampire literature was 'Braut von Korinth' (1797). Mario Praz in his *Romantic Agony*, the standard work on the Romantic Movement, says:

> The hero of Polidori's 'Vampyre' is a young libertine, Lord Ruthven, who is killed in Greece and becomes a vampire, seduces the sister of his friend Aubrey and suffocates her during the night which follows their wedding. A love-crime becomes an integral part of vampirism, though often in forms so far removed as to obscure the inner sense of the gruesome legend – Thus in *Melmoth the Wanderer*, the hero, who is a kind of Wandering Jew crossed with Byronic vampire, interrupts a wedding and terrifies everybody with the horrible fascination of his preternatural glare: soon after the bride dies and the bridegroom goes mad.

Byron and other Romantics took the crude Middle European legend of the vampire and transformed it. Praz remarks that Byron was largely responsible for the fashion of vampirism in literature. The desire to steal something valuable from his victims, whether it be blood, innocence or souls, is intrinsic to the Faustian/Byronic hero-villain. In later stories the hero-villain was transformed into a heroine-villainess – such as Le Fanu's 'Carmilla' (1871), the female vampire – who has since found her way into American popular literature to an unhealthy extent – remember her on the covers of planet stories or, whip in hand, on the more recent 'magazines for men' whose covers are beginning to brighten London bookstalls now?

Since the psychoanalysis of character-types is liable to produce dozens of different theories, I leave the reader to decide what all this means in sexual terms. Many young fantasy fans often share their enthusiasm for the genre with a taste for the erotic fantasies of Henry Miller, Jean Genet, William Burroughs and others. Certainly the link is obvious in Burroughs's *Naked Lunch*, *Ticket that Exploded* and *Soft Machine* which are works of sheer science fiction and the most brilliant ever to appear. *His* Faust is the whole human race rolled into one.

An interesting light on the classic hero-villain comes in J.G. Ballard's *Drowned World*, one of the best novels to appear since the

War. Ballard's hero-villain Strangman is not the central character of the book, but he tends to dominate the scenes he appears in.

> His handsome saturnine face regarding them with a mixture of suspicion and amused contempt, Strangman lounged back under the cool awning that shaded the poop deck of the depot ship...
>
> 'The trouble with you people is that you've been here for thirty million years and your perspectives are all wrong. You miss so much of the transitory beauty of life. I'm fascinated by the immediate past – the treasures of the Triassic compare pretty unfavourably with those of the closing years of the Second Millennium.'

Strangman's studied interest in things which seem to the other characters mere trivia shows us the Byronic hero-villain for what he probably is (if he exists in real life at all today): a brilliant, but bewildered man rebelling against the entire order of things, destroying them because they baffle him, fighting a lonely, hopeless battle against forces which are sure, in the end, to destroy him – even courting that destruction as Oscar Wilde did. Wilde, incidentally, changed his name to Sebastian Melmoth after his release from prison, seeing himself as the character created by Maturin, his kinsman. They all seem to have this quality – Marlowe's Faust, Milton's Satan, the Gothic villains – and Byron himself. We admire them because of it.

Elric: A Personality at War

(2008)

by Adrian Snook

I CAME TO *Elric* relatively late in life, picking up a copy of the Fantasy Masterworks edition for the first time at the age of forty-three.

As I ploughed into 'The Dreaming City' I began to feel that my first foray into the Moorcock Multiverse might not work out. Sword-wielding barbarian warriors have become something of a fantasy cliché and the whole treatment seemed a little, well, derivative. It was only when I checked the publication date that I realised 'The Dreaming City' was published in 1961, over forty-seven years ago! In other words it predates many other fantasy books that are now such established parts of the mainstream.

In time I realised that I was reading a work which had spawned so many pale imitations that some elements of Elric's world had almost become clichés. Once I realised this I was able to clear my mind and read on with a fresh palette, allowing the story to speak for itself.

In creating Elric, Moorcock did not pander to the reader's feelings. He is a hard character to like initially, but deeply fascinating nonetheless. A beguiling mixture of the vulnerable, heroic and tragic, your attachment for him grows almost imperceptibly as you turn the pages.

In a strange sense, Elric and his sword Stormbringer together represent a dysfunctional compound personality, unable to exist when separated but in constant conflict. In Freudian terms Elric represents a complex combination of Ego and Super-Ego, and Stormbringer the Id.

The id is a key element of our personality because it ensures that our basic needs are fulfilled from the moment of birth through our formative years. Sigmund Freud believed that the id operates purely on the pleasure principle. The id wants whatever feels good at that instant without consideration for morality or the potential consequences.

Acting as a metaphor for the id, Stormbringer's unquenchable desire to bury itself in the flesh of both men and of women drives Elric from the outset.

Interestingly, in chapter nine of *The Psychopathology of Everyday Life* (1901) Freud comments on the significance of the sword as a metaphor for a phallus. Moorcock's narrative documents Elric's losing battle with the powerful yet destructive urges of his sword/phallus, driven on by his id. The metaphor becomes quite explicit when the girl he loves dies 'screaming on the point of Stormbringer' at the end of chapter three of 'The Dreaming City'.

Within the first three years of life, a child interacts more and more with the family and the second part of the personality begins to develop. Freud called this the ego. The ego operates on the reality principle. The ego recognises that other people are fragile and that sometimes being impulsive, selfish or destructive can be destructive to them, and also to our best interests in the longer term.

Throughout the Elric saga the hero constantly struggles to meet the needs of Stormbringer (the id) in a controlled way, attempting to minimise the damage to those he cares for.

By the age of five the super-ego develops. The super-ego or conscience drives us to conform to the laws, moral and ethical restraints placed on us by our caregivers and society. If necessary this drives us to behave in ways that run counter to our desires and can even harm our self-interest in real terms.

In a healthy person, according to Freud, the ego needs to be the strongest element of the personality so that it can satisfy the needs of the id whilst striking compromises with the super-ego to reflect the practical realities of life. Not an easy job by any means. However, if the id becomes too dominant, impulses and self-gratification take over the person's life. As the stories make quite clear, Elric is not a healthy person and he loses the battle with the demands of his id many times.

It is Elric's weak ego that wins over the reader's sympathies and gives him his odd quality of vulnerability. We all know how hard it is to resist the insistent cravings of habitual pleasures.

As I followed Elric through the six tales that make up this volume there were sections which reminded me of Arthurian legend and other elements reminiscent of Norse mythology. However, what sets the Elric saga apart from action fiction of any period is the extent of the underpinning philosophical thought that evidently went into executing the war between the forces of Law and of Chaos and its outcome.

In a sense two parallel wars develop and are fought throughout the saga. One is the external war between Law and Chaos and the other is the parallel internal conflict within Elric's personality.

As the system of checks and balances that stabilise the cosmos fail and the Lords of Law and Chaos clash in increasingly bitter conflict, Elric's ego is increasingly losing the strength needed to successfully mediate the conflicting demands of his super-ego (the drive for moral law) and his rampaging id (the drive for moral chaos), culminating in the climactic final pages of *Stormbringer*.

In the closing paragraphs, cosmic balance is preserved because external victory for the Lords of Law is immediately offset by the internal collapse of Elric's ego and defeat of his super-ego. This results in total breakdown and 'his whole personality being drawn into the runesword'.

As the story concludes Elric is left 'a sprawled husk' whilst his id spears onwards and upwards. I can imagine Freud smiling knowingly at this final tour de force of phallic symbolism in a seminal work by an author called *Moorcock*.

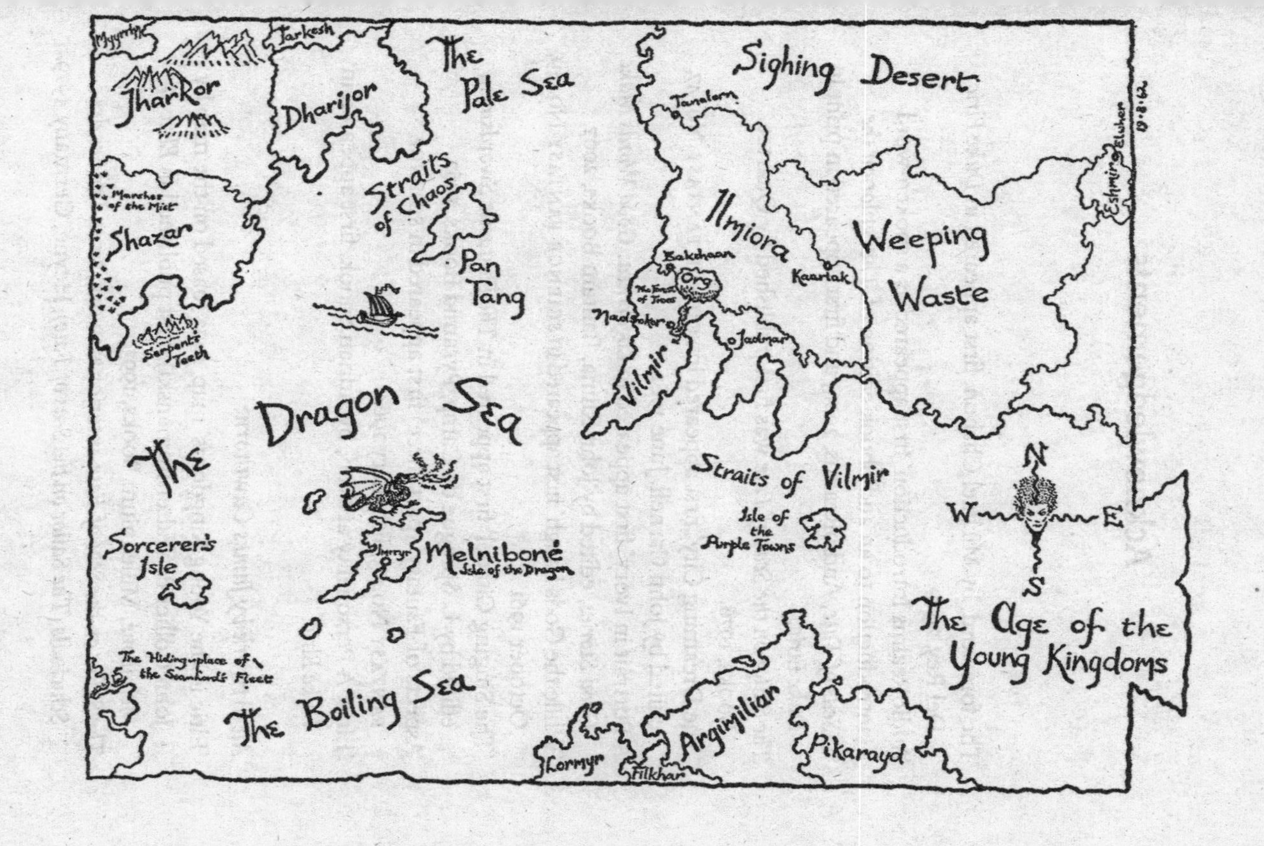

Myyrrhn
Jharkor
Tarkesh
Dharijor
The Pale Sea
Sighing Desert
Tanelorn
Marches of the Mist
Shazar
Straits of Chaos
Pan Tang
Serpent's Teeth
Ilmiora
Bakshaan
Org
The Forest of Troos
Kaarlak
Nadsokor
Jadmar
Weeping Waste
Vilmir
Eshmir
Elwher
19.8.62
The Dragon Sea
Straits of Vilmir
N
W
E
S
Isle of the Purple Towns
Sorcerer's Isle
Imrryr
Melniboné
Isle of the Dragon
The Age of the Young Kingdoms
The Hidingplace of the Sealord's Fleet
The Boiling Sea
Lormyr
Filkhar
Argimiliar
Pikarayd

Acknowledgements

The foreword, by Michael Chabon, first appeared in *Duke Elric*, Del Rey, 2009.

'AudioRealms Introduction' first appeared as a spoken-word introduction to an audiobook edition of *The Sailor on the Seas of Fate*, AudioRealms, 2006, and first appeared in print in *Duke Elric*.

The Sailor on the Seas of Fate was first published by Quartet Books, 1976.

'The Dreaming City' first appeared in SCIENCE FANTASY No. 47, edited by John Carnell, June 1961.

'A Portrait in Ivory' first appeared in *Logorrhea: Good Words Make Good Stories,* edited by John Klima, Bantam Books, 2007.

'While the Gods Laugh' first appeared in SCIENCE FANTASY No. 49, October 1961.

'The Singing Citadel' first appeared in *The Fantastic Swordsmen*, edited by L. Sprague de Camp, Pyramid Books, 1967.

'Aspects of Fantasy' (part three) first appeared in SCIENCE FANTASY No. 63, February 1964.

'Elric: A Personality at War', by Adrian Snook, first appeared in *Duke Elric*.

All artwork by James Cawthorn:

'Elric in the Young Kingdoms' map, 1992 (based on the map by John Collier & Walter Romanski), first published in *Elric of Melniboné*, Millennium Books, 1993.

The Sailor on the Seas of Fate, interior artwork, from *Die See des Schicksals (The Sailor on the Seas of Fate)*, Heyne, Germany, 1979.

ACKNOWLEDGEMENTS

'The Dreaming City', title page artwork, from the front cover of SCIENCE FANTASY No. 55, edited by John Carnell, October 1962.

'The Dreaming City', 'While the Gods Laugh' and 'The Singing Citadel', interior artwork, 1979, from *Der Zauber des Weissen Wolfs, (The Weird of the White Wolf)*, Heyne, Germany, 1980.

'The Age of the Young Kingdoms' map, 1962, first published in *The Fantastic Swordsmen,* edited by L. Sprague de Camp, Pyramid Books, 1967.

MICHAEL MOORCOCK (1939–) is one of the most important figures in British SF and Fantasy literature. The author of many literary novels and stories in practically every genre, he has won and been shortlisted for numerous awards including the Hugo, Nebula, World Fantasy, Whitbread and Guardian Fiction Prize. He is also a musician who performed in the seventies with his own band, the Deep Fix; and, as a member of the space-rock band, Hawkwind, won a platinum disc. His tenure as editor of NEW WORLDS magazine in the sixties and seventies is seen as the high watermark of SF editorship in the UK, and was crucial in the development of the SF New Wave. Michael Moorcock's literary creations include Hawkmoon, Corum, Von Bek, Jerry Cornelius and, of course, his most famous character, Elric. He has been compared to, among others, Balzac, Dumas, Dickens, James Joyce, Ian Fleming, J.R.R. Tolkien and Robert E. Howard. Although born in London, he now splits his time between homes in Texas and Paris.

For a more detailed biography, please see Michael Moorcock's entry in *The Encyclopedia of Science Fiction* at: http://www.sf-encyclopedia.com/

For further information about Michael Moorcock and his work, please visit www.multiverse.org, or send S.A.E. to The Nomads Of The Time Streams, Mo Dhachaidh, Loch Awe, Dalmally, Argyll, PA33 1AQ, Scotland, or P.O. Box 385716, Waikoloa, HI 96738, USA.